PERPETUAL

A Novel By

BRIAN HUEY

reSearch

Library of Congress Control Number: 2007909781
ISBN: Hardcover 978-1-4363-0842-7
Softcover 978-1-4363-0841-0

This is a work of fiction. Names, characters, places and incidents either are the product of the author's imagination or are used fictitiously, and any resemblance to any actual persons, living or dead, events, or locales is entirely coincidental.

Print information available on the last page.

Rev. date: 04/28/2015

To order additional copies of this book, contact:
Xlibris
1-888-795-4274
www.Xlibris.com
Orders@Xlibris.com
561393

Contents

PART FOUR PERPETUAL CONVERGENCE

Dedicated to

The Entrepreneurial Spirit

When bad men combine, the good must associate;
else they will fall one by one,
an unpitied sacrifice in a contemptible struggle.
– Edmund Burke

All of us failed to match our dreams of perfection.
So I rate us on the basis of our splendid failure
to do the impossible.
– William Faulkner

When I see a man on a bicycle, I do not despair for the future of the human race.
– H. G. Wells

What is the use of a house, if you haven't got a tolerable planet to put it on?
– Henry David Thoreau

Millinocket, ME
Orono, ME
Yale University
The Bronx, NY
Indiana Dunes, IN
Indianapolis, IN
Washington, DC
Wilson, NC
Camp Lejune, NC
South of the Border
Brunswick, GA
Jacksonville, FL
Destin, FL
Daytona Beach, FL
Liberty Square, FL
Miami, FL
Homestead, FL

CZECH REPUBLIC
GERMANY
SLOVAKIA
Vienna
AUSTRIA
SWITZERLAND
HUNGARY
ITALY
SLOVENIA

TURKEY
Kurdish Border
SYRIA
IRAN
IRAQ
JORDAN
SAUDI ARABIA
KUWAIT

UZBEKISTAN
TADSCHIKISTAN
TURKMENISTAN
CHINA
Khyber Pass
AFGHANISTAN
IRAN
PAKISTAN

PERPETUAL

reSearch

PROLOGUE

March 17, 1995

Revelations

MATTHEW THADDEUS EATON stepped up into the passenger side of the massive tow truck cab and sat beside Marcos, his nervous new friend. Marcos managed the Miami Beach Shell station where the VW bus hung off the back of the truck.

It was after midnight, and the faint sound of the South Beach nightlife was beginning to come alive a few blocks away. The prominent sound on the corner of Lincoln and Collins was the rumble of the large wrecker engine and the guffaws of an occasional set of drunken businessmen leaving the local strip bars. Matthew reached over and helped Maria in beside him. He turned his attention cattycorner and down a block from where they sat, to their other new friend who they knew as *Cracker Jack.* He was standing with two men Matthew believed were with the FBI. The FBI men were tall; Cracker Jack was more than a head taller. The three men were engaged in a heated discussion in front of the Cuban diner where Matthew and Maria spent the last hour mesmerized by Cracker Jack's tale of intrigue.

As Marcos maneuvered the wrecker out of the Shell lot, Matthew's VW bus in tow, the peaceful night erupted into gunfire.

Marcos yelled for them to duck and Matthew pushed Maria toward the floor as a bullet tore into the driver's side door. He ground the gears from first into second as more cracks of gunfire sounded.

"We're being shot at?" Maria screamed above the squeal of the truck and chaos going on outside.

"They must be stray shots. Why would anyone shoot at us?" Matthew shouted back. He put his hand on Maria's head and forced her down below the open window as a bullet buried itself into the seat behind them.

Matthew picked up a few of the words Marcos was muttering in Spanish. He seemed to be cussing at the truck for not accelerating fast enough. Then he looked at Matthew and, in clearer English than Matthew had heard him speak before, said, "You kids keep your heads down. We'll be out of here in no time." Marcos forced the stick into third gear, hit the gas, and the huge wrecker jerked forward.

Matthew looked up to make sure Marcos was going in a straight line. Then he looked out the window and his eyes met Cracker Jack's.

Everything appeared to be in slow motion. Somehow, Matthew felt this image would remain ingrained in his mind forever. Cracker Jack's eyes seemed to be saying, I'm depending on you.

Cracker Jack's last words in the diner came back to him: *I need your help; you might be my last chance.* Matthew stretched to keep his eyes on Cracker Jack and the two FBI agents defending him. One was kneeling at the corner of the building and firing across the street; the other had his back pressed up against Cracker Jack in the corner of the building, their only protection a palm tree. Matthew realized, though it was not all that comforting, that neither set of men were firing at the wrecker. The unfortunate trio was caught in the crossfire.

Matthew glanced at the two men taking cover behind a U.S. postal box on the other side of the street and firing on the three exposed men. He had seen them earlier and assumed they were yet more FBI agents. After all, Cracker Jack had said he was expecting replacements for his current *G-Men chaperones* that had him under *protective custody.*

"Stop the truck!" Matthew said, "We have to help!"

"Cracker Jack told me to get you kids out of here no matter what," Marcos retorted.

"I don't care what he said; he's out in the open."

With that, Marcos slammed on the brakes, bringing the rig to a screeching stop only a dozen feet past the shootout. Matthew reached over Maria to open the door; but before he could shout to Cracker Jack, he saw one of the agents with Cracker Jack go down. A bright patch of red appeared on Cracker Jack's right shoulder and on his chest, in vivid contrast to his white shirt. He flew backward as if yanked by an invisible chain and crashed into the wall of the building, bouncing off and hitting the ground face down. The two G-Men were already sprawled on the sand between the two buildings. "They shot them. Those other guys shot Cracker Jack and the FBI agents!" Matthew heard someone scream – and then realized it was his own voice. Under the street lamp the three men's bodies lay still, covered in blood.

"I have to help him," Matthew said, opening the door.

"No, Matthew, you'll be shot!" Maria put both hands on his chest to keep him from leaping out of the truck.

Marcos ground the truck into gear, the pungent smell of gasoline and exhaust filled the cab. With his voice shaking, Marcos said, "It's too late, *amigo*, it's too late."

Marcos tried to regain control as he barely missed a parked car on the narrow street. He careened first to the left, then to the right, and then to the left again until he got the rig under control.

They sped past hotels and retail shops two or three blocks from where Cracker Jack and the FBI agents went down when once again bullets began flying in their direction. The killers had chosen their next target. One bullet shattered the back window inches above Matthew's head, the glass spreading out in the cab like confetti.

"We have to go back, Marcos! We have to see if there's a chance he's alive."

Marcos erupted into Spanish. Matthew knew that he was saying 'No way in hell!' Then in English void of the slightest accent, Marcos said, "My job's to get you kids outta here, and that's what I'm gonna' do."

The rig was pushing forty as bullets twanged off the back. Before Matthew could yell, the truck barely missed hitting a grizzled old man holding a bottle to his lips in one hand and gripping his fully stacked shopping cart with the other. He froze in suspended animation a second before diving like an Olympic athlete out of their path. Marcos swerved and smashed two large garbage cans before regaining control.

Matthew looked out the shattered back window at a large green sedan that was catching up with the VW bus, which was bouncing around like a tetherball behind the wrecker. A man, who Cracker Jack had earlier called *Cue Ball,* leaned out of the passenger window. Matthew could see him smile as he pulled around the passenger side of the VW bus and leveled his gun out the driver's side window. Matthew leaned into Marcos and grabbed the wheel; Marcos was too shocked to object when Matthew swung the wheel hard left, barely missing a group of bar-hoppers who scattered to both sides of the street as bullets whizzed by off the passenger side. They careened into a small park area between their street and Ocean Drive with the VW bus still attached. They knocked over one forest green cast iron bench and then another while darting between palm trees.

The green sedan cut into the park in close pursuit. Marcos regained control, and Matthew let go of the wheel.

"*¡Hijos de puta!*" Marcos yelled and continued cussing at Matthew in English and Spanish even though he knew Matthew had saved at least one of them from taking a bullet.

"*¡Que locura!* There's no seat belts in this truck!" Maria said, waving her hands.

"Hey, it's not my truck. You can complain to my boss," Marcos shot back, "if we live through this!"

He growled something in Spanish and swung the wheel to the right directly in the path of the approaching green sedan.

Maria screamed, "What are you doing!"

Matthew looked into Cue Ball's wide eyes and then at the gun. He tensed, expecting a bullet. Before Cue Ball could shoot, the wrecker slammed into the sedan with such force Matthew thought the four-ton vehicle would flip. Instead, hood first, the sedan lifted high into the air, flipped, twisted, then hit flat on its top; crushing its passengers like potato chips in a bag. Sparks flew with the sound of metal scraping the pavement. Matthew craned to watch as the car looking like a Fourth of July sparkler, hit a short stone wall and rolled two, three, four times before finally landing right side up in the sand.

"¡Madre Santa de Dios!" Marcos whispered, crossing himself.

"That was close. Damn good gamble, Marcos," Matthew said. Maria also drew the sign of the cross, then held tighter to Matthew. The trio traveled west on Fifth Street, north on Alton and over the MacArthur Causeway, and then headed south on Route 1.

Part One

Perpetual Sun

CHAPTER 1

1955-1973

Invent

CAMERON T. JACKSON, a world-renowned quantum physicist and alternative energy pioneer, expanded on the concept that energy emanating from the sun captured into solar or photovoltaic cells would one day run all household lights, appliances, and more. In his book *Capturing the Sun* published in 1955, he warned of the inevitable depletion of our natural resources and the imminent dependence on foreign oil leading to geopolitical strife and imbalances. Dr. Jackson was an environmentalist long before the term became popular. He wrote:

> My mission is to advance the theory, development and application of naturally emulating energy sources such as solar, water or wind, and through quantum action combine emerging nano-science and other available technology with the distillation of atoms and neutrons, to create clean cost-effective self-renewing energy.

Although Jackson received international critical acclaim for his forward thinking theories, investors showed little interest in spending money on capturing energy from the sun when oil and coal were seemingly endless.

Hence, he was on his own to finance his research with family money and scant government energy research grants.

Jackson only allowed two things to come between him and his work: his son and an expensive bottle of cognac. After the questionable death of his wife Karen Carson Jackson in 1959, forced to become reclusive, Jackson focused on raising his son and laboring over his work. Meanwhile, perceptions about energy gradually changed. The oil embargo of 1973 caused a surge of interest in solar and other forms of alternative energy. People around the world began to embrace the reality that our natural resources were not only limited, but also rapidly depleting.

Genius that presents itself to the world before its time is often misunderstood and many times feared. While the world slowly changed, Jackson spent the ensuing decades outside of the public eye in his basement lab on a forty-acre lakeside ranch his wife had dubbed *Jackson's Place.* For more than a decade after Karen's death, the only visitors to the compound were Cameron's father in-law, a mysterious friend who lived on a sailboat off the panhandle of Florida, an unkempt FBI agent, and an occasional deliveryman.

Fourteen years after the first publishing of the then obscure *Capturing the Sun,* Jackson's publisher asked for an update. The second edition sold thousands of copies to libraries, universities, and researchers.

In 1965, a *TIME* magazine reporter compared Jackson's theories and contemporary predictions to the science fiction of Jules Verne's novel *From the Earth to the Moon,* which caused a fanatical anticipation of space flight in 1865. The comparison seemed to suit Jackson, and he found himself with a small cult-like following of scientists, students, and laymen. His detractors, mostly big business, purported that he was an alarmist, a troublemaker, and perhaps a mad scientist with unrealistic ideas.

The *Indianapolis Star* printed an editorial that stated,

> Cameron's revolutionary studies and sharp criticisms regarding our depleting energy resources have caused both positive and negative reactions throughout the country. If we are not careful, our own Mr. Jackson, son-in-law to the Carson industrial and political dynasty, is liable to cause widespread panic.

Imagine a reaction similar to the *War of the Worlds* hysteria. In 1938, the public was so superstitious that when Orson Welles read H. G. Wells' book over the radio on October 30, 1938, pandemonium ensued.

The New York Times reported, 'A wave of mass hysteria seized thousands of radio listeners between 8:15 and 9:30 o'clock last night when a broadcast of a dramatization of H. G. Wells' fantasy *The War of the Worlds* led thousands to believe an interplanetary conflict had started with invading Martians spreading death and destruction in New Jersey and New York.

Yale University
1969

Cameron Jackson enjoyed the criticism of his work and the comparison to Jules Verne and H. G. Wells. He was aware of the political and economic tension he was causing. Still, that didn't curb sharp criticisms, especially when he proved that less expensive, environment friendly forms of energy could be developed within a few decades should the funds be appropriated. During rare college speaking engagements the *TIME* magazine comparison often appeared in his introductions.

In May of 1969, his first speaking engagement in three years, Cameron presented to academe the next phase of his research. His work in solar energy spurred the idea for what became CJ Energy and led him to his most amazing discovery: energy *could* replicate itself, saving as much as ninety-eight percent of the current energy costs per household or business with no ozone or other negative environmental effect.

Two months before Apollo 11 would land two men on the moon and return them safely to Earth, the marquee at the door of Davies Auditorium read:

Dr. Cameron Jackson
The Jules Verne of Energy
Presenting: The Alternative Energy Revolution
Featuring updates to his book *Capturing the Sun*

The Dean of Engineering and the School of Physics stood at the podium and said, "It's no coincidence that we chose Dr. Jackson for this occasion just weeks before Americans land on the moon. As a man before his time, Jules Verne predicted submarines, flying machines, skyscrapers, and the most preposterous – a landing on the moon. Dr. Jackson has the similar audacity to suggest we will one day derive all energy from limitless sources. Perhaps another dean will stand here one day and compare a new visionary with the great Dr. Jackson."

Jackson sat to the speaker's right looking out into the crowd. He sensed his shadows were here. They're here. They're always here, he thought. He knew he was a threat to some and an object of interest to others. He knew they were willing to kill to get his research. Though he had proof, he was hesitant to risk his son's and in-laws' safety. He had taken precautions for his son to carry on the work if something should happen to him; but Tremont was still so young, and there was so much more to be done.

"Ladies and gentlemen," the dean of Physics continued, please join me in welcoming the Jules Verne of alternative energy with PhDs from Harvard and MIT; and most important, an honorary doctorate from Yale University. You know we don't give those to Harvard boys lightly." A chuckle spread through the crowd with a few student cheers. "I give you Dr. Cameron Jackson." The ovation erupted and lasted several minutes.

Dr. Jackson stepped to the podium. He put a hand to his brow and squinted, straining to see the back of the hall where two stern-faced men in sunglasses and dark suits stood. His Shadows showed up no matter where he went; he only felt safe at home, at Jackson's Place.

His speech was short but eloquent. He reviewed the past, present, and future of alternative energy sources, emphasizing both the positive and negative attributes; and he closed with the announcement that before the end of this century it was highly probable that he would introduce an entirely new, potentially limitless energy source. Though many in the crowd were expecting something new and astounding from this reclusive researcher, the claim of a new *renewable energy source* caused a skeptical buzz.

"Within thirty years? Impossible," whispered Raymond Shu, the dean of Mechanical Engineering, to another associate.

"It appears the good Dr. Jackson is ahead of his time by more than a few centuries," Yale President Kingman Brewster Jr. whispered to a colleague.

His colleague replied with a smile, "This comes from the man who implemented coeducation at Yale this very year?"

President Brewster grinned. Though many alumni objected, he had pushed the idea since becoming president in 1963. If Yale was to attract the best minds in the country, it was imperative to open the school to women.

"This is science fiction indeed," whispered Paul Penfield to another associate. Penfield, a former classmate and friend, current professor of Electrical Engineering and Quantum Physics, and a renowned author, was Jackson's greatest detractor.

"Where will they obtain the grants to fund such a daunting feat?" asked a scientist from Ukraine.

"Perhaps from NASA," said an academic sitting next to him. They both laughed.

Dr. Jackson was used to the skepticism. He was happy to let his colleagues think he was speaking of solar-based energy and not a new form of clean energy emulation.

But the hour was now, not ten or a hundred years away. The questions that irritated Dr. Jackson's mind were when, where, and how to roll out the discovery. What should the first prototypes be? Perhaps home heating and cooling? Electronic power sources? Automobiles? He frowned. On the other hand, the bigger question is whether to reveal his research at all. Before Karen died, before she was murdered, he swore no corporation or government would control CJ Energy Cells. It will be available to the whole world equally, or to no one at all!

Cameron felt dizzy and was sweating in the cool hall like he had a fever. He reached into his coat pocket and took out a multi-colored flask. He turned as if he were going to cough and took a long pull. Cameron screwed the cap back on while smiling sheepishly at a colleague who was looking wide-eyed at him from the other side of the podium.

While the dean rambled on, Cameron's mind drifted to his brilliant ten-year-old son, Tremont, and, other than his research, the only reason for living. He had done all he could to keep him safe at his lake front high security compound. But he had buckled to his strong-willed in-laws who insisted Tremont attend school in Indianapolis, where he was top of his class and played basketball. He worried day and night during each school year even though his in-laws, the high profile Carson family, had presidential-type security complete with secret service agents and private bodyguards.

Each time he goes public with information about his research, the chance increases that they, whoever *they* are, might follow through on their threats. The most recent anonymous letter, accompanied by a chilling videotape, said that if he offers his research to anyone but *them*, his son would be next. He didn't even know who *them* was. Government? The oil cartels? Independent parties? There were many factions threatened by his research. If *they* knew what he had really discovered, there's no telling to what lengths they would go. The letters and tapes came by express mail, and he could not risk turning them over to the authorities. He rubbed his forehead and felt the usual pain in his chest. The first letter had come after his book made headlines. When he didn't take it seriously – he lost Karen.

He looked around nervously. Why had he accepted this engagement? He stood up from his chair without looking at the dean or the crowd and stumbled off the stage. He needed to call the Carsons and check on his son. He needed a drink.

CHAPTER 2

1973

Threat

TWELVE MEN, WHO all but one was robed in white, occupied the extravagant conference room in the basement of the Vienna, Austria OPEC building. They inhaled khubz, pita bread, hummus, kaitaif, baba ghanoush, and Um Ali. They chased the mezze, or appetizers with dark Arabic coffee and Shai tea.

The men were in good spirits and engaging in discussions – except for one. He sat alone and rigid at the far end of the immaculate table, his black robe in contrast to the group. The founders in the early sixties called their organization Hafiz-OPEC Saumba Shokran, meaning, Protectors of OPEC Stability and Longevity.

Sheik Mohammed bin Bandar, a robust man of fifty-some years, stood at the head of the table, raised his hand, and smiled. "I would first like to welcome our two new members to this important meeting at this critical juncture in our history: Sheik Hassan Al-Fawza of Saudi Arabia representing the royal family – " He indicated an equally robust man to the center left who gave a slight nod. Sheik Bandar then turned toward the tall man in the black robes and said, "Please welcome Omar bin Taliffan representing the newly formed United Arab Emirates.

"As you know, I have been asked to be the spokesperson to the world for OPEC. "I come here today to emphasize to you how important it is that we all stand together for the sake of each of our countries and Islam, when we turn the world upside down with the upcoming announcement."

The men in the room knew what he was going to say; nonetheless, anticipation choked the air.

"Nearly all OPEC member countries will not ship petroleum to countries that support Israel." He paused and said, "Inshallah," meaning, *if Allah wills.*

The room erupted in chatter. He raised his hands. "Our target countries are the United States and their allies. Your importance, the importance of this group, will multiply exponentially, my friends."

The representative from Syria, a clean-shaven elder statesman, said, "The U.S. and the U.K. will not sit idly by."

"There is not much they can do, Mustafa," countered the representative from Iran.

"I disagree, General Daneshvar. Once we make this announcement, we will set in motion what has been on the table for over a hundred years. America and many European countries will increase their efforts to lessen their child-like dependency that fuels our economic growth."

The General nodded in understanding. "Yes, the U.S. will step up exploration in the Gulf and Alaska . . . but this will take many decades."

The leader of the group interrupted. "You are both correct and have reiterated our potential predicament, which leads to the purpose of our meeting today. We now have a forum, a majority of OPEC member states, and the most propitious of timing. For twelve years, OPEC has been successful in creating continuity between our member states. The mission of Hafiz-OPEC Saumba Shokran has been covert to maintain OPEC's stability while protecting our interests worldwide. Over the last couple of years, we have added many more states to OPEC's membership, giving us collective control of over thirty percent of the world's oil reserves." All but one in the room voiced boisterous affirmations. "Much of OPEC's success can be attributed to efforts put forth by this small group and your associates. We have all worked behind political, economic, and social agendas with great success. Our mission will not change with the upcoming embargoes against the West. Our mission becomes more important to our collective future.

General Daneshvar lifted a page from a stack of newspapers. "Our small group, Hafiz-OPEC Saumba Shokran, Protectors of OPEC Stability and Longevity, has truly met the challenges of the past and has much to be proud of. If we allow our brothers to fall asleep at the feet of prosperity, then in the end, we have failed. With the changing world economy and aggressive activity to develop alternative energy sources, our responsibility grows. In 1960, most of the world, especially members of the American Oil Federation, the Seven Sisters, said OPEC would not last five years. In 1965, they assured themselves we would not survive the decade. They are now paying for their skepticism."

Sheik Bandar took over, "OPEC has made a strategic move this very month toward a substantial increase in the base barrel price." He grinned. "Reverberations throughout the world financial markets have been deafening, far greater than our expectations. Today, the world is paying a premium for our natural resource. The Seven Sisters along with western governments now know to respect the Organization of Petroleum Exporting Countries. Instead of looking at us as overpaid camel salesmen, we will be recognized as a formidable force to deal with for generations." The group then rewarded him with nods of approval and praises to Allah.

"This aggressive move does not come without a cost," he continued. "Already the American and British governments, and private citizens like the Ralph Nader group have convened their various energy councils. They will renew their efforts toward combating our control of their addiction. All will intensify with the embargo announcement. Regardless of our sectarian differences, it is our mandate to secure the longevity of our lands and our peoples. We must now step up our defensive measures against this competitive pressure."

One member did not seem to be in step with his counterparts. He stood and stretched to his full six feet, two inches. A deep sound like the growl of a lowering dog came from his throat, quelling the festive mood in the room.

As was their custom, the leader took his seat, and their newest member had the floor. "You are wise not to deceive yourselves with a false sense of security, my friends." The speaker was the youngest in the room by ten years. His black garb, accented in gray, extended from the top of his turban to the bottom of his sandals. Whether this style of dress, representative of Islamic religious leaders or scholars, was worn intentionally, who could say? But he did make a vivid first impression.

Omar bin Taliffan was attending the meeting at the bequest of the United Arab Emirates (UAE) formed two years earlier in 1972. Once the emirates had learned of Hafiz-OPEC Saumba Shokran, they pressed the native Yemen bin Taliffan family to join the tight group and protect their interests. Omar's father, Mohammed, prior to his death in a plane crash, required his son to attend. The UAE leadership could not have been more pleased hearing that the eldest son and patriarch of the family would be their man. Omar bin Taliffan's father, a self-educated man, had been one of the most powerful and wealthiest Middle East businessmen in memory. He was also a close friend and ally of the Saudi royal family. Omar had three key business interests: the UAE members who contract with the bin Taliffan Construction Group to build their cities; his company and family; and the Saudi royal family. He accepted this challenge with one reservation; all three priorities conflicted with his much larger purpose.

After a number of formalities, thanking the leadership for inviting the UAE and himself to the meeting, Omar bin Taliffan folded his hands against his chest and said, "We sit in our lavish estates and palaces across the great deserts living sheltered lives while millions of Muslim people remain in poverty and ignorance. We open our kingdoms and businesses to the western ideology and lose our identity.

"Do you think the heathen Christians in America, the UK, and their sheep in Europe, Israel, Canada, and Japan are sitting by waiting for us to bankrupt their economies with higher oil prices while we gain economic and political strength? If so, then you have become exactly what many have said: foolish old men who have lost their way and their vision." He went on to quote from the Koran. Then he closed his eyes and pressed his hands together while reciting a prayer.

A few of the men in the room were clearly agitated by the direction bin Taliffan was taking. When the young man finished his prayer, the representative from Saudi Arabia began to stand. Sheik Bandar raised his hand palm out at the end of the table – as if to say, *you will have your chance.* In contrast, the representatives from Iran and Iraq, though no love was lost between them, were smiling.

Bin Taliffan opened his eyes and waited for the pantomime between the other members to cease before continuing. "You – and even the old men of the country of my father's birth – have become fat and happy on the immense wealth we have all acquired while western ideas, technology, and capitalism creep into our cities, schools, and homes." His voice was steady but held an icy tone. "You say this group is set up to protect the interests of our people and our future. At the same time, your industry leaders are discussing contracts and partnerships with AT&T, IBM, McDonald's, and K-Mart. Make no mistake, these companies represent the devil's doorways into Islam." He pointed his finger at the representative from Saudi Arabia and said, "You allow cancers to lodge themselves in greedy bellies. You give your Western infidel partners sanctuary in your bowels allowing them to eat away at our way of living."

The representative from Saudi Arabia balled his hands into fists and his eyes contained a fire desiring to consume his accuser. Even so, he kept his seat. He understood the economic and political power this twenty-five-year-old heir wielded. Though he himself a Saudi prince, he was not ready to put the royal family at odds with the bin Taliffan family, one of two families that had bailed the Saudi government out of its mid-sixties bankruptcy in return for multiple billion-dollar construction contracts.

A slight turn at the corner of the young speaker's mouth indicated a bit of amusement toward his victim. "Let us not be lulled into a hypnotic state by the opium of wealth. Do not forget, the infidels' supreme objective has always been to convert others that do not accept their Christ and their democracy. They will not be satisfied until we are like them. Is today different than the days of their crusades when they invaded our lands and murdered millions of our people in the name of their God?"

He walked to the wall behind him and slapped his hand against a picture of an oil well in Saudi Arabia. "The raw crude under our feet is not our greatest asset. As a family that has assisted many of your governments along with my father's association with Mohamed bin Laden, and has benefited by building civilizations above these rich wells, we are humbled with the knowledge we gain strength from the resources that Allah provides to our people." He clapped his hands together. "This blessing can also become our greatest curse. We have been in a holy war with the West for a millennium. It won't be long, maybe a century, maybe two, before we are lost."

The leader recognized an opening. "Thank you, Omar. As always, your passion is commendable. Your family is one of the most respected in the world. As a young engineer only a few years out of George Washington University, I worked with your father and Mohamed bin Laden to design bridges, buildings, mosques, and much of the infrastructure in Saudi Arabia, Syria, and Kuwait.

We were all saddened by the loss of your father and uncle in that tragic aircraft accident."

Omar nodded. Discomfort left a hairline crack in his stone-like posture.

Prince Hammad Outed of Qatar, whose country sat upon one of the richest veins of oil in the Middle East, stood to say, "I agree with your assessment. Though I would like to offer a suggestion that we move today's meeting along as I know more than one member has a flight out of Austria later this afternoon." Omar sat down.

As one of the most respected Middle East leaders by government and industrial leaders around the world, Outed, heir-apparent, along with his five younger brothers, would inherit the majority share of his country's oil deposit. He looked to the head of the table and said, "The bylaws of this committee, Hafiz-OPEC Saumba Shokran, were drafted in 1960 by my grandfather, King Shaikh Ahmad bin Ali bin Abdullah Al-Thani, Sheik Bandar, and other members of OPEC. These bylaws stated that once we have a majority of OPEC members as members of this organization, we would elect officers. Giving more formality to our group is a step toward assuring our collective business survival that could be in jeopardy from outside forces. OPEC cannot be associated with what we do from this room to protect our region of the world."

He looked around the room and, not finding an objection beyond the ever-piercing black eyes of young Omar, continued, "It is my opinion that as Sheik Bandar and Omar bin Taliffan have pointed out in two very different ways, we have awakened a divisive force – a sleeping giant. If we do not begin to take evasive action, our grandchildren may find themselves herding camels and selling rugs at the market. I have counted your votes and Sheik Bandar will act as our Secretary General. I will act as his assistant."

The representative from Iran, General Velayatollah Daneshvar, who was known to be anything but a friend to the West, yet a dutiful soldier of the pro-Western Iranian Monarchy, asked, "And who is your sleeping giant, Hamaad? The USA? They have been awake and meddling in our affairs since 1948. Perhaps you refer to my good friend Richard Nixon?" A few of the men chuckled.

"Mr. Nixon is exceedingly busy with East Asia and his own internal strife in Washington; he is the least of our worries. As with much of the invention and ingenuity of the twentieth century, the U.S. is the chief harbor for this threat."

"You leave us in suspense," said Sheik Bandar.

The Iraqi representative, Ibrahim al-Maliki, a Baghdad-born Sunni Oil Minister under Saddam Hussein, agreed. "We are at your mercy."

Prince Outed raised his eyebrows and smiled. He was about to speak when there was a light knock on the door. A teenage boy rolled in a cart and placed it against the wall. He first handed a note to Sheik Bandar, and then with a nervous crackle in his voice, spoke in perfect Farsi, "Sweet and spice black bread and the finest Yemen green mocha coffee – for your pleasure." He backed out of the door. The rich aroma of the oldest known cultivated coffee in the world, grown at altitudes greater than 4,500 feet above sea level, filled the room.

Sheik Bandar read the note and said, "It seems Dr. Jean-Paul Dominique Esquirol, the leading physicist in fuel cell research, has had an unfortunate accident. He received a medication overdose while in the hospital and is severely incapacitated."

"How tragic," Omar Taliffan interjected. "Without Esquirol, western fuel cell development could be set back a decade." All eyes were on Taliffan who then said, "Allah smiles upon us this day."

Ignoring the refreshments, Prince Outed walked to the far wall where a large white screen was lowering from the ceiling. Above Sheik Bandar, a small shutter opened to reveal a projector lens. The lens came alive with light, and the first slide took the men to a California style home displaying four large rectangular objects on the roof. The next slide revealed contemporary windmills lining a typical desert backdrop. The next revealed a face very familiar to men of industry. Dick Gertenberg, a small man in stature, stood next to an unusual looking automobile. Typeset on a sign above the car was the words *GM Electric Car (1973): Prototype of the Future.* The next slide revealed a quote in bold white letters on a pitch-black background:

> At a recent energy summit, the Big Three, General Motors, Ford, and Chrysler agreed to work together to reduce the cost of driving for the average American.

The next slide showed a quote by an unnamed industry official:

> We will combat rising oil prices and the increasing threat of America being held hostage by the Middle East. We will do this by producing

> more energy efficient automobiles and engineering new alternative forms of energy to power the future. Our combined efforts will lead to less dependence on foreign natural resources and ensure affordable transportation for future generations.

Prince Hamaad Outed left the damning quote on the screen for a few minutes and then followed by a dozen more frames depicting other experimental forms of energy in action around the world. Without saying a word, he had driven the point home. The sleeping giant was not a country but a concept they all understood: inexpensive alternative forms of energy. The next slide image appeared and stayed up on the screen. A black and white picture revealed, behind a podium, a man of unusual height, in relation to the men standing to his right and left. He wore an open-collared shirt and a tweed jacket common for Ivy League professors. The podium read *Yale University*. Prince Hamaad walked over to a beverage table. He poured a cup of the rich Yemen brew. The other men began standing and stretching their legs, filling their coffee cups, and adding sweet and spicy desserts to their plates. They expected a reason for the picture of the speaker still on the wall.

Omar remained in his chair and said, "You are a master of the cliff-hanger, Prince Hamaad. But we are not at your monthly book club meeting. What is his identity and how does he relate to our meeting today? I assume he has something to do with alternative energy development?"

Once every member had taken his seat, Prince Hamaad explained, "That man is one of energy's most respected modern fathers – a physicist without peer. His alma mater is the Massachusetts Institute of Technology and his research, articles, and popular book are causing a resurgence of interest within the science and business communities. Since his days at MIT, he has been researching and developing practical uses of solar energy. Though Ericsson and Kemp, both Americans, experimented and implemented many successful solar products, it was this man and his colleagues at MIT that proposed wide use of solar cells called photovoltaic in the late fifties."

The Iranian general responded, "Surely you are not saying that solar energy is our primary concern. It is cost prohibitive. It isn't efficient. It will take two hundred years for scientists to develop it to be competitive with fossil fuels. We should be more concerned with the expansion of nuclear energy and the latest developments in fuel cells." But there seemed to be a question and concern in his tone.

Sheik Bandar looked to Prince Hamaad before beginning in a slow and steady voice. "You may be correct about solar energy as we know it today. As it is, solar is not our challenge. You are correct that fuel cell advances could be a more pervasive technology, but like the quest for cost-effective use of solar energy, scientists have been trying to develop a marketable fuel cell for over one hundred and fifty years." OPEC's assistant secretary general put his finger into the line of light from the projector behind him and pointed to the man at the podium.

"While other scientists toil over solar and fuel cell technology, Cameron Jackson has been researching and perhaps already developing something of far greater consequence. He may be the preeminent threat to the longevity of the oil industry and Islam. Our initial task is to learn as much as possible about his research. What is the concept? How far along is he? Who else is he working with? We suspect the American government or NASA, but we don't know. Will his final product be cost-effective? How soon could he speed up the product to market?"

"There must be quite a bit of his research already published," said the Iraq oil minister.

"That is the quandary. Mr. Jackson is extremely secretive about his work. He lives and works like a recluse in a secured compound southeast of Chicago."

Omar bin Taliffan growled, "If your suspicions can be verified, *inshallah,* then we should pray for misfortune to befall Mr. Jackson, don't you agree?"

Sheik Bandar blanched, but did not interrupt.

Prince Hamaad Outed placed his hands on the table as he leaned in to the group. He lost his affable demeanor. "Yes, Omar. *Inshallah.* Whatever it takes, Mr. Jackson must be stopped."

CHAPTER 3

1983

Anguish

MATTHEW LOOKED UP from the little black-haired girl to the thick dark clouds covering the sky from the northern mountains to the southern pine tree-lined horizon. Even for Millinocket, Maine, it was a most miserable, unseasonably cold, rainy April night. Lightning spread across the sky, lighting up the hill for a brief moment. He took a deep breath through his nose and recognized the sweet scent of ozone, produced, he knew, each time lightning flashed and split two parts of oxygen, $O_{2,}$ into three atoms of unstable oxygen called O_3. He also knew people were destroying this natural occurrence; and he wanted to do something about it, when he grew up, of course. He also knew kids his age didn't typically know that kind of stuff, much less understand the chemistry behind it, or so he was told. He loved that smell.

His eyes returned to Maria Valdeorras and didn't move from her again until the priest began the graveside service.

Right when the service started, ominous streaks of lightning followed the crack of distant thunder to the northeast over the sprawling Great Northern Paper Mill. Most of the people on this hill, alive or dead, had worked at the mill.

When the next bolt of lightning struck up north, he could clearly see the outline of Mount Katahdin. For a second, he thought he saw the outline of a moose with wings – the Penobscot Indian Spirit! The thought made his heart race. His brother, and his friend Pete who was half Micmac American Indian, had told Matthew many stories about an angry spirit that was responsible for all kinds of tragedies. They told him this spirit devoured complete hunting parties for simply climbing the forbidden mountain. What was it? Poma . . . Pama . . . Pamola, that's it. He knew most of the tribes of Northern Maine believed Pamola lived at the top of Mount Katahdin.

Matthew counted the seconds between the thunder and the lightning: *one one thousand, two one thousand, three one thousand.* The heart of the storm was getting closer.

Science was his thing. His father would brag that at barely seven, Matthew knew more about meteorology than the weatherman on Channel Five. He could hear his father's bass voice as he said Matthew knew "a hell-of-a-lot more than that damn cheese-head trying to pretend he's a patriot!" He had no idea what that meant, but it made him happy.

A large crowd had assembled at the Willow Run Cemetery. They stood in a long semicircle under a huge oak tree, one of the largest Matthew had ever seen. He didn't see any willow trees. I wonder why they call it Willow Run. Maybe they meant Widow Run and someone just wrote it down wrong, he thought. Every male in the Eaton family knew trees before he knew proper sentence structure and algebra. Matthew's father owned one of the most successful timber and logging businesses in North America.

The Eatons, their employees, and most of the town of Millinocket came to the wake and viewing held earlier at St. Martin of Tours Parish, the only Catholic church in town. Nearly everyone knew and liked – if not loved – the deceased and wished to pay respect to the family. Not to mention, she was Mr. Eaton's executive administrator for over twenty years.

She was also Maria's mother. Matthew didn't quite understand the gossip he had heard from his friends' parents, but the gist was rumors that Matthew's father and Maria's mother had something more than a casual working relationship.

Matthew stood holding the hands of his father and mother. Behind the three, standing tall in marine uniform with one hand on Matthew's shoulder and the other holding a large black umbrella over the entire family was his brother Sean. He was home on leave from special assignment in the Middle East.

Matthew glanced over at two men next to the Eaton family. One he knew was Dennis Weaver, the strange lanky Katahdin Sporting Lodge innkeeper to whom his mother often said not to pay any attention. The other, much shorter *newcomer* to the small mill town, was Mr. Estebanez, who was staying at the lodge. The town folks were buzzing about the stranger's desire to invest in the town's revitalization program, particularly in scholastics.

Matthew had heard that the old-timers grumbling about "*carpetbaggers,* outsiders trying to take over their *backyard,*" and make changes too quickly, for one reason: to line their pockets with green, for the sake of green. Whatever they meant by that. In the end, the consensus was, the women liked Mr. Estebanez and the men disliked him. Matthew's mother said the men were even more suspicious than usual because the women were attracted to the stranger. In the end, the new development brought jobs to the area and the newspaper reports were mostly positive about his large donation toward building Maine's first science center, devoted strictly to the environment and alternative energy. Matthew had the same reaction to this news that other kids his age would have if Disney were building a park in the neighborhood!

The only other funeral Matthew had been to in his short life was the unceremonious burial of Mr. Pibbs on a hill behind the family ranch. Mr. Pibbs had been his father's old lumber mill dog, a Chow-Pit Bull mix. That darn dog didn't like anyone except Matthew and was shot twice by hunters, and twice nearly died after taking on a lynx and another time a bobcat. The veterinarian who put over a hundred stitches in Mr. Pibbs was amazed he was alive, and said, "I'd hate to see the other guy." Surviving all of that, Mr. Pibbs met his final demise when hit by a company vehicle down at one of the Eaton's pulp mills.

Matthew had been absorbing all the activity since the wake started hours earlier. He was very sad, but he didn't think Maria looked sad. He could not see anything in Maria's blank expression. He heard one woman say, "Maria is still in shock and would not realize her mother was really gone for quite some time." When Mrs. Valdeorras was around Matthew, he may as well have had another mother. She had kept an eye on him many times when his mother traveled to see family at Martha's Vineyard and lately had been teaching him Spanish, which she said he picked up rather easily. That was not surprising to his mother, father, or teachers, as he seemed to have a knack for French and Italian. Besides the small Valdeorras family, people from Spanish-speaking countries were rare in Northern Maine. Over the last century, many French Canadians moved in to find work, and the Italians built the mills. Many of the Italians still cluster around *Little Italy* on the southwest corner of town.

Matthew looked around at all the people with dark shadows across their faces donned in black and holding black umbrellas over their heads. Of the thousand – nearly one-fifth of the town's population – that signed the register at the wake, more than a hundred had braved the weather. Matthew had heard his father say that the priest and a number of wealthy family members had flown in from Spain. The town had lost somebody special.

He didn't know how to express his emotions. Maybe he was in shock too. He studied each person, and though he recognized many, no one stood out to him. They looked like the zombies he saw on a black and white movie not long ago. His eyes kept returning to Maria. This time he was startled – she was staring back at him. It was dusk and quite a distance to the other side of the large semicircle around the gravesite. Her eyes seemed to penetrate right through him. He felt a dull pain in his chest. Perhaps, he thought, this is what my mother means when she says, "You're breaking my heart." It was difficult to take his eyes away from this petite black-haired creature. He saw the huge hand on her shoulder pressing her against the thigh and hip of a large man. When he looked back at Maria, she was still staring at him. He decided she didn't look like a zombie at all. She looked like a princess caught in a rainstorm. Though at least three umbrellas covered her, she was still soaked from head to toe. Her black veil could not contain her tight curls cascading halfway down her little body. In her hands, in contrast to the surroundings, she held close to her chest a bouquet of colorful flowers.

His little heart began to hurt even more; he was sure now it was truly breaking. He wondered if you could really die from a broken heart as his mother said his great-grandfather had done after Matthew's great-grandmother died. He remembered feeling a little like this when he touched Mr. Pibbs for the last time. If he felt this way, how much worse must the surly man and his daughter feel? She continued to stare at him, and he knew he was feeling the pain in the little girl's eyes like it was his own.

Their eyes remained on each other throughout the service as the plump priest, who had flown in with family members from Spain, who reminded him of Friar Tuck in *Robin Hood*, spoke in another language that Matthew recognized as the Spanish Mrs. Valdeorras spoke.

Two men lowered the casket into the muddy gravesite as the priest spoke now in a funnier but even more melodic language. The two women closest to Maria and her father began wailing, he had heard they were Maria's aunts from Spain. Still, not a tear fell from the girl's eyes. Matthew felt like crying, but he decided he would try to be like the stiff shouldered, stoic Maine men, and the oak tree. As Maria stared at him, he felt like she was taking something from him: strength, oak strength perhaps.

The rain had died down. The rotund priest concluded by crossing himself, and people began lining up to say a few words to the family. Matthew's father shook the big surly man's hand with both of his, said some things Matthew could not hear, and walked with his mother and brother down the steep hillside to their cars. Matthew didn't follow. Instead, he drifted toward a thousand blazing eyes of the Great Northern Paper Mill. The mill lay across the river and dominated the view northward like an old monster waiting to consume the small town and its residents. A streak of lighting brightened the sky to the northwest of the factory, revealing Mount Katahdin overshadowing the monstrous mill and everything else in the region. He tried to shake off the queer ominous feeling and knelt down next to the ancient oak tree.

"Hello, Matthew."

Matthew was startled to see the newcomer, Mr. Estebanez, standing in the dark a few feet away.

He knelt down next to Matthew. "Do you know who I am?"

Matthew nodded.

"I found some neat games put out by Scientific America. Thought you might like them. My particular favorites are the crossword puzzles." He handed a plastic bag to Matthew and gave him a soft punch on the chin. "Nice weather you have up here. Reminds me of spring in Moscow." Mr. Estebanez stood up and walked down the hill.

Matthew took out the pocketknife his brother had brought to him from Kuwait. He smiled, *the knife that was supposed to never leave the house*. He began carving into the tree.

A few minutes later, someone touched his shoulder, and he thought he was in big trouble either for carving on the big oak or for keeping the family from leaving. He was still kneeling, frozen with his pocketknife half imbedded in the tree when Maria leaned in, kissed him lightly on the cheek, handed him a yellow rose, and then ran down the hill along a cobblestone path toward the cars.

Matthew turned around to finish his carving when he heard his father and brother yell his name as the rain picked up in intensity. He completed his task and surveyed his work. Satisfied, he picked up the bag full of magazines and ran down the hill toward two angry parents and a brother that swatted him in the back of the head as he sprang into the back seat of his father's GMC Jimmy.

"Here."

Sean handed Matthew a package wrapped in corrugated paper.

"What's this?"

"Some books my friend Tree thought you would like."

Matthew tore off the paper and stared at his new treasure. It would be safe to say that no other child his age understood the value of what he held in his hands.

Over the next few years, Matthew spotted Maria around the town and at her father's restaurant. He had known Mrs. Valdeorras had a child; but until the funeral, they had never met. Emblazoned on his mind was the memory of Willow Run. More than once when passing each other, Maria and Matthew's eyes locked and time seemed to stand still until his oblivious parents or her three doting aunts shuffled them off to one place or another, breaking the spell. When he was ten, he rode his bike past her house and caught her watching him out of an upstairs window. He clipped her mailbox with the handle of his bike and tumbled into the grass. Besides a small dent in his pride, he was uninjured, and nearly lost control again as he could hear her laughing all the way down the next block. He felt like a klutz, but the sound of her laughter stayed with him. For the next few days he felt like doing handstands and somersaults.

As she attended the Catholic school and he, a private prep school, they did not see each other much, though he thought of her often. The vision of her piercing bold black eyes nearly unnerved him. One night, he and his parents were having dinner at her father's restaurant. Mr. Valdeorras mentioned that Maria would begin classes at the public middle school in the fall.

After weeks of incessant begging, he finally talked his mother into allowing him to transfer schools. His father had a surge in business while in the process of building an addition on their house and was too preoccupied to put up much of a fight.

His first day, Matthew walked down the deserted hall of the Millinocket middle school and into Mrs. Pulaski's sixth and seventh grade combined English class. Like a magnet, he caught a familiar girl smiling at him. He became lightheaded and thought he should retreat and come back tomorrow.

Mrs. Pulaski guided him to his chair two rows away from Maria, who boldly stared at him and smiled. His face felt sunburned, and it seemed like a frog was doing back flips in his stomach. He seriously considered leaving the class so he could dunk his head into a sink.

Mrs. Pulaski looked at a card she held in her hand and with concern in her voice said, "Matthew, did you bring your pills?"

Matthew reached into his pocket to be sure and produced a small silver container, he replied, "Yes, ma'am," and took his seat.

During lunch behind the small school, while the cool fall breeze spun leaves like small tornados around their feet, they sat together without saying a word.

The silences didn't last long. After a few weeks, they had to keep apologizing for interrupting each other as they could not stop talking. Since Maria got in the majority of verbiage, which was fine with him, he learned a lot he didn't know about her. For instance, her full name would be very hard to remember, but he made a point of writing it down in case she ever quizzed him: Maria Teresa Bierzo Valdeorras.

"My father's name is even more difficult: Felipe Juan Carlos Bierzo Valdeorras, but everyone in town just calls him Phil. Our names have historical meaning, relating to the region of my parents' homeland. My father's family owned hundreds of acres of vineyards; and my mother, a Bierzo, was the only daughter of the governor of the same region. They left Spain in a hurry due to a family feud between the Bierzos and the Valdeorras. Isn't that romantic?" Her face lit up when she smiled, and Matthew was speechless again. They stopped at a park bench and Matthew set down the two stacks of books he insisted on carrying.

"So they came to Boston when they were eighteen, got married, and opened Godello's Spanish Cuisine Restaurant." Godello's was a popular landmark in north central Maine. "The name Godello's comes from the area where my grandparents, uncles, aunts, and cousins still live. I can't wait to go visit. It's also the name of the type of grapes my father's family grows." She took a deep breath and looked over at Matthew who was leaning up against a tree to keep from passing out while trying to look nonchalant with his hands folded behind his head. She threw her hands up in what became a familiar expressive action to Matthew. "I'm a motor mouth. I'm sorry."

She's amazing, Matthew thought, smiling like a cheshire cat. It had taken them five years to share the same lunch table, and have some freedom from their vulture like parents and relatives; but from that day on, they were inseparable. They never talked about that stormy night at the cemetery on Willow Run. Matthew figured Maria didn't want to go there because of the pain of losing her mother.

As for the newcomer, Mr. Estebanez, whom Matthew had met in the rain by the large oak tree, he had become his tutor of sorts. They met often at the new Katahdin Environmental Science Center or in the kitchen at the Eaton home west of town, a mile off the Golden Road, which cuts through one hundred miles of Maine's north woods from Millinocket to the Canadian border. They also spent an increasing amount of time studying at the Katahdin Sporting Lodge where Mr. Estebanez stayed when in Maine. Matthew's father, Parker, was not too keen on the unusual relationship but his mother, Kate, seemed intrigued by the mysterious philanthropist. After all, she would say, Estebanez seems to be the only person in the region that was able to challenge their son academically.

While Matthew grew up in the remote mill town, powers beyond his wildest imagination were converging on his world.

CHAPTER 4

August 1989

Resolve

TWELVE HUNDRED MILES away from northern Maine on the shores of Lake Michigan, a father and son were working together at the Charleston style home, complete with a wraparound porch, ornamental trim, and stained glass windows, they called Jackson's Place. They were together for the first time in nearly a decade in a basement lab more elaborate and equipped than MIT's finest.

"Dad, I was going over these figures and if I'm calculating correctly, the tests have come out with less than a .003 margin of error? You've come a long way while I was overseas."

His father didn't look up from the microscope, but he could not hide his excitement, "And, I have been able to stabilize the metals, oxidation, and atomic exchange down to the same margin. The little molecule buggers are still renegades, but as long as they are contained, they never dissipate." He looked up and said, "I think this calls for a drink."

Tremont was born with exceptional bloodlines – on both sides of the family – dating back to the American Revolution. On his father's side, there was

Andrew Jackson, the ninth president. On his mother's side, there was Lindsey Carson, the father of twelve children, including the frontiersman, Kit Carson. Coupled with that daunting family history is his grandfather's, the honorable Senator Stephen John Carson. Last but not least, there's his mythical father who some say rivaled Einstein in his theories.

Tremont never knew his mother, Karen Carson Jackson. She died during childbirth. After a short investigation, the Indianapolis coroner's office ruled her death an accident stating that she received an incorrect drug combination. Tremont was unaware of his father's allegations of foul play.

Cameron never recovered from her death, but, with the painkilling assistance of scotch and cognac, made raising his only son one of his two greatest endeavors.

Cameron and Tremont spent the last few weeks of July 1989, together working in the lab, running or playing with the dogs along the beach, enjoying fine meals, wine and cognac in the evenings. Life was as good as it gets, like Tremont remembered things to be until he left Indiana for graduate school at Yale nearly nine years earlier.

The big day they both anticipated was fast approaching. His father would present his research to the governing body over alternative energy in DC. Contrary to his best instincts, his father convinced him to book separate flights. Tremont took the opportunity to spend a few days with his grandparents while his father flew off to meet a friend in New York City.

After checking the settings on the extensive security system, and putting the cover on his new Mustang GLX, they put the dogs in the GMC Jimmy SUV and headed out for the city three hours south of their Indiana Dunes compound. Tremont dropped his father at the airport and reminded him of the appointed time they would meet at the Washington International baggage claim in DC on Tuesday. "The Senate Travel Department already has a limo set up for us, so I guess we'll be arriving in style."

"As it should be," his father said.

Two days later Tremont left the sprawling Carson estate and drove to the Indianapolis International Airport. He was excited about joining his father in Washington where his dad would finally reveal and shock the government and the world with his life's work. He knew it was dangerous, but with the high security around the Senate and seeing that now he himself could keep a close eye on his father . . . all should be well. He hoped. So why did I let him go to New York without me? He did not wish to put a damper on the excitement but something was definitely making the hair raise on the back of his neck. He shook it off and tried to focus on the occasion. His father would be unveiling the greatest energy miracle since electricity.

Part Two

Perpetual Journey

CHAPTER 5

Summer 1994

Spirit

BEFORE LEAVING MILLINOCKET for college, Matthew had purchased a 1967 Volkswagen bus for the price of moving it off deceased Mr. Pelletier's small mountainside place. The family had an estate auction prior to converting the quaint turn-of-the-century home into yet another bed and breakfast. There were already six B&Bs in the Katahdin region, three of which were in Millinocket, as the small town of less than 5,000 year-round residents was considered by many to be the gateway to an outdoor playground. Millinocket was close to Interstate 95 and boasted dozens of campgrounds, as well as hunting, fishing, and sporting camps.

Sean was home on leave between missions in eastern Asia. Off the record, he told Matthew it was undercover work in North Korea. Something about acting as a businessman in order to get coordinates on a target. Matthew asked what kind of target, and Sean made a vague response and changed the subject.

"I looked for you last night, and waited up until one," Matthew said as Sean drove the big company vehicle northeast on Millinocket Road.

"Sorry about that. You can blame it on Pete Marks. Excuse me, *Ranger* Pete Marks. The Blue Ox Saloon is the best thing to happen to our deteriorating town."

Realization hit Matthew. Sean was out drinking all night. He didn't look the worse for wear, he thought. It must be part of the military training.

"John St. John says they've been open just a year, but the place looks and feels like it's been there forever. I was over there before eight knocking down Molson Golden's, nobody was in the place, and John was trying to decide which hat to put on the big moose head on the wall. By nine, you'd have thought Ben & Jerry came into town again. The place was packed and everyone was buying me beers. After we wore the old timers out, Pete Marks, John, and me – we sat there trading old Indian stories. Pete started going on and on about Pamola – "

"That's the god of thunder who lives on top of Mount Katahdin."

"Right, anyhow, nobody knows folklore better than Pete – he spent his life at the foot of the old Micmac chief – can't think of his name – but he's truly a modern day witch doctor."

"Chief Tanner. I've spent some time with him; his deep soft voice seems to cause you to go into a trance, and it's as if you are transported back hundreds of years."

"I remember. He used to do the same thing to Pete and me when we were kids. Do you get those dreams?"

"More like nightmares!" Matthew exclaimed and they both laughed.

Sean cussed as he passed the cutoff to Pelletier's place. He threw the truck into reverse and said, "I'll tell you one thing, if we ever did get into a pinch with Pamola, all we would have to do is sic Pete on him – he would talk the great *moose bird spirit* to death."

The Pelletier's place looked abandoned. They pulled up to the garage and Matthew jumped out and opened the door. They loaded the classic faded, what must have been green at one time, VW bus onto the Eaton Logging and Forestry fixed bed truck. Sean adjusted the controls on a mammoth 8,000-pound super-winch. Matthew thought the two of them could have pushed the bus up the ramp, but it was kind of fun using the winch for something other than trees and cut lumber.

Maine did not have titles on vehicles until the mid-eighties, so they drove away from the future B&B with Matthew's new toy bouncing along behind. Sean steered west on Fire Road 13, turning right on Fire Road 15, and finally reaching a dirt road carved through a dense wall of trees. When they came out into the open, there stood five dilapidated buildings. On the front of a tremendous barn was a weathered sign: Eaton Logging and Forestry, est. 1937. The sawmill, built by Sean and Matthew's grandfather, was abandoned when newer equipment was needed to compete with larger companies. They drove up to the mammoth old barn and Sean backed the rig up to the doors. Following Sean's signal, Matthew jumped out and opened the two barn doors.

"I remember Dad saying something about this old place," Matthew said. He looked around with his jaw hanging low at what appeared to be an active mechanics shop with a late model Corvette, and two 60s Mustangs. "Who do these belong to?"

"Ah, Mr. Johnson has been coming up here for years to get away from Mrs. Johnson. I used to sneak off with him when our old man was kicking my ass about one thing or another."

"I was robbed! I've worked with Mr. Johnson in the East Millinocket shop for ten years and he never mentioned this place, not once."

Sean unchained the VW and lowered it to the stone tiled floor.

Matthew could not hide the grin on his face.

"What?" Sean said.

"Nothing. Let's get to work!" Matthew could not be more excited about the bus and working with his big brother. With any luck, they would soon know if it was salvageable.

The brothers completely ripped the engine apart, cleaning each piece meticulously and filing down rough edges where appropriate. While they worked, Matthew couldn't help noticing his brother's mood swings from jovial to downright surly. Matthew tried to bring it up, but Sean ignored his probing questions. Sean was much worse with his parents, older relatives, and friends. In fact, it was obvious he preferred Matthew's company, which made up for his sullen demeanor.

They drove to Bangor the next day in search of parts and a set of new tires; and over the next week, they worked long hours to put the engine back together. Late on the seventh day, they replaced the clutch, brake pads and shoes, and the bus was ready for a test drive.

"When do you have to leave?" Matthew asked as he rolled out from under the bus on the six-wheeled mechanics creeper.

"I'm sorry bro, I received a change of plans this morning. I have to fly out of Boston back to Bangkok tomorrow. We'll have to put our hiking trip on hold until next time." He tightened the nuts on the battery and chuckled for the first time since he had been home. "I would love to see the look on the old man's face when he sees this old *peace mobile.*" They both knew that their father, who served tours of duty during both the Korean conflict and the Vietnam War, had strong feelings about those who protested the war. In his words, "College kids were riding around in hippie mobiles spitting on the graves of brave men and women who were helping to provide their precious freedom of speech."

Matthew wiped his greasy hands on his overalls and mopped sweat from his brow with a shop cloth. He crouched down and stared into the little engine. "Will it run?"

Sean handed him an ice cold *Sea Dog Old Gollywobbler Ale.* They sipped the tart brew and Sean asked, "Where did the old man get this? I thought you could only buy it at the coast?"

"They just opened another brewery in Bangor." Matthew grinned as he took a long swig. "Just in time, too."

Sean squinted with one eye and pointed his beer at Matthew. "You go down there and study your ass off, little brother. Don't be drinking yourself under the table every night like my buddy and I did down at Yale. You hear me?"

"Sure, Sean, no problem. Hey, that's the first time you've mentioned your friend since I was a kid. I've always been confused about a few things . . ."

Sean avoided Matthew's eyes, picked up a can of gas, and began to pour it into the tank. "You're still a kid." Sean seemed to consider his answer. "He and I grew apart years ago."

"But you guys were thick as thieves in the Marines, right?"

"I said we grew apart," Sean snapped at him.

"All right, all right," Matthew said, and thought, what got between them? The quick anger was exactly what he had witnessed between Sean and his father. Unlike Matthew, of course, Mr. Eaton didn't let Sean off with a short answer. They would both push until a fierce fight broke out. This had been going on every night since he arrived. The small family would sit down to a meal fit for royalty, and usually before the first slice of turkey was on the plate, the two of them were at it full tilt. Really, it wasn't much different than when Sean was growing up, but the intensity now bordered on violence.

The good news was Sean's mood could change in a heartbeat. "Okay, little brother, here goes." Sean turned the key. Nothing. He turned it again, and the engine tumbled. He pumped the gas twice and turned the key again. There was a quiet little rumble, the VW bus shook, and then the sweetest sound emerged as the engine came to life and held. Sean jumped out of the front seat, whooped, and clicked his heels. He grabbed Matthew around the shoulders and gave him a strong, quick hug. Matthew was in so much shock watching his brother's transformation that it took a minute to register that their thirty hours of hard work had paid off. Somehow, he knew this memory with his brother would be one of his best.

Sean left for Asia, and Matthew worked on the VW's interior and exterior appearance as authentic parts came in from as far away as San Diego. Besides patching a few rusty spots, he didn't alter the original pastel paint job. He liked the bus the way it was. But before he sprang it on his father, he wanted it to look and smell as good as it ran.

Maria met him at the barn. "So this is where you have been hiding all these weeks." She walked around and around making little hmms and ahs. She opened the doors and sat in the seat, and then she crawled back into the back.

Matthew lifted the back hatch and looked at her with anticipation. "Well?"

"All we need back here is a blanket."

"You vixen."

She grabbed the front of his gray coveralls to pull him into the vehicle. "I think your little van is so, so, so cute." She kissed him on the lips.

He pulled away. It might not have been so bad if she hadn't used the high-pitched, cartoon-like cutesy voice. "Cute? That's all you can say, cute? It's a work of art, a piece of New England and American history. And it's a bus. Not a van. A bus."

"Okay, I love your cute little civil rights and love-not-war bus."

Matthew was not amused and went around to the front of the shop to open two large double doors. "It's D-day. Time to lay this one on Dad."

Seeing that Matthew was preoccupied, Maria drove back to her father's restaurant. Matthew threw his road bike in the back of the VW bus and headed toward home, reciting over and over what he would say to his father. "He's not going to like it," he admitted aloud. He pulled up to his parent's estate, and as he shifted into park, it backfired.

His mother met him with a smile and said she fell in love with the bus at first site. "It reminds me of a van my sister's boyfriend Luke had when we were in college. They were the oldest hippies at the Cape. In '69, they drove it to Woodstock filled with a dozen other free spirits."

His father, on the other hand, was predictable. Mr. Eaton was standing on the porch with Mr. Johnson, a grizzled, leather skinned, heavy smoking mechanic from the shop who had taught Sean and Matthew everything they knew about engines.

His father said, "What are you going to do with this piece of junk – paint flowers on the side and go to Oregon to join a commune? And how safe is a vehicle with one thin piece of metal between you and the guy coming at you?" His father barked and grumbled more questions and complaints at him without opening a door or kicking a tire.

"It's a classic, Dad. Not a piece of junk." And after his father went into the house, he said, "And I thought I would put off joining the commune until after college."

Mr. Johnson shrugged as if to say "I tried" and walked down the steps toward them. "I stopped at the shop in the old barn last week." He must have sensed Matthew's surprise and said, "Don't worry, I'm probably the only one who remembers the place exists. Why do you think I've left all that equipment there? As you saw, I often have a little auto project of my own and it's the one place even my wife would never think to look." He chuckled and then said, "You and Sean did a good job, Matt."

Matthew beamed. "We had a good teacher."

Kate Eaton walked up to the pair. "I'm sorry, honey," his mother said. "You have to understand that while your father was on his second tour of Vietnam, all the anti-war demonstrations were going on, and this," she ran her hand across the side of the bus, "represented everything he detested. So perhaps you could just let it go?"

His father came back out and snorted, "If every cop from here to Bangor stops you to search for wacky-tabacky, don't come crying to me to pay your tickets." He turned and walked back into the house.

"If I drove up in a four-wheel drive pickup, he would still find something wrong with it."

Mr. Johnson said, "Sorry, Matt. I told him how you and your brother worked your tails off and miraculously put life back into this relic. You know, the fact is the VW bus, though revered for its legacy by many, was rated as one of the top ten worst vehicles ever, right up there with the PACER, Gremlin, Pinto, Chevette, and the all time no contest winner – the Vega. I had me one of them Pintos and nearly fried like chicken when I got hit in the back. Damn thing burst into flames. So you be careful there, Matt. You be careful." Mr. Johnson lit up a smoke, got into his company truck, and drove down the long Eaton drive.

A few weeks later Matthew loaded up the bus and left to begin his college career at UMaine.

Spring Break
March 15, 1995

March delivered record cold temperatures and like thousands of their peers across the nation, the students at the University of Maine were looking forward to the prospects of spring break – preferably somewhere blazing hot.

Matthew replaced the phone on the hook outside his dorm room and shook his head. That was weird, he thought, I wonder if my mother put him up to that. The call was from an uncle who lived in Homestead, south of Miami. Uncle Carl was his father's estranged youngest brother whom Matthew had not seen since he was a boy.

Matthew was so busy with finals and training as captain of the rowing team, he hadn't considered a destination for Maria and himself. He finished two freshman term papers, turned them in that morning, and focused his attention on addressing an Express Mail. He reached for the envelope on the shelf above him and bumped a row of books into a domino effect. The books came crashing down on top of his head. He swore and began picking them up when his eyes caught a familiar worn title, *Capturing the Sun* by Cameron T. Jackson. He opened the jacket and read the handwritten inscription in blue ink on the inside cover:

> Matthew, the answers surround you in every atom and neutron. Look to your environment, and deep within.

It was signed Cameron T. Jackson, PhD.

His brother, Sean, had brought it to him while on leave from the Marines when Matthew was very young. Sean never said how he had obtained it or how he was able to get a personal signature from the great Cameron Jackson. At least Matthew didn't think he had. He made a mental note to ask him the next time he saw him.

Matthew held the book like it was the Word. To him, it was the next best thing. He opened the front cover and removed a folded sheet of paper. He smiled. It was a note from his mentor, Mr. Estebanez, back home. Mr. E was a philanthropic eccentric science buff who had donated large sums of money to enhance the school systems science programs and had taken an interest in Matthew. The note said:

> Matthew;
>
> I wish you well at UMaine and your MIT correspondence work. Never lose focus. Remember, whatever you can imagine is possible, and believe with all of your heart, you can achieve. Think long term. You are unique and in a good position to help solve the impending energy crisis, and you will have all the assistance you need in your endeavor. If you need anything, leave a message with Weaver at the lodge.
>
> Warm regards,
> Estebanez

Matthew folded the note and carefully placed it back in the jacket of the book. He then replaced the old book and returned to the project at hand. The stack of papers in front of him held the results of his nine-month-long independent energy science lab, which he entitled *Solar Energy: Advances in the Nineties.* The term paper was part and parcel of maintaining a full six-year UMaine and MIT combined scholarship grant he won his senior year of high school. He had to maintain at least a 3.5 GPA and complete quarterly labs and projects to keep his scholarship. He had considered going out of state with MIT as his first choice. Though he had many scholastic and athletic scholarship offers, leaving Maine and being far away from Maria didn't feel right to him. When UMaine, one hour south of Millinocket and nearly in Bangor, offered him a full scholarship plus complete access to labs and technology, it was an easy decision.

The first semester flew by, and Matthew had not returned to Millinocket except for Thanksgiving and then again for a few days including Christmas. Though they didn't talk about it much because they hardly talked about anything, Matthew knew his father wanted him to come home on the weekends to work in the office of Eaton Logging and Forestry. Since Sean was dedicating his life to the military, the burden of one day taking over the family business would likely fall on the younger son. He frowned at the thought.

Matthew stretched his arms behind his back and thought how glad he was that the 1994-95 Black Bears swimming season was finally finished. He was somewhat satisfied with his success though he knew he could do better, and would, next season. Matthew, nationally ranked, had set school records in the 200-yard butterfly and the 400-yard individual-medley. Though Matthew felt like he needed a break in order to concentrate on this huge project and his other studies, he was never one to allow such a respite. He was already entrenched in early morning workouts with twelve other members of the Black Bear Club Rowing crew. Their workouts began at 4:00 a.m. on the Penobscot and Stillwater Rivers, and ended circling the sixty-two acre Ayers Island. When they had time, they would travel ten miles northwest on Pushaw Lake.

Though he was in peak shape, he was retraining a different set of muscles. Today he felt as if one of his father's skid-steer tractors ran him over. Matthew reached in a drawer in his desk and opened a bottle of anti-inflammatory, to pop 800 mg. He chased it with a chug of a thick, vitamin-packed, strawberry flavored energy drink. Stuffing the thick solar energy study in the express envelope, he rushed out of the dorm, down its granite steps two at a time, and dodged large ice encrusted puddles on the sidewalk. While he ran he looked toward the Memorial Union post office across campus and then at the clock on a nearby building. He had ten minutes to get it in today's mail. He pushed spring break to the back of his mind and sprinted. When he was sure the package was on its way, he could focus his attention on Maria and having fun. Once inside the bustling student union, with five minutes to spare, he reread the address on his package and dropped it in the mail chute. He went to the post office window and, finding the seat behind the counter empty, decided he could check back later to be sure the package went out on time.

Outside, he began jogging back up the hill when without warning he had to stop. He bent over, putting his hands on his knees. Not again, he thought with a grimace. After a moment, he shook his head, took a deep breath, looked at the clock tower, and started walking slower and a bit unsteady. Not expecting Maria until that evening, he could take his time on the way back and maybe stop at the infirmary, he thought.

"Matthew!" A voice hailed him from behind.

He turned to see Chase, one of his buddies from the rowing crew, running to catch up. They connected with a handshake, first palms together, then fists and thumbs, and finally the fists together.

Chase was a talker and went on about a girl he met, how hard his midterms were, and how sore he was from the hard week of rowing. He finally finished with a question. "So what're you doing for break?"

"I've just now been able to think about it. We were going to hit Boston and the Cape."

"With Maria? You mean with Maria, right? Man, she is hot. Isn't she your girlfriend?"

"Yeah, Maria. She's a girl, and she's my friend, so I guess that qualifies her as a girlfriend."

Chase laughed, misinterpreting as usual. "Sure, sure, you're trying to keep your options open, eh?"

"I wouldn't say that." He realized he wasn't sure what he was saying. Perhaps Maria was his girlfriend. They had become more intimate since Maria nearly attacked what's-her-name he was sort of seeing last fall. They had somehow transformed from friends, which might explain the physical experience he had every time she was around. That never – well, rarely – happened when they were growing up. Chase chatted away and then asked him something.

"What? I'm sorry. I was zoning out."

"I said, so you and Maria are going to stay in New England then?"

"Well, actually my uncle has been bugging me to fly to Miami and visit. It's kind of weird because it's not like we've been close. He's cool though, very adventurous." Matthew was thinking about the last call from his uncle that morning. He had sounded close to pleading when he asked Matthew to visit. He said he had some things to show him from his years of flying cargo to Central America. What could possibly be so important he couldn't tell him what it was over the phone? Besides, he'd only seen his uncle twice, maybe three times in the last nineteen years. "He's sort of the black sheep on my father's side of the family."

"So why not go?"

"I couldn't justify the funds to fly, and it's probably too late to buy tickets, but I'm thinking my VW bus could get us there and back. Maybe we will. See you on the water when I get back, Chase."

Matthew began to jog up the hill toward his dorm when a wave of dizziness overtook him. He stopped and leaned up against a lamppost, then bent over and vomited. He looked around, put his back to the post and slid down to the ground. He closed his eyes and reached into his pocket, retrieving a small silver case. He took out a tiny white pill.

Maria was in the last semester of her senior year in Millinocket and making frequent weekend trips south to UMaine to see Matthew. She packed two large suitcases, a backpack, and a cosmetic bag. In her mind, she would not be coming home until after UMaine's spring break. This meant missing a week of school and deceiving her ultra-traditional father.

As she drove her '88 Mazda Protégé south, she thought about the intense feelings for Matthew she'd had these past months. While she grappled with what she thought might be a subtle change from puppy love to real love, she decided it would be best not to leave Matthew alone for long stretches of time with a candy store of college girls. "They just take advantage of his naive good nature," she had often told her friends.

What caused her to have to deal with her feelings was an eye-opening first visit to UMaine last fall when she found Matthew kissing *that, that, that other girl.* She felt the blood in her body heat up with the thought of it. She looked at the little stuffed black bear Matthew had given her at Christmas. It stared back at her from the dashboard of her car. "I mean, it's up to me to keep him out of harm's way. Isn't it?" The black bear didn't reply, but she took his silence as an affirmation. "Thank god I was able to shake him loose from that rich Boston floozy. There was nothing *real* about that girl except maybe her money. I'm sure she even had a boob job. How else could she be that thin with those perfectly round breasts trying to split right out of her extra small t-shirt? What was he thinking? *¿Dios mio que es lo que estaba pensando este hombre?"* The UMaine mascot remained silent. Maybe he didn't understand Castilian Spanish. The bear knew Maria reverted to her father's native dialect when she was angry.

"Well, I can tell you this. Matthew shouldn't be left alone for long without me, that's for sure. He's simply too naive when it comes to girls. I mean, no commitments have been made, but the idea of him with any other girl, *me vuelve loca!* That socialite only wanted a handsome athletic trophy to escort her around campus." She drove in silence down Highway 95 deep in her thoughts. They had both been so busy with school, sports, and work they had only spoken a few times on the phone and had last seen each other over the Christmas vacation. She worried that maybe, again, he had found someone else to take her place.

But when she saw the signs for Orono, her insides felt like butterflies bursting out of their cocoons by the thousands. "He's really an amazing person, isn't he? I'm so excited to see him I could scream." She scooped up the bear and kissed it. "I *so* have to pee! I've been holding it since we left home!"

The door was open. I know I closed that door, didn't I? Matthew asked himself, worried about the stereo system his brother sent him from Japan or Korea or wherever he was the past winter. Matthew stepped into his dorm room to find Maria sitting on the bed with her back up against a large stack of pillows, legs crossed, drinking from a bottle of French spring water. She couldn't be more beautiful. She appeared completely absorbed in *The Mind of the Serial Killer*.

"There you are, handsome." She bounced off the bed and gave him a big hug. "I parked up on the hill and saw Floyd on the way down to the dorm. He wanted to know what your plans were for spring break; for that matter, so do I!"

"I was talking to Chase. You met Chase last time you were here, didn't you? He thinks you're *hot*." He frowned and didn't wait for her to answer. "I was telling him how it's the funniest thing – do you remember me telling you how my dad's brother Carl has been bugging me for months to go to his place south of Miami?" Matthew sat on the bed and put his hands on his head.

"Bad?"

"Not too bad. I took a pill a few minutes ago."

She sat beside him. "You were saying about Uncle Carl? I remember. You thought it was kind of strange after all these years."

"I still do, but heck, what do you think? We can stop at beaches all along the way. It'll be fun." Matthew's voice was rising. He wasn't sure if it was the closeness of her body or making the decision to go to Florida.

"Florida! I'm all packed, ready for anything except I need to go shopping for a suit, maybe in Boston?" She sat back on the bed with wide eyes and biting down on her bottom lip. Matthew thought she looked like a child on Christmas morning.

"Great." He had made a decision to go even before he saw Maria. But was it his decision? Something nagged at his pragmatic mind. It was as if he was *supposed to be* in Florida for spring break. Spring break should be about gawking at wet t-shirt contests, attending keg parties, or enjoying the simple rapport with thousands of college kids from around the country. But he couldn't shake the feeling of something surreal, even spiritual, about this trip. He thought aloud, "Going with no sleep for three days can sure make a guy wacky."

Misunderstanding his comment, Maria said, "No, it's not wacky at all. Florida sounds great. Definitely! When can we leave? Do you want to drive my car?"

"I was thinking of taking the bus. It's been driving great, and it was made for this type of road trip."

"So what do you think?" Maria asked now perched on the edge of the bed.

"Well, you know I'm a devout follower of Dr. Nike's philosophy."

"What's that?"

"'Just do it,'" Matthew said with enthusiasm.

She threw her arms around his neck and kissed him hard on the lips. Matthew grinned, pulled back, and stared at her.

She studied his face. "What?"

"Nothing, it's all good. So you're all packed, huh? What did you tell the old man?"

"Oh, he'll be okay."

Matthew knew her father would definitely *not* be okay, but he decided not to say anything.

"You know what I love about you?" Maria asked.

"And what is that?"

"Never mind. Your ego is big enough."

"I was just thinking the same thing about you."

"Go ahead, say it, you want to say it, you do." When he just grinned in reply, she reached back to smack him, and he caught her wrist. "Why don't you say it?" she asked pouting.

"You're fishing," he said, letting go of her wrist and putting both hands together and throwing them over his right shoulder then forward as if he was tossing the line of a fishing rod out in front of him. He pretended to reel it in.

"You're darn right I am." She poked him in the chest. "Where's that romantic guy I know is hiding down deep in there?" She pursed her lips and her left eye closed slightly.

Matthew adored this unique expression of hers when she was mad at him or teasing. Trying to discern which was which, that was the challenge. He was having a hard time coming up with the words he wanted to say so he changed the subject, "You're going to miss home, aren't you?"

"Suffocating little Millinocket? Not on your life, mister, especially without you there."

Matthew looked into her eyes, "Oh, I don't know, I have missed being home. Man, oh man, we had some intense adventures. Do you realize we've known each other most of our lives? I appreciate you always being there for me." There, I said it, he thought wryly. That's kind of like saying the four-letter word.

Maria had a satisfied look on her face and walked to the other end of the dorm room, less than eight paces. "I always said I would go where you go, just so it was out of the Katahdin region. I mean, I love it up there, and I love my papa, but there's so much to see and do outside of that boring town."

He felt a strong attachment to his hometown of Millinocket and the mountainous Katahdin region of northern Maine. He had enjoyed more than a lifetime of adventures with Maria, his best guy-friend Johnny Fazio, and his older brother, Sean. Much to her father's chagrin, Sean had often taken the three kids hiking and camping into the Katahdin wild.

The hundreds of memories he had experienced with this feisty black-haired girl seemed to take on another dimension entirely. "I don't know. You would miss it, Maria. What about the weekends we spent sitting together on the rocks above Little Niagara Falls? There's nowhere else in the world like that."

Maria unwrapped a present she brought for Matthew and put the compact disk soundtrack from the new *Batman* movie into his stereo. Seal's "A Kiss from the Rose" came through the speakers. She picked up her book and sat cross-legged on the floor.

"We have got to go to that movie during spring break," Matthew said as he searched for a Red Sox hat. "I see you are still reading the same gruesome stuff."

"You got a problem with that, mister?"

"You are a strange bird, always having a book with you about someone murdering someone in repugnant ways in woods just like the ones we were in."

"Scaredy cat."

"You really need to meet Stephen King one of these days. You two have a lot in common."

"You know he lives in Hermon. We should go visit."

In actuality, Matthew knew the books Maria read were not just horror stories but also about criminal psychology or forensic medicine. Though science was *his* thing, the whole idea gave him the willies.

Changing the subject, Maria said, "Yep, you used to talk about all the things you wanted to do and places you wanted to see."

"I didn't think you were listening."

"I never missed a word. Don't you know by now women are born to multitask?"

Matthew remembered how he would go on and on about his dreams, inventions, and aspirations while she read. He could see her on the moss near a stream, sitting cross-legged, eating an apple, and without looking up from her engrossing, or better yet *gross* book, and say, "That sounds good to me too, Matthew." He was the dreamer, and she seemed perfectly content to be a part of his dreams. She told him many times that, along with following him to the ends of the earth, she had her heart set on becoming a forensic medical examiner or crime scene investigator and solving the world's worst crimes. Meanwhile, he had no problem with biology or anatomy, even dissecting. It was the gory stuff people could do to other people that made Matthew's stomach turn. He rarely went to a horror movie even if local mega-author King wrote the screenplay, and only then if Maria insisted.

Maria shook her shoulders as if she had a chill and hugged herself. "Do you remember when we were on Millinocket Lake after I finished reading about the Savannah serial killer who drowned all his victims?"

"I think so. That was the day you freaked out, and made me row us back in, like the Loch Ness Monster was chasing us. I believe you said you had a vision of drowning."

"I still have that vision. It's so real, I see it in the day and then again in my dreams." She rubbed her temples and closed her eyes tight.

"Maybe you should not read that stuff, or go to those movies, and maybe why you should not be going into forensics. But I know you will anyhow."

"You just don't understand. This was different. I don't dream about anything else I've read, but the vision of you and I in the lake in a storm was so real I could feel the water pouring down on us, and it was as clear a day as today. We were thrown over by a wave and then," she closed her eyes, "I drowned."

In truth, Matthew did understand. He had the same type of dreams after he met with Chief Tanner. "I thought psychologists agree that you cannot die in a dream."

"They are not dreams. I have visions."

"Ah. Like the difference between a bus and a van?"

Maria lightened up and tried to pinch and twist his skin as he pulled away successfully. They both laughed.

One time she snuck them into *Silence of the Lambs.* Matthew agreed to go, thinking he would be her knight in shining armor. Instead, he scrunched down in the seat while wide-eyed Maria munched away on popcorn and said, "Cool!" "Neat!" and "I want to be just like Clarice Starling!" He woke more than once in a sweat from a dream that Dr. Hannibal "The Cannibal" Lecter was unraveling his skin as he slept.

"What are you thinking about?"

"How you like to face your fears, and how much fun we've had. How you would suddenly throw caution to the wind. Sometimes you're so conservative and analytical. And then, WHAM! You're sneaking us in the back door of the movie theater. Do you remember when we hiked the mountain trail in Baxter State Park and then you suggested we cross through little Niagara? Even my brother would think twice before that."

She smiled at the backhanded compliment. "It's true. I would never have considered doing that myself, but I knew you would protect me. I think that's why my dad didn't put up such a fuss today. He knows you'll keep us safe." She laughed. "Do you remember three summers ago when you were working nights for the shopping center, and I had an insatiable craving for chocolate?" It was terribly tempting and convenient that Matthew had keys to Mrs. McGregory's confectionary store. They still argued whose idea it was to go in for chocolate. But they lost track of time while dipping their fingers in the slowly churning mixing vat full of dark chocolate. "Things sort of got out of hand when you smeared chocolate in my face."

"Hey, you smeared chocolate in my face first."

"Whatever," she said. Within minutes, the playful smearing had turned into an all-out chocolate fight. They found themselves covered in chocolate from head to foot. Laughing like hyenas, they cleaned up as best they could and drove up to the southern edge of Millinocket Lake.

"I can still feel that ice-cold water," Maria said. "I think that was the last time we skinny dipped together. Why was that?"

Matthew smiled sheepishly. It was different when they were pre-teens. That night the realization set in that his best friend had developed a woman's body. He was shocked and embarrassed about the reaction he had. He was almost sure she didn't notice, but then again, it was difficult to hide in the bright moonlight. After they swam, he stayed in the water until she had her undergarments on, and her back was turned. Then he rushed onto the bank and pulled his jeans on without bothering with the towel.

Dropping her last question, he said, "We were careless, eh? We should've taken our clothes in the water and removed all the evidence. We were caught naked with the contraband."

"That was so embarrassing." Maria put her hands to her face. "I barely had my bra on when," she paused to salute and change to a deep voice, "Deputy Dubois appeared out of woods. I still wonder how long he was standing there." Officer Dubois was like a Dutch uncle to most of the kids in the small town and close friends with both Mr. Eaton and Mr. Valdeorras.

"At his age, you should've given him a heart attack, which would have saved us a lot of trouble."

"I think it was more excitement than he's had since McGrath stole the hat right off his head at the Homecoming game. He sure spent a lot of time looking for evidence when it really wasn't hard to find." There had been just enough chocolate behind their ears and plenty on their clothes for irrefutable evidence. Their punishment, besides having to deal with the consternation of their parents, was to work over at Mrs. McGregory's for a month without pay.

"The punishment wasn't all that bad, but it took me a month to lose the extra five pounds I gained," said Maria. "Now hurry up and pack your two pairs of jeans and all four of your t-shirts."

While he packed, she talked on and on about the things they would do in Florida. Eventually, he interrupted to say, "You know, I really appreciate how you motivate me."

"Hmm? How do you mean, sexy man?" she asked with a wink.

"I mean regarding my inventions. You encourage me to pursue my dreams with a vengeance. I would've never entered the MIT scholarship had it not been for you." She always listened intently regarding one alternative energy invention or another even when most of the details had to be boring. "You, my dear, are my secret weapon, spurring me on to do more than I might on my own."

"I don't know what you're talking about."

"Right. How about when you entered me into the Smithsonian Science contest?"

"You mean for the national competition? You know that I didn't do that on my own. Mr. Estebanez used me to get you and your parents to fill out the entry forms. The competition you won, I might add, and then won how many times since, four, five?"

"Six actually. Mr. E has really been there for me, that's for sure. He can be quite persuasive."

"Have you heard from him lately? He left Millinocket when you left for school in September and hasn't been back since."

"Only once since I left for college." Matthew reached up to the set of books that had fallen on his head just hours ago. "He sent me some interesting studies on fuel cells currently being conducted in Germany. He thinks they're flawed and wanted me to look them over and send him my suggestions. He said they'd pay me for my time. Imagine that."

"He's a strange man, isn't he?"

Matthew laughed. "I guess you could say that."

"Mysterious even. I overheard Mr. Fazio telling my father he thought Mr. Estebanez was working for the government. It was odd that he took such an interest in you and your studies. But I think he's harmless.

"That was the night I went home early, and you met me at my house. My father shouldn't have been home for at least another hour. Oh my god, he nearly caught us. What were we thinking?"

"Thinking had nothing to do with it," Matthew said.

"Father is steeped in traditional values. He would have killed us!" Maria said.

"No, he would have killed me. You, he would have locked in the wine cellar until you were thirty. It's your fault for being so damn irresistible," he said, snapping a wet towel in her direction. Her left eye closed and she pursed her lips. Man, he loved when she did that. He put his hands up in surrender and balled up the towel, then put it in his bag. She was about to scold him for that when he jumped on the bed, grabbed her around her tiny waist, and pulled her to him. "Do you remember the day we met?" Just as soon as he said it, he regretted it. Maria's face turned dark.

Matthew drew her tighter to his chest. "I'm sorry. I was just thinking about how we connected that day."

"I know. It's still hard for me to talk about it."

He took her hand, picked up his two bags, and locked the door. On the elevator, he said, "Sorry to bum you out. Once we get on the road, you'll feel better."

She put on a brave smile and said, "Hey, once we get in the bug, it's all about finding a bathing suit and getting a tan."

Bus, he thought. It's not a *bug*, not a *van;* it's a *bus.* They hiked up the hill to Matthew's four-wheel treasure, parked next to Maria's Mazda.

CHAPTER 6

1981

Bond

TREMONT SAT ON the bench lacing up his shoes. He contemplated why he was here and where he was going once he graduated. Though joining his father at Jackson's Place was the unquestionable eventuality, he had at least one detour to make before he settled into the sedate scientist's lifestyle.

Ever since he could remember, he held the solemn ideal that it was his duty to serve his country in the military. In time, he formulated an objective along the lines of national security. He knew the micro technology was available to protect every vulnerable area of the country, like commercial airlines, border security, or public utilities; but few in business or government were taking the steps to make changes. He also knew it was a huge bureaucracy, and the cogs in the wheel of change encompassed complicated issues. But that didn't mean that he could sit back and do nothing about it. It was every patriotic able-bodied man's God-given responsibility. Those aren't my words, Tremont thought with a grin. He could hear his grandfather's baritone voice reverberating through his brain. "Not only a patriot's responsibility, but a Carson imperative." Tremont was nearly overwhelmed with his post-graduate work in applied physics and computer science at Yale and work on a masters degree through MIT's

Engineering Department. He wasn't sure he could make the decision to enlist in two years.

His thoughts evaporated as he hit the ground so hard it knocked the wind out of him. He lay in two inches of mud gasping. He found himself looking into the familiar sparkling blue eyes of his muddy attacker. He was not surprised to see Sean Eaton, from Mill-something, Maine, with a triumphant grin. Sean took Tremont's hand and jerked him to his feet. When he could finally gulp in a breath, Tremont squeaked out, "That was a cheap shot, Eaton. You better watch your back."

"I always do, Tree. I always do." He laughed and ran back to huddle with his team.

Club rugby was a sadistic alternative to an NCAA sanctioned collegiate sport. Tough, hard-hitting, unpadded, screaming, scrambling students came together to rattle each other's brains outside of the classroom at the one-hundred-year-old Yale University Rugby Football Club. Today, Sean, six inches shorter and twenty pounds lighter, put Tremont in the mud twice. Tremont retaliated with two borderline illegal tackles. After the last tackle that ended the game, Sean could have gotten mad. Instead, he began to laugh, with Tremont following suit. Soon both teams were guffawing like drunks at a bachelor party.

For the next two years, they were inseparable. Every weekend they executed an adventure – including the Ironman Canada competition, scuba diving off the Florida Keys and mountain climbing wherever they could find a mountain. Their Legal Ethics professor grew frustrated with them missing almost every Monday morning class or sleeping through it when they graced him with their presence. He nicknamed the delinquent pair Huck and Tom after Mark Twain's famed adventurers.

They had met when Sean was working toward a degree in law with specialization in criminal justice, criminology, and law enforcement. Though having had a tough time in high school with fighting and controlling his hyperactivity, Sean excelled at the University of Maine and graduated with a pre-law degree in criminal justice. When accepted into Yale's Law School, everyone was quite surprised back home. Like his father and grandfathers, Sean intended on going into the military with the hopes of working his way into military intelligence. Unlike his friend Tremont, he did not have grand ideas of patriotism but wanted the opportunity for nonstop excitement, danger, and intrigue. Sean revealed to Tremont his long-term plan to work for the CIA or another branch of the secret service once discharged from the military, as a hero of course, like his father and grandfathers.

Just months before graduation, they were navigating their kayaks down a full day journey on the Gauley River, infamous for some of the wildest rapids in the Eastern United States. Half way through what some river guides call "The Marathon, "Tremont and Sean stopped to rest prior to taking on the challenging Pillow Rock between two level five rapids. The pair sat on top of a tremendous boulder that seemed to be suspended in mid air.

Tremont had come to a decision. "I'll go with you."

Sean took a large bite out of a baloney sandwich on white bread, void of condiments. "What the hell are you talking about? You are with me."

"I'll go with you," Tremont said between inhaling his sandwich while opening another.

"Where?"

"The Marines, brainless. Someone's got to keep an eye on you."

Sean said a few choice cuss words and laughed. "You can't do that. All you've talked about for two years is getting back to research with your old man. What kind of crap are you shoveling?"

"I talked it over with my dad last night, and he supports my decision." Though thinking back to his conversation with his father, he could not help feeling a sharp pain in his heart. The things his father didn't say said the most. "I'm sure he's worried with all the unrest in the Middle East," he said referring to an escalation in terrorist activities overseas and the taking of western hostages by Iranian extremists. "And he won't say it, but he's disappointed that I won't be at Jackson's Place this summer. But he's okay with my decision," he offered unconvincingly. "Like he said, saving the world from a catastrophic energy crisis can wait."

Sean laughed and almost choked on his baloney. "You two really believe you're onto something, don't you?"

"It's all theory," he said though he knew that was not entirely true, "but yeah, the work is exciting. Ironically, the hard sell will be my mother's family, but the Senator can't argue with patriotism."

"Yeah, that's right. Like me, you come from a long line of war heroes, only you also have a slew of sleazy politicians," Sean mocked, his strong upper Maine brogue rolling off his tongue like custard.

Tremont laughed. "Look who's talking." He stood and reached high over his head to stretch his long body from fingers to sandals. "Let's get going, bud. Those rapids aren't going to wait all day, and there's still Sweet's Falls. Shoot, there might not be anything left of either one of us to deliver to the Marines."

Sean picked up the trash and asked, "Would you join anyhow?" He finished pulling on his neoprene wetsuit, picked up his kayak over his shoulder and walked down to the water edge. "I mean, if I wasn't joining?"

"Yeah, I would. I want to do a lot of things, but this is an experience I feel compelled to have before I check back into the world of science and discovery. My whole life I've been doing what everyone else wants. Don't get me wrong, I love basketball; the scouts are still calling me to go pro, which just isn't in the cards for me. And I miss working with my father." He changed the subject. "I can't wait for you to meet him. He's the most intelligent and insightful man I'll ever know."

"Don't take this wrong but he sounds a bit obsessive, compulsive, and reclusive to me."

"Obsessive yes, but not compulsive. All great inventors in history were obsessed about their product. If they weren't, they couldn't take the hundreds of failures it takes before reaching success." Tremont was tempted to reveal more about his fathers work, but decided against it. "It's safe to say he's on the verge of more amazing discoveries."

"You don't say a lot about the nature of his work. I mean, I know what I've read, but what's he working on now?"

Tremont set his kayak into the water. "All I can tell you is that solar energy panels will pale in comparison." Tremont, feeling that he said too much already, hoped Sean would change the subject. To move the conversation to a close, he slipped into the compartment seat of his kayak and began to stretch his jacket around the circumference to seal out the water.

Sean didn't pursue it. Instead with a rare show of emotion he said, "You remind me of my brother – or he reminds me of you. It would have made more sense for him to be born in your family rather than with a bunch of loggers. Matthew constantly talks about solar power, electricity, fission, and anything science related. A year ago, I was home during break and went with him to the Stearns High School science show; he was just in kindergarten. It was all we could do to get him out of the gym hours after it ended. I remember him giving suggestions to one teacher that he felt was incorrectly helping a student. I think it was a hydro-energy experiment. I'm sure the teacher thought he was humoring my brother as they debated for a while, and it turned out Matthew was right.

"Call it silly or a sense of fate, but I don't think it's an accident that you and I met. Next week we'll run up to Maine so you can meet Matthew, my mom, and of course my old man." He shook his head and then spit. "That will be an experience. For my mom's sake, I have to tell him about joining the service in person. He'll probably lose it, especially when he hears I'm not going to practice law."

"You don't talk about him much," Tremont said.

"Not much to tell. He's like an old bear with his foot caught in a steel trap."

"You two don't get along I take it."

"We have our good days. Like when we are at least two hundred miles apart."

"I look forward to meeting him, your mother, and your little brother. Maybe someday he can come out to Indiana and play in my father's lab. You'll get a kick out of the security; it's tighter than Fort Knox. Until then, looks like it will be my job to keep you from getting your lily white ass shot off."

Sean shook his head as he finished locking himself into his kayak. "It will be the other way around, chump. There's not a tank big enough to hide your hulking frame. We'll have to keep you in camouflage twenty-four-seven."

They pushed off their kayaks into the gushing river. Seconds later, the current drew them up ten feet above the water level sideways along the smooth surface of Pillow Rock where the water converged from all sides. They had to balance, push off with their paddles, and pray. A surge of water threw the fiberglass shells and human cargo so fast and so hard against the rock that they hung in suspended animation nearly upside down for a moment before the force of the water slammed them forward and down into the roaring river. Though they couldn't hear anything above the thundering waves, they screamed like madmen, wide-eyed with smiles from ear to ear.

CHAPTER 7

March 15, 1995 10:00 A.M.

Ramble

MATTHEW PUT MARIA'S bags into the bus. He tried not to say anything, but she caught him rolling his eyes.

"What? I didn't want to forget anything." She stood back to look at the VW bus. "It'll be fun going down the highway in this old thing."

"Like I told my dad last summer . . ."

"I know. It's a classic."

"Right. Remember the bus in the Harvard movie *With Honors*? They used my bus!"

"They didn't use your bus."

"They might as well have used my bus."

They drove down the hill toward Memorial student union. Maria talked, and Matthew grew quiet. He parked and began to get out.

She tugged on his shirt sleeve. "Hey, mister, and where were you just now?"

Matthew hadn't realized he'd phased out – the one thing that bothered her most about him. "What were you saying?"

"I knew it. You weren't listening. I swear I'm going to have to write a paper on the male attention span. No, that wouldn't do; it would be a blank page!"

"You should be a stand-up comic instead. Step aside, Seinfeld!"

"Very funny. Those are shows about nothing, and we're something. Aren't we?" Maria asked.

"We are. I was actually thinking about your father. He already thinks I'm a bad influence on you. Little does he know you planned most of the mischief, and I got all the blame. I wonder if we should let him know that we're going to Florida," Matthew said with a grin.

"Since losing my mother, to say that he's overprotective would be a huge understatement. I know I don't have to tell you that being a first generation Spanish immigrant, and a devout Catholic, things are done a certain way – his way."

Matthew raised his eyebrows, and thought, I'm toast.

Maria chuckled, "Don't you worry about it, punkin. I'll handle Papa."

In the back of the student union parking lot, a man sat in his idling large gray sedan. After Matthew walked past, he turned and sauntered over to a pair of freestanding pay phones.

"So far, so good," he mumbled into the receiver. "I can't tell you for sure, but it appears everything is going according to plan." He paused to listen. "You know me. They won't see me unless I want them to see me. I'll keep in touch."

He returned to his car and smiled as he watched Maria get out of the van, open the back hatch, and begin rearranging the luggage. "Aye, what a pretty lass," he said, "Mr. Eaton is a lucky young man; he has the luck of the Irish, he does." Without the mock accent he said, "He'll need it." He stuck a piece of gum in his mouth and laid his head back on the rest. "Lots of it."

Matthew jogged into the student union and up to the postal desk. "Sandy, I'm glad you're here," he said to the tiny girl behind the counter, "did express mail pick up on time? My package has to be in Boston in the morning." If she said no, he had a contingency plan to deliver it himself since they were essentially going right by MIT on the way south.

When Sandy went to the back to check, he saw two girls he knew from the UMaine swim team. They seemed to be quite upset. "Hey, Donna. Hello, Darma. What's up?" He looked over their shoulders at the bulletin board to read one of many advertisements for roommates, furniture, and books. One of those notes had phone numbers written on the bottom to tear off. None were missing. The note said: URGENT! NEED RIDE TO FLORIDA! (Preferably near Daytona.) WILL PAY FOR GAS! Darma Swenson and Donna Fisher

He observed the suitcases at the two girls' feet. Donna was from upscale Greenwich, Connecticut, and the daughter of a prominent Wall Street attorney. Darma was from the much-celebrated 90210 zip code in Los Angeles and daughter of a movie industry executive, director, or some such professional.

"I'm heading to Florida." Right when he said it, he realized his blunder. Maria would kill him. Please, please say no, he thought, but he knew he was cooked.

The girls' screams nearly broke Matthew's eardrums. They threw their arms around his neck and kissed him on both cheeks.

"We had a ride with a friend to Jacksonville, and my aunt was going to pick us up and take us to her house near Daytona. Anyhow, the plans fell through yesterday, and it was too late to get a decent flight," Donna said. "Matthew! You've saved spring break."

"Matthew, you're a doll! We'll be in your debt."

"Well, if you and Darma can throw in a couple hundred for the trip, that will be thanks enough." Matthew held out a slim hope the money would be a barrier.

"Like, not a problem," Donna said. "I have a little money with me, and my aunt will give you plenty when we get to Daytona. She's, like, totally loaded."

Sandy frowned when she saw the two blonde girls and confirmed the package was safely on the way to Boston. Relieved to have that burden behind him, Matthew focused on the new challenge. He carried one bag under each arm and one in each hand as the two bottle blondes followed behind carrying backpacks seemingly made out of animals. Both girls had shoulder length hair pulled back into ponytails, chalk white skin, bright red lipstick, and blue eyes. His buddy Floyd called them the Doublemint Chewing Gum girls.

As they approached the VW bus, Matthew smiled at Maria but knew, judging by her body language, she was not happy. If her eyes were lasers, she would have cut him and the Doublemints in half. Afraid to put the bags down and give Maria an open target, he made the introductions and explanations.

Darma and Donna seemed oblivious to Maria's anger. They were not as concerned with Maria as they were their mode of transportation to Florida. They stared at Matthew's bus with a sour twist to their faces.

"Are you sure this thing can make it to Florida and back? I'm not sure it'll make it to Greenwich," Darma said.

"Will the authorities let it cross the state border?" Donna added.

Maria beat Matthew to his little speech. "Hey, this is a classic, and Matthew rebuilt the engine himself. This van will take us to hell and back if Matthew asks it to."

"That's what I'm afraid of," Donna quipped.

Matthew arranged their huge suitcases in the back of the bus, covering everything with old moving blankets. His father used to do that when they travelled. He had said, why tempt thieves. What they can't see won't hurt them or you.

Matthew closed the side doors and overheard Darma whisper to Donna, "Let's humor the lumberjack, and when we get to Daytona, we can make other arrangements to get back." He shot them an angry look, and they shrugged.

Matthew tried to give Maria a hug. She pushed him away and said, "Who the hell are these *Baywatch* chicks? I'm not happy sharing you or the trip with anyone." Then letting him off the hook, she put her arms around his neck and said, "But I'm way too excited about my first major road trip past Boston, so let's get this show on the road."

He decided he wouldn't push his luck, as there was already enough high-test estrogen in the vicinity to fuel the space shuttle. After lifting the hidden back seats and storing their luggage behind he was about to get in the VW bus when he saw Floyd standing at the curb with a huge sports bag slung over his shoulder. He knew Floyd would be waiting on the team bus to take him and the track team to Boston to catch a flight to the elite Olympic training camp in Colorado Springs. He caught sight of Matthew and hustled over to the bus. "You look like you're heading to Woodstock instead of Florida." Through the window, he could see Darma and Donna roll their eyes. They were so completely embarrassed anyone, especially the popular and handsome Floyd Schmidt, would see them in this contraption.

Maria smiled and gave Floyd a big hug. Always ready to add fuel to the fire, Floyd said, "You know, dude, you had all these things you could have done this week, and you chose a half-baked idea like going to Florida in your flower power van with three beautiful ladies. Whatever were you thinking?"

"Bus," Matthew corrected and raised his eyebrows.

Floyd ignored the correction and reconsidered. "I see your point. I'm going to Colorado to lift weights and train with fifty skinny, sweaty, and horny guys. I actually like your idea. Any extra room?" Everyone laughed.

"We'll be thinking of you when we hit the beaches in Daytona and Fort Lauderdale, and I'll still get in my swimming and running, so you don't have to worry about getting too far ahead of me."

"You may be able to kick my butt in the pool, dude, but on the field, you'll always be toast." Floyd couldn't swim two lengths of the pool, but though Matthew was a good runner, he was no match for Floyd, an All-American decathlete. "Just be sure to bring me back something interesting from the beach, like one of those southern belles from Charleston or Savannah." With that, he spun around and walked back to the curb just in time to meet the Athletic Department bus. He tossed the sports bag in with the others and climbed on.

Maria stepped up into the front passenger seat, the valley girls nervously fastened the seatbelts Matthew installed last summer, and they headed for the highway on a nearly two-thousand-mile adventure to Miami. On the way out of the parking lot, Matthew caught the eye of a man in a disheveled suit leaning up against a large gray car. The man quickly turned away. Matthew thought he had seen him before in Millinocket at the hunting lodge while studying with Mr. Estebanez. In fact, he was sure of it.

March 15, 1995 11:00 a.m.

The four travelers left Orono and drove down Interstate 95 past Bangor. Matthew felt the thick, cold sheet of tension engulfing the bus. He decided to break the ice. Though he had taken quite a few family vacations and accompanied his father on business trips, Maria had never ventured farther than the Maine coast and one or two school trips to Boston. So when Matthew asked his other passengers about their travel experiences, they dominated the conversation for the next few hours, talking non-stop about all the things they had done and seen as well as expounding on their expansive inventory of possessions. Darma and Donna had gone around the world before the VW bus reached New York City. Matthew and Maria were ready to leave their valley girl passengers at Donna's estate along the shore of Long Island Sound. As they passed Greenwich, Matthew thought about asking them why they couldn't stop and pick up the Lincoln Navigator from the Swenson fleet Donna was bragging about, but he decided against creating a black cloud. He had a feeling Donna's parents were not aware of the Florida trip.

When they stopped for gas, Maria mumbled in Spanish next to him. He was afraid to ask. Instead, he watched the gallons turn over on the meter. He then noticed a gray Cadillac Seville similar to the one he had seen the familiar man leaning on. It was not so much the car, as there were plenty of Cadillacs on the road, but he could see the outline of the driver still in the vehicle through the tinted windows. The driver had not gone into the store after filling up his tank. He just sat in the parking space in his car.

"Do you need anything in the store?" Darma asked. They all went in. When they came out a good twenty minutes later, the Cadillac was gone. "Must be my imagination," Matthew thought aloud.

"What's that?" Maria asked.

"Nothing. I thought I saw someone we knew." On their way out of the parking lot, he looked in all directions and did not see the car. But it bothered him. "There are no coincidences," his brother often said.

In New Jersey, the blondes tired of the aria of themselves, the conversation turned into an inquisition about Maria: her beautiful dark features, her heritage, the loss of her mother, her father's restaurant, and what it was like growing up in a small lumberjack town like Millinocket.

Matthew was surprised to hear Maria elaborate, especially about her mother. The bus's social environment was changing. Maybe talking about the loss would be good for her.

"My father didn't venture far from home; and after my mother died, he lost heart in anything but taking care of me and being the proprietor of *Restaurante de Godello's*."

"Doesn't *Godello* have something to do with wine?" asked Donna.

"My father named the restaurant after the grape his family harvested for generations in *Ourense* in the northwestern region of Spain called Galicia."

Matthew decided to throw in his knowledge. "Godello's is a very popular Spanish restaurant. People come from New Hampshire, Vermont, and Boston because it's so unique. My father says that in Millinocket where Spanish speaking people are scarce, Mr. Valdeorras's cooking made him a hit with the French Canadians, Italians, and even us hard headed Scotch-Irish."

Darma said, "Oh, we loved the food in Spain. My father filmed in Spain one summer, and Mummy and I spent an entire month traveling and eating. I don't think we got to Glacier."

Maria overlooked the mispronunciation of Galicia. "You would love the dishes at my restaurant: *Mariscos*, which is a shellfish dish, and *Mecoras*, a delicious spider crab entrée . . . the *santisguinnos* is which they call crayfish here. And of course, what Northwestern Spain has in common with Maine is our many lobster dishes."

"Do you think that's why your father picked Maine?" Matthew asked to keep in the conversation. Some of what Maria was saying was familiar, but much of it was new.

"I think being close to the ocean was very important for him; and there were too many restaurants on the coast, so he picked a small town that would not have an upscale Spanish restaurant. That was many years ago, when the town was three times the size it is now. If we didn't lose my mother – ," Maria paused, then said more quietly, "Papa had talked about moving to Boston and opening a restaurant."

Matthew sensed the mood swing and said, "Maria, tell them about your favorite dish, besides me, of course."

Maria brightened, "Oh, my favorites are wine marinated scallops and stewed octopus." The other girls both winced. Matthew, who could stomach about anything, was not quite that adventurous, he thought.

"Didn't you tell me that west of where your folks were from there were restaurants that specialized in octopus?"

"They're called *Pulperiias*. Where we go to a steakhouse, the locals in Galacia go to octopus-house restaurant." They all laughed at this peculiarity.

The discussion was still on food when they passed signs for Baltimore and Washington. Matthew was having hunger pains. He'd already finished two packages of Fig Newtons, and was working on a box of Nilla Wafers.

"We also serve classic Spanish dishes like *Paella* – a thick gumbo-like chicken and tomato based soup accompanied by *Tortilla de Patatas, Gazpacho,* and *Horchata de Chufa*."

"'The drink of the gods,'" Matthew quoted from the menu.

"What is it?" Donna asked.

"A thick, rich substitute for milk, coffee, or other dinner drinks prepared with *chufa,* the rare tiger nut from Spain, which my father had his cousins shipped because it's too expensive through normal channels." Her father would get very dark if he had to substitute *Horchata de Almendra* when he ran out of Chufa. "Then we top off the night with sweet flan."

"Oh," Darma exhaled, "I've had that in Spain. It's sinfully delicious cake. I love the caramel."

"Try to control yourself, darling. Save the orgasms for Florida," Donna chided.

"Very good, Darma. When you come to visit, you can have all the flan you desire, or you might want Matthew's favorite, *churros.*"

"What's that?"

"Keep talking, and I'm turning around and heading back to Millinocket!" Matthew said. He wasn't sure if the food was turning him on or the three girls discussing food like they were talking about something else entirely.

"*Churros* are fried dough sprinkled with sugar and served with a cup of thick hot chocolate. But even better than the desserts is the bread!"

"I'm way sorry, but bread over dessert?" said Donna.

"Yes, ma'am," Matthew said, "people from around the world come to Maria's little restaurant in the Katahdin region just for the authentic *Pan de Horno* bread. My uncle had him ship it all the way to Miami for the holidays. It's very difficult to make and impossible to reproduce without a good recipe, which, *en la cabeza de Señor Valledoras.*"

"It's true. The recipes go back many generations. My father took to cooking with his mother very early in life."

Matthew couldn't help thinking this trip would be good for both Maria and her father, though he shuddered to think about seeing her father in person upon their return.

March 15, 1995, 9:00 p.m.

While in training, Matthew had been used to eating four or five times a day. He was famished. His first experience with the southern style Cracker Barrel restaurant was a scene fit for a commercial. He ordered a full breakfast of hickory smoked country ham, eggs over easy, grits, biscuits and gravy, hash-browns, and, since it was on the menu, wild Maine blueberry pancakes! Matthew was about as happy as he had ever been. The girls ate light and shook their heads in amazement that anyone could eat that much food in one sitting. But they got even.

Matthew turned to the hard task of getting the girls out of the gift shop. He had hoped to make Miami before tomorrow afternoon, but they had lost a lot of time. The girls were finally in the bus when he noticed another Cadillac. This time he locked the girls in and trotted across the parking lot toward the car. It has to be the same car, he thought. He was halfway to the car when the driver began pulling away. Matthew picked up his speed, and the driver took off. What the hell, he thought. Maybe he's watching the girls? He had heard that college girls had been abducted on spring break. "Crazy world," he said and cussed under his breath. He almost told them when he got into the bus, but the three of them were singing Beach Boys songs and laughing. He'd tell them at the next stop. He relaxed some as they played music and continued to sing late into the evening.

They drove all night through Virginia and down into the Carolinas. The girls fell asleep while Matthew enjoyed the peace and quiet until it was time to gas up again. The highlight of the next morning, after passing dozens of colorful billboards, eighteen hours after leaving the University, was coming upon a gaudy tourist attraction in South Carolina, "South of the Border."

Maria awoke, rubbed her eyes, and said, "Matthew! I think you made a wrong turn. How did we get to Mexico?" Approaching the entrance, they stared up at an eclectically painted cartoon wearing a sombrero and holding a South of the Border sign. Painted in bright colors, all the buildings sported high false fronts. Along the highway and flanking the buildings on all sides were sky-high billboards advertising peanuts, fireworks, sombreros, sunglasses, and sandals. All the signs used poorly structured English, such as "Pedro ver' glad you come" and "Pedro got 112 meelion Amigos who stay weeth heem."

"How awfully demeaning," Maria commented.

"Someone really needs a lesson in color coordination. Yech," Darma said. "This place reminds me of going with my mom to Tijuana to shop."

The three girls got out to stretch their legs and went into the shop. Matthew looked at the fireworks but made sure the girls were in eyesight at all times.

Maria called to him from the changing rooms and he stood at the corner trying to keep an eye on Darma and Donna.

"So what do you think, handsome?" Maria said with one hand on her hip and the other in the air in a seductive pose, brandishing her new multi-color bikini.

"I have to admit, that beats all the fireworks in the store *and* in China, hands down."

Maria smiled. "Right answer, Mister."

While Maria changed, Matthew walked over to look at sunglasses. Suddenly someone grabbed him just above the elbow.

"Please come with me, Matthew."

Matthew tried to pull his arm away, but the man had him in a vice grip. He pushed Matthew out the side door and toward the back of the building. With one quick move, Matthew pressed back on the man and forced him against the stucco wall. "I'm not going any further unless you tell me what this is about." Matthew turned ready to defend himself and looked right into very familiar eyes. He was speechless.

"Hello, Matthew. Sorry about the strong arm, but I didn't want Maria to see me. Let's go behind the building."

When they turned the corner, Matthew said, "Mr. Estebanez! What are you doing here?"

"Sorry to have to track you down like this. I thought I would catch you at your college, but I missed you by a couple hours. I have an urgent matter to discuss with you."

Thursday, March 16, 8:00 a.m.

After a final handshake and a quick guy hug, Estebanez walked away. Matthew, worried about the girls, rushed back to the souvenir store. Still baffled, he started thinking. Mr. E wasn't the one in the Caddy. How did he get here? If he was willing to come all the way to South Carolina, why didn't he handle the situation himself or send it express mail? And why me? He returned to the back of the building, and Estebanez was gone. He ran down the length of the building and looked into the parking lot, then in the front, and then to the side. Gone.

He went back inside. The girls were gone, and goose bumps popped up all over his arms and back. He ran through the large store and out to the VW bus. They were inside. He leaned over and put his hands on his knees. He thought he was going to throw up. What about the gray Cadillac Seville? Perhaps the guy was with Mr. Estebanez, but something told him he wasn't. He should have thought to ask what Estebanez was driving. And if the guy in the Caddy was with Estebanez, then why didn't one of them give him the package earlier? Why play the cat and mouse game all the way to South Carolina?

In the VW bus, the girls were comparing items from their shopping spree. Matthew opened the doors at the side of the bus and removed the heavy moving blankets. He then lifted up a few suitcases and placed the large envelope underneath. After replacing the suitcases and the moving blankets, he climbed in next to Maria and started the engine. "Hey, did you buy fireworks?" Maria asked. Matthew didn't respond. She tapped him on the arm. "What's the matter? You look troubled."

"Nothing. I decided we could get the fireworks on the way back." He feigned a laugh. "This way I won't be tempted to shoot them off. I wouldn't want to get arrested in Georgia or Florida." Matthew suddenly felt dizzy and blinked at the prisms that appeared in front of his eyes. Not again, he thought.

Maria reached for her purse and took out a familiar silver case. She handed Matthew a small white pill and a bottle of water.

"Then what did you put in the back?" Darma asked.

"A pair of sunglasses in one of my bags," he lied, putting the pill in his mouth and taking a quick gulp.

"Won't you need them to drive?" Darma persisted.

Matthew was in no mood for twenty questions. "If I need them, I'll get them later, thank you." He laid his head back on the seat and closed his eyes.

"Well, excuse me," Darma said.

Matthew drove around the huge parking lot of South of the Border looking for the gray sedan and Estebanez. Nothing. Maria stared at him. She didn't ask, so he didn't try to explain.

They drove through Georgia until Matthew saw blue lights in his mirror. He cussed quietly, but all three girls heard him and looked behind to see the police approaching fast.

Matthew pulled over and, from his side mirror, watched in amazement as the stereotypical *Dukes of Hazard*-type officer approached.

"This trip is getting more interesting by the minute," he sighed.

The heavyset man wrote down their license plate number, looked into the back window, and then leaned on Matthew's windowsill. His face was close enough for Matthew to smell the chewing tobacco.

"You know how fast you was goin', boy?"

"I'm sure it was within the speed limit, officer."

"Don't you go gettin' smart with me. Where did you get this hippie mobile anyhow? I haven't seen one of these in quite a spell," he said as he wrote out the ticket on what looked to be a spiral notepad instead of the usual citation on a clipboard.

"I found it on a farm near my home in Maine. My brother and I, he's serving overseas now, rebuilt the engine and fixed it up."

"Still needs some work, and try paintin' it a normal color." He handed Matthew the paper, which simply showed the name of the county, a charge of going twenty over the speed limit, and one hundred dollars next to the amount due. Matthew was about to argue his VW bus could not go twenty over the speed limit, but he sensed that it would be futile. "Can I write you a check?"

"Sure thang," he drawled. "Just make out the check to Buster Pawley."

"Who is he?"

"You Yankee college kids ask too many questions. He's the local Brunswick Magistrate. 'Course, you could just come down with me to the county jail and see Magistrate Pawley in the morning to state your case." He reached to take back the makeshift ticket, and Matthew pulled it away.

"No, that's all right. Here you go." Matthew handed him the check. He secretly hoped the check bounced but knew his mother had deposited a thousand dollars in his account at the beginning of the semester. He figured since he wasn't speeding, Boss Hog saw the Maine plates on the VW bus and that was justification enough to issue a ticket, real or fake.

"Very wise, young man. You pick up on things real quick. But you really have to remember one thing."

"What's that, sir?"

"There're two types of Yankees. There's regular Yankees, and there's damn Yankees. Now, a Yankee comes to the South and passes through without too much of a fuss. A damn Yankee, well, he comes to the South and stays."

Darma laughed. Donna hit her so hard she yelped.

Boss Hog furrowed his brow and leaned in close to Matthew. The rancid smell of the chewing tobacco was making him nauseated. Out of the corner of his eye, he could see it begin to drip down the Hog's chin.

"Now which are you, boy? A regular Yankee or a damn Yankee?"

"Today we're just regular Yankees, sir."

"Good, good. Now y'all get your Yankee tails out of my county and slow this mule down while you go."

Matthew drove away and didn't start breathing normally until he saw Boss Hog's blue lights disappear in his rear view mirror.

"So it's not a van. It's not a bus. It's a mule," Maria said.

"I totally didn't think people like him existed," Darma said. "My father actually reviewed the script to do a remake of *Dukes of Hazard.* He turned it down."

Donna was laughing uncontrollably while mimicking the last words Boss Hog said. She finally said more seriously, "My father says there are certain states that he's always glad to get through, and Georgia is one of them. He says they're ticket-happy. When they need money, the out-of-state drivers bring revenues up to speed."

Matthew chewed two antacid pills. He had heard stories of people disappearing in the South, and though it wasn't 1960, he got a shiver up his spine. He looked at the girls and feigned a lackadaisical smile. The responsibility for the safety of Maria and the Bobbsey twins was weighing on his rolling stomach: first the gray Cadillac, then Estebanez, now this. Things come in threes, he thought. Bobbsey twins? Who the hell were the Bobbsey twins anyhow?

He decided he would focus his attention on getting to Miami without any other incidents, enjoy the beach, visit his uncle, drop off the package, and then return to Maine – a simple plan.

CHAPTER 8

1981

Patriot

UPON GRADUATING FROM Yale with a masters in physics, computer science and an associate PhD in energy engineering from MIT, Tremont joined the Marines with his good friend Sean Eaton. First came boot camp, and then according to their recruiter, they would be assigned to a special operations unit based in California. The Carson family went into shock. The senator took pride in his grandson's decision, but under pressure from his wife back in Indiana, he had to get involved. Cameron Jackson on the other hand, though perhaps disappointed in not having his son's companionship, remained supportive of his decision.

Though he was the Senate majority leader with the Senate in session, Tremont's grandfather arranged to fly to Hartford's Bradley Airport from DC. He called a contact in the State Department from the plane to assist in heading off the enlistment papers before administration logged Tremont permanently into the system. Once at Bradley, a limo met him. He directed the driver to make double time to New Haven. The double resulted in a ticket passing through New Britain, the billboard-slated home of Stanley Tools. The disingenuous highway patrolman treated the Senator like a common criminal and became belligerent when the Senator referenced his friendship to Connecticut Governor William O'Neill.

Once they were back on the road, he returned his thoughts to his grandson, the living memory of his beloved Karen. Though he was a staunch supporter of the military and sat on the Senate Armed Services Committee, he never considered the military an option for Tremont. He felt certain he could talk him out of this whim, this temporary insanity. Little did he know that his own repetitive monologues about the Carson military history to Tremont, and anyone else within a quarter mile of his deep voice, contributed to an integral part of Tremont's patriotic character.

Tremont met his grandfather at the McDougal Graduate Student Center and they embraced. They had always been close. Along with his father, the Carson family offered his closest connection to his mother's memory. Over coffee – Tremont with an extra large white mocha latte and the Senator, "coffee, strong, and black" – , they talked about everything from Washington politics to Indiana basketball, which had gone into a slump after many of the championship team members graduated. They skirted around the military issue until Tremont rattled off an explanation on his own.

His grandfather listened, offering an "I see" or "uh huh" without interrupting. The evening waned, they switched to decaf, and Senator Stephen John Carson resigned himself to his grandson's decision. "You know, you truly are your mother's son. She was, and you are, even more stubborn than me. When I talk to you, I think of Karen, and my heart wells up with pride." The Senator stared at his coffee grounds. He said, "The past twenty years seem like a day."

"Not a day goes by, Grandpa, that I don't wish I had even one day to know her. That's not to say I don't appreciate how you and Dad have kept her memory alive."

"She was the only person who could see right through me. Your mother knew what I was thinking before I thought it. She called me out on any issue that didn't add up in her mind or that she disagreed with. Do you know how much she loved to argue with me? I always said she would have made a good legislator up on the Hill. I suppose a military career wouldn't hurt if you should ever have a desire to enter politics."

"I'll keep that in mind," Tremont said with a grin, "but if I qualify for special operations, I'll be busy trying to use my computer science and engineering skills to devise protections against terrorist plots."

"Abroad?"

"And here in the States, Grandpa. It's only a matter of time before the fanaticism gets to our shores. We need to protect our energy sources, water systems, air-space, and borders. Right now, we're sitting ducks."

"You've given this a lot of thought, haven't you?"

"Yes, sir. It's been running around in my brain since I was a kid. I needed to get enough education to make the most impact when I enlisted. I may get in there and not be able to make much of it for four, six, or eight years, but I intend to do all I can. When I get out, I'll work with my father to devise products to ensure our country's safety. I can already see that along with my father's work – " Tremont paused as he always did when discussing his dad, "along with his work in alternative energy solutions, we can start a company whose primary focus is security."

When Tremont finished outlining his long-term plans and sat back to take a breath, the senator said, "It's obvious you've developed a passion about our country's security; and by God, if I didn't know better, I would think you were tapping into the closed door sessions of the Senate Armed Services Committee."

Tremont chuckled. "Maybe I have, Grandpa. Maybe I have."

"All the issues you raised are on our plate every month, but I'll be damned if I can get the Democrats to move the necessary funds from social programs to defense and security. I'm afraid it will take a major breach of security before everyone wakes up."

"I wrote a paper on that my senior year. Did you read it?" The Senator smiled and nodded. "I compared our current apathy regarding terrorist organizations to the same sentiments the country displayed prior to the bombing of Pearl Harbor." Tremont perked up. "I think I just had an epiphany." He took a notebook from his backpack and began to write and talk at the same time. "When it comes down to it, Grandpa, everything Dad has dedicated his life to is directly correlated to our national security."

"How do you figure?"

"It's all about oil. Successful, cost-effective alternative energy sources would lessen our dependence on foreign oil and put us into an even stronger economic and strategic position in the world."

"I can't say you're not on target. Every year, we battle over the proportion of funds that the Senate and Congress should direct toward energy research.

Every year, we shelve energy for more immediate and tangible priorities. So, how do you see that all these energy issues directly affect our national security, or more precisely, how is it intertwined with a potential terrorist threat?" the Senator asked. Tremont was too engrossed in his writing to reply.

Senator Carson flew to Indianapolis for the weekend. When he arrived at the Carson estate, he walked into a full house of anxious family members. He lumbered into the great room and announced, "As usual, Tremont is going to do what Tremont wants to do. If he wants to use his talents and brains to help protect the future of our country, how can I or anyone else fault him in that?" The Senator hoped to close the matter without delving into too much of the details.

"That's not good enough, Stephen. Did you try to talk some sense into him?" his wife asked.

He sat down in his soft black leather chair in which no one else would dare sit, took a deep breath, and said, "How on earth could I argue with him? Nearly every Carson man has served our country in the armed forces. Many sacrificed life or limb during one war or another." He explained some of what Tremont had told him, leaving out the military secret service and special operations details.

Mrs. Carson shook her head. "I'd better call Cameron. He so looked forward to having Tremont back with him to work on his precious science projects. He'll be extremely disappointed." She walked out of the room.

Six grandchildren under the age of ten converged on their grandfather like bees on honey. He pulled them onto his lap like Santa Claus. "John, could you grab the bag next to my coat? I just might have something in there for these rascals."

John, his youngest son and the city manager for Indianapolis, retrieved the bag full of goodies and handed it to his father. He stood swirling his drink and said, "You know, Mother always favored Cameron and seems to be the only one who understands his quirky and eccentric ways."

"I think what bothers you, John, is like any of us, she doesn't have a clue as to what's so important that it must be kept behind his shroud of secrecy?"

"Exactly, Father. But she dotes on him and Tremont ten times more than any of us."

The Senator handed out the toys he had picked up at the airport. After a few minutes of smiles and laughs, he looked up at his expectant son. "I know you don't understand Cameron. None of us really do; but let me tell you, Son, one day that eccentric scientist's work is going to change this world in a way measured to Einstein, Bell, or Franklin. Mark my words."

CHAPTER 9

1981

Security

THE DELIVERY VAN pulled up to the solid steel gate. The driver reviewed his delivery manifest. He was new on this route that included no more than five stops, with the first being over sixty miles from his hub location. His ten-hour day included dropping packages here, the state park ranger's office to the east, and some sparse residential locations inland. The man leaned out of his truck and pressed the button below the speaker. While he waited for a response, he reread his route notes. "Be very careful dealing with the security system and the owner." He did not read the rest. He looked to the right and left, impressed with the heavy gauge steel link fence that disappeared into the pine forest. He took note of three rows of barbed wire gracing the top of the fence perhaps ten feet off the ground. He noted that the gate in front of him had heavier reinforcement than the White House gates. The compound only lacked armed marines and executive service officers, though he got the feeling they might appear at any time. The soft female computer voice surprised him. "Please state your name and your business."

"John Lomax, Government Express. I have a package for Mr. Jackson that requires his signature."

"Please type in your security code."

John typed in the code listed on the manifest that he knew changed with each delivery.

"Thank you, Government Express. Please retype your security code." He typed it again.

"Thank you, Government Express. Please type in the package air-bill number." Lomax was not expecting this, and he was a man that didn't like surprises. He typed in the air-bill number, after a long pause the latch clicked, and the gate began to open. The mechanical voice stated, "You may enter, Mr. Lomax. Your vehicle will be under constant surveillance. Please wait in your vehicle near the house until you receive further instruction." Lomax thought that command a little strange.

While interviewing for this assignment, he learned that he would deliver envelopes and boxes, and occasionally highly insured wooden crates. One crate, marked fragile, earlier this year had a fifty thousand dollar insurance policy. Lomax grinned, thinking he might have been tempted to drop the box just to see if the insurance would pay that ridiculous amount, and at the same time, he could get a look at what was so damn valuable.

He drove down the blacktop driveway, taking in the lay of the land. He felt a chill run up his spine as the gate closed behind him. Tall pines eventually opened to a clearing bordering the drive. There stood a magnificent white Charleston-style home with beautifully detailed moldings and trim. On the wraparound porch were four Red Oak Brumby rockers, planters empty of foliage, and two peculiar statues that reminded him of satanic beasts in *The Omen.* John Lomax opened his door and approached, ignoring the computer's command to stay in his truck. He heard a muffled rumbling on his right and then another on his left. He cussed and began to back up slowly. His eyes darted to the sign on the landing: *Beware of Dogs. They don't bite. They gnarl.*

"Nice dogs. I'm a good guy," Lomax said, wishing he had brought along his doggie biscuit box or the handgun tucked under his seat. The monster dogs stood up and stretched almost casually, as if killing delivery drivers were all in a day's work. He heard static coming from a speaker on the corner of the house, then, "Please remain in your vehicle until further instruction. Thank you for your cooperation."

Lomax cussed still retreating as the beasts lumbered down the steps. He had police dog training and knew it was important to remain calm, but he was panicking. He had confronted the enemy in Vietnam, eliminated terrorists in Bosnia, and chased down criminals in dark alleys, but they had all been predictable. Finally, his back touched the delivery truck. He dropped the package, opened the door, and jumped in, slamming and locking the door just as both beasts bounded and straddled their front legs all the way up to the window. He leaned over to the passenger seat with one hand on the power window switch. He could feel their hot breath as they barked and the window closed. "You boys are even bigger than I thought. Damn. What is it your master is hiding behind those mahogany doors?" He had seen what he needed to see. For now. He needed to keep this job. For now.

He didn't wait to see what the next instruction would have been. He'd finish his deliveries, find out what he could from the park rangers who managed most of the dunes and property along the lake, and then endure the long drive back to the station. No wonder it was so easy to request this route when he moved to the Chicago station. They had not been able to keep a driver on this special delivery. He would report in and meet the owner of this secret hide-away next time. Lomax knew this was a long-term assignment. He was tired of the daily pressures in Washington anyhow. Studying this state-of-the-art center and the eccentric owner would be a pleasant break. He took one last look at the dogs. "A challenge," he said as one who enjoyed a challenge.

Back at the porch, the two dogs, one with the large package clenched in his mouth, returned to their posts. The one dog placed the package on one of the Brumby rocking chairs; the other was already lying down, eyes closed, satisfied with the nice stretch.

The two wide-jawed, full-grown Rottweilers were an obvious deterrent to any visitor who might not heed the clear message to stay in the vehicle.

Above the dogs and the stained glass windows accenting the mahogany door, a carefully carved and delicately painted sign creaked. On the sign were the words "Jackson's Place."

About one hundred yards to the right of the house stood a large electrical transformer more commonly seen in a city than in the geography of rural farmland and sandy beaches. Multiple cables ran a few hundred feet across the width of the property and threaded through three telephone poles before hooking into this out-of-place house. On both sides of the house were six-by-ten feet freestanding solar panels, with more adorning the roof. In spite of his quick exit, Lomax could not have missed a dozen or more windmills at least thirty feet in height in the distance behind the house and scattered along the three football fields' length of the property. Though surrounded by a thick green coniferous forest on the south, west, and east, with Lake Michigan on the north, the sandy compound had been cleared of trees to make room for these man-made monstrosities. Close to the back porch of the house, visible above the roofline, a forty-feet old-fashioned oak waterwheel turned slowly in the water of a stream cutting across the property before emptying into Lake Michigan. The contrast of old world and new world energy technology was palpable.

Within a few yards of the northeast corner of Jackson's Place, a park ranger guided a tour of nature enthusiasts. With his back to the tall fence, he said, "Ladies and gentlemen, you have seen half of the Dunes that have marveled naturalists for nearly a century. A most diverse area, this 15,000-acre sanctuary is described as the land where prairie, marsh, and forest meet."

A woman walked down to the water to take pictures of the windmills.

"I wouldn't go down there, ma'am," he ranger said.

One man asked, "Is it true a famous scientist lives behind that fence?"

"Yes, his name is Dr. Cameron Jackson. Though the good doctor has never given an official version, a few of us rangers have done some research. How does someone carve out such a large section of Indiana Dunes, our prized national lakeshore? One story is that Dr. Jackson is the great, great, great grandson of Andrew Jackson. They say Jackson received a thousand year lease on this land. One of President Jackson's descendants donated most of the land back to the government but kept this prime real estate."

The tourist said, "No matter how he obtained the property, he obviously prefers his tranquility and privacy."

"As a scientist he certainly has a place where he can submerge himself completely in his research."

The woman with the large zoom lens on her camera continued to wade into the water as the ranger went on to tell about how another ranger climbed the high rock wall that stretched a dozen yards out into the lake. He ended his story by saying, "An air-raid siren blasted out a sound so loud he could not hear for hours. Then a commanding voice stated, 'You are trespassing on private property protected by watch dogs, electric fencing, motion sensors, and video surveillance. Enter at your own risk.'"

"What do you think he's hiding?" another naturalist asked.

"Of course I'm only speculating, but my guess is that he works on highly sensitive government projects; he's a physicist, so maybe it's nuclear related? Who knows, but it would have to be something very important to have more security than the president."

When the woman began to climb the rocks, the siren split the air, ending conversation, sending the group in full retreat with hands covering their ears.

Dr. Jackson was sitting in the den of the house his wife designed, contracted, and decorated three decades before, when the northern property siren went off. That was the third time this month. He spun his chair and pointed a remote control toward the large wall of monitors. He chuckled as he saw the young woman splash into the water though he felt bad about her camera flying into the air and splintering on the rocks. He recognized the young ranger holding his ears and running to save her.

He spun back around to the scrapbook that held his attention and took another sip of cognac. His current page depicted the house that inspired Jackson's Place. The Market Inn, in historic Charleston, South Carolina, was the bed and breakfast where he and his Karen had honeymooned thirty years before.

He closed the book and placed it gingerly on the mahogany shelves, right of the monitors and security-system control center. Since everything in the house reminded him of Karen, he stayed busy with his work. He spent the majority of his time developing his proprietary solutions to the inevitable depletion of natural fossil energy resources.

On rare occasions he traveled to universities and government agencies to raise grant money. He preached about the necessity of accelerating the development of alternative energy sources. From those necessary fund-raising tours, curiosity percolated from advocates and detractors alike. Advocates joined in his mantra calling for change. Detractors feared disruption of the status quo.

Jackson had proved he could deliver with advanced solar technologies, but what if he could come up with a better source that was compact and cost-effective. It could cost the oil and automotive industries billions.

The scientist swirled his drink and shook his head. The world was making progress but at a snails pace; and if they could not help themselves, he would have to give them a push. He was nearly ready to give the world of science a push. He just had a little more work to do in the most sophisticated energy lab on the planet right there, below ground, at Jackson's Place.

He sat in his favorite leather easy chair nursing another glass of Hennessy cognac. He swirled deep in thought after a disturbing phone conversation with his son, Tremont. He was aware that another delivery van braved the compound and that Popeye and Brutus were keeping watch over the package. As with the tour of would-be naturalists, he had watched it on one of the screens on the wall of plasma monitors across the room. He had monitors placed throughout the house so he would be able to look at any part of the property from the labs, the kitchen, or his bedroom. Each monitor displayed eight views of the expansive compound in rotation. Motion and sound sensors triggered alarms if anything over the weight of a large raccoon should come within sixty feet of the electrified fencing surrounding the property. Often a deer or a black bear sounded the alarm at night, but that was all right. He was glad to wake and review the projections from the infrared night video cameras. Proof of the system's effectiveness gave him comfort.

In fact, the alarm had gone off at 5:00 a.m. this morning. On a monitor, he saw a family of deer feeding close to the western fence. He looked at the digital clock on the screen and decided to head down to the lab. The coffee maker turned on automatically at six; and by seven, he was in the lab. While he dressed, he pictured, instead of a family of deer, a well-trained team of Iranian terrorists crossing from Canada, storming Jackson's Place to kill him and steal his work. A few years ago he might have expected the Russians, but now the threat could come from a plethora of sources.

He possessed a number of weapons, but his favorite was a custom-made .45 caliber handgun engraved with the initials "CJ" on both sides of the grip. His father gave the pistol to him when he retired from the Marines just after Karen died. Though he and his father were estranged, they became quite close after Tremont was born. Cameron wished he and his father had shared the kind of relationship he had with his son Tremont. Cameron always kept the gun near him whether in the basement lab, drinking himself silly in the den or walking the compound with the dogs.

After Karen's funeral in '59, his closest friend helped him obtain much of the compound's security equipment. He also had help from an agent with the FBI, whom he preferred would leave him be. Both his friend and the agent had also suggested that Cameron keep a gun close. His friend was godfather to Tremont and along with the FBI agent were the only other people convinced that Karen's death was intentional; a warning, with fatal consequences. He poured another glass of cognac and cursed. The other believer, agent Flannigan of the FBI, could have prevented it, if he had only listened. Cameron tossed down the shot trying to erase the thought.

He stared at a picture on the wall of himself on a large sailboat, arm in arm with a handsome shorter man. What was it his closest friend called himself now? Cameron had laughed when he received the last wooden case holding a bottle of expensive rare wine, with its note from his old friend bearing a new pseudonym. There were a number of times over the past three decades that, had his friend not intervened, Cameron might not be here to continue his work. But even his friend could not stop them when it counted the most. Even he had not been able to save Karen.

The next morning Cameron woke in his easy chair and barely noticing the effects of the alcohol that rarely left his system, he showered, went to the kitchen, made a pitcher of Bloody Marys and pushed a large red button next to an oversized dumbwaiter. "Down you go, Mary." He filled two large bowls with kibbles and was in the lab before 6:00 a.m.

Ten hours later he wrote that it had been a good day in the lab. Cameron made a habit of denoting the day's progress and any thoughts or clues about where to start the next day in his volumes of journals. No matter how sure he was that he would remember the next day, he would be lost without those notes the next time he sat down at the desk. Scientific creativity came and went like waking from a dream. The vision could be gone in moments.

He considered going back up in the dumbwaiter, both he and Tremont had done it more than once over the years. Instead, he stood, stretched, and climbed two flights of stairs, stopping to set the security system at each level. He was out of breath when he reached the main floor.

Cameron walked to the kitchen bay window overlooking the back of the property, the beautiful water wheel and Lake Michigan off in the distance. He stared at the windmills. The twelve posts full of halogen lamps lit up the compound like an evening Chicago Cubs game. The giant guardians cascaded toward the sandy beaches. He opened the door to the deck and stepped into the evening air. Cameron thought of how he enjoyed his daily walks with his son along the untouched beaches throwing sticks into the lake for Brutus and Popeye to retrieve. They had not done it since Tremont went to Yale. Besides his nightly cognac, his son and the oversized Rottweilers were his source of joy outside of work. He whistled for the boys; and, though stiff and tired, he walked down the steps and off toward the shoreline. Brutus and Popeye came around the house. "You miss our walks too, don't you, boys?" They responded with boisterous yelps and tumbled over each other as they sped to the lake. Cameron joined them and picked up sticks to begin their old ritual. Though the boys could keep this up all night, Cameron tired and settled on a shelf of Bedford limestone estimated to have been deposited thousands of years ago – or millions, depending on whether you were talking to an evolutionist or a creationist. Off to the west, he could see the Chicago skyline sitting north of the obtrusive Gary, Indiana steel mills. To the east, he could see the lights of Michigan City. Brutus jumped on the rocks and rubbed against his leg. Cameron smiled and scratched behind his ears. Jealous, Popeye appeared on the other side for his equal share. "It's not such a bad life. I have you guys, and I have my Jackson's Place refuge."

He sat with his pair of man's best friends and stared at his habitat. Jackson's Place was bequeathed to Cameron Jackson by his father who inherited it from his father who inherited it from his father who, as the story goes, inherited it from his grandfather – Andrew Jackson. The seventh president of the United States, though a Tennessean, purchased it from the French Canadian farming family that owned the entire 15,000 acres running twenty-five miles along the Lake Michigan shore a few years before Indiana became a state in 1816.

Revitalized by the fresh lake air, Cameron and his four legged companions walked the gradual grade to the house. This was another of many nights the renowned Dr. Cameron Jackson didn't feel like saving the world, and allowed himself to get blind drunk, more drunk than usual, smoke Cuban cigars, and reminisce about what could have been. His son had phoned from Yale to let him know he would not be back this summer to help carry the cross. Of all the crazy patriotic things to do, Tremont had enlisted in the Marines. He knew it was a possibility in Tremont's long term plans, though they hadn't discussed it often. But he'd privately hoped Tremont would return home after graduate school. He looked at a picture of Karen on the desk and said, "Sometimes there's too much of your father – and mine – in that boy," and then as if she replied, "I know, honey, just one more sip and I'm off to bed. I'll cut back. I promise." He made this promise nearly every night.

After a few hours, Brutus and Popeye slipped in the door as he stumbled to the front porch. He leaned onto the porch railing for support noticing a familiar red and yellow, slightly gnarled, express mail package left the day before by yet another agent who could not follow simple directions. He grinned at the memory of the look on the face of the otherwise capable deliveryman as Brutus and Popeye announced their presence.

The dogs lumbered to the kitchen to wolf down two large bowls of dry chow, their fourth helping for the day. Cameron sat hard into one of the Brumby rockers and tore the package open. He pulled out an unmarked videotape and a letter typed on plain white paper. Not again, he thought.

> WE ARE STILL WATCHING, MR. JACKSON. YOU CAN RESEARCH. YOU CAN DEVELOP. BUT WE EXPECT RIGHT OF FIRST REFUSAL ON PURCHASING ALL OF YOUR RESEARCH. OUR OFFER REMAINS THE SAME. TEN MILLION DOLLARS. HALF PAID WHEN YOU DELIVER. HALF PAID WHEN PROTOTYPES ARE OPERATIONAL. AND OF COURSE THE ADDED BONUS: YOU AND YOUR SON LIVE. TIME IS RUNNING OUT. WE ARE NOT IMPRESSED WITH YOUR EVER ADVANCING SECURITY SYSTEMS. TO US, IT'S A MINOR INCONVENIENCE. IF WE WANTED TO BE WITH YOU IN THE HOUSE DRINKING COGNAC AND SMOKING CIGARS, WE WOULD BE. BUT WHO CAN WORK EFFICIENTLY WITH A GUN TO THEIR HEAD? LET'S BE PRACTICAL. THE FBI HAS ALREADY PROVEN THEY

CANNOT PROTECT YOU OR YOUR LOVED ONES. THEY COULD NOT PROTECT HER. AND EVEN THE MARINES CANNOT PROTECT YOUR OTHER MOST PRICELESS ASSET. TIME IS WASTING. WHEN YOU ARE FINISHED SIMPLY REMOVE THE JACKSON'S PLACE SIGN FROM THE PORCH, AND WE WILL BE IN CONTACT.

Cameron knew the same person, for the last twenty years, had typed these letters. They had the same tone and tenor on the same old Smith and Corona typewriter displaying a weakness with the "n" and "t" keys. After Karen's sudden death, officially deemed as natural during labor, he presented the letters to homicide detectives with the Indianapolis Police Department, and then to inspector Flannigan. He wanted revenge, but against whom? He had to protect his son first. As the letters and videos continued to show up, he kept them to himself. Not even Tremont was aware of their content. He had planned to reveal it all to him this summer. That would have to wait.

He perspired even in the cool night air. His face was hot. It was a threat. Yet it was nothing. As usual, the return address was a Washington DC post office box that had proved to be a bogus location upon investigation. The videotape was generic and untraceable, he and his closest friend, who had connections, had tried. Cameron's vision blurred as he stared toward the front of the property. He knew they could not know the depth or even the premise of his research. They couldn't know that CJ Energy Cells would one day be produced so easily and at such a low cost that a child could replicate them.

They were guessing but obviously felt what he was working on would have a major impact. Ten million dollars was a lot of money. If they planned to obtain anything from him with intimidation and threats, they were sorely mistaken. Either the whole world would benefit equally, or he would bury a life's work with him. No monopoly would control the future of energy.

He wobbled from the Brumby into the house. He made his way to a cozy, acoustically perfect room where Tremont and he had installed their audio and video systems. He inserted the tape and sat back on the corner of a chair. The video revealed soundless scenes of him playing with the dogs on the beach, Tremont walking on the Yale campus, Senator Carson on the steps of the

Capitol, nieces and nephews at play on their school campuses, and other family members shopping at the mall or working in their offices.

He shut off the television, pulled out the VHS tape, wrapped the letter around it with a rubber band, and set it on the desk. He would place it in a cabinet down in the lab along with the others. He shook his head and said, "It's been twenty years, you bastards." Then, never sure if even Jackson's Place could be bugged, he thought, One day soon, you'll pay. The dogs came into the room and sat at the foot of his leather armchair. He affectionately rubbed their ears. Before he fell asleep, he thought of his son, his wife Karen, and his life's work. He grumbled, "I'll do it, or I'll die trying."

CHAPTER 10

March 16, 1995 Noon

Quest

IT WAS LATE morning when they saw the signs for Jacksonville, Florida. Matthew looked at the odometer. It had been thirteen hundred miles since they'd left Maine.

"All right!" they all cheered with a surge of energy. Unfortunately, they were under the illusion that, being in Florida, they were almost there. Matthew somehow missed the sign that read 357 miles to Miami. The girls slept at least half of the trip, and he was running on what was at the bottom of his adrenalin tank. He had planned to stop on Daytona so they could see the Speedway and drive on the beach; but when he saw that it was fifty miles off the highway and more than 288 miles to Miami, he changed his mind.

The next stop was to drop off Darma and Donna just south of Daytona, in Port Orange. After getting lost a few times, Matthew pulled up to the gated community. Getting through the gate was tough. Matthew was sure the security guard was not used to seeing disheveled teenagers in late model VW buses.

"You kids just get back from Woodstock?" the guard asked.

"Well, you're close, sir. We just drove in from Maine. I'm dropping off my Baywatch friends with their aunt, and then we'll be on our way." The guard opened the gate, and they drove down the long lush drive flanked by majestic palm trees. Impressed, Matthew pulled into the driveway of a very nice Spanish-style home with a perfectly manicured Florida-style lawn and a premium ocean view.

Once Matthew unloaded their bags, he had the chore of asking Donna and Darma for gas money again. He was down to his last few dollars and, out of sheer stubbornness, planned to hold off stopping at an ATM or using his American Express until they got to Miami. He considered letting it go, but after all, the whole reason for taking along passengers was to share in the cost of the trip. It was the principal of the matter. Sometimes his frugality ended up costing him in the end.

Matthew and Maria were leaning up against the VW soaking up the sun when Donna came prancing down the front steps.

"My aunt isn't home, Matt." She smiled and batted her eyes. "Can I get you some cash when you come to pick us up next week?"

Like I have any choice, Matthew thought. He nodded his head. Donna pranced back to the porch and into the house without looking back. He and Maria got in the VW and headed out of the neighborhood.

Matthew stopped at a Publix and pulled money out of the ATM before stopping at Waffle House. After yet another heavy breakfast, the "All-Star Special," they were back on the highway, pushing the VW hard all the way down the long stretch to Fort Lauderdale. The speeding ticket in Georgia was now a distant memory. The bus didn't sound good. There was a strange rattle in the back.

When they filled up in Fort Lauderdale, Maria said, "Matthew, it's time for me to learn to drive the van."

"Bus."

"Whatever. I know you're tired. I'll drive the rest of the way to your Uncle Carl's house."

"Something is not feeling or sounding right. Do you hear that noise in the back? How about we wait until we get to Carl's? I'll teach you to shift gears in their neighborhood, though a few cat's lives may be at risk."

She folded her arms and slid down in her seat. Matthew winced seeing her all too familiar pout. They drove the next few miles with the only sound being the cling-clang growing louder in the engine.

Carl Eaton stepped out of his quiet suburban home, stared down the well-lit street and looked at his watch. The Eatons lived in the Homestead area just south of Miami. Carl was a pilot for a cargo airline and had the dubious distinction of logging the most hours, without incident, while transporting cargo to and from South American countries. That is, until mountain-based guerillas shot his plane out of the sky over El Salvador, most likely mistaking them for the CIA or DEA. His copilot died on impact, and he spent the next few years in rehabilitation. A back page Miami Herald news article started a short-lived rumor linking Carl Eaton to the CIA. The Herald later retracted their story but with no apology. After months of rehab, Uncle Carl recovered and had to give up flying. He made a small fortune in real estate and continued in the import-export business. As a sideline he collected and worked on vintage cars.

His wife, Carol came out of the house and said, "You look worried."

He looked at his watch again and muttered, "I'll give them another hour, and if they aren't here, I'm either going to have to call the state police or get up in the air and look for them. That old washed out VW bus Kate described should be fairly easy to locate along 95."

"It's too early to worry, honey. They probably got tired and stopped to rest."

"I guess." But it was what he knew, that she didn't know, that worried him.

"I'm on my second wind. But the bus is getting worse." When she didn't respond, he said, "I'm sorry about making a joke about the cats." She gave him an extra evil look and then smiled and they both laughed.

Earlier, Matthew had retrieved the express mail envelope from the back, and he felt for it under the seat. He wanted to deliver the package but was torn between his promise to Mr. E, and getting to his uncle's house before the engine blew. He had also told his uncle he would be there by dinnertime, and it was well past that. With less confidence than he felt, he said, "We'll sleep on the Biscayne beaches all day tomorrow. How does that sound?"

"Wonderful. I can learn to drive standard anytime. It's so nice just to have you all to myself." Maria gave him a hug and kiss, then crawled into the backseat and fell fast asleep.

They still had an hour or more to go. The VW bus sounded like a steam engine. Matthew was beyond tired. Sometimes I really am my father, stubborn as hell. I should have let her drive. Though he had great respect for his father, the thought of being like him didn't bode well. He stopped and checked the engine every ten miles. Come on, just a few miles farther. Now he was not just worried about gas money. The mechanic's bill would kill his budget for the semester. The last thing he wanted to do was call home to hear "I told you so."

Maria awoke refreshed and bounced into the front seat, animated like a kid seeing Disney World for the first time. They had actually discussed going to Disney for at least a day, maybe on the way back. He decided to gamble that the engine would hold up at least until they reached his uncle's house and said, "Hey, you woke up just in time, I have to drop something off in Miami Beach."

"Drop something off? You never mentioned anything about that."

"I didn't? It's nothing, just a package."

"Something from your father?" Maria asked skeptically.

"Something like that."

She frowned at him. "What-ev-er," she drawled, imitating their former passengers. Then she saw the sign again. "There's the Miami Beach exit! Don't miss it. Let's run down to the ocean while we're there, just for a few minutes. I'm still mad at you for missing Daytona. Hey, do you know who lives in Miami Beach?"

"A whole lot of people from New York?"

"Yes, and one of them is Thomas Harris."

Matthew raised his eyebrows and cocked his head.

"You know, he wrote the Hannibal Lecter books. Maybe we'll run into him."

"Sure, *Clarice*, maybe he'll be walking down the beach in the middle of the night," he said, and then flinched as she punched him in the shoulder. He smiled at her exuberance. He wasn't sure why he felt the compulsion to lie to her. Until this trip, he could not remember ever having done that. Until he sorted out what Mr. Estebanez was up to, he didn't want to get Maria involved. "I think it's a good idea to let the engine rest a bit anyhow. We'll deliver the letter, and we can sleep in the bus for a few hours. It's really too late to drive on to my uncle's house anyhow." As if on cue, the engine whistled and sighed. "I don't know how much more the bus can take."

Maria seemed not to be listening as she leaned her head out the window. "I think I can smell the ocean and hear the waves. Let's go walk on the beach before dropping off your precious package."

He followed the signs from I-95 to 195 East, onto Arthur Godfrey which dead ended on Collins. He turned onto a side road between two condominium complexes thinking the beach must be somewhere in that direction. The bus sounded worse. It was pitch dark, about midnight. Suddenly, a terrible grinding sound came from the back of the bus sounding like lug nuts rattling in a coffee can. Then there was a loud bang and the whole bus shook like they'd hit a roadside bomb.

Smoke billowed out from the rear of the bus. Matthew laid his head on the steering wheel, and then got out to investigate. When he dropped the door to the engine, he was nearly blown over by the smoke.

"Pretty bad, huh?"

"Yeah, pretty bad. I don't get it. Sean and I overhauled the whole engine!"

Matthew slammed the hood and stormed down the alley toward the beach, leaving Maria five steps behind. He ran down the boardwalk steps and out onto the beach. At the water's edge he clenched his fists, and shook them at the sky.

Matthew saw that Maria had caught up with him; she stood at the top of the boardwalk stairs and watched as he kicked the sand and waved his arms like a lunatic.

"You're going to bring on an episode, Matthew," she yelled.

Matthew, disconcerted, sat down on the wet sand and stared out at the luminous waves, the half moon, and the bright stars that seemed to hang within his reach. He recalled the chastisement from his father who said Matthew's sudden outbursts came from his mother's Scotch-Irish family. She and Matthew shared the kind of temperament that was like a slow burning fuse, which without warning, reached the TNT followed by a tremendous explosion. Back home, he seemed to be able to keep his emotions under control most of the time. Here, for the first time, he was on his own. It's time to grow up, he thought.

He took a deep breath and turned to see Maria sitting at the top of the boardwalk, looking adorable with her knees pulled up to her chest. The look on her face was one of amusement. Matthew was embarrassed.

She had seen a hint of his Irish before. A few meaningless quarrels, a few schoolboy fights after school; and just this semester, Matthew and his friend

Floyd defended her from a couple of drunken football players. But Maria must have thought this maniacal display was off the chart.

Matthew liked to be in control of his emotions as well as the situation. At least that way, when things went wrong, there was only himself to blame. He was blaming himself and God this time. He had never been particularly religious so he surprised himself, adding God like that.

Once he released his stress through his immature display, he was ready to tackle this seemingly hopeless situation. In the past, he had Mr. Johnson at the shop and his brother Sean to lean on. He was good with engines himself, but he didn't have any tools. It was late in the evening, and the chance of finding a shop was slim. He walked back up to the boardwalk and smiled at Maria.

"Matthew, Matthew, Matthew. Feel better?" She reached out to hand him something. He took the pill and put it in his mouth.

"Immensely, I'm fine now. We're broken down in a dark alley in a strange town where we don't know anyone. No worries," he said as they walked hand in hand across the boardwalk and back onto the street. The bus looked to Matthew like one of those dead cartoons, with large Xs for eyes on the headlights. The only sign of life was the smoke still rising from the rear.

Matthew feared hallucination as a lanky man dressed like a character from Miami Vice emerged from the smoke. The man posed an eerie sight with the smoke creating a halo around his body in the lamplight and incited a sixth sense of potential danger. Matthew looked around for some kind of weapon, but there wasn't anything except concrete, buildings and large green dumpsters. He started playing fight scenarios through his mind and decided that if there was trouble he would have to fight in close to avoid what appeared to be an NBA center's reach. *I'll just fight dirty; kick and punch first and ask questions later.*

Maria seemed curious but not scared. She said quietly, "This tall fellow reminds me of someone, a singer maybe."

The spindly but not quite gangly man leaned in the shadows against the driver's side door of the bus with his head *and* shoulders above the roof of the at least six-foot-high VW. As they drew closer, they noticed he held in one hand a box of Cracker Jacks.

A guess would put him somewhere in his early to mid-thirties. He was clean-shaven with khaki pants and an un-tucked white silk short sleeve shirt. His unruly hair had tight, dark curls. His prominent nose reminded Matthew of Larry Bird, the former center for the Boston Celtics. When he saw them coming, he pushed off the bus and into the moonlight with his face brightening into a broad smile.

"That's it," Maria said just loud enough so only Matthew could hear.

"That's what?" Matthew said, not taking his eyes off the man and preparing himself to dive in punching and kicking.

"Barry Manilow."

"What?"

"That's who he looks like. Barry Manilow, except a lot taller."

"Larry Bird."

"Who?"

"Larry Bird. You know, the Celtics center. He's now a coach."

The man interrupted their little argument. "Hi, I'm Cracker Jack," he said with an even broader smile. "Looks like you kids have some major problems with this classic."

Well, Matthew thought, he's the first person to recognize the VW bus as a classic. He kept his guard up all the same. For all he knew, this guy could be a psycho killer. Still, something about him seemed familiar. To hide his tension, he laughed. "Is that the first name you could come up with? The name off the box?"

"Well, young fella, it just happens to be the handle I go by these days. And you're right. I was nicknamed after the snack. I never could get enough of the damn stuff, and now it just makes me think of better days."

The stranger shook Matthew's hand and did a little bow as he took Maria's hand. Matthew was thinking that he did appear to be harmless, but his brother had often said to him to beware of the friendly raccoon, he'll turn out to be rabid.

Matthew followed behind as they walked to the back of the VW while Maria explained how they ended up here. She finished by saying, "Matthew had this package to deliver, and I was insistent that we stop and see the ocean first."

The stranger sauntered to the back and opened the engine flap. The smoke had settled down. He reached behind his back and under his shirt to take out a Mag-Lite.

Matthew wondered aloud, "Why would a guy have a huge flashlight tucked in his belt?"

"Listen, kid. Do you know where you are? A Mag-Lite makes a decent deterrent to crime. If you're going to make a habit of breaking down in dark, crime-ridden alleys, you should have one too." Shining the light on the engine, he cussed under his breath when he burned his hand.

Matthew leaned in beside him, still wary and ready to block if the stranger swung the heavy flashlight. Standing like this reminded him of standing with his older brother while they studied an engine problem together.

"Hmmmm, I'm afraid we are going to need a mechanics bay area, a lift, and a lot of parts." Cracker Jack went on and on with a list of parts that would be needed, and the two of them discussed how to fix the bus. All Matthew heard was expensive and more expensive.

"I could fix most of the problems if I had the right tools and a shop to put her up on a lift. But that seems to be a problem," Matthew said, looking around at the alley.

Maria stood quietly behind, but Matthew knew she was bursting with questions and was already profiling the man as a potential gentleman criminal: *pretty much harmless, but possibly into high-end theft of diamonds and furs or perhaps securities fraud.*

"Any suggestions, Mister – ," he paused, "Jack?" Matthew laughed. He could not bring himself to say the outlandish name. Cracker Jack looked over Matthew's shoulder at Maria and smiled. The light from a street lamp shone on his face. He looks so familiar, Matthew thought, like I've seen him somewhere a very long time ago. When a thought came to mind, he quickly dispelled it as impossible.

Matthew had turned to the engine and was not paying close attention when Cracker Jack suggested that they go over to see his friend at the Shell station and see if he could give them a tow. When Cracker Jack said his friend's name, Matthew turned sharply.

Matthew was about to ask him what he said the gas station attendant's name was, especially his last name, when Maria nudged in between them.

"Maria, my name is Maria." Never one to be left out, she offered her hand and shook his firmly. "It's a pleasure to meet you, Mr. Cracker Jack."

Maria could charm the rattle off a snake, and Cracker Jack came under her spell, or was it something more?

"So you are Maria. It's a pleasure to meet you as well. You two kids go over there and tell Marcos that it would be a favor for me, and he will do whatever he can do to help. Let's say he owes me a favor or two."

"What did you say Marcos's last name was?"

Cracker Jack didn't miss a beat, "I don't think I did say, but it's *Estefon*."

"Oh, Estefon, right."

Maria looked at Matthew with an inquisitive expression.

"I could have sworn he said Estebanez," Matthew whispered. If he did, why did he now say Estefon, Matthew thought. Estebanez did not sound to him like a common Cuban name, though maybe it was. I've got to get some sleep.

Cracker Jack was so charismatic that they found themselves talking for quite some time. "I have to make a call, and I'll ring Marcos at the Shell. I'll be right back." And he sauntered around the corner.

"He asked me an awful lot of questions, and I can't believe how we've rattled on about ourselves. There's something really familiar about this Cracker."

"His name is Cracker Jack," Maria said with a smile. "I think he's charming. How old do you think he is?"

"I was figuring around Sean's age." In a short amount of time, he had told the Cracker about his dreams, schooling, and life in general – even his entrepreneurial hopes and aspirations outside of his father's business that he had not discussed with anyone but Maria. Feeling embarrassed about running on, he said, "I read that people have a tendency to talk easily about themselves if you just ask a lot of leading open-ended questions."

"What's an open ended question?"

"The kind you can't answer with a No or Yes. I think that's what he was doing to me."

"In psych class, I learned a great interviewing technique," Maria said. "By changing every sentence of the conversation into a question, people will tell a perfect stranger their middle name, social security number, and bra size."

"Thank goodness he left before you could reveal that."

"Very funny. But, I know what you mean, I felt like he was analyzing us."

"Or interviewing," Matthew agreed.

"I think you and he may have a lot in common."

Cracker Jack came back around the corner. "Sorry, guys. I had to check in with my G-Men. You two looked famished. After you talk to Marcos, come over to the all-night diner." He turned and pointed. "It's around the corner on the end of this building. My apartment, compliments of the U.S. government, is right above the diner. My friend Juanita is there now and she'll take care of you. I'll meet you there in a bit." He spun around and disappeared around the corner.

Matthew looked at Maria, who looked back with the same quizzical expression. "G-Men? Doesn't that mean the FBI or something?"

"Yeah, that's what they used to call them, but maybe he meant something else. I don't like the sounds of any of this Maria, but I don't know that we have a choice, do you?"

"I think it's exciting and I think you are misjudging Cracker Jack. He's a character, but harmless, at least, harmless to us."

"You're the psychologist. Okay, let's go over and meet Marcos before we get some food."

They walked out of the alley across the street to the Shell station. Miami Beach was predominantly retired New Yorkers and the extremely eclectic, but Matthew knew, it could also be very dangerous at night. The Shell station looked like it had for thirty years. The backlit sign was in the shape of a shell, and the cement building was probably painted white at some point but now was all different shades of grime and dirt. Two gas pumps stood out front like a couple of tin soldiers with red bodies and round yellow heads. Sitting in the office with his legs on a desk, reading a racing magazine, was a short man wearing a freshly pressed gray shirt with red pin stripes and a Shell patch just below the name George.

"Hi, I'm Matthew, and this is Maria. This guy told us to see you . . ." Matthew said pointing back in the direction of the bus.

He laughed and said in broken English, "Hi, I'm Marcos and that old Cracker Jack, he sure knows his engines like nobody business. He may seem *loco*, but he sure is a smart about things. He help me out many times so I do what I can, *chicos*."

While noting his neat appearance and lack of grease or even a little dirt on his hands and under his fingernails, something else occurred to Matthew, "Do you think he has ever been in Maine? I have this nagging feeling I know him or have seen him before."

"Don't know about that, Mr. Eaton. He been around the world I think, but been down here in Miami for a while."

Matthew cocked his head and tried to think if he had told Cracker Jack his last name. He didn't think so. And why would he have a shirt that says George? He was about to ask but Marcos spoke first.

"My mechanic, he not here today, and since it's *Domingo,* we would not be able to get parts from Miami until Monday. So Cracker Jack, he says you have family in Homestead?"

"Yes, my uncle."

Marcos walked to the gray metal desk and punched some keys on a worn out adding machine. "Then for *cuarenta dólares,* I take you *esta noche.*"

Matthew turned to go, then did an about face and said, "Marcos. What is your last name?"

Marcos turned, smiled and said, "Estefan. *¿Porque?*"

"I just misunderstood what your friend said. That's all. Thanks."

While they waited for Marcos to get off work or finish reading his racing magazine, they walked back to the VW bus. Maria laughed when she opened her door. On her seat was a twenty-four ounce box of Cracker Jack's.

"Is this guy for real, Matthew?"

"My guess is that he's a little bit crazy."

Matthew leaned up against the bus and closed his eyes. He could see his father, arms folded, shaking his head, not saying a word and walking back into their house. I think I'll keep this happenstance to myself, he thought grimly. He locked the smoldering casualty of their long journey. They walked away from the Shell and the bus toward the all night Cuban diner, first passing a number of busy bars.

As they passed The Executive Club, two men were walking toward them, taking up the whole sidewalk. Matthew stepped aside but still bumped into one of two well-dressed men that Matthew assumed were leaving the upscale strip bar. One scowled at him and the other smiled and said in a strange Middle Eastern yet sort of German accent, "Please excuse my brother and I. I'm afraid we have had far too many Cuban *Mojito's.*" With a slight bow, he put a hand on his brother's shoulder and directed him across the street. Matthew took Maria's arm and held her close. He was irritated with the attention she was getting from the men standing outside the clubs. They entered the dimly lit diner.

CHAPTER 11

1981

Remember

STILL FEELING THE effects of more than double his usual glasses of Hennessy cognac, Cameron arrived at the Carson family cemetery on the far eastern side of their estate in Indianapolis. He sat in the spring rain next to his wife's grave on a well-worn MIT imprinted folding-stool. Though the journey was nearly three hundred miles round trip, he visited at least twice a month. Under duress from her suspicious sudden death and pressure from her father, the Senator, he had succumbed to burying Karen in the Carson family cemetery. He had since regretted that decision as he would have preferred to have her close to him at Jackson's Place.

Wet and chilled to the bone, he took a long warming pull of Hennessy. He stared blurry-eyed at the beautifully designed Moravian ceramic flask given to him over thirty years ago by the German physicist Wolfgang Pauli.

"Sweetheart, do you remember the story about this flask?" he asked the tombstone. "No? Well, I'll tell you again if you won't be too bored by the details. This great man, Pauli, won a Nobel Prize for the Exclusion Principle, the *Pauli* Exclusion Principle. It gets a bit dicey to the layman, but simply the electrons, neutrons, and protons can possess the same energy or quantum state in an atom. Anyhow, Pauli gave the flask to me in 1956 while he was attending the

International Energy Conference. I suppose he was listening to some young cocky college student present a halfway credible case for the potential of cost-effectively harnessing energy from the sun." He chuckled, thinking how idealistic he was up on that stage, back then. He took a drink.

"You know, Pauli was ailing and died only two years later at the age of fifty-six, the age I am now," he said. "He walked up to me and handed me this flask." Cameron scrunched up his face and said in his best German accent, "'Young man, if you intend to go against the establishment, you are going to need this.' Then we just stared at each other. I didn't know what to say, so he said, 'This has served me well over the years,'" and walked away.

"'Do you know who that was?' my good friend Michael Craigo said to me. I told him he looked like someone I saw in a textbook. Michael said, 'He's Wolfgang Pauli – perhaps this century's greatest mind in quantum physics.' I just stared at this exquisite multi-colored bottle, screwed off the top, and sniffed. My head reeled backward, and my eyes watered – what an intoxicating aroma. Much to your chagrin, Karen, I've been hooked ever since.

"I had one problem after another in the lab this week and something occurred to me. Pauli was also infamous for The Pauli Effect. I cause the same thing every time I'm in a lab – catastrophe! Old Wolfgang Pauli had the legendary reputation of walking into a lab only to watch the experiment in process self-destruct." He sat quietly for a few minutes.

"Where was I, dear? Oh yes, I stood there looking at my new trophy – this flask. It was full to the top of what must have been expensive cognac; at that time, I wouldn't have known the difference, not having developed the discriminating taste I now have. Besides, if a beverage simply had alcohol content, it was okay with most of us guys at MIT."

Cameron kept the flask full in honor of the strange German genius and the quality of the brew got better as time and funds improved. "When Pauli died, the entire department of teachers and students met on the roof of the Hayden Barker Science Library and toasted his passing. We sent our glasses and bottles crashing to the alley below." Cameron pushed himself off his MIT stool, raised the flask to the sky, and toasted Wolfgang Pauli and all the great scientists before him. Then he knelt down at the tombstone. He began to weep. He told her the latest about their amazing son. How Tremont did this and Tremont did that and how Tremont had ten times the potential he ever had. "I know you're proud of him too." He always spoke to her in present tense as if she had never departed. "Even with him joining the Marines. I know I don't have to worry because I know Tremont has his own guardian angel.

"I really don't have much motivation to work without him here. I didn't tell him that of course. What Tremont doesn't know is that CJ Energy is ready to go. I could have revealed the results a few years ago, but I was waiting for Tremont to finish his studies. I don't know, maybe I'll never release it – if I'd only done what they asked you'd still be here with me." He sat down on the stool and buried his head in his hands. "Tell me what to do, Kay." As if she answered him, he took out a handkerchief and wiped his nose and face. "You're right, Kay, I have plenty of corporate work to do on solar cells and whatnot. When Tremont gets home for good, then we'll see what the world thinks of CJ Energy. Once it's made public, they should have no reason to hurt Tremont or me."

He stood and folded the chair. "Thanks for keeping an eye on him, Kay. You know how he is. He's bullheaded and impetuous like me and an idealist like you."

He paused for a long time without feeling the chilly rain that had seeped through his coat and flannel shirt. He had a hard time leaving her. "God I miss you, Kay. I miss you more every day. I'm still keeping the place up nice. I know you find it hard to believe that I can use a vacuum and mop, but it still looks like it did back then. Not much has changed except the lab and all the security shit. Sorry." She hated profanity. "But I'm still a lonely son of a bitch. Sorry again, honey. But I'll be seeing you when my work is finished here." He kissed her tombstone, apologized for drinking too much, promised to quit soon, and brushed away some dirt from the glistening white marble. The inscription read:

> The Perfect Wife and Friend
> Karen "Kay" Jackson
> Born March 3, 1935
> Gone to help God organize heaven, August 17, 1959

Cameron dropped the stool; he reached down to pick it up and stumbled. He cussed. While attempting to stand, something or someone caught his eye out in the dimly lit parking lot. He withdrew his .45. "Who's there? By god, I'll . . ." When he stumbled into the parking lot, tires screeched and he watched the taillights of a large SUV disappear around the corner.

CHAPTER 12

1981

Genius

MATTHEW WAS A child when Tremont visited Millinocket, Maine, with his closest friend Sean. After an introduction in the kitchen with Sean's father and mother, Tremont recognized that Sean needed some time with his parents and stepped out on the porch where Matthew had already positioned himself with a pencil and paper. A scruffy, longhaired collie mix lay next to him. The dog's eyes followed Tremont's every move. They were both quiet, and Matthew seemed not to notice the skinny giant. Tremont stood on the opposite end of the porch leaning against one of the six two-story-high oak posts holding up a massive overhang, which surrounded the front of the colonial style house. He observed Matthew struggling over some complicated problem and several minutes went by before Tremont spoke. "I've heard a lot about you from your brother. Are you working on something I can help you with?"

Sean Eaton was inside the house having a heart-to-heart discussion with his father about joining the Marines. By now both voices were bellowing accusations and insults. Matthew didn't flinch, but Tremont was disturbed. He could not remember one single cross word exchanged between him and his father though he had witnessed many altercations between his father and his grandfather, Senator Carson. Young Matthew did not reply and continued to focus on the task in front of him. Tremont edged over toward the boy and leaned on the next closest towering post. Something crashed inside the house. Mrs. Eaton reprimanded and tried to console the two men at the same time. "Please don't fight, and please be careful of my mother's china. Those plates are irreplaceable! They made it through four generations and how they made it twenty years with the two of you, I'll never know! Now sit down and have some cobbler." She stepped to the door and said, "Tremont, would you like some apple cobbler and coffee or tea?" The dog's ears rose when he heard the word cobbler, but he did not move, though his eyes focused on Mrs. Eaton.

"No, ma'am, but thank you just the same," Tremont said.

"Matthew?"

"Do you have any cake? German chocolate?"

"No, you know I only make that on your birthday. But I made carrot cake Sunday, and I believe there's a piece with your name on it."

Matthew frowned, not looking up from his paper. "No, thank you, Mom."

She handed him a glass of milk and a small white pill that Matthew took dutifully, draining the glass of milk and wiping the white mustache onto his sleeve.

Mrs. Eaton went back to the sparring match. Over the last few months, Tremont had formed the impression that Sean had a long time adversarial relationship with his father and that he and his mother were very close. The current drama gave plenty of credence to that assumption. Tremont noted that Matthew seemed to be oblivious to the whole scene: He's really focused, like I was at that age when I got working on something important. Since Matthew had not acknowledged his presence on the porch, Tremont sat down next to the boy and pretended not to look over his shoulder. Someone pounded on the table and another crash was heard in the house. Sean's father said, "You never think of anyone but yourself. What if something should happen to me? Who would oversee things at the mills?"

Sean met his father's modulation and replied, "Nothing is going to happen to you, old man. You're too damn ornery to die before your time. Besides, the way we are, we'd kill each other inside of a year."

Over Matthew's shoulder, Tremont studied a drawing of what appeared to be a windmill much like the ones his father installed and modified in the back of his family home at Jackson's Place. Except, Matthew's drawing included auxiliary solar panels, indicated by an arrow pointing at large rectangles running vertically down each side of the pole with the words scribbled "solar panels." This justified Tremont's suspicions that, just as Sean had said, Matthew was a short version of himself.

"Do you often sit around designing and inventing . . . drawing like this?"

Matthew looked up and smiled. "Every day."

"What are you trying to solve here? I see these are solar panels. What do you know about solar energy?" Tremont asked while bending his lanky body to sit down next to Matthew on the porch. He thought he would intimidate the boy, but quite the contrary, Matthew looked him right in the eye and seemed to be analyzing Tremont while Tremont was querying him.

"You're the science genius my brother told me about. I've wanted to talk to you for a long time," Matthew said.

Tremont nearly chuckled aloud. He thought, What could be a long time in a six-year-old's life?

"I heard him call you Tree," Matthew said and turned back to his drawing.

"You should hear what my father and grandfather call me – "

Before he could tell him, Matthew interjected with an answer to his earlier question, "Well, I was thinking that all those windmills in California don't work all the time, but they have sun all the time. So if we can get energy from the sun, the windmills would run all day and then have enough power to continue through the night."

Tremont was used to being around intelligent people but the kid was more than he expected by far. He was not only intelligent; he had a clear affinity for science, energy science at that. Tremont couldn't wait to tell his father about Matthew.

"How did you get interested in windmills and solar panels?" Tremont asked.

Matthew shrugged.

Having forgotten that he was talking to a child barely out of kindergarten, Tremont changed the subject. "I noticed when I walked out on the porch that you seemed to be perplexed about something."

Matthew gave him an incredulous look.

"I mean something seemed to bother you about your design."

He paused and ran his pencil from the bottom of the windmill to the top. "They're too big."

"Meaning?"

"There must be a way to make the same power with something a whole lot smaller. Kind of like my dad's computer. Did you know they used to fill up a whole building, and now it sits on his desk?"

"You use your dad's computer?"

"I mean, if someone can shrink . . . Did you see that black and white movie where the guy had this big machine and he shrunk everything and everyone around him? I love that movie. Sometimes I think that's how they shrunk the computer."

The path of this child's logic enthralled Tremont. "My father has spent his entire life trying to do just what you've described, Matthew. Take the power of the sun or the wind or the chemical action in water and capture it into a small vessel."

"Vessel?"

"A cabinet like what houses the computer or a box or a cylinder like a battery but with the ability to regenerate itself and not wear out," Tremont continued, encouraged by the look of understanding on his young pupil's face. They talked for a while longer and then he asked Matthew what books he had on alternative energy.

"I have some kids' books, and have asked my teachers for some real books – "

"Real books," Tremont said, amused.

"I asked her for a book on solar panels. She never got it for me."

"I bet she mistakenly didn't think you'd be able to understand the concepts. I'll send you a few books that I think you'll enjoy and some others you can keep for when you get older." Though, he thought, I have a feeling in a couple of years you'll be able to comprehend most of *Capturing the Sun.*

As the evening waned on, Tremont found it easy to talk to this youngster about world events, archeology, geography, politics, and their mutual favorite subject of science and inventions. Though parts of the conversation kept to a juvenile level, Matthew's critical thinking and analytical abilities rivaled many of Tremont's classmates in high school and even some at Yale. Tremont knew he himself had a special gift and was not much different from Matthew when he was the same age. He never thought of himself as different from his classmates and fit in well in the classroom, on the basketball court, and in social situations. He had a feeling that Matthew would be much the same in this rural setting, provided he had enough guidance. Perhaps I can help keep him focused, he thought, but he couldn't imagine how this would be possible from a distance, especially now. One way or another, he would keep an eye on him.

The sun was setting over the forest to their left and the two unlikely chums faced the northern mountain ranges of Maine toward the border of Canada. The Eaton's home was set on the highest elevation close to town and they could clearly see Mount Katahdin far off in the distance. An hour had passed. Sean and his father were still arguing. Sean's mother interjected a few times to mediate the tension. Tremont revealed portions of his father's work to see what the fresh young mind would bounce back. He glimpsed a rudimentary understanding in Matthew's eyes. The voices in the house began to crescendo again. A few minutes later, Sean came barreling out and nearly slammed the screen door off its hinges, startling Tremont and Matthew.

"Let's go, Tree. He's an ass and always will be." Sean reached down and put his hand on Matthew's head. "I'll see you later, little brother. I promise to write. Be sure to send me letters with copies of your drawings, okay?"

Matthew looked up with tears forming in his eyes.

Sean knelt down beside his kid brother and said, "Sorry we couldn't do one of our hiking trips. Next time, I promise." When Sean tried to ruffle his hair, Matthew ducked to pat the dog's head. Sean stormed down the steps and out to the Land Cruiser.

Tremont turned to Matthew, who was now drawing imaginary lines into the pine floorboards. "Listen, kid, your brother talks about you constantly. Why do you think I knew so much about you and how much we have in common? You two have a special bond. Hey, I'll be back, we'll both be back soon with lots of good stories." Matthew still didn't look up and he caught a glimpse of Mrs. Eaton standing in the doorway listening. "You and I are going to be great friends. I guarantee it. And I'll write you too, and send you some ideas for your class science projects. Would you like that?"

Matthew smiled, wiped a tear from his eye and nodded. Tremont gave him his signature grin and ruffled Matthew's curly hair. Matthew didn't duck his head this time.

As Tremont stepped off the porch, Matthew said, "I'll draw a picture of my rain-catching machine for you. I think it will work, but I don't know. I'm only five, you know."

Tremont walked away shaking his head. He muttered, "Yeah, only five – a genius kid who loves alternative energy projects. What's the chance of that?"

Matthew watched the SUV plow down the long ranch driveway screaming its driver's anger back to the house. Parker James Eaton came out of the house, crossed his arms, and stared after the SUV, not saying a word. He walked back into the house rubbing one hand across his forehead.

Kate edged past Parker and stepped out on the porch. "He's angry, Matthew, but you have to know he is also proud of Sean and more than a little scared about him going into the Marines." She patted his shoulder then retreated into the house to face her bear of a husband.

Matthew looked at his paper and said, "You know, Nuke, I think Tree really liked my drawings and ideas."

Matthew didn't hear from or see the man his brother called Tree for fourteen years.

CHAPTER 13

1982

Honor

AFTER LEAVING MILLINOCKET, Sean and Tremont returned to New Haven where they packed all of their belongings into Tremont's 1975 white Toyota Land Cruiser, safari-style with a rack on the top and a black iron grill on the front to deflect a charging rhino. They bid a final good-bye to Yale and traveled the seven hundred miles south to Camp Lejeune in Jacksonville, North Carolina.

Both Sean and Tremont could not have been in better physical condition and flew right through boot camp although Sean had more than a few problems with Sergeant Schmoltz who Sean said reminded him way too much of his father and the principal at Stearns High School. They had one week of R&R, which Tremont spent at Jackson's Place and Indianapolis. Sean maximized his time getting to know the ladies and bartenders in North Myrtle Beach, over two hours south of thc base. Though he had booked a hotel for the week, the local sheriff's department provided Sean accommodations on two separate nights.

When they returned, they shipped out to Miramar, California, where they were attached to the Third Marine Aircraft Wing. In Miramar, they received a promotion and new orders placing them with a newly formed secret Marine Anti-Terrorist Intelligence group. They and two dozen other young marines spent a month in the desert training with seasoned military intelligence and civilian CIA personnel. They were now officially marine military intelligence officers.

Within weeks of completing their training, they shipped out to Kuwait to deal with an upsurge in the taking of U.S. and NATO hostages in Iran and Syria by Islamic extremists. They arrived in the most dangerous part of the world as Iran was embroiled in another bitter war against neighboring Iraq. In Kuwait, they learned Farsi, recruited informants and trained Islamic moderates to infiltrate terrorist cells. They were part of, and soon led, covert missions throughout the region.

As the border war heightened, hostage taking lessened and they received new orders placing them in southern Pakistan. Tremont thought it ironic that their unwritten mission was to work *with* an extreme Islamic fundamentalist group called the Taliban in an effort to undermine the Soviet occupation of Afghanistan.

Tremont sat alone next to a small fire outside of Jalalabad, capital of the Nangarhar province of Afghanistan. He used to love to study the history of this ancient place near the Khyber Pass. Now he just wondered how he got here. He positioned himself in the shadows with his back to the fire, never wanting to blind his night vision or to be a target for a communist sniper. Sitting around the fire also at least four to five feet from the flames were a dozen Afghani Mujahideen and Pakistani Taliban freedom fighters. Tremont did not like their company. In his opinion, the Taliban would be a far worse regime than the communists could ever be. If human rights, particularly women's rights, were not already horrendous, the Taliban would set Afghanistan back to the Stone Age. He shared these instincts with his superiors and heard his observations were passed on to military intelligence at the Pentagon or discussed at length with President Reagan in cabinet meetings.

Meanwhile, the current U.S. Executive branch covertly placed many other domestic and military secret service agents around the world. The long-term goal was spreading the ideal of freedom and democracy throughout the world, taking the fight to the terrorists before they brought it to the U.S. Tremont struggled in the firelight to write his weekly letter to his father. He wrote that it would take a couple hundred years after planting these seeds to see results, to affect centuries of tribal and hard-line religious societies of the Middle East. "We are seed planters," Tremont said aloud, pleased with himself.

"What was that?"

Sean was trying to sleep with his head on a rock a few feet deeper in the dark than Tremont.

"I was thinking about whether what we are doing has any value or if we're spinning our wheels. If these Pakistani extreme Islamic zealots take over Kabul as planned, I think the country will step back five centuries in human rights."

"Fortunately, that's not our decision to make. The White House wants the Soviets out. They would rather fight the Taliban ten or twenty years from now than have to try to beat the Soviets in this part of the world alone."

"So it's the Soviets out and anyone in."

"Exactly."

Tremont laughed. "We're pawns."

"Damn dangerous pawns, my friend. What are you writing?"

"Letter to my dad. I'm letting him know to say when, and I'm out of here."

"You're signed on for a few more tours."

"Ah, that's where you're wrong. I added an addendum to my reenlistment. I'm month-to-month, brother. When my father's ready to put me to work full time, I'll be heading home and trading in my rifle for a soldering gun."

It was Sean's turn to laugh. "Not me, man. I'm in for the duration. Death or retirement, I'm getting kind of used to these rocks and my American-hating buddies."

Tremont knew where this dialogue was heading, so he let it rest and returned to his letter.

"Hey, man, is your father still working on the same project you told me about back at Yale?" Sean asked.

"Same project."

"You still a believer?"

"Still a believer."

"That's great, man. I still think it's weird that my little brother's a sci-fi nut like you and your crazy old man. I gave him those books and you would have thought I bought him Disneyland."

"That's great, I'm glad he liked them," Tremont said and held his breath until he could hear Sean's heavy breathing. Once again, he was pleased that the conversation hadn't gone any further. He was tired of lying to Sean about how much he knew about his genius little brother Matthew. The last he had heard Matthew had come up with a new form of hydro energy conversion system. In concept it wasn't bad. It had been explored at MIT and other energy conservatories. In fact, his father had worked with a team of hydro energy researchers back in the fifties. But for a child to consider the possibilities of hydroelectric energy on his own and develop a prototype was more than astounding. If Matthew could do that before he was in middle school, what could he accomplish in college and beyond? Tremont couldn't have picked a better protégé. Is that what he was? A protégé? Or something more? Insurance perhaps? He felt a little guilty about working behind the scenes in the boy's life without his parent's knowledge. Considering the weight of his father's work, and the impact on the future of civilization, he could live with a little guilt.

Tremont shone a pen light on the letter he was writing to his father. He signed his nickname and chuckled as he remembered his father telling him, at six-foot-four and only fourteen years old, that all the sugar from the massive quantities of snack foods he consumed was going to stunt his growth.

He knew his father was nearing completion of his experiments and would soon be ready to develop a prototype. He would ask for a discharge from the Marines when that time came, and perhaps maintain his active status with the National Guard. Tremont was committed to throwing himself into his father's energy inventions full time. Imagine, he thought as he folded the letter and addressed the envelope, if the U.S. and other developed countries were no longer dependent on Middle East oil but could be independently secure in their energy consumption without depleting another iota of their natural resources.

He closed his eyes only to be awakened minutes later to the sound of gunfire. He dove for his M-249 Squad Automatic Weapon (SAW). Sean was already throwing dirt on the fire, and they retreated to the rocks as bullets ricocheted around them. He could hear the screams of the hard-fighting Pakistani Taliban as the enemy, firing American-made M-16s similar to his own, and the distinctive Russian Kalashnikov Assault Rifles, the AK-47s, picked his allies off on the west side of the fire.

As he leaned against a boulder unable to move right or left, he cussed the politicians that were responsible for U.S.-made weapons killing U.S. soldiers and allies. He knew all to well how that could happen. Before being deployed to Afghanistan, Tremont and Sean were providing security in Geneva for a high level meeting which included the head of the CIA, William Casey, Vice President George Bush, and Iranian Prime Minister Banisadr.

Looking back, Tremont could see why they were pulled from the region. In 1980, a deal allegedly had been made to trade weapons for the return of hostages. A mysterious Defense Intelligence Agency, DIA, officer Tremont only knew as *Ollie* told them U.S. arms had been filtering through Iran since Jimmy Carter's inability to free fifty-two American hostages before the end of his administration. Carter was defeated, and not surprisingly, President Reagan gained the captives' release only months later. Ollie said the secret meetings continued with one exception: the Iranians were trading oil instead of hostages.

Tremont, Sean, and half a dozen of their men kept tight to their cover. They all agreed their best chance of survival was staying put until daylight. They used their night vision goggles and traded sentry duty for the next eight hours. In the morning, they checked on the dead and wounded. Their assailants had disappeared in the night.

"This is getting old," Tremont said.

CHAPTER 14

1983

Terror

"A UNIVERSITY STUDENT, a mother, and her small child died in the blast. Hundreds have been hospitalized with injuries," reported the dark-eyed Austrian News Network (ANN) anchor. She went on to say that the car bomb in Israel was the third bombing against civilians in crowded retail shopping areas in a month. She stopped in mid-sentence and put a hand to her ear. A sheet of paper appeared to the reporter's right. She smoothed the edges while reading. Looking into the camera, she said, "Sheik Mohammed bin Bandar, the assistant secretary general of OPEC." She rechecked the paper. "Sheik Bandar has been assassinated in Egypt. According to a source inside OPEC, Mohammed bin Bandar had been in a heated battle with other OPEC members over what some considered his overly conservative pro-Western positions. Here at ANN, we have been covering this controversy for a number of years and – " She put her hand to her ear. "We now have a live feed outside the Hotel El Houssain where the assistant secretary was gunned down minutes ago at the Khan El-Khalili bazaar. Sudir? What are the authorities telling you? Were there any other injuries or casualties?"

Two blocks from the Austrian News Network headquarters, twenty men sat around an ornate marble table. The room displayed a colorful Middle Eastern silk tapestry, huge Persian carpets, and hand-carved marble furniture. Original oil paintings hung on two walls. One depicted desert landscapes, and another showed three medieval Islamic empires. On a third wall were dozens of contemporary photographs of modern oil fields and refineries. Affixed to the bottom of each framed and matted picture was a silver engraved tag giving the picture locations as Bahrain, Kuwait, Qatar, Iran, Iraq, Saudi Arabia, Egypt, Syria, and various states or emirates of the United Arab Emirates – the UAE. Sitting in this monumental room, one would never know he was in the basement of OPEC's worldwide headquarters, a modern four-story marble building at Donaustrasse 93 in downtown Vienna, Austria, with IBM to the left and an Austrian bank to the right.

Were it not for the six Austrian "GEK Cobra" military police soldiers standing guard – two at the door to the basement conference room, and four at the base of the front steps, all carrying StG77 automatic rifles – one would not be able to differentiate this building from any other of its type in Europe. These men were part of the same GEK Cobra formed in 1972 to protect Jewish immigrants after the attack on Jewish athletes at the Munich Olympics. Their other major distinction was their assistance in 1975 that ended a siege led by the infamous assassin, the Jackal.

The two Cobra guards on duty outside the conference room, though Austrian citizens, were clearly not of European descent. Earlier, as each man exited the elevator, they greeted these two professional soldiers by name, *Ahmed and Saleh Jobrani Maher.*

Inside the conference room, the seat at the head of the table was vacant. The two screens on the wall transfixed the men. One screen featured the local Austrian news with the sound turned down and subtitles showing in Farsi. The other screen blared with the Al-Jezeera news report.

"It is a great tragedy," said one man as he touched his forehead, lips, and his chest before bowing his head. "He was a great man – a very great man with the hand of Allah on his shoulder. May he find his peace and guide us through these difficult times."

Most of the men nodded in agreement, except one tall, dark man in his mid-thirties who seemed not to be disturbed by the news.

Before the reporter concluded, the tall figure with a medium-length graying beard, long black and gray robes, sandals, and turban made the News Network reporters vanish. All eyes were on him as he paced around the room.

"Most of us agree that Mohammed bin Bandar was weak when it came to making many policy decisions that affect our profits, our stability, and our very existence.

"We have been playing right into the hands of the West. All that I had predicted when I first attended your meeting as a representative of the United Arab Emirates has come about. OPEC is weakening as development in the Gulf of Mexico and the North Sea continues. Exploration in Alaska, Siberia, and China is on the horizon. Fossil fuel faces extinction as the dinosaur of energy in the nuclear age. Some estimates give our dominance less than fifty years; others say as much as one hundred. Since my father and uncles helped form these councils, this group's mission was to provide stability, protection, and balance. Is this not what Hafiz-OPEC Saumba Shokran means in its most holy understanding?"

The familiar growl prefaced Omar bin Taliffan's next statement. "What have we done in the past decade to assure our corporate future? Since the formation of Hafiz-OPEC Saumba Shokran, what have we accomplished?" A few of the members shuffled through papers preparing to respond with details of their hard work over the years, but he didn't give them a chance. "Nothing, my friends. Nothing!"

Since 1973, the group had doubled in size from its original twelve-country membership. Assistant Secretary General bin Bandar had led its political and commercial activities while turning a blind eye to its members' suspected illegal deals, assassinations, and perhaps sponsored terrorism. With bin Bandar out of the picture, there was only one elder statesman left to object. The Sheiks, Ministers of Oil, and princes of this secret society had been replaced by younger family members who were more easily influenced by the strangely charismatic and powerful Omar bin Taliffan who had become an outspoken Islamic leader. Many in the West believed the only difference between him and his extremist relatives was that he directed his network from boardrooms and pulpits rather than from desert terrorism training camps and caves.

All but the elder statesman, Sheik Hassan Al-Fawza, was now giving Omar bin Taliffan, who recently appointed himself leader, positive affirmations.

There came a knock at the door. Taliffan signaled Nafed, a young page who was preparing coffee and pastries. It is safe to say nobody matching the description of the two men ushered in by the Cobra guard ever before set foot on this floor of OPEC's Vienna international headquarters. The two Anglo men looked out of place. The first had short sandy brown hair, striking blue eyes, gray at the temples, and a prominent cleft chin. He was dressed in long Docker shorts, a Dallas Cowboys cap, flip-flop sandals, and a wrinkled short-sleeve button-down shirt. Were it not for the three thick manila folders he withdrew from a worn canvas satchel, he would have passed for a Western tourist on the beaches in front of the Emirates Palace Hotel in Abuh Dabi. The second looked closer to the part of a businessman or politician. He had short-cropped black hair and wore a black pinstriped suit, white shirt, and a silver silk tie. He took out a legal pad and pen, placed them on the table, and then set his brown leather briefcase at his side. They took their seats as their black robed host stalked around the room.

When he reached the front, Omar bin Taliffan made a ceremonious show of taking his seat at the head of the table.

Sheik Hassan Al-Fawza of Saudi Arabia, the lone elder statesman and one of the group's founders, stood. "I demand to know what is going on!" he said to Omar bin Taliffan. "Did you have anything to do with Bandar's murder?" The room became deadly silent. The Sheik cleared his throat. "You cannot take Sheik Mohammed bin Bandar's position without a vote. We will not stand for it." He looked around the room and found no support. "And what are these men doing here? This is a closed session. If I have to, I will take this up with the OPEC membership later today."

"Please sit down, my dear uncle. How long had you and my father been business partners and friends? Forty years? Please drink and eat. All will unfold within the hour, I promise you."

Taliffan stood behind the old sheik, "You are not looking well, Uncle. Can I have Nayef get you something from the infirmary?"

Though the room was quite cool, the Sheik mopped the sweat from his head. He replied, voice cracking, "I am feeling fine, but why are you – "

Taliffan spread his spider-like fingers over the man's shoulders. "All will be revealed in good time, Inshallah."

Taliffan returned to the head of the table. "Let me introduce Senator Wayne Green from Texas and his associate," he paused while his and the other man's eyes locked, "Mr. Smith. They represent those in the United States who share our objectives. In order to continue to increase our growing dominance in the world market, we must avoid the mistakes of the past, such as the failed embargo of the early seventies. The unexpected result was the empowerment of nuclear energy proponents and alternative energy conservationists, creating a quiet but deadly enemy of our way of life – "

All eyes turned to the elder Sheik as he stood, grabbed his chest, and fell hard on the marble table.

Taliffan's message was clear. It didn't matter who you were, if you got in the way of the cause, you were expendable. Unfazed, the man next to the Sheik looked at Taliffan for direction.

"Yes, of course, Mahmoud, check on our uncle."

Mahmoud had joined the secret society to replace General Daneshvar, who had taken ill and died in Vienna the previous year. General Daneshvar had disagreed with the radical actions of some members of Hafiz-OPEC Saumba Shokran, meaning Protectors of OPEC Stability and Longevity. As with Secretary General bin Bandar, the media had alluded to foul play, but an investigation by the Vienna police and the Iranian government was inconclusive.

Mahmoud put two fingers along the side of the Sheik's neck. "He is dead."

As if on cue the door opened and the two Cobras entered the room. Taliffan shook his head. "Our uncle will be missed. Please, help Nayef take him to the infirmary until we have time to take him to the hospital." They lifted the Sheik's body and carried him out of the room.

Taliffan motioned to the Americans.

The Senator wrung his hands, took a deep breath, and replaced his glasses. He pressed his shaking hands over his yellow pad as if he were forcing wrinkles out of a shirt. "Gentlemen, as Prince Taliffan said, we have much in common. Our goals are similar to yours." He launched into the current global political and economic situation as it related to the oil industry. We must maintain the flow of oil and wealth far into the next century," he said. "If we sit back and allow men like Jackson to succeed, our best experts agree you may be looking at only fifty years before the United States and Europe are energy source independent. Already, France has initiated construction of the largest nuclear plant in Europe. They hope to be fossil fuel free by 2005. In summary, we must work together to assure our *constituents* – "

"The Seven Sisters," Taliffan interrupted to clarify.

"In part, yes, our constituents include hundreds of other companies and many governments who depend on the stability of the oil industry." The Senator looked back down at his yellow pad, flipped a page, and said, "We must keep competing supplies of crude oil from gaining availability to make sure our demand for *your* oil remains a constant – through legislative and economic means. So far my constituents have been holding up their end of the bargain. We must also continue to curtail fuel cell and solar energy progress. As I chair the Committee on Energy and Commerce, we have been successful in slowing their progress by not appropriating funds to research and development. That could change should the Democrats win the Oval Office or gain a majority in the elections next year.

We must further hinder the growth of other forms of alternative energy. This is the area that worries me the most – the unknown. We are monitoring each situation, and we appreciate your help around the world. You'll note that Doctor Jean-Paul Dominique Esquirol is now a permanent resident of hotel-Dieu de Mental du fou. His foundation's advances in micro-hydro energy have been set back more than a decade. As I said earlier, the only threat we have not been able to get our hands on is in our own country. John?"

Smith opened and rubbed his eyes. He looked around the room. "Don't worry, folks. I have dear Cameron Jackson under round-the-clock surveillance." He chuckled. "I needed a break from his incessant classical music collection, though I must say, I'm becoming quite the Tchaikovsky and Mendelssohn fan." He looked at their blank stares and cleared his throat, "If he leaves his compound with his mysterious little energy experiment and heads to Washington, we'll know it. You boys hold up your end of keeping a juicy supply of oil available, and we'll keep your competition in line – Mr. Jackson will remain my own personal project."

CHAPTER 15

March 17, 1995 1:00 a.m.

Transfer

JUST AS MARIA said, "I wonder if Cracker Jack will be coming back," he walked through the door. They heard his melodic voice say, "*Juanita, hola guapa.* These kids must be famished, fix them up with whatever their hearts desire."

Juanita was a compact dark Latin girl in her mid twenties, and a full foot shorter than Cracker Jack, "*Si, mi querido, enseguida.* It will be my pleasure," she said.

"*Gracias, mi amor. Tan bella y amable como siempre.* Put it on my tab, or better yet, put it on you-know-who's tab. They can afford it."

Juanita smiled slyly at Cracker Jack, and Maria whispered to Matthew, "Something is going on between those two, and it's not just bacon and eggs."

Cracker Jack came over and sat down next to Matthew. He stretched his long legs out away from the table and gave them a radiant smile.

When Juanita took their large order, Cracker Jack chuckled. "I thought you two looked famished."

"One can't live on Cracker Jack alone," Maria said, "but it sure looks like Juanita could."

"Hey, the only difference between me and a prisoner is that I do have conjugal visits." He laughed aloud to see the surprised looks on their faces.

"Seriously." His smile disappeared, and he leaned over his face only inches from theirs. "I'm going to tell you the most incredible story. What I say, you cannot repeat to anyone – ever. Just having met me, it's too late to turn back. Knowing what I'm about to tell you will put you at risk even further." He had their undivided attention.

Though intrigued, Matthew tried to sound aloof, "I think to some extent you're kidding around with us; but for your help, and breakfast, the least we can do is be good ears and," Matthew put up his right hand with three fingers and thumb over pinky, "scout's honor, it's our secret."

Cracker Jack smiled. "Breakfast is nothing, and it's my pleasure to help out a couple of great kids. I know it's hard to conceive, but you may be my last chance to save decades of research."

"You said earlier that you had to check in with your G-Men? That's the FBI, right?" Maria asked.

"That's right."

"Have they formally arrested you?"

"No, they are holding me under an obscure national security risk law. It's bogus, I'm sure, but they've had me under apartment arrest. I haven't been charged, but I can't use the restroom without their permission."

Matthew was intrigued but skeptical, "It hardly seems legal or American for that matter."

"My lawyers are doing all they can, but this is the first chance I've had to talk to anyone, but Marcos, in weeks. The most important thing now is to get my father's life work into safe hands in a safe place."

"Why not entrust it with the FBI?" Maria asked.

"They may in fact have good intentions, but the research is far from secure with them. Nor am I – secure, I mean. If you will agree to help me, Marcos will know what to do, and he'll see to it that you're compensated. Money is no object."

Maria raised her hands to shoulder height. "I'm confused, Cracker Jack. Why on earth would you want two inexperienced college kids to help you? Why would you think we even could?"

Cracker Jack continued telling about his father's nearly obsessive need for the highest of security. He feared that one day someone or some institution would either steal or destroy his life's work on alternative energy sources, either for personal gain or because his research threatened their business or government.

Matthew thought parts of what he was saying sounded familiar. He was able to follow the technical side of the discussion and noted everything Cracker Jack said was plausible and feasible. This late night breakfast, at the very least, was the most fascinating he had ever had. The man was either crazy or the son of a genius or maybe both. It's funny, he thought. If he were talking about solar energy . . . it couldn't be!

"How long have they been holding you?" Maria asked.

"For the last three months. *For my own protection,* until someone decides what to do with me." Cracker Jack paused and took a deep breath, "Or I have a convenient accident." He put his hands behind his head and looked up at the ceiling.

It occurred to Matthew that if Cracker Jack was in danger then anyone around him might be in danger.

They dug into a second helping of scrambled eggs while Cracker Jack continued, "I grew up working with my father. The two labs in our house were my playground. He has over a hundred patents on alternative energy products including some of the first effective solar panels."

"Solar panels!" Matthew exclaimed with a full mouth of eggs. "What's his name?"

Cracker Jack put up a hand. "All in good time Watson, all in good time."

"I . . . I . . . I . . ."

"Matthew?" Maria said.

Matthew looked like he would choke, wiped his mouth with a napkin, turned to Maria and said, "You know that book you're always picking up and asking me if you could buy me another one because – "

"The jacket is so worn?"

"Yes! That's the one. I think the author is *his* father!" Matthew could barely contain his excitement. "I've read a lot about your father's research. *Mr. Jackson.*" Looking back to Maria, "Cameron Jackson cut the path for every other alternative energy scientist and never really got the credit for being the first to develop an effective solar panel."

Cracker Jack smiled and nodded. "Russel Ohl actually patented the first solar cells in 1946, and my father went on to patent specific improvements in new generations of photo-electrochemical, polymer, and most recently nano-crystal cells. He has been involved in research and development of nearly every type of alternative energy source you can imagine and some that no ordinary person could imagine. He was one of the pioneers of fuel cells but when the organizations he was consulting began heading in the wrong direction and spending billions in taxpayers' money, he left the corporate world to concentrate on what he called *the final answer*. He was out of the limelight for quite a few years while he worked on something that would have had more impact on the world than anything since the invention of electricity."

Maria was shaking her head. "You could not be spinning a story that would be more pertinent to Matthew. He dreams of inventing something within the same field that . . . Ow!" Matthew kicked her under the table. She hit him in the shoulder, and they exchanged a look most likely not lost on Cracker Jack. Maria continued, "He wants to do something that would change the world for the better – every project through school related to one form of energy or another, like solar panels, windmills, electricity, hydro electricity, and fuel cells. He even won a national Smithsonian . . ."

"Maria . . . ?" Matthew said, not happy with sharing his bio with a stranger.

"I know." Cracker Jack paused, "I mean, I assumed that would be the case earlier as you talked about your major at UMaine and your course selection."

Matthew looked quizzically at Cracker Jack. Something wasn't quite right, he thought. "I've considered working in some form of energy engineering and quantum physics. That's how my scholarships are designated." Matthew looked over at Maria, who was transfixed on Cracker Jack. Matthew knew what she was doing. She may have found the perfect subject to study, Matthew thought, besides me. "So Mr. Cracker Jack Jackson, what is your first name? I think I read it somewhere once but I cannot recall. Terry or Trevor?" Matthew noticed a slight hesitation.

"I'm actually named after my father. Cameron," which was actually true, as Cameron is his middle name.

Cracker Jack changed the subject much too quickly Matthew decided.

"To a great many people, my father was the mad scientist of Indiana, the son-in-law to the rich Carson political heritage."

"Senator Carson. I think he had more tenure in the Senate than Strom Thurmond?" Maria said.

"You know your American government," Cracker Jack observed.

"Not really. I just remember that he and Thurmond wielded a lot of power and helped defeat a lot of progressive legislation."

"You mean *liberal* legislation," Matthew interjected and received a kick for his insolence.

He then said to Cracker Jack, "Hence the inheritance."

Cracker Jack nodded, "He passed away only a few years ago. As to my father, anyone who could appreciate gains in alternative energy science knew he's not mad . . ."

"He's a science icon," Matthew said.

Cracker Jack nodded, clearly pleased with the compliment. "Think about the many forms of energy we depend upon today: electrical energy reformation, solar, wind, hydro, and nuclear. My father had been involved in all of these areas, contributing while he was at MIT and for all these years since. His particular bent was harnessing natural forms of energy. It's clean, neat,and potentially less costly if critical mass can be reached."

"Critical mass?" Maria asked.

Matthew chimed in, "That's the point at the top of a bell curve or where two axis cross on a graph where the benefit equals the cost or demand equals supply; and thereafter the product takes off like it has a mind of its own. Kind of like, one day there were no personal computers, and it seemed like the next they were on most every desk in the world."

"Excellent!" Cracker Jack exclaimed, like a proud professor to a student who answered correctly. "The problem is, critical mass could take decades in any one of the clean alternative energy sources, maybe longer. My father is partly responsible for hundreds of government-subsidized projects around the world. Before I was born, he built a compound on a large piece of land left to him by his father. After my mother died, he spent his life researching and developing energy systems, most of which have never been seen by the public."

"You lost your mother," Maria said. "I'm sorry."

"She died in childbirth."

Cracker Jack sat up straight, stretched his long arms, and said, "But all this is another part of the very long story. We might not have a lot of time for me to get to why I need you tonight.

"Our compound was covered with his experimentations. He installed dozens of wind turbines in our backyard. We had enough solar panels to illuminate New York City, and, my favorite, Dad built an old time Danish-style water mill. That was a sight to see."

Maria was about to comment, probably on the water mill, when Matthew jumped in. "You mentioned fuel cells?"

"Dad rebuilt an old tractor that ran completely on a twenty kilowatt hydrogen and oxygen fuel cell. It was as reliable as the sun coming up in the morning. The concept and first working models have been around since the mid 1840s. My father, along with a bright staff of researchers, developed many of the modern variations now used in space, in prototype cars, and hundreds of other test markets. But he came to the conclusion that the cost was prohibitive, and there was a slim chance of making a final product that was stable and marketable. He began telling people to save their money. Since then, government and private industries have invested billions. The very people he helped put into business ostracized him."

"They have a lot to lose," Maria observed.

"Yes. After discarding fuel cells as an inevitable dead end, he turned his attention back to using the same concept of capturing energy from the most natural source, the reaction between neutrons and protons in a stable environment agitated by the perfect set of solids which – ," Cracker leaned forward, folded his hands together and pointed his two index fingers toward Matthew, " – which causes not only electrical energy, but energy that reproduces itself."

Matthew's heart was pounding. "It sounds like you're saying he wanted to invent a self-replenishing energy source."

Cracker Jack smiled. He sat back in his seat and drummed on the table. "That is exactly what he proposed: energy that does not depend upon refueling . . . ever. *True perpetual energy.*" He paused for effect. Matthew's jaw dropped. Cracker Jack leaned his long frame across the table until his face was over Matthew's eggs.

"My father spent decades creating true perpetual energy."

Matthew took a breath. "I knew it. I just knew it." He couldn't think of another scientist in the world that could match Cameron Jackson's brilliance. If anyone could do it, he could.

They sipped on a strong, ultra-sweet brew of Cuban coffee.

"What have you been doing since your father's death?" Matthew asked, hoping this would bring the discussion back to Cracker Jack's interest in Maria and him.

Maria was clearly startled and said, "I'm sorry. I didn't realize – "

Cracker Jack acknowledged her sympathy with an appreciative smile. He then said, "These last few years, I've picked up where my father left off. I spent a number of years in the military with the intention of coming home and helping my father with his research. I lost a lot of quality time with him.

Anyhow, back to the future, as they say. They watch me too closely to get anything accomplished, and I have something that needs finishing – " his voice trailed off.

"What is it?" Maria said.

He considered his answer, "I need to focus my attention on taking care of some very bad people."

"The one's who are trying to steal your father's research and inventions?" Maria asked. Cracker Jack nodded somberly.

Matthew sensed that if Cracker Jack had anything to say about it, his enemies would never see a courtroom, maybe a coffin, but not a courtroom.

"While I concentrate on that, providing I can shake my hosts, I have to pass the ball."

"Pass the ball?" Maria said.

"My father didn't die in vain. Quietly, his underlying goal had always been to catch and contain the natural energy found in water, air, and the sun. Then transfer that energy into an unlimited power supply."

Maria interjected, "My parents always said if they could bottle my energy, they could make millions." Matthew sat speechless; his heart was racing.

Cracker Jack showed the most disarming smile. "Actually, that reminds me of my father. Whenever there was a gusty wind blowing off Lake Michigan, my father would step to the porch and watch our windmills. He would say, 'I can bottle that energy, son, and use it whenever I wish.' And that is what he has been doing ever since I can remember."

"That's nothing new, of course. There is the battery." That was a stupid thing to say, Matthew thought.

"Yes, the battery was the first step, placing finite chemical energy into a cylinder which can only be maximized combined with electricity. What has been the obvious problem since batteries were introduced in Baghdad over two thousand years ago?"

"Consistent and quick energy loss."

"Right, which leads to disposable waste of billions of batteries," Maria said distastefully. "What about rechargeable?"

"That was the logical next step. It could have been a grand one if consumers were willing to take the time to recharge. But, like fuel cells, it's still a band-aid, not a cure."

"Right. Rechargeable batteries, similar to our discussion about fuel cells, have a finite life," Matthew said.

"True, and people, particularly Americans, are trained to throw things away. So instead of trying to change consumer perception and habits, industry has to come up with more disposable solutions. For instance, every two years, the entire supply of the world's computers becomes obsolete. Our own innovation creates a need for more and more recycling solutions."

Maria interjected, "Even so, only less than one percent of total waste is currently recycled."

"That's another issue you two can work on next." Cracker Jack laughed.

Matthew frowned. "Next?"

"Listen, my father dedicated his life to finding solutions to the depletion of our natural energy resources. The positive spin-off effects are endless, such as substantially reducing carbon dioxide emissions and other harmful byproduct waste."

"But can a cost-effective solution be perfected and taken to market in our lifetime? It's my dream. But I highly doubt it."

"My father thought so. And he found the ultimate solution."

"Perpetual energy." Matthew had been dying to say it again. He had years of vivid dreams about the possibilities. If what Cracker Jack said was true . . .

Cracker Jack sat back in the booth with a satisfied smile.

Maria broke the extended silence. "You know, the unspoken synergy is intriguing. I suspect you two have more in common than just your love for alternative energy."

Cracker Jack deflected the observation with humor. "Perhaps we are brothers from a different mother, eh Matthew?" Matthew returned his smile.

Maria frowned, "I'm serious, guys. Have you never heard of the theory of Five Degrees of Separation?"

"I think it's six degrees," Matthew corrected and flinched, expecting another punch in the shoulder. Instead, Cracker Jack mediated.

"Well, actually you are both right. Everyone on earth connects through a chain of acquaintances with no more than five intermediaries. At one time it was called the five degrees of separation, and was later changed to the six degrees in order to include the subject."

"Fascinating," Maria said while giving Matthew *the look.* She changed the subject. "You're saying your father came up with the invention of the century, possibly slowing or solving global warming, something that could help millions around the world. What could anyone possibly gain from stopping you?"

"That's quite a leap to solving global warming, but to answer your question, many companies and industry's have a lot to lose. People will kill over a wallet or road rage. Imagine what they are willing to do when billions of dollars are at stake," Cracker Jack said.

Matthew sensed they were in danger even now and worried staying would increase the risk of putting Maria in harm's way. But he was too fascinated to leave. "Did you work with your father on the research?"

"Until I went into the Marines. Like I said earlier, I could have been working with him."

Matthew noted that Cracker Jack's eyes were glossy with tears. He was about to ask him about his military background. But it could wait.

Cracker Jack rubbed his eyes and said, "The next stage was to make a working prototype and begin a beta test project. I was ready to do that a few years ago, when my uncle – ," his brief hesitation was not lost on Matthew, " – when I was informed that I was under surveillance. A few weeks later, someone ransacked my apartment."

"By the FBI, huh?" said Maria.

"Perhaps, but there's a long list of companies, governments, and criminals interested in obtaining my father's work. Whoever *they* were, they kept him under surveillance all those years, but they had a tough time keeping up with my fathers' extensive security system.

"I found out the hard way that even the delivery driver was a mole. When my uncle ran a background check on him, it came up with a long history of military and secret service work. I had an altercation with him before I headed for Miami.

"There were two major security break-ins over the years. The first time they tried not to leave a trace while my father was in DC. The second time they destroyed the place, but that's another story. Both times the silent alarms were tripped and the hidden cameras – "

"So you got them on camera?" Maria interrupted.

Cracker Jack shook his head. "They wore black stealth gear. It covered their faces and heads."

"They sound like ninjas!" Maria exclaimed. Cracker Jack smiled.

"Maria watches a lot of movies," Matthew said apologetically, and he dodged another knuckle punch.

"More like U.S. Special Forces. Navy Seals training is my best guess."

Matthew interjected, "So they came off the lake?"

"They even neutralized my dad's dogs."

"Killed them?" Maria asked.

"No, thank god, just anesthetized them, both times they were walking sideways for weeks. But they would have to have known that Popeye and Brutus were there."

"Perhaps the delivery man?"

"Popeye and Brutus?" Maria asked with a laugh. Matthew and Cracker Jack laughed too, breaking the tension for a moment.

"Did they get all of your research?" Matthew asked.

Cracker Jack laughed again. "They thought they did, but my father outsmarted them with his multiple layers of security."

"Talk about effective preplanning!" Matthew exclaimed.

"Even if they could copy the files from our server, which I doubt, and photograph Dad's journals, which I'm certain they never found, they couldn't pick up anything significant. It would take a consortium of MIT grad students a decade to piece together my father's work. Even then, they would only be half-right. Much of my father's research was in his head."

"And now in yours," Matthew concluded.

Cracker Jack smiled, appreciating his perception. "Yes."

"Where have you been? I mean before you came to Miami?" Maria asked.

"After they broke into my father's place, *they* followed me here to Miami where I barely escaped. From there I've lived in London, San Francisco, and most recently Scotland."

"Where is your place in the U.K.?" Matthew asked.

"It's on an island, the ends of the earth," he said with a grin. "I'll tell you about that enchanting place another time.

I'd still be there had my mother's family not been placed under investigation. I knew it was a ruse to corner me. My uncle found tracking devices in all of their cars and even on my grandfather's yacht. Then the FBI cornered me, and I've been stuck here since."

"Who else do you suspect, besides the FBI?" Maria asked. "I have a mind to contact a few civil rights groups."

"I wish my illegal detainment was the worse of my problems. There are major conglomerates with endless resources and unscrupulous governments that would do just about anything to be first on the market with the answer to the impending energy crisis.

"And, like you said, those that might prefer to destroy your product, before it destroyed them."

"Precisely. The oil industry is in a twist and they are not even sure what we have. Through my lawyers, I continue to be solicited by companies and governments who want first right of refusal. They have offered seven digits as a signing bonus. Behind their offers is the desire to own my father's discoveries exclusively. One country or group could hold the rest of the world hostage."

"In a way, the oil industry does that now," Matthew interjected. "My professor at MIT predicts gas prices to triple in the next decade, and oil company profits to skyrocket. He says they use scare tactics like the Gulf War to temporarily jack prices up."

Maria queried, "I don't understand, if they don't know what your product is, why all the attention?"

"They just know he made major advances in energy technology, they know Dad was first to accelerate with solar and fuel cell energy, and they want whatever it is that he was working on for the last few decades. If they knew what we had, there's no telling how much would be invested to get to me."

"*¡Esos ladrones avariciosos!*" Maria exclaimed, pounding her fist on the table.

Matthew muttered, "Greedy thieves is right," as he reached to catch a glass before it hit the floor.

Maria barely noticed as Matthew cleaned up the water. She said, "Something like this belongs to the entire world, don't you think? Not any one single company, government, or person?"

Cracker Jack nodded showing obvious approval and then more seriously said, "Precisely, my dear Maria. Precisely."

Part Three

Perpetual Tragedy

CHAPTER 16

spring 1987

Tutor

MATTHEW WAS IN the fourth grade when his mother success-fully dragged his father to a parent teacher's conference. As he put the large dual rear wheeled truck they called the mule, into gear, he grumbled, "I don't see why we have to hear what we already know. The boy has never had anything but the top score in his class since kindergarten."

Kate was clearly frazzled and said to Parker, "You really should enjoy these; at least everything is positive. The only trips to school when Sean was growing up were when he was in trouble."

"Damn right," Parker grumbled, "Sean might as well have had a permanent seat in detention."

Matthew sat quietly in the back seat of the Ford 350. He was used to their bickering, and though he knew it was not a good time to tell them he was quite old enough to stay at home alone, he tried one more time to deliver what he thought was a good argument. He took his best shot while his father turned the truck off their long gravel drive onto the Golden Road toward Millinocket. As expected his father's voice boomed inside the truck cab, "If you ask again, little man, you will not be able to sit down for a week."

His mother always came to his defense, "Don't be so hard on him, Parker," and then told Matthew, "Maybe next time, dear."

Once they arrived at the school Matthew sat on a cold metal chair outside his classroom while his parents talked to his teacher, Shirley Reading. He thought how nobody believed that was her *real* name, and amused himself by putting various last names with her first. Shirley Arithmetic, Shirley Writing, Shirley Quantum Physics. He liked the last one best. After all, she is a *science* teacher, and not a *reading* teacher.

Out of his back pocket, he retrieved a rolled and torn Scientific America puzzle magazine given to him by Mr. Estebanez. On the front was a picture of the latest Nobel Prize winners in Physics. Georg Bednorz and Alexander Muller won the prestigious prize for their breakthrough in ceramic superconductivity. Bednorz appeared so young, Matthew thought. "I'd like to win that," he said aloud. He turned the pages until he came to a crossword puzzle entitled "Names of Great Scientists," and went to work.

On the way home, Matthew was curious as to why his mother and father were arguing about Mr. Estebanez. His mother didn't see why his father had a problem with a man that was providing much needed equipment, desks, and lab supplies for many of the schools in the area. His father said that he had no problem with any of his philanthropy, but did have a problem with a strange man getting too interested in his family, particularly his impressionable son. Matthew decided he was not impressionable and that his mother was right on this one, and, most every other one, for that matter.

A deer leapt across the trucks path. Parker swerved just barely missing the tall buck. He cussed, then said, "And what do you think about him living up there at the sporting lodge with that eccentric old kook, Weaver? I hear all they do is smoke cigars and drink wine all day long."

"I highly doubt that," his mother said, "I think it's quite wonderful that he can live the life he chooses. Not everything is a conspiracy, dear."

"Miss Reading sure thinks he walks on water. I thought the conference was about Matthew. The two of you talked more about that Cuban than – "

"So does every other woman in town," Kate said which ignited another grumble from his father.

Finding an opening, Matthew said, "I like him. He gave me a stack of great magazines last time he was at school. I gave him some of my drawings and he's going to make some notes on them when he has time. And he's the only person I know that is interested in alternative energy science."

"I don't know what the big deal is anyhow. What's wrong with nuclear energy and oil?" Parker Eaton asked.

Matthew sat forward until his head and shoulders were nearly in the front seat, it was rare that his father asked him about his studies. They talked a lot about the forestry business, engines, and fishing, but never about science. "Oil pollutes and we are going to run out of it soon anyhow. And, nuclear is good but it's dangerous," he paused, "and, we have no solution for the waste byproduct. Mr. Estebanez and I are interested in solar, fuel cells, wind and hydro energy. I want to design the next generation of solar panels using wind – and water, as a backup source. It's all been done before, but my models are smaller, more energy efficient, and will cost less."

"All this makes perfect sense to you, doesn't it, honey," his mother said proudly.

When Matthew didn't reply, Parker said, "So how do you figure Estebanez fits into your plans?" He was obviously still annoyed, but curious.

His mother chimed in, "When Mr. Estebanez finishes his project, Matthew will have quite a place to study until he goes off to college. He's been underwriting and obtaining grants for the region's first environmental science center. There won't be anything like it this side of Boston. It will add some life to this dying town."

Parker grumbled something about a waste of taxpayer's money.

Kate turned in her seat and flipped on the light above Matthew's head. "Mrs. Reading said that when Mr. Estebanez is at the school, you two strike up conversations about windmills and solar panels." Matthew nodded and smiled as he turned a page in his magazine. His mother continued, "She said it's quite remarkable that you can hold an adult conversation about many things, and when it comes to science she has to concentrate to keep up with you. I know just what she means."

They arrived back at the expansive Eaton property just before nine. Matthew ran straight to the freezer, pulled a pint of Ben & Jerry's, Cherry Amour ice cream, and sat at the table before his father could demand that he go to bed.

Whenever he ate Ben & Jerry's ice cream, a vision came to mind of Sean taking him to see the largest ice cream sundae in the world, over in St. Albans, Vermont. Best of all, Joe Fazio, their biggest fan, literally, convinced the *Cowmobile,* driven by Ben and Jerry themselves, to add Millinocket to their tour. Afterwards the Cowmobile made a stop in Bangor and Boston and then proceeded west until *somehow* burning up in Cleveland!

"I wonder what the Cowmobile looked like on fire?"

"What honey?" his mother asked.

Matthew imagined what Godello's Spanish Restaurant called *fried ice cream.*

His mother picked up on his train of thought, "How Joe Fazio convinced them to add Millinocket to their cross-country tour, I can't imagine."

"He's their biggest fan, Mom!" They both laughed.

Matthew smiled into his half-eaten pint. He admired the ice cream makers and swore he would one day build a business like Ben & Jerry's; except he will make miniature solar powered windmills to generate the electricity, to freeze the ice cream.

His mother settled at the table and began writing on a white lined pad. Parker returned to the kitchen, took a beer from the fridge, and leaned against the counter. His mother began asking questions about their annual company picnic. His father said to keep the cost down and that he didn't want to have to deal with any of the details. He said he had enough to worry about with lumber sales and pulp volume at an all time low.

"I could sure use Sean's help. Do you think he will re-enlist? He will be up for an honorable discharge at the end of this year."

"You should tell him that you are proud of him and that you need him," Kate said.

"He knows."

"I'm not so sure. You should tell him. You hardly ever talk to him when he calls." When Parker didn't respond she said, "I've noticed Sean is changing, slowly, subtly but it has not been for the better. He snaps about nearly everything, and other times he is despondent and distant."

Matthew was about three-quarters through the Cherry Amour. He listened intently. He missed him and hoped that he would come home for good so they could spend more time backpacking and working on engines.

His father turned and sat down in a chair opposite Kate, but within reach of Matthew. "He's always had a chip on his shoulder," his father said without his usual edge. "The kind of work he's doing, either makes you tougher or spits you out. When I was *in country*," he said, referring to Korea and Vietnam, "we could identify our enemy, though it was tough to fish them out of dense jungles. Searching the desert and caves for terrorists is a whole new ball game. It takes men like Sean."

When he was nine, Matthew overheard his mother talking to a neighbor here in their kitchen about how his father knew firsthand the kind of stress front-line military combatants endured and how it changed a man. She had said that Parker was not now the man she knew at Boston College before the Marines, or even the man she married a few years later. She had said, much of his hard exterior was how he dealt with leagues of demons from his years with the DIA and that she was all too familiar with what Special Forces intelligence missions could do to a man's psyche. Matthew had looked up the Defense Intelligence Agency and Marine Special Forces at the library and envisioned his father as a hero. Matthew received quite a scolding for going through his father's things when he had made the mistake of asking his father about the medals in the shape of a heart and a star. He knew his father had the rank of Colonel, which was high up in his estimation. He also knew, from overhearing conversations between his father and uncles, that the Marines had discharged his father when Matthew's grandfather died suddenly of a massive aneurysm. His father was the only brother in a position to take over the saw and pulp mills. Matthew wondered what his father experienced that caused his ranting nightmares waking him more than a couple times a week. His mother had told the neighbor that the nightmares were bad after Korea, and grew worse after Vietnam.

Matthew was startled when his father barked, "Shouldn't you be in bed?" Matthew looked down into the empty pint and wondered where it went. His father finished his beer and stood at the sink looking out at the bright waning gibbous moon hanging over the Katahdin Mountains. "I'll talk to him next time he calls. Like I said, I could sure use his help around here. I don't see getting any use out of Matthew for another ten years," he said, as if Matthew wasn't in the room, "and it doesn't look like I can depend on my brothers. Jim's constantly battling one ailment or another, Darrell will probably retire soon from teaching forestry at Springfield College. He could be the most help to us. And damn that Carl, he hasn't had the decency to come visit in what . . . five years?"

Matthew's mother reminded his father that he paid to put his older brother through college and grad school, which is what got him the teaching position, and that his stubbornness had kept the distance between himself and his youngest brother Carl, who had been a pilot in the Air Force and was now flying cargo between Miami and Central America.

His father seemed not to be listening. "I see the pulp industry getting a lot worse before it gets better and if anything ever happens to me . . . if anything happens to me, you can sell everything and that should be enough to take care of you and Matthew for life."

Matthew pretended to try to scoop more ice cream from the bottom of the empty carton. It was a lot more comfortable sitting here and listening to the latest family news than at the top of the stairs, he thought.

His mother changed the subject and said, "I don't know about Matthew coming into the business. I wouldn't be surprised if he went on to study engineering and physics at MIT, maybe on full scholarship."

"He's a bright boy, I'll give him that. I guess you're saying I shouldn't wait around for him to take over Eaton Logging and Forestry?"

Matthew wanted to say that he was sitting right here, but thought better of it. He was now scraping the cardboard raw.

"It's because of your hard work, dear, that he'll have the opportunity to follow his dreams?"

"Dreams. He's only ten years old, Kate. What could he possibly know about what he wants to do with his life. I was working ten hours a day sweeping the saw mill floors when I was his age."

I just told you in the truck what I planned to do, he thought with a touch of anger.

Parker went to the bar and poured a tall Scotch whiskey.

"*I do* know," Kate said, as if she were reading Matthew's thoughts. "A look at his library of books and his many tablets of drawings of windmills and other contraptions would tell you all you need to know about your son. Miss Reading had simply reinforced what I, and you, should already know."

His father pointed a thick index finger at him and then pointed up the stairs.

"Yes, sir," Matthew said, throwing the beat up carton in the trash. When his father was out of earshot, he said to his mother, "Do you really think I have a chance of getting a scholarship to MIT?"

"Of course, dear. You'll probably be able to choose wherever you would like to go. Though I dare say, you could not do better than MIT. And you would be close to home."

"What about Mr. Estebanez. What do you think of him?"

"You mean that handsome, smooth-talking man? I think he's harmless but could charm the jewels off the Queen." Matthew frowned thinking that was a strange thing to say about Mr. Estebanez. His mother blushed like a schoolgirl, turned away from Matthew, and took her teacup to the sink saying something further. Matthew thought she said, *Parker used to make me feel that way.*

Matthew lay in bed thinking of how Mr. Estebanez really was out of place and peculiar to the Eatons and the little town of Millinocket. Even at his young age, he could see the similarities between Mr. Estebanez and his mother. His mother grew up in an affluent family around the wealthy at Martha's Vineyard and attended the best prep schools. The frequent appearance of this dark, lean, charismatic stranger who signed into the Katahdin Sporting Lodge as Estebanez a few years ago had single handedly put a spark back into their community. He appeared often in town and showed an unusual interest in the region's educational opportunities for youth, particularly the sciences. Besides helping to bring the environmental science center, he had also sponsored science competitions and helped bring a Smithsonian competition to the state. When Matthew stood out far above the rest, he took a personal interest in him and his family, offering and eventually taking Matthew to the national competition in Washington DC. What could be wrong about that? Matthew thought.

One local private investigator aimed to find out. Joseph Fazio, with dark olive Sicilian features, standing half as wide as he was tall, walked into the foyer of the Katahdin Sporting Lodge with a young nervous looking county deputy. With the look of a pallbearer in a Mafia funeral, Fazio approached Estebanez and the proprietor, Dennis Weaver, as they played chess in the library.

Fazio asked Weaver if he and the deputy could have a few minutes with Mr. Estebanez.

Weaver, older than Methuselah, over six foot and skinny, studied the board, pointed a long bony finger at Estebanez, smiled, and retreated to the front desk. Fazio turned a darkly stained heavy solid oak chair around backwards and sat his at least three hundred pound bulk down, while the town deputy walked around the large library pretending to study the titles of the old books.

The chair complained under Fazio's weight as Estebanez lit up a long cigar and extended one toward his visitor, who waved it off.

"Those legal?" Fazio said.

"The good ones are never legal."

"Wine?" Estebanez offered. "This is a very good Cabernet Sauvignon you should appreciate; it's a 1968 Tuscan Sassicaia, the first vintage offered to the public. It will warm the Italian cockles of your soul."

"My cockles are fine, and I'm a beer and whiskey man."

"An Italian who doesn't drink wine?"

"I didn't say I don't drink wine, but it has to be accompanied by antipasti and a plate full of risotto, lasagna, and eggplant *parmigiano*."

"Suit yourself," Estebanez said as he poured another small glass of port.

"You know, when I came to town, I was considered a *carpetbagger* just like you, except over in Little Italy of course," he chuckled, "and many people looked at me cross-eyed. Hell, they still do. What's your story?"

"Actually, I feel quite welcome," he said, clearly avoiding the question. "It must make you miss the fun in Chicago – murders, rapes, robberies – family ties?"

"I see you have been doing your homework on me."

"People talk."

"Well, therein lies the mystery, Mr. Estebanez. People do talk, but they don't seem to know anything about you, except that you have adopted the town and its favorite son."

"What can I say, Mr. Fazio. Science is my life."

"Perhaps. It seems more like wine, women, and cigars."

Estebanez smiled. "I like a good song too."

Fazio returned his smile. "Do me a favor. Keep your distance from Kate. She's a good woman but not your type."

"What's my type?"

Fazio ignored the bait and said, "The Eatons are not only important citizens in this area, but also my good friends. Any improper advances toward Kate . . ."

Temper flaring, Estebanez leaned in toward Fazio. And then, like turning off a switch, he sat back and puffed on his cigar. "I hold all of the Eatons in the highest regard; you are way off base, *paisan*."

Fazio stared at Estebanez for a long uncomfortable moment, reached into his back pocket and took out a notebook. He asked him another twenty questions, receiving more and more obtuse answers. He finally motioned to the deputy, who was roughly flipping through a first edition copy of *A Connecticut Yankee in King Arthur's Court*, that it was time to go.

"That crazy old Weaver let you down in his wine cellar yet?" Fazio asked, in a hushed voice.

"Let me ask you, Fazio, is everyone in this region as contentious as old Weaver and the men in town?" Estebanez didn't seem to have any problem with the women. "It seems that people up here love a debate more than the Senate and Congress combined."

Fazio grunted, "I thought we were argumentative in Chicago. The good people of Millinocket will debate over which way the sun will come up in the morning and then, if it suits them, change their mind about where it will go down. And let me tell you, being an outsider, if you, your father, and your grandfather cannot prove roots in the area, your opinion is not worth crap."

Estebanez took a long drag on his cigar and blew smoke rings toward the ceiling. "No. He hasn't taken me into the secret cellar yet, but I'm working on him."

"Don't hold your breath. The way he protects it, even obsesses over it, some say he's got silver and gold buried down there."

The lanky innkeeper, after chastising the deputy, returned to retake his chair across from Estebanez, who poured another dark glass of wine and moved his bishop, taking Weaver's queen and saying simply, "Check and mate."

Outside, Fazio said to the young deputy, "I can see why so many people like the guy, but I can see through him. He's a player, Randy. He's a guy with a lot to hide, and certainly not someone that would be here unless he had an ulterior motive."

"What is that?"

"I did an extensive background check on what I had on this guy and in the system, he barely exists."

"I could book him and get some fingerprints. Or maybe we could do like they do on *Law and Order* and get his wine glass?"

"I already did that. That's how I got the little information I have. Tell you what, if you can catch him jaywalking, then by all means take him in; but until then, I think we'll just have to keep an eye on Mister Smooth."

A week later Fazio decided it was time to discuss his informal "lack of findings" with the Eatons.

The boys had just finished playing in an American Legion little league baseball game. Matthew and Johnny Fazio were leaning up against the concession stand talking to Maria and another girl while Joe Fazio inhaled a second foot-long ballpark frank and a large box of fries as he sat across from Parker and Kate Eaton at a picnic table.

Mrs. Eaton called for Matthew who ran quickly over to his parents. "How are you feeling?"

"Great, Mom. Great," he said a little out of breath.

She whispered in his ear.

"Not right now, Mom, really, I feel pretty good and you know how they make me drowsy," he said, looking over his shoulder.

"You let me know if you need one."

"Yes, ma'am, can I go back to my game?"

She smiled and kissed him on the cheek. He didn't pull back like many his age would do. Instead he returned her kiss and ran back to his friends.

Fazio said, "So what do you know about this Estebanez?"

"The fella that's building the science lab addition onto the high school?" Parker asked.

"That's the one. Doesn't it strike you as funny that a guy not from around here would invest so much time, attention, and money into an off-the-map mill town?"

“I never really thought about it,” Kate said, “but I will say the women in town have nothing else to talk about than the charming Mr. Estebanez.”

Parker frowned at his wife’s comment and said, “What are you getting at, Joe? When you came to Millinocket, there wasn’t anything normal about a former Chicago cop picking up his family and moving clear across the country.”

Fazio laughed, “This is true.” He dipped his ballpark dog into a pool of mustard. He licked his fingers and took a long swallow of AJ Stephan’s soda, a local favorite. He didn’t try to suppress a burp. “Man, that’s good birch beer, reminds me of going with my dad to White Castle back in the Windy City.” He wiped his mouth and took a small spiral notebook from his hip pocket. “You’re right, Parker. People come to the simple life of the Katahdin region for a lot of reasons.” He paused as he studied his notes. “Outdoor sports, retirement, a need to get out of the city, but scholastic philanthropy is not one of them, and then there’s Matthew . . .”

Kate craned her neck toward the little notebook. “What is it about Estebanez and Matthew that bothers you?”

Fazio explained to the Eatons that he didn’t think Estebanez was a threat to their son, but he didn’t like having a mysterious outsider in his town for an extended period of time with no clear explanation for his presence, not to mention his journalistic polling of the Millinocket citizens. “Isn’t it peculiar that this philanthropist, for lack of a better title, would choose Millinocket to be a benefactor? Why wouldn’t he pick Miami, Jacksonville, Atlanta, or his own Gulf Coast region? While I was checking up on him, I could not find much in a background check, but I did find that he resided in a small town in the Florida panhandle called Destin.” He paused for emphasis. “On a sailboat.”

The Eatons both looked surprised. Mrs. Eaton smiled and said, “How mysterious and romantic.” Her husband grunted his disapproval and spat.

“Let’s just say that I get bored easily. Like I said, Millinocket is a sleepy mill town leaving much to be desired to an old homicide detective from the streets of Chicago. As a detective in Chicago, I developed a good sense of when someone was out of place and up to something. So last year I decided I would make Mr. Estebanez my own personal responsibility.”

“So what did you uncover?” Mr. Eaton asked while wiping mustard from his mouth.

“Nothing. Absolutely nothing. The man has no history.”

"No record?"

"*Nada*."

"So what's the problem?"

"That's the problem. A man doesn't live half a century in the United States and not create a measurable trail, unless he has something to hide. And if science really is his life as he states, then why is it no one in the science world has ever heard of him? There're too many holes in his story, that's all I'm saying."

"Then why would he create such a high profile here? It seems to me that someone who is running away from something would keep low," Kate said. "And Matthew?"

Fazio closed the notebook and rolled his massive frame to one side to return it to his back pocket. "All I'm saying is that someone has gone to a lot of trouble to eliminate any record of a man's past, and that can only mean one of two things: government or criminal – or maybe both."

Kate repeated, "And Matthew?"

"When he started paying so much attention to Matthew, it piqued my interest more." He looked over to the boys who were sitting at another picnic table with Maria and her friend. They were trying to impress the girls with their French fry food fight skills. "I wouldn't want to see anything happen to Matthew."

"You think Matthew might be in danger?" Kate asked. "Mr. Estebanez didn't show any interest in Matthew until Matthew won each of the competitions he sponsored."

Fazio raised his eyebrows and cocked his head. Parker Eaton picked up on the signal. "Joe. Are you saying Estebanez has an ulterior motive that somehow involves my son?"

"I'm making no accusation, Parker. What I'm saying is that, from the day he arrived at the Lodge, he began asking questions about your son. Since he seems to have an unusual interest in the sciences, he might have read about Matthew's uncanny intelligence and that led to curiosity, but one might also say everything has been orchestrated for a purpose."

The Eatons looked at Fazio like he had suggested their son was an alien from outer space that Estebanez had under a microscope. They asked in unison, "What purpose?"

"I don't have a clue."

Mr. Eaton got up from the table shaking his head. "Well, if you do get a clue, you know where I'll be. It's good to see you, Joe. Your boy saved the game with that throw to second off that bunt. I think he's got quite a future in the game." With that, he walked by Matthew and snapped his fingers. "Let's go, Spaceman," Parker said, referring to Bill Lee, a former Red Sox pitcher who retired in Vermont, due west of Millinocket. Bill "Spaceman" Lee came to Millinocket to buy slow growing ash, maple, and yellow birch from the Eatons' timber business.

Matthew jumped up to follow his father. "Matthew," his father boomed, "don't forget your bat. Bill Lee made that special for you, and if you lose it, I'll tan your hide."

Kate stared at Fazio as if she was trying to make up her mind. "Thank you, Joe. I appreciate you keeping an eye on Mr. Estebanez. I'll talk to him as well. He's supposed to come over for tea sometime next week with some books for Matthew. What do you suggest we do in the meantime?" She fumbled through her purse.

Fazio slipped to the end of the bench and labored to pull himself out of the table. "They really need to leave more room between the bench and the tabletop," he grumbled, "Kate, at the very least, I wouldn't let Matthew go anywhere alone with the man, and as far as the next national competition in Washington, DC, you or Parker should go along. Maybe it's nothing, Kate, but there are too many holes to be plugged before this ship goes out of port."

Fazio watched Kate walk off in the direction of her husband and son. "Fine looking woman," he said quietly. He pulled out the notebook again and flipped half way through. "Oh, and Kate?" When she turned, he said, "Have you heard of a scientist by the name of Cameron Jackson?"

She paused. "The name sounds familiar. I think he's an author of a book on solar energy." Her eyes rolled toward the sky, "Yes, Matthew has the book in his library."

"He has a library."

"He might as well. There are hundreds of books in his room, but this particular book means a lot to him. Why?"

"I'm not sure. It's just like a name that came up in conjunction with Estebanez, and he mailed a few packages out to his place in Indiana. Another name that came up was that old Indiana Senator," he looked at his notes,

"Carson." He could see that didn't ring any bells. "I'll let you know." He made a notation and walked over to his son who was showing the girls how he could spin the baseball on his index finger. "Ok, Casanova, your mom had sauce simmering all day. Let's go get some dinner."

"We just had hotdogs, Dad."

"Appetizers, son, those were just appetizers."

Estebanez sat in the lobby of the lodge flipping through a copy of *Field and Stream.* He was getting used to the relaxed lifestyle at the lodge, nestled on the border of wilderness and civilization. He loved the mountains and outdoor sports nearly as much as he did the freedom of living on a yacht. Unfortunately, he thought, you can't have it both ways. He chuckled. Then again, maybe you can. He had extended each stay well after he gained the surveillance data he came to obtain. He tried to convince himself that it had nothing to do with Matthew's charming and beautiful mother, Kate Eaton. But he knew better. The thing that bothered him, no, intrigued him, the most was that she was closer to his age than any woman he had courted in the last twenty years. Until now, he stuck with his principles. They had to be young, unmarried, and only interested in his money. There was something about this beautiful, sophisticated woman, hidden up here in logging country, which he could not shake.

As for all the attention he was attracting from the local authorities, especially the robust private investigator, he was unfettered and went about his business dissecting the town. He kicked his feet up on the solid oak coffee table block in front of him. He had many assignments in his life of espionage, in the military and with the government, as a civilian extracting political prisoners from third world countries, a criminal justice professor, a paramilitary trainer, a wine broker on the side, and a weapons broker (sometimes official, sometimes not). He even had a stint as a private investigator, like Fazio, but keeping an eye on a kid was a new twist. He thought this would be a boring gig, but he owed it to an old friend. He noticed the greatest benefit so far was how the low-key atmosphere began to iron out the hard lines inside and out. He now felt like he was taking a vacation every few months. He rather liked the people of this region, and the kid's mother was a great bonus. A man of deep Catholic convictions, he didn't look at it as adulterous thinking, not at all. This was the first time he looked at an attractive woman when sex was not even part of the equation.

His mentoring mission was quite simple. It helped that everyone, save Fazio, was so accommodating. All of his teachers, friends, and even strangers were quick to brag about their young science genius. And, most wanted to be known as Mr. Estebanez's friend. If you were going to be a spy, he thought, you have to use all of your strengths. One of his was his charismatic personality and charm-he knew it was quite effective. Some of his informants he slept with, others he had to kill-and of course, he always regretted it. The killing, that is. It was nice to have an assignment in which there were no hits scheduled, at least not yet.

"Are you quite comfortable, Mr. Estebanez? Is there anything I can get you?"

Estebanez looked up to see the proprietor of the sporting lodge where he made his residence when in Maine. Though sometimes the lanky gray-haired innkeeper could get on his nerves, he kept to himself for the most part, respecting his patron's privacy. Upon his first visit a few years ago, he got the general overview, like the prelude to a laborious book. The proprietor took him everywhere except where he wanted to go the most – the wine cellar. Weaver had told Estebanez that he was the fourth generation owner of the pre-Revolutionary War establishment, and his name was Dennis Weaver. "Not to be confused with the actor," he was quick to say, "Though I've been told that I look and sound a lot like him." As he took Estebanez through the immense lodge, peppered with the actor's memorabilia, collages of Northeastern American and Native American history, Dennis Weaver let him in on his lifelong dream: one day soon, the actor would be staying at his lodge, and they would get a picture together. He was quick to point out that they corresponded regularly. Estebanez learned from the townsfolk, that to be more precise, the lodge owner sent so many postcards and letters to the actor he was on a short list of stalkers.

"Everything is splendid, Mr. Weaver, just splendid. I was wondering if you would be kind enough to take me on a tour of your wine reserves."

The proprietor feigned a look of shock and said, "You know those cellars have had few visitors over the years other than me and my father before me and his father before him. However, sir, I have given this much thought. You have been so patient, and the most frequent visitor to the lodge since Milton

Bradley, one of Maine's favorite sons. In 1860 he developed *The Checkered Game of Life* sitting in this library."

"You don't say," Estebanez said patiently.

"My great grandfather gave Bradley a similar game that was left in the library by a Brit. The next thing he knew, Bradley had changed his lithography shop into a game board company. The rest is history. I'm sorry, there I go again, where were we?"

"The wine cellar."

"Ah, yes. I do think it's time for you to be among the elite." He made a partial bow and said, "If you will follow me, monsieur."

He quickly put the magazine on the coffee table and followed his host. The real humor in the moment wasn't only Weaver's illusions of grandeur, but also that this wasn't his first trip to the hallowed cellar as Estebanez had found the false wall the night of his first visit to Millinocket and had been *borrowing* exquisite bottles of wine ever since. With their shared extensive knowledge about the fermented grape elixir, the two unlikely friends spent many hours late into the evening playing chess, smoking cigars, and drinking. Estebanez found Weaver, though bordering on schizophrenic, to be quite intelligent, with an encyclopedic knowledge of anything to do with the region and its people. As a trained spy, he knew most everyone loves to talk about themselves and what they know. A pro lets them.

Weaver opened the false wall behind a four-foot section of the massive library bookcase revealing a glistening black rock wall and an ancient looking black oval topped door. He lifted a silver necklace over his head and inserted the skeleton key into the keyhole. The two walked down a steep set of steps into a natural rock walled cellar. At the bottom of the steps, Weaver pulled on a huge oak door comparable to one leading into a medieval dungeon. Endorphins spiked as Estebanez stepped into the familiar presence of the largest wine cellar in the country. Though he now knew his way around with his eyes closed, he pretended to grope along the cold slate shelves lit only by the light from the library behind them.

Weaver took pleasure in providing the aura of history by lighting the oil lamps positioned throughout the cellar. Estebanez could tell Weaver relished seeing the expressions of an informed wine connoisseur, so he didn't disappoint and gave a wide-eyed show of amazement as the cellar unfolded before him.

"You know, I ascertained you were a professional wine connoisseur, though you never said as much. Your knowledge of wine far exceeds that of the casual customer." As they walked, Weaver began his oration like a docent. "In 1774, this wonderful cellar and the original lodge were built by General Gage, the antagonistic leader of the British Army who personified their cocky presence in the New England territories. Gage claimed King George had granted him the entire Katahdin region. Having a love for the vine, he imported hundreds of cases of the most expensive wines of the day into this cellar. Many of the bottles are still on the shelves. Though called back to England in 1775, Gage continued to finance construction of the lodge. Consider this twist of irony: upon completion, the northwest cornerstone was engraved on July 4, 1776!" He pulled a bottle out of the mahogany shelving and presented it, holding the neck with one hand and laying the body of the bottle across his palm.

Estebanez's eyes widened as he observed the dusty 1770 bottle of Chablis from a famous Bousquette vineyard in the south of France. How could he have missed that one? The spirit may have long ago turned to vinegar, though that did not in the least effect its nearly priceless value.

Weaver grinned, looked a bit ominous in the flickering light, and didn't miss a beat. "This bottle was already in Boston when the Revolutionary War began on April 18, 1775 rung in by the famous midnight ride of Paul Revere." He quoted Longfellow:

A hurry of hoofs in a village street,
A shape in the moonlight, a bulk in the dark,
And beneath, from the pebbles, in passing, a spark
Stuck out by a steed flying fearless, and fleet:
That was all! And yet, through the gloom and the light, the fate of a nation was riding that night.

"Fascinating," Estebanez said, ever intrigued with the story behind any bottle he purchased, borrowed, or stole. He was compelled to correct the proprietor regarding the facts of the story, particularly the part where Paul Revere was in prison at midnight. Instead, noticing that Weaver was counting bottles in the same rack from which he had pilfered a rare bottle to sell at Sotheby's, he said, "May I offer to purchase this bottle, Mr. Weaver? Please, name your price."

Weaver could not hide his immense pleasure. "Why, Mr. Estebanez, we rarely sell bottles from this area of the cellar. We would soon lose the museum quality preserved by my family for many generations."

An expert in the art of negotiation derived by bargaining for hostages or terrorizing hostages, Estebanez remained quiet while returning the bottle to Weaver.

Weaver soon found his vocal cords. "I dare say, even the few bottles that have been sold," he said, while looking up at the slate ceiling for theatrical emphasis, "to my ancestors' holy indignation were auctioned at Sotheby's."

Damn, Estebanez thought, I should have known Weaver had been selling at Sotheby's. He's not getting any younger and he's always talking about buying a ranch in Wyoming next to his actor idol. So far, the Sotheby auctioneer staff had not questioned him as to where he obtained his rare bottles, perhaps assuming they were from his private collection.

Weaver nearly dropped the priceless bottle as he added, "Oh, how they brought a pretty price!"

Recognizing a familiar glint of greed in Weaver's eyes, Estebanez raised one eyebrow.

And Weaver took the bait. "However, I think an exception could be made. Let me make some inquiries into the bottle's market value."

Estebanez hid his disappointment. Stealing the bottle would have been a lot more fun, much less costly and would be adding to his Swiss bank accounts, instead of detracting from them. He shook his head at the irony. He seemed to always trade one vice for another. For instance, the lovely Mrs. Eaton was causing him to curb one while causing another, and paying an exorbitant price for a bottle of wine fed one vice, while stealing it fed another. "I'm a very sick man," he said a bit louder than he intended.

"Excuse me?" Weaver asked.

"I think I may need to lie down. Perhaps the cool air and excitement have the best of me." As he turned he noticed a stack of barrels and junk in the back corner. He wandered in that direction and felt a breeze coming from between the cracks of the neat stacks. "What is behind here?"

Weaver stuttered and said, "Just the back wall. We really should be going, I have to tend to the other guests," and he turned and walked away while muttering that he really needed to do an inventory.

Estebanez stared a bit longer at the wall. He felt a strange sensation and then a shiver. He turned and followed Weaver up the stairs.

Once they went through the process of extinguishing the lamps, locking up the cellar doors, and closing up the false bookshelves, Estebanez followed Weaver through the library where, instead of pricey wines, there were walls of vintage poetry and prose. In an adjacent room, Weaver placed the bottle into a wooden box surrounded by enough straw and bubble wrap to secure nitroglycerin.

"I need to make a few calls," Weaver said. He left the room. Estebanez reasoned that he was off pretending to be researching the bottle's value. He knew Weaver knew what he wanted for the rich jewel of the vine. He returned with an apology, wrote a number on a lodge postcard, and handed it to Estebanez, who looked at it, frowned, wrote another number, and handed it back. Weaver made a face, wrote another number, and handed it to Estebanez. This process went on until Weaver finally said, "You, sir, drive a hard bargain. Congratulations. This exquisite bottle of Chablis is yours."

I'll have to sell four of Weaver's bottles at Sotheby's to make up for this one, he thought wryly. The idea that Weaver might do an inventory didn't worry him. He always tried to pilfer bottles that would not stand out to Weaver and those that had more than one sister on the rack. Anyhow, he doubted the senile old man could ever complete such a huge task unless he hired an army of accountants.

As if Weaver had read his mind, he said, "Have you ever been to Sotheby's?"

"Never. Why?"

"I was just on the phone with Pierre from New York, he handles the wine opportunities, though wine auctions are only held in London. He said they might auction the Andrew Lloyd Webber collection soon, which isn't half as rich as the Weaver collection. He says Webber's collection should go for over five million."

Estebanez saw that sparkle of *greed* again. He wished Weaver would get to the point, so he could deny the truth, again.

"The London department appraised my collection in '79. Pierre hopes to auction the entire Weaver cellar one day. They can dream on," he said without conviction. "He said that Serena in London called recently and asked why I was not selling individual bottles directly through Sotheby's, yet they were showing up through a broker."

"That *is* strange."

"That's what I told him. I asked him to describe the broker – "

Estebanez smelled a bluff and gave Weaver a quizzical look.

"He then said he had already spoken out of turn, and went on to point out the confidentiality that protects all buyers and sellers, yada, yada."

Weaver sealed the crate with a waxy substance and affixed many *fragile* stickers on all sides of the crate. He studied the obscure Indiana address Estebanez had written on the bill of lading envelope. He said he had relatives in Indiana; but like most people in the area, he had only been out of the region a few times in his life-once to serve in Japan during the Korean War, and another to attend weddings and funerals in other parts of New England. Weaver strained to read what his eccentric guest jotted down on a Millinocket post card before stuffing it in the slit at the top of the bill of lading: *C; For your safekeeping. M.E. continues to excel – better than expected. Send my best to T. See you soon. Z*

CHAPTER 17

Summer 1988

Suspect

FAZIO HUFFED AND puffed up the back stairwell to his office above Danny's Nook, a small café in the center of town. He walked down the dark hallway to a single door at the end. He entered his small office, not much more than a couple of walk-in closets. He switched on a brass and green attorney's lamp at the desk and sat to turn on his new computer. He loved technology and any tool of the trade that allowed him to research cases and keep in touch with his old cronies in Chicago and DC in and out of law enforcement. The computer, along with a fax, and a good answering machine saved him the cost of a secretary to boot.

He pulled a couple faxes from the tray behind him. Upon further investigation by his friends in the FBI and the Chicago police department, there was very little on Estebanez, but what they did have came up clean. He shook his head and reached into his desk drawer for a pound bag of peanut M&Ms. The FBI profile consisted of a picture and one short personal history. It stated that Cuban immigrant Estebanez is an energy industry consultant, MIT and Stanford schooled, without a criminal record, with a clean two-tour stint in the Marine Corps, and tight with quite a few Washington Republican politicians and numerous Pentagon officials.

Fazio thought it strange that a man in his fifties did not have a more detailed record. It was one of the shortest veteran background checks he'd seen, more in line with someone who retired to a West Virginia mountain cabin. Or, he thought, someone who went through a witness protection program. He had some experience in that area, having worked with many mob informants while on the Chicago police force. Being Sicilian on a mostly Irish police force in the sixties caused him quite a bit of turmoil and pitted him against his own family and friends. Today, things were different. Organized crime was shifting to other ethnic groups that had much less honor and scruples than the Italians, in his opinion. The Russian mob would kill their own and their families, without a reason. At least when the mafia had to kill another Italian in their own family, they took care of the rest of the family like it was their own. The Chinese human trafficking was becoming a big business, and the Central and South American drug trade was expanding faster than the DEA could calculate. He thought of his father, killed by a mob hit-man in the seventies while eating at his favorite restaurant. His two older brothers took their revenge and ended up in prison where they still sit.

He tapped a pen against the green light shade while he stared at the faxes. Or Estebanez could be a CIA operative. He smiled as he concluded that Mr. Estebanez is a spy somehow linked to national intelligence. The more he thought about it, the more it made sense to Fazio. Over his career he'd worked with the CIA on numerous cases and came across a few CIA spooks when he was in Nam. Estebanez's actions were very smooth, too smooth. He always sat with his back against the wall, his eyes were always scanning the room from left to right, and he always answered a question with a question. Fazio faxed his suspicions to his contacts in DC and Chicago, shut everything down, and turned out the light. When he stepped into the night air, his thoughts were on Matthew Eaton.

After Fazio turned the corner, a dark figure stepped out of the shadows of the stairwell and went up to Fazio's office. He picked the lock with one quick move, put on leather gloves, and pulled the shade on the window looking over Main Street. He turned on the computer and, careful to keep everything in its exact place, he began sifting through drawers and files, looking over each fax, and then snapping pictures with a miniature camera. He sat behind the desk and leaned back at ease as he waited for the computer to reboot. After a quick search of Fazio's files, he came upon what he was looking for. The file named ME was quite large. He plugged in a hard drive to the machine and downloaded the file. He shut down the computer and quietly went out of the office. Turning at the bottom of the stairs the thief heard something and turned in time to see his assailant. "You!" he yelled as a club of some sort came down on the head.

The assailant grabbed the hard drive and slipped out into the night.

That same evening Matthew and his mother answered the ringing phone at the same time. "Parker, it's Sean," his mother yelled up the steps. Matthew was supposed to be asleep hours ago; he sat on the floor in the dark hallway hoping his father didn't wake up. Conversations with his brother always went better that way.

Kate asked Sean a number of questions. When she only received two and three syllable answers, she filled the void with details about the new art gallery in town run by a woman who grew up in the region but moved to DC when she was young, and how she must have lost her mind to return all these years later. She lamented about Aunt Cassandra's cancer, and bragged on how Uncle Ken sold his bookbindery business in Boston, and then bought a bed and breakfast in Gatlinburg, Tennessee.

Matthew was bored and about to hang up when his mother asked, "Sean, do you know anything about that handsome man Estebanez that was at Salina Valdeorras's funeral?" All she got in return was a brooding silence – something Matthew and his mother had noticed was becoming more frequent as time passed. "He's donated a lot of time and money to the school system, all in the areas of science. And he's taken quite an interest in your little brother."

That got Sean's attention. "How so?"

"Matthew is becoming quite a local celebrity winning those science competitions. Mr. Estebanez says that since he'll be around quite a bit while building the new science wing on the high school, he'd like to spend time tutoring Matthew."

"What do you know about him?" Sean asked.

"Just that he's a philanthropist and energy consultant."

"Did you say energy? Now *that's* interesting."

"He also says he's a naturalist, so Millinocket is a perfect place to build a world-class research lab. The alternate benefit could help foundering old Millinocket get back on its feet. It's rather exciting. Everyone on MAGIC – "

"What's Magic?"

"Millinocket Area Growth and Investment Council. I'm on the Board. Anyhow, everyone is very excited. Most everyone likes him, and you know people are not that accepting of strangers. Along with the outdoor recreation business, this could really bring the attention the region needs. The only other idea anyone had was to add a moose zoo near the entrance to town."

That brought a chuckle from Sean. "Not that idea again," he said. "You can't cage a moose." He asked how Matthew was doing with his studies, then said, "Don't push him too hard, Mom. He has to enjoy his childhood too. Where's the old man? I only have a few more minutes on the government's nickel."

"I think I can hear him snoring through the floorboards, honey. He's had a long week at the mills, and the economic downturn is putting the pulp industry into a tailspin."

"He'll pull through, Mom. If he can't sell the wood, he'll make wooden nickels and sell them on the corner." There was no humor in his tone. "I'll call again next month. Keep an eye on that Spanish guy. What's his name?" Before his mother could answer, he raised his voice and said, "Goodnight, Matt, we'll go hiking around Sandy Stream Pond when I get home. Don't you let Pop catch you – he'll tan your hide."

"What makes you think he's on the phone, he went to bed hours ago?"

"He's always listening in on the upstairs phone, Mom."

Matthew slipped the phone on the receiver. As he closed his door, he could hear his father's heavy footsteps. A moose zoo, he thought, now that's a good idea!

He peered out a crack in the door until he was sure the coast was clear. It bothered him that his father was so hard on Sean. His mother had confessed to him that she wished her two bull-headed men could communicate better. She said she knew they loved each other but had no idea how to show it. Love and hate, she had said, were two emotions so close to each other that they could be confused.

Too many times, he witnessed her sitting in the chair next to the phone, place her arms on the closed roll-top desk, and cry.

Matthew found it strange that during the conversation she decided to use her limited time to talk about Mr. Estebanez. He knew she liked him as she always put on one of her special dresses and looked in the mirror an awful lot, fixing her hair and makeup, whenever he was visiting. She would do the same thing and then they would run into him at places like the library or post office.

He crept out into the hallway and sat on the first step.

Parker followed her into the kitchen. "What did Sean have to say?"

"You were awake? Why didn't you talk to him?"

"There's no use getting into another argument. I talked to him last month about not re-enlisting, and he flew off the handle."

"You could have told him how much you needed him here. It would make a difference."

"Sean will do what he wants to do. It doesn't matter what I say. As long as he keeps his head down, that's what counts."

They began to argue, as they always did after Sean called. Kate asked him to keep his voice down because he would wake Matthew.

"He was sitting in the hallway listening on the extension."

Matthew held his breath.

"I want you to stay away from that smooth-talking fancy pants *gusano*." His father said.

"I know what that means, and it's a horrible thing to say. That's what Castro called Cubans that have come to America. The same way your grandfather and mine did from England and Ireland."

He sat down at the table and waved his hand like he was swatting a fly. "The next thing you know you'll be voting for a Kennedy and queers getting married. Anyhow, there's something about him that I cannot quite place, but Fazio and I are having him checked out."

"You are what? You leave that to Joe. Don't you dare get involved! What if Estebanez finds out? He's probably the best thing that has happened to this area in decades, and I will not have you and Joe running him out of town like you did those nice boys who had the knick-knack shop."

"Knick-knack, my ass. They were a couple of drug dealers."

Kate took his peach cobbler from the table and put it in the refrigerator saying, "You're impossible."

Parker grunted, picked up his tea, retrieved his cobbler, and retired to his study, but not before pouring a large shot of scotch into the hot tea and saying, "Get your butt back into bed," without looking Matthew's way.

Once he heard Johnny Carson delivering his monologue, Matthew tiptoed down the steps and into the kitchen. "Everything okay, Mom?"

"Oh sure, honey."

"Yeah. Sean seems okay," he said as more of a question than a statement.

"I think so. He's so quiet these days."

"Don't worry about me and Mr. Estebanez. He knows so much about so many things. He likes my ideas on solar panels in windmills, and I think he was in the FBI or something."

His mother dropped the dish that was in her hand. It didn't break but rolled around in the sink. "What would make you say that?"

"Some of the things he says about his life remind me of James Bond movies, that's all. He also knows a lot about science, and I think he's met one of the authors of my energy books, which is pretty cool." Before his mother could ask which one, Matthew said, "Goodnight, Mom. Try not to worry."

She leaned in to give him a hug and a kiss. "You are getting so tall, Matthew. I'll be looking up at you in no time. I love you, sweetheart. Now get some sleep." She looked up at the clock. "School starts in eight hours." Matthew had just opened his mouth when she said, "And no, you cannot watch Johnny Carson! Goodnight."

Matthew lay in bed with a penlight shining on page sixty-eight of his prize possession, a signed copy of *Capturing the Sun* by Dr. Cameron Jackson. He could not remember the name of Sean's college friend who must have given the book to Sean to give to him. He'd ask Sean next time he called. He dreamed of someday meeting Dr. Jackson to show him his solar-paneled windmill ideas.

His mother came into the room to find Matthew fast asleep with the book across his chest and the penlight dimming from low batteries. She picked up the book, kissed him, and ran her hand through his dark, wavy hair. She whispered, "Most kids are reading Tom Sawyer or the Hardy Boys, and you read books over my head and everyone else's – except maybe Mr. Estebanez. Sleep and dream of windmills, my sweet boy."

Back in town, Fazio remembered something and returned to his office. As he came around the corner, he bumped head on into a man. He instinctively reached out and grabbed the man's arm. "Hey, fella, are you okay?"

The man was holding the top of his head. With a strong Middle-Eastern accent, he grumbled that he was fine. The man stumbled down the street, and Fazio stared after him as he disappeared into the night.

"Joe, is that you? What the heck ya doing out here this late at night?"

Fazio turned to see Officer Franklin Dubois walking his usual beat. Though crime was rare, he checked all the retailers' doors each night.

"I was working late and forgot something. How have you been, Frank?"

"Good, Joe, you?"

"Good, thanks. Hey, did you see a lanky and lean stranger, black hair, black shirt and pants, in town today?"

"Nope, can't say as I've seen a stranger in town today. What did he look like?"

"Didn't see his face but Middle Eastern by his accent was my estimation. He was either drunk as a skunk or sick as a dog. Or both." They heard the engine start and looked in the direction the man had gone. A large vehicle screeched out from an alley two blocks down and sped out of town. "You're not going after him?" Fazio asked."

"There's not much chance of me catching up on him, Joe. You have a good night. Give my best to your wife and little Johnny."

Fazio walked up to his office and turned on the lights. Everything looked normal. He picked up a bag filled with bagels that were on the shelf next to the window. I could have sworn I left those on the desk, he thought.

CHAPTER 18

1989

Declare

TREMONT SAT ON a canvas stool staring out the front flap at the shimmering desert. Often when he woke, he could not remember where he was until he heard someone speak the native Middle Eastern language or dialect. He realized he would never grow accustomed to trying to relax in a sweltering tent, below a scorching sun, ten thousand miles away from Jackson's Place. He could imagine the cool wind coming off the lake as he, Brutus, and Popeye ran and played on the beach. Today was the scheduled day once a week when he spoke to his father on the satellite phone, which was strictly reserved for government business. Unofficial phone calls home were one of the few perks of being on unofficial special assignment. He looked at his watch. It would be near dinnertime back home.

"So you're finally announcing to your chums your plans to change the world, Dad?" Tremont said, referring to his father's fellow academics.

"I don't know, son. Some days yes, some days no. I could have launched a prototype product years ago, but you understand my reservations better than anyone. Even half of my friends thought I was crazy the last time I stood on a podium and suggested a future without a dependence on fossil fuels."

"Dad, I was thinking how when I was a boy, and Grandfather said, if you could only bottle that energy you could run a city on it. Do you remember what you told him?" Tremont knew his father would be sitting on a stool in his lab at Jackson's Place. He would close one eye and put his index finger to his chin.

"I do remember. I said, 'Senator, that's exactly what I intend to do.'"

"I remember everyone laughed, and you just smiled. You knew what you had all the way back then, didn't you?"

"Yes, I did. But I wondered then and still wonder if anyone in that room would be alive when our energy designs are placed into action. It's one thing to have the technology. It's another to implement it in an environment that is dependent on fossil-fuel energy.

Tremont said, "I guess I've always known this day would come." He wiped his forehead with the khaki-colored handkerchief that hung around his neck. "I could use one here to power a few high velocity fans."

"That could be done. I could use the miniature fan design we did for the computer industry, make it pocket size, and plug in a CJ Energy chip."

"You would."

"Indeed." They both laughed. "You always cheer me up, son."

"How do you think you'll launch the first chip? Computers? I understand Stephen Jobs is planning to launch a line of smaller computers and one of my technicians in Cairo showed me a design for a computer smaller than a briefcase that you could carry around, if only a battery were made that could power it. I had to hold my tongue."

"You should meet this Stephen Jobs and his genius partner, what's his name, Wozniak? When you get home perhaps the two of you can work something out. The sky is the limit. Every day, I think of a new application. It's funny how things change. It seems like yesterday, I was imagining we would launch our product in transistor radios. Who could imagine that a mainframe computer that took up a New York block would be the size of a breadbox? Though I want the world to benefit from this discovery as quickly as possible, I'm more concerned now than ever about CJ Energy falling into the wrong hands. Greed is a dangerous and invisible enemy to progress. I'm not sure the world is ready for us to let the cat out of the bag."

Tremont often sensed his father was not telling him something. "Have you had more threats?"

"There's no need to worry, son. Wait until you see some of the security additions to Jackson's Place. I added infrared motion detectors outside and inside the fence line and upgraded the visual surveillance system." He laughed. "The den looks like a television studio control room. Sometimes I'll sit in there with a glass of cognac and watch the deer feed and the rangers from the national park. It's therapy." He chuckled again.

"So, you have had more threats."

"I'm not worried . . . just being careful."

"I'll be home soon, and you'll have your own government trained Special Forces security guard. Then we'll give the oil industry and anyone else that wants to buck us, a real Jackson in-your-face run for their money – just like we always planned, Dad." They had to keep their talks short, so Tremont wished his father luck with his presentation and said he would see him in June.

"Are you sure they're going to let you out?" Cameron asked. The last time Tremont thought he was coming home; the Marines extended his tour due to *unforeseen security risks* in the region.

"I didn't give them a choice this time, Dad. I've served my country, survived, and I'm proud of *most* of the work Sean and I have done over here. Some of my guys have not been as lucky. We lost little John and a dozen other guys last month." Tremont got quiet as he thought about the guys he left California with eight years ago. Most went home in caskets. "We take three steps forward and two backwards, Dad."

His father said, "Speaking of holding things back, what's on your mind?"

"You can read me like a book, Dad. I'll tell you more about what led to my decision when I'm home. It's safe to say that I know my place is back with you."

"I'm proud of you, son," Cameron said. "I'll see you soon. We'll prepare the final presentation together and then storm Washington."

"We'll turn the world upside down."

Washington National Airport
March 1989

Cameron rode the escalator down to ground transportation. He carried an overnight bag and a briefcase. The limo driver was a little too easy to spot as he was waving one of those annoying white signs printed with large letter: CAMERON JACKSON. Cameron looked around nervously, smiled at the driver and took the sign out of his hand.

As they drove, he thought why he was here and what he would say. After years of turning down requests from around the world, Cameron bent to pressure from his colleagues to speak in Washington. The Georgetown Physics Department molded the symposium around Dr. Jackson's schedule. Cameron reasoned that if he got in and out of Washington in twenty-four hours, *they* . . . those bastards . . . *they* would not even know he was there.

A black Suburban SUV followed closely behind Cameron's limo. The four passengers had been in the baggage claim area when Cameron arrived. Just before they went out the sliding doors behind Cameron, one of them had signaled to a man wearing khaki shorts and a Dallas Cowboys cap that stood at the top of the escalator.

"Damn it, you are too close! Follow three cars behind. We know where Jackson is staying and we know where he'll be tomorrow, so there's no need to rush."

"You got it, boss, it's your show." The driver said revealing a heavy Eastern European accent. "I still don't understand how that old man can be such a threat, that they pay us each ten thousand American dollars to keep an eye on him."

"Klaus, you are not paid to think – or talk." The man said, displaying a rich Bronx-like accent.

"Still, what does he got in that briefcase, DelGercio, a nuclear bomb?"

"Just drive."

It had been nearly twenty years since Cameron last made bold claims to a skeptical crowd. Since then, he'd toned down, and when the subject of perpetual energy came up, he brushed it aside as a topic for the future. Now that Tremont was coming home, he decided it was time – now or never. He wasn't getting any younger and lately he'd been gaining a deeper sense of his mortality. He didn't want to leave the burden and danger to Tremont, though he had a feeling anyone that tried to mess with his son now, would be all the worse for it. He also realized the invention of the century was too big for them to handle alone. I guess I always knew that, he thought, but everything in life involves timing, the right timing.

If he could gain unilateral support from the members of the World Council on Alternative Sources of Energy (WCASE), he could place CJ Energy Cells in their protective custody. There would be one stipulation: CJ Energy Cells would have to be available equally to all. Without that, he would rather destroy it all. Perhaps the animals, the murderers, who have been hounding him for thirty years would have no choice but to leave him, and Tremont, alone. Or they might finish him off out of spite. Either way, he was tired of hiding.

After checking in and taking a short nap, Cameron left his hotel and walked two blocks along Reservoir Road, then into the Georgetown University Conference Hotel. When he arrived at the auditorium, he stopped and stared at the large crowd of students and his contemporaries. He took a swig of cognac. Would they accept his predictions, and most of all, his announcement, if he should decide to make the announcement? He considered how the technological world had changed in fifteen years. Typewriters, IBM key-punch machines, and transistor AM radios had a small spot in the Smithsonian. Instead of a phonograph in your home, kids listened to music on small players they carried around like a set of keys. Computers were small enough to sit on a desk or a kitchen counter. Microwaves and VHS video were normal household items. And all the while, he had been developing the power source that would run the technological revolution into the next century. He looked at the crowd and considered how most were expecting a repeat of his now historical Jules Verne *The Alternative Energy Revolution* speech, published in textbooks from MIT to Stanford.

But today's speech was different. This day he was mere weeks away from changing his presentation from theory to fact. Only Cameron and Tremont knew – though some obviously suspected – that all the years of hibernation would produce something significant. When he made his presentation to WCASE in August, a host of patents and research would prove beyond a shadow of doubt that perpetual energy was not only possible, but would be reality before the turn of the century. If all went well, they would obtain enough grant money to develop prototypes. Though Cameron had much of his inherited wealth available and nearly all the royalties earned on his expired solar energy patents, he did not wish to delve into his private funds further. That was for Tremont.

Of course, he thought, it was probable that those who had proven they were willing to go as far as murder to obtain his research would only step up their efforts. One way or another all hell would break loose. Or *they* would lock him up in the loony bin like they did Dr. Jean-Paul Dominique Esquirol, just prior to releasing his new form of fuel cell technology. Mysteriously, the French physicists work burned in an electrical fire.

Or *they* would kill him.

Cameron nervously held onto the lip of the podium. It had been years since he was out in public at all, let alone in front of a crowd of academics and media. He also suspected that *they* would be out there. The crowd applauded for over five minutes standing in honor of their great colleague. As he waited for the ovation to die down, he felt waves of mixed emotions and the weight of the random events coming together that had led him to this moment.

Then, as always, his excitement abated as he thought about how the only love of his life should be with him. *They* took her from him. *They* had to pay. It had been twenty-six years, yet it seemed like days. The work and the cognac, though both were rewarding, were really just an anesthetic for his pain. The authorities had long since stopped taking his calls and replying to his letters, passing him off as a conspiracy theorist. Only one lone agent had taken him seriously, when Cameron insisted their lives were in danger: but he got there too late. When Flannigan bucked his superiors, then and many times since he nearly lost his job. Cameron had a feeling Flannigan was in the audience tonight.

He spoke for two hours. As he drew charts on the blackboard behind him, he became more animated than he had ever been in front of a crowd. The academic and alternative energy conscious crowd had been awaiting this for years. He turned to them, both hands firmly planted on the podium, and said, "Ladies and gentlemen, if given the funds, we will all see the result of my life's work in action: the world's first source of perpetual energy." As he said it, he even shocked himself. He had not meant to use the damning word *perpetual.* It just came out.

The crowd took a corporate breath and then seemed to let it out all at one time, jumping to their feet and making more noise than a capacity crowd in a football stadium.

Reporters headed for the door to call in the news. "Cameron 'Jules Verne' Jackson is at it again."

Cameron could not help noticing two familiar men – shadows from his nightmares – depart the hall. There was no holding back now. They could try and stop him, or they could get on board. He thought most of the pressure he had been under these last years came indirectly from the fuel cell and oil industries. They had the most to lose. He had upped the ante, and his adversaries would now include anyone who wanted his research for their own profit. That was a much larger list.

After the speech to the Georgetown University crowd, Dr. Jackson was overwhelmed with congratulatory praise and questions. Seeing that their friend was in distress, a few of his closest allies known as the *fraternal brothers of energy* led him out of the building. Once they had him safely back in his hotel room, he agreed to meet and greet at the black tie event that evening at the chancellor's home. Cameron gave each one of his old friends a two-handed handshake and thanked them for saving him from the smothering crowd.

That evening, at the reception attended by senators, congressmen and woman, business leaders, and academics from around the world, his closest friends once again surrounded him.

"Do the crowds still bother you the way they used to, Cameron?" The familiar deep voice resonated over his shoulder.

"Brewster, you old son of a gun. I thought you'd retired to London, and we'd never see your flaming liberal face again," Cameron said, taking his old friend, Kingman Brewster, who had been President of Yale until he retired in 1977, by the arm.

"Cameron Jackson, without liberals like me, you save-the-earth, energy conservation, tree-huggers wouldn't have a platform at all." He took Cameron's hand and said, "We have all missed you immensely. The President asked about you the last time I was with him."

"Please give him my best."

"I will. You know that speech earlier today sounded very similar to the one I was skeptical of back in 1969." Kingman had returned this week from Oxford, England, to see his old friend Cameron and visit the White House where he often served as an education consultant. "So Cameron, where is that genius son?

I expected him to be right by your side. He's been missed at Yale. There was never a dull moment with him and that lumberjack."

"Sean Eaton. The boys have been raising Cain somewhere in the Middle East. My son is due home this summer. I must say I've missed him. He's always been my right hand man in the lab."

"How about those monster dogs, what were their names, Popeye and Brutus?"

"They have been hopeless without him as well."

"I'm not saying this because you're my friend, Cameron. God knows I wouldn't do that." Many in the group chuckled. "But I overheard reports that your son was the brightest student in his class, one of the brightest and most accomplished that has ever attended the university. Yale and MIT – and I don't know how many other universities – are still using the software program he developed to track experiment progress and analyze data. We don't offer an energy science degree," he said for the benefit of others in the group, "so he crafted his own in association with your old alma mater. Why he went into the military, I'll never know."

There was a chorus of agreement from the group around Cameron, which had swelled to more than a dozen. Cameron drank down another gin and tonic and was clearly enjoying the discussion about his son.

"Patriotism, impulsiveness, and maybe a sense of adventure. Some kids go to Italy for a semester; my son had to see the world from a Huey helicopter."

"What area did he specialize in?" one of the *fraternal brothers of energy*, Randall Parez, asked.

"He started out in the Marines involved in a CIA and military intelligence study. His recommendations on counteracting potential terrorist threats to disbursed, renewable, and domestic supplies of fuels, electricity, and nuclear sources were presented to a bipartisan committee on antiterrorism."

Brewster interrupted, "I saw that Tremont's work is detailed in an Anti-terrorism Act before Congress this year."

Cameron beamed. It was easy to be humble about his own accomplishments, but not when it involved Tremont.

These disclosures about Cameron's son raised questions, and the conversation segued into ways to tap into various funding sources for energy research and development. Cameron listened and hoped that very thing would be the result of his presentation to the World Council on Alternative Sources of Energy this summer.

Randall Parez asked, "What led Tremont into the Marines? Was it a push from the old Senator? I understand the military is as much a tradition in your two families as turkey on Thanksgiving."

"He became friends with a wild kid from upstate Maine, the young man Kingman mentioned. Sean and Tremont got to talking about their mutual interest in national security and military intelligence. They considered each branch and chose the Marines."

"What do you know about the work they've been doing?" Parez asked.

Cameron avoided the sensitive, even top-secret subject. "For the past few years, the details are sketchy at best."

"Weren't you surprised he chose the military with such a promising future assisting you in your research?" the former Yale President asked.

"At first, yes. But both of his grandfathers were in World War Two and we can trace the Jackson's and Carson's leading battles all the way back to the Revolutionary War and I served in Korea, so I guess it's in his blood. He's seeing the world while he serves his country; his last three postcards were sent from Baghdad, Budapest, and Seoul."

"Does he ever regret his decision?" asked his friend Sergio, an Italian nuclear physicist.

"I asked him recently if he regretted leaving science for weeding out terrorist organizations. He told me he was applying his knowledge where it would count the most. He said he sometimes wishes he didn't have such integral knowledge about the terrorist threat to our nation, but he will never regret the opportunity to protect his country from this eminent threat.

"He and Sean were being trained by military intelligence and Special Forces. Tremont was able to stay immersed in research learning things that will accelerate our work when he returns." He paused, fearing that he might reveal too much about his son's sensitive position. He concluded with a simple, "His plate's been full."

"So Dr. Jackson, your son is a military spook," blurted out one of the younger men in the ever-expanding group around Cameron. "I understand he's in the DIA?"

Cameron Jackson laughed. "I don't know about that. What I do know is that he's a soldier working with thousands of other young men and women around the globe to keep our country free."

The young man persisted. "I don't think we'll ever have to worry about terrorists here in our country, but there's always going to be dissension against the U.S. in third world and Arab nations because we incite them to anger over our arrogant and often covert actions. We need to understand their culture better and not kindle their anger against Americans. I mean, look at our audacity in the West Bank."

"Listen," Cameron broke in, "we are not as safe as you and most American's think. If we don't step up our efforts to protect against terrorism, we're going to get bit right here on our own soil. Security should be our nation's number one priority."

The young man took another jab. "I understand you take security very seriously – don't you think it looks a bit paranoid living on a compound more secure than Fort Knox?"

Randall Parez broke in, "Here's to national security and alternative forms of energy." Many in the group raised their glasses to toast.

Cameron caught Randall's eye. They had a mutual understanding. Randall Parez's thirty-plus year career networked his particular acumen within government agencies relating to technological advances in utility efficiencies. The stranger turned his attention on Parez.

"Mr. Parez, are you still focused on security issues relating to the overburdened electricity grids?"

"Yes, indeed, Ralph Nadar and I have consulted Congress on many occasions emphasizing that our interlocking grids with Canada and Mexico are facing an inevitable overload. Worse yet, is how vulnerable all of our resources are, including our deteriorating water system, to terrorist tampering."

Another man in the growing crowd said, "I find it hard to believe given the facts, you are not receiving a tremendous amount of support."

"It's all politics. Until enough citizens realize the enormity of the danger, it will remain a minor issue bounced around like a ping-pong ball in the halls of the legislature. Those that are aware of the threat are hoping the system will hold until either they are out of office or someone poses a magic solution."

A woman with an accent indicating she was from India or Pakistan said, "It's an economic issue. The cost of change is overwhelming. It's hard to imagine how many billions will need to be invested every year for many decades to upgrade the infrastructure."

Parez nodded in agreement, "To say we cannot afford the change is ludicrous. We cannot afford to stand still, especially in sensitive markets like Washington, New York, and our exposed borders."

Brewster, the former Yale President interjected, "Historically, when there is an ongoing political gridlock such as this, some catastrophic event has to happen to force change."

"I hope that day never comes," chimed in Francesca, an energy researcher from Quebec. "I agree we are exposed in many areas along our mutual borders and through our connecting flights. It seems our greatest mutual strength is our greatest weakness: freedom."

Francesca's comment drew a chorus of affirmations from the group.

The young stranger folded his arms and said, "That sounds like a cop out. I look around the room filled with some of the greatest scientific minds of our century. There must be something that can be done."

"Ah," Parez said with a chuckle, "now you have circled back to the importance of this day. Dr. Jackson and physicists like him give us all hope. He has focused all of his resources, indeed his entire life, toward an ultimate solution."

Privy to Tremont's work, Cameron knew more than anyone in this circle about the dangers America was facing. He was not able to say much since Tremont was in a sensitive area dealing with classified information. He knew his son's missions were top secret but also knew part of it had to do with infiltrating terrorist groups like Al-Qaeda and Al-Jihad. Cameron would not be happy until his son was back in Indiana.

Changing the subject, someone out of Cameron's view asked, "Dr. Jackson, I could have sworn you were intimating that perpetual energy was a fact rather than just a possibility. Are you indeed working on this, and when will we get something more than speculation?"

Cameron looked around at his expanding audience noting there were a number of strangers. *They are here,* he thought. He called them shadows because they followed him around, and had been doing so as far back as his days at MIT and Harvard. But things were different now. Danger increased proportionally the closer he came to launching his discovery. He looked back at the sandy-haired man and thought he recognized him, but not as a threat. Asking follow-up questions before Cameron had a chance to answer the first was a sure sign he was a reporter. Cameron had a lot of experience over the years with dodging the media. He humored the man by saying, "When I know, you will know, Mr . . ."

"Ackerman, Kip Ackerman with the *New York Times*."

Cameron almost laughed aloud as his friends and colleagues took one-step back from the journalist like he had a contagious disease. If Mr. Ackerman were with *Science America* or a trade magazine, it would be one thing, but the fact that he was with a major newspaper raised their blood pressure. One misplaced article positioning their field in a bad light could cost them research funds. Most agreed it was better not to talk to outsiders at all.

Cameron was feeling the effects of his third gin. He said, "What if, and of course, I'm just hypothesizing . . ."

"Oh, here it comes," interrupted Sergio Magiano, a member of the energy fraternity, "more science fiction from our very own Jules Verne."

A server came over to refresh drinks for many in the group, including Cameron, who made a mental note this would be his last. "First of all, my dear Sergio, the origin of our family name is English. The suggestion of any relationship to the French Jules Verne would have been enough provocation to call you out for a duel. If you remember, I didn't take on that manacle. I believe it was the media, ey? As I was saying, it's just a hypothesis, but what if we were to create a way to capture unlimited volumes of energy for one hundredth or even one thousandth the cost of fossil fuel energy?" With that, Cameron realized the alcohol was doing more and more of the talking. He had counseled his son over and over not to get cornered into this very situation. What the hell, he thought, I can give in to the demons for once. I'm only months from the point of no return anyhow. Then let the cards fall where they may.

Sergio crossed his arms, leaned in toward his eccentric friend, and in a heavy Italian accent whispered, "Jules, I know what you're thinking, and you'd better keep it to yourself or risk the consternation of everyone who is invested in any other source. We all have much to lose if you are right."

Cameron sensed more than friendly advice from Sergio. Maybe it was the liquor, but there was a tone of warning in Sergio's reprimand, perhaps bordering on a threat. Is he one of them?

The crowd around Cameron, now burgeoning to over fifty, was in a feeding frenzy. The discussion had led to the possibility of the icon revealing some of his scientific improbabilities, and they were not going to let it rest. Zaffar Ahmed, an India-born Princeton and Harvard educated geologist and consultant to the oil industry said, "If what you are proposing is possible – and for the record, I'm not saying that it is – " Ahmed looked around nervously, cleared his throat and lowered his voice. If you are proposing perpetual solar energy, I would have to agree; you're making yourself a target."

Cameron noticed Ahmed wink at the *Times* reporter. He's definitely one of them. He knew the intellectual conversation to follow would have a life of its own whether he was involved or not. Johnson was staring at him; the reporter smiled and raised his glass with a wink. Cameron frowned. Over Johnson's shoulder, he noticed the two men he'd seen in the auditorium earlier as they exited the group. There they are, Cameron thought, satisfied his intuition had been correct.

Dimitri Yanovsky, a Russian scientist with leather-like skin and eyebrows rivaling the fur of a black bear, was known for advancing nuclear energy component modifications and was once Russian Deputy Energy Minister. He said, "It is true, my friend. The oil industry and their respective governments have not been concerned with us. They know the cost of nuclear energy production continues to escalate along with the fear of security failure. We cannot compete in consumer industries and most industrial applications. Were I to succeed in miniaturizing the nuclear process and reducing the cost to a nominal figure, I would be a target, no? It would be wise to surround myself with bodyguards and check my vehicles for explosive devices!"

Another threat? Cameron thought.

Then Yanovsky chuckled. "But of course, my friend, we are not even close. I will not have to change my name and ask for political asylum in the great U. S. of A. anytime soon." Everyone in the large group laughed and looked to Dr. Cameron Jackson for a reply.

"Amen, my Russian friend, it's a dangerous world in which we challenge the status quo." Then he whispered, "Here's to you, my son. Come home safely." He tossed down the balance of his drink and slipped away from the increasingly argumentative crowd.

On his way out the door, he saw an unshaven rough-looking man wearing a wrinkled brown suit and dirty white shirt leaning up against a lamppost. Cameron recognized him immediately, older, but the same man. "Why Mr. Flannigan, it is good to see you again."

"And you, Mr. Jackson."

"Still with the Bureau?"

"Much to Director Harrington's chagrin. Do you mind if I walk with you back to your hotel?"

"Actually, I would prefer that you did."

They walked a couple blocks and took a right on Wisconsin Avenue toward Cameron's Four Seasons hotel. Flannigan offered Cameron a cigarette, "Sorry, I don't carry cigars with me."

"I quit years ago, but I must admit the cigars are still a vice. Thank you anyhow."

"So Mr. Jackson, you saw them too, I take it."

"I was beginning to think I was being paranoid. Yes, there were two men at the back of the auditorium. I've seen them before, in Indianapolis and once at one of Tremont's basketball games a number of years ago."

"I notice you didn't stay at the Conference Center on campus, probably a good idea. I wish you would let me know when you were venturing out from Jackson's Place, I still have some pull and could have a man keeping an eye on you. Also, I have access to new wireless surveillance technology I would be more than happy to let you test out at your compound."

"I might take you up on that. Thank you."

"If Colin – you remember old Colin Jester – if he wasn't an alumnus of Georgetown, in theology of all things," – that got a raised eyebrow and a smile from Cameron, "I would not have heard you would be here today."

They talked casually for the rest of the walk.

"Well, it certainly was a pleasure seeing you again, Mr. Flannigan. Thank you for your concern." Cameron had turned to walk up the stairs when Flannigan touched him on the shoulder. "Yes?"

"I believed you, even before the hospital. You know that, don't you?"

"Yes, I know, you were only following orders. You're the only one, Mr. – "

"Call me Patrick. Please."

"You're the only one, Mr. Flannigan. And your help with obtaining the best security systems and helping to keep an eye on Tremont through the years has been appreciated. I only wish you and the bureau had found out who was responsible for her death, and who has kept me in fear for my son's life all these years."

"It's been my life mission ever since you called before she went into the hospital." Flannigan looked away, "And they, we, didn't take your call seriously enough."

"You weren't alone, agent Flannigan," Cameron said. "But your help these three decades has kept Tremont and I alive, I'm sure of that."

"Are you sure about going public with your research?"

"As sure as I'll ever be, I suppose."

"Then let us help you. Keep me apprised of your every move. When is the WCASE presentation that I overheard you discussing?"

"August. I'll fax you the details once they're set. Tremont will be coming with me."

"He's grown into a fine man, Mr. Jackson. You should be very proud. If you didn't need him, we might be looking to bring him into the bureau. He's developed quite a record on antiterrorism, the kind of intel I have a feeling we are going to need desperately over the next few decades."

"I am very proud of him, Agent Flannigan. Thank you again."

When Cameron got to the bellman at the top of the stairs, he looked at Flannigan's receding figure and a rush of pain shot through his body as if he had lost Karen this very day. He remembered Flannigan showing up at the hospital. His words rang in his head. *Mr. Jackson, I'm so terribly sorry. We should have taken your calls more seriously these last months. Is there anything I can do?* He'd told Patrick Flannigan that he could help him make sure they didn't get to his son or his wife's family. Before Flannigan left the hospital he'd said, *I will never rest until I find out who did this. I promise you that.*

CHAPTER 19

May 21, 1989

Free

TREMONT LOOKED AT his watch and then at the Atlantic ocean out the window of the C-130 Hercules military transport plane. He could barely believe nearly a decade had passed since he and Sean were battling the Gauley River and made the decision to join the Marines.

He was excited to be heading back to help his father accelerate the launch of CJ Energy Cells. He smiled, appreciating the name his father had chosen for the future of energy, then thought about the lengths people would go to, to keep the product from success. He was increasingly worried about his father's safety. It took facing the realities of life and death, and witnessing the extreme lengths fanatics were willing to go to achieve their objectives, for him to see clearly his father's dangerous circumstances. He wanted to ask his dad some tough questions about his mother's death and numerous peculiar events that hadn't seemed real, but now he suspected were. His father avoided his questions during their long distance conversations. Tremont knew the things his father wasn't saying were more important than those he was. He wondered how desperate his father's enemies had become, and how far they were willing to go.

Many times while serving his country in the Middle East, Tremont had wondered if he chose badly; and if he could have been more useful by going straight back to Jackson's Place after finishing his graduate studies. On the other hand, the things he'd learned and the people he'd met would be an asset once they were ready to go to market. And he was fairly sure that, if he had gone right back into the lab after graduate school, he would not have the same sense of urgency that he did now. He'd experienced firsthand to what extent religious zealots would go to undermine the infidel Westerners' influence over their region. He also marveled at how the capitalist Arabs' oligopoly on the world's oil supply used supply and demand like the slide on a trombone, throwing western economies and stock markets into flux.

Tremont was surer than ever it was time to launch CJ Energy. To work toward making the free countries of the world independent of the need for foreign oil, and to make low cost energy available to third world and developing countries.

Tremont landed on the tarmac of the McCutcheon New River Marine Air Station, part of Camp Lejeune, North Carolina. His first task and last order, at least for now, was to attend a lengthy debriefing. He then met with the base commander at his impressive Emerald Isle second home. He spent two hours over a lunch of surf and turf thwarting one bribe after another. The Marines wanted him to reenlist. How he got out of that meeting in civilian clothes, he thought, he'd never know.

Back on base, Tremont looked at his watch, threw his duffel bag over his shoulder, and jogged to the MP Station. He had a note from the Commander directing the MP to drop him off at the Ford dealer in Jacksonville. Tremont smiled all the way down Marine Boulevard as the MP chatted on about who knows what. He was a free man, and he coveted one car for as long as he could remember.

He waved to the MP, set his duffel bag next to the reception desk inside the dealership, and walked over to a new black Mustang GLX convertible. He didn't bother taking it for a test drive. He looked at the sticker, took off ten percent, and wrote a check.

A stocky salesman walked over. "That particular car has more under the hood than Dale Earnhardt's Mach 5."

"I'll take it," Tremont said, handing the young man the check and a copy of his military ID.

"Ummm, I'll have to check with . . . I'll be right back." A few minutes later, the salesman came back, accompanied by an older man wearing a starched white shirt and burgundy-striped tie. They both wore broad grins. The sales manager said, "Mr. Jackson, I like to meet a man on a mission. Congratulations on your discharge today. I did the same thing many years ago when I got back from Korea, except I bought a new Ford Fairlane. It wasn't until 1964 that the first Mustang came off the assembly line, or I *guaran-damn-tee* I would have bought that."

Tremont smiled and shook both men's hands. He figured they'd called the base to check the validity of the check and, at the same time, get his active duty status.

"Tell you what," the manager continued, "we're not even going to haggle over the price. You've cut a fair deal here." He handed Tremont the keys. "Step over to Kent's office, and he'll get the title paperwork in order, and you can be on your way. Which way you headed, son?"

"Off to the Florida panhandle, then up to Indiana."

"You're going to enjoy the scenery much better now, I *guaran-damn-tee-it*."

"I don't doubt it one bit."

A half hour later, Tremont pulled out onto Highway 74 heading west. He had studied a map while at the dealer and memorized the simple directions. He would take I-95 south, connect to I-20 west to Atlanta, and then it was all-downhill to the Gulf Coast. The Mustang was the first new car he had ever owned. As he cruised through one small North and South Carolina town after another, his thoughts kept slipping to his protégé. The kid had become a major part of his long-term backup plan. He worried he was obsessing but knew the chance of finding another young person with Matthew's savant-like understanding of energy engineering and physics was unlikely.

Up until this morning, he'd considered going north and checking in on the kid, but Sean's suspicions were already heightened. He had left Sean on such a bad note that he decided making contact with Matthew could wait. Besides, he thought, his uncle had kept close tabs on his development. He smiled because, as ridiculous as it would sound aloud, he felt a kinship to Matthew, like he was his own brother or son. He listened as Sean boasted of Matthew's accomplishments when postcards arrived from his parents. He didn't think Sean was wise to his own Matthew Eaton surveillance program but couldn't be certain. There were those times when talking about his brother that Sean quipped, "But you knew that, didn't you?" or "Well, you probably have more intel on that than I do."

Then he would laugh and change the subject. Sean had become more cryptic and aggressive toward him, which Tremont attributed to battle stress resulting from their covert assignments. They were not as close as they'd once been.

Tremont couldn't help noticing the drastic changes in personality Sean went through while they were together in Special Ops and Intel. Soldiers responded to the stress, the intensity of extractions, and in Sean's case, unauthorized assassinations, in different ways. All intelligence, special ops, and Special Forces soldiers had to undergo psychological evaluations on regular intervals. Though the doctors concluded that both he and Sean were suffering from post-traumatic stress disorder, their work was too valuable to pull them from the field.

Special ops superiors often overlooked the medical advice of psychiatrists and Marine MDs. Tremont thought Sean was taking more than a little joy in what should be the undesirable part of their various assignments.

One night after they had infiltrated an Al-Qaeda training camp in Egypt, killed a half dozen alleged terrorists, and extracted European and American hostages, Tremont suggested Sean get out of the service before he lost it completely.

Sean said, "It's my life, and I would definitely rather die by the sword . . ."

Tremont was tired of hearing Sean repeat this often misquoted idiom. "Do you know who said that and why?"

"It's in the Bible," Sean said, obviously irritated to get another literary lesson from his all-too-smart friend. "Though I suppose you're going to enlighten me."

Tremont didn't miss a beat. "Your favorite Biblical quote was first spoken by Jesus. After Judas betrayed Jesus and the crowd came up to arrest Him, the Apostle Peter attacked a guard with his sword, according to Matthew 26:52 . . ."

Sean threw a pebble into the fire, scattering sparks in all directions. "You even know the blasted verse."

" . . . Jesus said to Peter, and I'm paraphrasing the King James, to put his sword away, for all those who take up the sword perish by the sword."

"You missed your calling, Pastor Tree," Sean grumbled. They had both retreated to their own thoughts.

Tremont put the Mustang on cruise heading out of Atlanta. His thoughts meandered to what he had learned while dodging bullets these past years. He felt he had contributed quite a bit to America's security, though there was so much more to do. Someone else would have to fill in where he left off. He re-engineered security systems for power grids in Kuwait and later on Saudi oil fields. He consulted with politicians and scientist on anti-terrorism mechanisms for domestic U.S. and international cities. In their spare time, he and Sean were personally responsible for taking out dozens of potential terrorists in the suspects' own backyards while setting up a network of Arab-Muslim informants and spies who continue to infiltrate hidden terrorist cells and provide data leading to undocumented air strikes on terrorist training camps in Afghanistan, Libya, Syria, and Iraq.

He pulled off for fuel near Columbus, Georgia. While filling the tank he looked across the highway at the signs for Fort Benning which reminded him of Little John, a soldier who died in his arms. It was not too many months ago, Tremont's itch to opt out of the Marines was further scratched while on a fact-finding mission in the northeastern corner of Iraq on the corner of the borders of Turkey, Iraq, and Iran.

It was the hottest part of the summer, two clicks from the Turkish border. Sean and Tremont sat with their unofficial Kurdish rebel company having finished setting up a temporary camp on top of a ridge with low profile camouflage tents. The group of eleven Kurds, six Army GI's, and two military consultants took up positions a dozen feet away from the center of camp. Out of habit, one Kurd prepared a makeshift fire, though they all knew it could not be lit. The rest of the team ceremoniously cleaned their weapons while waiting for dark. They were planning to infiltrate a potential terrorist camp the next day, so there would be no fire, and it would be Turkish-made canned rations and some U.S. GI energy snacks not surprisingly branded *Hooah!First Strike Booster Nutrition Bars.* Sean and Tremont obtained a large supply of these fresh out of the lab test in the last field air drop before they left the Kurdish capital city of Mosul a month earlier.

To break the uncomfortable silence, Tremont threw an oatmeal and raisin *Hooah!* to Sean whose reflexes were so sharp, even at dusk, he caught it with one hand while not even looking in his direction. Tremont said, "I know you don't want to hear it, but I think it's time for the both of us to go back to the States. We've done more in a couple years than the CIA has in ten toward our mission. I think we're taking too many chances, and the statistics are going to catch up with us. Not to mention, our mission was never intended to include assassinating public figures, which has been made illegal by Congress during the Carter Administration."

"Carter! Another nansy-pansy! Half the reason we are in this predicament is because of his weakness on foreign policy. The old Gipper," referring to then President Ronald Reagan, "isn't afraid of Russia or God almighty for that matter."

"Hey, I didn't say I agreed with the law or Carter's politics. It is what it is. I will say, Carter is becoming more effective out of office than he was in. I think he's becoming a hell of a diplomat and humanitarian."

"Mr. Carter and his bleeding heart liberal pals are delusional to think these religious fanatics care one bit about diplomacy. Mark my words, Tree, while politicians are trying to negotiate for oil, the fanatics like that lunatic bin Laden are working behind the scenes to find ways to disrupt any progress we have made. The work you and I are doing is invaluable."

Without his realizing it, Sean had raised his voice. All the Kurds had stopped talking and were looking across the unlit stack of wood and up the hill at their two American consultants. "We can't put our sword up on the mantle until every one of these freedom hating whackos is wiped off the face of the earth!" Sean stood up, put his hands on his hips, and gave the Kurds a "what the hell are you looking at" glare. One made a comment, which brought on a chuckle from the group. Afterward, they went back to their task while some lay down to sleep. Sean ignored them and turned back to debate with his college buddy. He cleared his throat and spit, then said, "If criminal psychopaths anywhere in the world are considered enemies of America and democracy, and they get in the way of me completing my mission and setting up my network . . ."

Tremont couldn't help noticing how Sean now referred to their part in military sanctioned missions in the first person. Marine psychologists call it a symptom of battle fatigue where the fight has become so personal that the soldier cannot differentiate between their egocentric need for power and their job. The soldier is brought in for debriefing and, more than likely, put on long-term medical leave or discharged from the service. Sean's time for debriefing had long come and gone. Tremont figured the powers that be wanted the results coming out of special-ops teams like theirs but also wanted to claim plausible-deniability should things go wrong or become public. In that case, he thought, Sean and anyone within range, namely moi, would become the designated scapegoats.

"Hey!" Sean said, pointing his rifle in Tremont's direction, "are you listening to me?"

"Whoa, point that SAW elsewhere, man. I zoned out for a minute. What were you saying?"

Realization lit up on Sean's face, and he set his gun against a rock. "You're losing it, Tree."

That's the pot calling the kettle black, Tremont thought.

"What I said was that we have an obligation to do what we have to do. If that includes ridding the world of a cockroach here or there, so be it." He sat on the hard ground between some rocks and picked up his new ultra-light M249 Squad Automatic Weapon (SAW) to lay it across his lap. Soldiers kept their weapons close for obvious reasons, but they never let these state-of-the-art weapons out of their sight, as their camping buddies would replace them with some ancient trinket or a less accurate, slower rate of fire Russian AK-47 dating back to WWII. Of course, in the morning, the Kurds would have seen nothing, and in the thief's mind, he would have rationalized it as a decent trade.

Tremont was determined not to go into a dialog that neither of them could win. He had been down that road with Sean too many times these past months. An uncomfortable silence passed before he said, "I wish I could do something with the Saddam directive." He paused realizing that at the mention of Saddam Hussein's name, he again had the attention of his pals in arms. He spoke to them in a fluent Northern Kurdish dialect known as Kurmanji or Badinani. At least half of the worlds estimated thirty million Kurdish-speaking people speak this dialect. Sean said, "I would get that bastard, and then I would bring his ugly head to the center of Mosul and mount it on a pole for all to see as the skin bakes and peels in the sun until only the skull remained." Though most of his Kurdish cohorts spoke a more centralized dialect called

Sorani and more specifically Xushnaw, they got the gist of what Sean said and rewarded him with grunts of affirmation. The rare sense of fellowship was shattered when Sean began to laugh and pointed his M249 SAW at the group of Kurds across the camp who were staring his way and talking about their American sponsors. He made the sound of bullets discharging. "Pow, pow, pow, pow." The Kurds turned away and ignored him. "I wouldn't miss, even if I was taken out."

Tremont looked at the Kurds and then over to the small Army platoon off to their right, with their oldest member, a sergeant, who was no more than twenty-five. Though knowing the Kurds would take offense, their hatred of Saddam Hussein would overshadow any mistrust they might have of the Americans. He realized it would take a lot more to aggravate these war-seasoned guerrillas, especially since the Americans brought them weapons and provided intelligence support on Sunni Islamic insurgents from neighboring Iran, and other countries. The slaughter of dozens of their Kurdish brothers and sisters by Saddam's death squads after a foiled assassination plot in 1981 remained palpable. Their biggest fear was that Saddam would use chemical weapons against their people in an effort to remove their threat to his reign.

"Let's be honest. It's not only about the terrorists; it's about oil," Tremont said.

"Oh! He has an opinion! Sure, it's about oil," Sean replied. "It's always been about oil, and if two *amigos* like you and me are sitting around a campfire outside of Mosul ten twenty or thirty years from now, it will still be about oil."

"The Islamic extremists want to eliminate us, and the Arab capitalists want to rob us blind by reducing supply and raising prices."

Not if my father has anything to say about it, Tremont thought.

"Bastards," Sean said, along with a few more choice words.

"So maybe you can see how much more important it is that I finish my work with my father," Tremont said, and Sean grumbled and turned to study a map of the Iraqi airport where they were to observe a potential terrorist leader arriving to meet with the Iraq President.

With legs crossed and elbows on his knees, Tremont rubbed his eyes, ran his fingers through his wavy hair, and said, "One of these days we're going to lose the game of probabilities. I don't need you adding to the danger," he lifted his chin toward the Kurds, "with our freedom fighters."

"You worry way too much, Nancy." Sean's increasing sarcasm and insults were not lost on Tremont. The Kurdish and Afghan rebels they traveled with on different missions had labels for Sean. *Chatichat metooraf* translated to "psychotic American" or, more precisely, "you piece of crazy," along with a few other hard to translate insults tagged on.

It wasn't hard to determine Sean's state of mind. Two years ago they were assigned to Paris. Their mission was to locate a Palestinian leader allegedly responsible for masterminding the deaths of Israeli athletes at the 1972 Munich games. These terrorists were purportedly planning a repeat performance during the upcoming Olympics. Two members of the infamous Mossad, the Israeli counterpart to the CIA, accompanied Sean and Tremont. During their month together with the Mossad agents, Sean was dubbed *Halev Mistagya.* Sean, who had a knack for picking up languages, smiled and touched his forehead while bowing slightly. Tremont turned to one of the Mossad who spoke fluent English and asked what the term meant.

"It is hard to translate," he replied, "but the two words mean 'crazy heart.'"

Tremont thought back to that simple assessment and wondered if what was becoming so apparent to him now had been inherent in Sean all along. Probably, he thought sadly.

Sean broke into his reverie. "Hey, what are you looking so glum about?"

"Sometimes I wonder if I should have joined up at all," Tremont said with a sigh.

"Damn, Tree. You and my brother Matthew were sure cut from the same root."

Tremont looked up and frowned. Now where did that come from?

"You both belong in a science lab. Not that it's such a bad thing. Mom was telling me about an invention that they say is sure to win an award at some Smithsonian contest in DC. How about that? I'll bet you won one of those things, didn't you?"

Tremont studied Sean's face and wondered just what he knew about his own covert relationship. Sometimes, he was sure Sean was savvy, and other times, like now, he was sure of the opposite. Through his uncle's documentation and support of Matthew's education, Tremont kept abreast of Matthew's successes and the coveted Smithsonian inventor's award program. Sean was right about another thing: Matthew was sure to win not just his own age-group level but the overall award as well. His intricate design of incorporating wind, solar, and electrical energy sources into a modified windmill, in concept, rivaled even the most sophisticated models coming out of MIT. He simply replied, "Man, that's great about Matthew. I look forward to seeing him again one day. Maybe you can bring him out to the Indiana Dunes and introduce him to my father."

Sean returned to his mission. "Speaking of your father, you can't believe that working on your dad's secret energy project could be more important than protecting him, your family, and all Americans from terrorist scum?"

"I thought that I would be doing both. I got a deeper understanding of applications for his inventions, helped secure our country from terrorist threats to our energy sources and natural resource supplies, and joined a long lineage of Carsons and Jacksons in service to my country."

Sean clapped his hands together, "Bravo. Bravo. A real live American hero."

"All I can say, Sean, is what seemed so clear back there on the Gauley River while we were preparing to go over Sweet's Falls has become awful cloudy."

Once again, Sean ignored his rafting buddy's concerns and logic. "Hang in there, bro. We'll have the worst of them dead or in custody in no time."

"It seems that we take out one, and we get ten more."

Sean didn't even try to hide his aggravation. "We're making a dent. We can develop better security measures the more we know about their plans. Wiping out terrorist cells is just icing on the cake. I do the dirty work, and you write the reports, Nancy. What a team!"

One more jab like that and I might have to teach him a lesson, Tremont thought. I can still kick his Rambo butt. But he didn't voice his objection knowing one of them had to stay above the rising tensions between them. Instead, he said, "What is your long term plan, Sean?"

"Just doing what we're doing. I figure while we're here gathering information, we might as well rid the world of every terrorist down to the potential suicide bomber who we know is waiting for his orders to take out a school bus full of Israeli children."

The two boys from Yale who had been playing rugby only a few years ago with their biggest problem being how they were going to survive semester finals had collected an incredible amount of intel, which translated into dozens of recommended security measures to Congress. They confiscated documents detailing Al-Qaeda and other terrorist cell plans to hit train stations, embassies, and even U.S. targets, such as the White House, Pentagon, and Wall Street. Other plans used biological threats within water systems and airborne chemical plots. Most of the plans were unsophisticated, but given time and the lackadaisical attitude in Congress about protecting U.S. borders, they could succeed.

At that moment on the rocks in northern Iraq, Tremont made his decision. It was time to go home.

Suddenly, a brigade of at least one hundred troops from Saddam's elite Republican Guard attacked from all sides. The firefight lasted twenty minutes; in the meantime, the Guard diced their group down from fourteen to five; Sean and Tremont, two Kurds, and one Army infantry soldier, nineteen-year-old private first class, John Imbrognio, "Little John".

The five remaining men had retreated down a dry ravine while the Republican Guard swarmed the camp. Little John insisted on taking up the rear as the rest of the beleaguered team crab-crawled down the ravine. At the bottom, Tremont whispered for them to hold up and wait for Little John. A few minutes later the big kid stumbled right into Tremont knocking him, Sean, and one of the Kurds flat on the ground, Sean on the bottom.

"You big assed son of a . . . ," Sean said quietly but with menace.

"Shut up, Sean," Tremont whispered. At that moment he did not think he could feel more contempt for any human being. "Little John, are you hit?" Tremont felt for a pulse, it was weak and when he took his hand away it was dripping with blood. "Damn." He put his hand back on his neck and applied pressure.

"We can't sit here and wait for the *Saddamites* to catch up with us. Let's go."

"You go ahead. I'll catch up."

"I'm not leaving you here, Tree. We're Huck and Tom, remember?" For a long moment, they stared at each other.

"Go. We'll have a better chance split up anyhow."

Tremont knew that by the amount of blood that the bullet had hit the carotid artery. He knew even with access to a medical facility that Little John didn't have a chance. He wrapped the wound as tight as he could without cutting off his air and put Little John's hand on his neck. "Press down as tight as you can right here." Tremont jumped to his feet and looked for somewhere they could hide.

As luck would have it he found a hole and knowing he could not carry Little John even on a good day, he forced him to get to his feet and put the other arm around his shoulders. They were near equal in height and if anyone saw the two of them standing in the dark desert against the moonlit sky, they would have thought a couple of giants were passing through. He got Little John in behind the huge boulder and down into the hole. He pulled sun burnt brush in around them and he lay curled up against his dying young friend. A bit of moonlight glistened off his face. Little John was smiling. "Aw guess," he said in his southern Alabama drawl, as blood gurgled deep in his throat, "I got a ticket home, eh, Corporal."

"You okay, man?"

Tremont looked up to see that he was standing in front of the cashier inside the BP Station.

"We ain't got nobody named Little John around here man. Hey, you play for the Hawks?" the young cashier said looking up at Tremont.

"I'm fine, and no, I don't." He handed the boy a fifty for twenty-five dollars of gas and didn't bother to get the change.

Tremont pulled out of the gas station and saluted the base for a long moment as he passed by.

Back on the highway, he crossed into Alabama and noted the "Pensacola 192 miles" sign. He rubbed his eyes and wondered if he would ever be able to get the blood, gore, and death of the past few years out of his head. He doubted it. He flipped through his limited collection of cassettes and put a new one in the player. He frowned as he thought about who gave him the tape. Another ghost, he thought sadly. Brad was a southern boy he served with in the Middle East. Brad's armored Jeep hit a roadside mine not fifty feet from the base gate where Tremont was waiting to greet him. When Tremont got to the smoldering mass of metal, none of the four soldiers were recognizable.

Tremont closed his eyes tight and said a quiet prayer. When he opened them, he sharply turned the wheel to avoid hitting a slow moving dump truck.

The likable kid was a former football player for the University of Georgia, no more than twenty, fresh out of boot camp, and had only been in Tremont's reconnaissance unit for a few weeks. He played a mean guitar and had plans after a few years in the service of returning to UGA to pursue a degree in business and music and play out his remaining years of eligibility with the Bulldogs. He would not have been in the armed services had it not been for the financial pressures causing him to work two jobs to support his ailing mother and younger siblings. Though smart as a whip, he was unable to keep his grades up to stay eligible to play for the Bulldogs, so he decided to enlist.

Tremont listened sadly to the music. The kid had told him this band would be a huge success. He was right on the money. Athens, Georgia's R.E.M. had taken the charts by storm.

As a song from their second album, *Murmur*, played, the lyrics struck home. It rang true that one person couldn't or at least shouldn't carry the weight of the world on his shoulder. Tremont tried to focus on the future instead of the past. That lasted about five minutes until in his mind he was back in another part of the Middle East and then another, and then another. The next thing he knew the sun began to rise to his left and he was pulling up in front of the central Destin boat dock. He looked out on to his Uncle's two-hundred-foot floating residence.

CHAPTER 20

May 22, 1989

Chill

"HE HAS MORE potential than any kid I've ever met," Tremont said, sitting back on his chair and sipping on a glass of Pinot Gris as they sailed west along the panhandle of Florida on a perfectly clear, calm day. His uncle went on about how the world was finally becoming post Chardonnay and that while Chardonnay and Sauvignon Blanc go well with fish, a Pinot Gris *enhances* the taste and is less oaky, has less alcohol, less acidity and creates a balance with the food.

That was all well and good, Tremont thought, but he would have enjoyed the moment, especially after years in the desert, if he was drinking Lambrusco and eating a BK Big Fish sandwich. Of course, he didn't reveal that to the man who defined aficionado.

"I have trained many young men twice his age in language, self-defense, weaponry, and," his uncle paused, put his nose deep in his glass and inhaled, "and fine wine. Besides you, I've never come across a lad who absorbed information quicker. It won't be long before the tutor becomes the student."

Tremont chuckled. "So the crash course in quantum physics my father put you through is running its course?"

"I've confounded highly trained KGB agents with less effort." They both laughed.

He and his uncle enjoyed a gourmet lunch of baked lime-dill wild salmon on spring greens with Sichuan cucumber salad, served by a gorgeous young female chef fresh out of The Culinary Institute of America. When she wasn't serving or pouring, she was massaging his uncle's shoulders. Tremont talked about first meeting Matthew and how intently he focused on his drawings of the multiple resource alternative energy windmills. "He was smarter and sharper when I first met him than I was at twice his age."

After lunch they walked around the expansive yacht, *The Karen*, named after Tremont's mother, which was the square footage of his father's home on Lake Michigan. Though his uncle had sent specs and pictures of the floating mansion to Tremont while he was overseas, he repeated the dimensions and weight again for good measure.

Tremont realized he was not paying attention and tuned back in as his uncle, whom he knew as Zebo, was finishing with, "Yes, unlike your petite mother, Karen, the ship is over 400 tons of steel, wood, and accessories; one hundred seventy-eight feet in length. *Pero jovencito*, where the ocean vessel Karen is so very similar to your dear departed mother, is in her beauty. *Tu madre era la mujer más hermosa que yo he conocido en toda mi vida*." he said quietly while touching two fingers and his thumb to his lips, kissing them, and opening his hand quickly to the air.

"She was very beautiful, wasn't she?" Tremont said, as more of a statement than a question.

They both sat quietly out of respect for Karen Carson Jackson's name. In Tremont's case, the mention of his mother's name unleashed a flood of regrets shooting like an electrical current from his brain to his heart and then back upwards to his eyes. Tremont wiped his eyes and broke the silence.

"How is Marcos? Is he still in school at FSU?"

His uncle beamed with the mention of his nephew's name. He had taken Marcos under his wing when he was only five, the only survivor of a botched escape from Cuba in 1964. Years ago, Marcos told Tremont that Zebo never forgave himself for not being there for his brother and his family. He was on a mission five thousand miles away at the time, and his brother never indicated what he was planning. As the story goes, the Coast Guard picked up the little boy miles from where the boat overturned in a storm. Marcos told them he was going to swim to Miami to find his uncle. Ironically, the Captain of the Coast Guard Cutter served with his uncle during The Bay of Pigs incident and was able to find Zebo through their mutual government connections.

Zebo said, "You know Marcos looks up to you like an older brother."

Tremont nodded.

"He asks about you often. Did you get his letters?"

"Yes, there were dozens, and as witty and dry humored as always. I know he wants to be a pilot, but he really should consider the stage." They both laughed.

"Along with logging hours in the sky, he's finishing his degree in criminal justice. I fear he wishes to follow in his old man's footsteps – and now yours."

"So, he wants to be a sailor and wine connoisseur?"

"Exactly." Zebo clicked glasses with Tremont. "To family."

"To family."

"Anyhow, I got him an interview with the CIA and the FBI. They both offered him a job when he finishes his masters. Marcos called them amateurs and said that maybe he would start his own agency. Smart-ass. The other option he investigated was Defense Intelligence. I was actually hoping you would talk him out of that."

"Will do."

Zebo returned to his natural jovial demeanor. He snapped his fingers. "Anthony?" he called, and a man appeared from seemingly nowhere at his uncle's side. "Would you please bring me the last bottle I shipped to you when I was up in Maine?" Anthony raised his eyebrows, nodded, and turned to retrieve the bottle.

The man Zebo called Anthony was unfamiliar to Tremont, but the type of man was not. He was definitely military and probably a trained intelligence professional. His uncle always seemed to have dangerous-looking employees. Tremont came to accept this strange fact when he was a child visiting one houseboat or another. Anthony was a hulk of a man, not much older than Tremont, with a neck like a medium-sized tree trunk and muscles bulging out of a navy blue suit. The unmistakable impression of a shoulder holster was evident under his left arm. As Tremont remembered from his childhood, this was a common tool carried by his uncle's crew.

It was about fifteen years ago, the yacht was called *The Presidents* and much smaller than *The Karen.* His uncle named the vessel in 1974 when he joined the Presidential detail. Then Vice President Ford specifically requested Uncle Zebo when it was clear President Nixon was heading for impeachment in the face of the Watergate scandal. It was a short assignment. When Carter replaced Ford, the somewhat liberal southern Democrat could not tolerate Zebo's reputation as an outspoken conservative Republican. Tremont smiled. His uncle could not keep his views to himself. It must be contagious, he thought.

One day when Tremont and Marcos were fishing off the stern of *The Presidents,* one of the crew, Stephan, was making repairs on the rigging above the mainstay when a crosswind forced the boats beam against the waves in what sailors call a broach. Stephan all but fell from his perch twenty feet in the air. His nickel-plated .38-caliber revolver slid the entire length of the deck to land at Tremont and Marcos's feet. Though they were trying to hold onto the bulwark with one hand and their fishing rods with the other, Tremont decided to hand his fishing pole to Marcos and dive for the gun. He caught it as the boat lurched up to right itself and threw Tremont onto his back.

He held up his prize in Marcos's direction only to feel a vice-grip on his wrist while being pulled to his feet in one swift motion. Stephan took the gun out of Tremont's grip, checked the load, and then holstered it behind his back. He said, "If you boys would like a lesson, you can ask your uncle. Otherwise, never touch another man's gun unless he offers. Do you understand?" The boys both nodded, and he returned to his work on the rigging.

"What are you thinking about?" his uncle asked.

"The first time I held a gun," Tremont replied.

Tremont and Uncle Zebo, uncle by choice instead of blood, smoked Cuban Cigars, drank a priceless glass of Merlot from the cellars of the Katahdin Sporting Lodge, and talked about the future. They discussed the past few years and their secret pact to keep a closer protective eye on Tremont's Dad, who rarely left Jackson's Place except to visit Karen's grave.

Zebo lit another cigar and offered one to Tremont who declined. "Your father has layers and layers of sophisticated security, Flannigan and I have made sure of that – but there are people that can get in there if they want to. I think they are just waiting."

"Waiting for him to finish."

"Or indicate that he's finished."

"You don't think they would hurt him? I mean without Dad, there is no research. No product. Nothing."

"I don't know," Zebo said thoughtfully. "I do know this, when your father completes his work, there is no end to the depths of power and money that will be thrown at him to buy, stop, or steal the research."

Tremont felt a familiar wave of anxiety flood over him. He decided he would not only be his father's full-time assistant but his bodyguard twenty-four-seven.

"You know," Zebo said, "before I forget, I knew the northern Maine Eaton name sounded familiar, so I checked the Agency's records and found something uncanny." Zebo leaned on the forward bow railing as the two of them watched the huge triple mast yacht ride high and cut through the water like butter. Zebo puffed on his cigar and then stared at it for a minute. "I was on a mission to Nicaragua with his Uncle Carl; I was Seals and he was Air Force. Miraculously he got us out safely with three of four engines shot out. How he landed that huge cargo plane we used as cover, I'll never know."

"You've got to be kidding. Six degrees of separation, huh."

"Six degrees. Anyhow, I thought it was too coincidental too, but I looked him up, and he's living in Miami. I gave him a call and it turns out he and his brother are somewhat estranged, something to do with him not being interested in the forestry business. I didn't tell him much, except that I came across the kid while doing business up in Maine. He asked that I keep him informed, that besides an annual call and card from Kate –" He paused at the mention of her name.

"What?"

Zebo grinned and raised his eyebrows. "I don't know. There's just something about that woman."

Tremont brushed off his initial thought. He knew that Kate Eaton was far out of his uncles preferred female age range. Uncle Zebo was never without a model-like *young* woman around.

They spoke in depth about Matthew Eaton, prodigy of Tremont and kid brother of his former best friend, Sean Eaton.

"Former best friend?"

"Sean crossed over to the dark side."

"How long has it been since he was stateside to get a psych evaluation, debriefing, and some R&R?"

"Not once since we shipped out in '82. I know that's crazy, but he's been on some very sensitive missions and . . . ," Tremont stopped himself, realizing that his uncle may or may not be cleared for this particular highly classified information. And even if he was, there were only four people alive who were privy to Sean and Tremont's orders. He changed the subject. "By the time the kid is in college, he could know more about centrifuge and nuclear fission than ten capable veteran energy scientists combined."

Zebo threw a picture of Matthew Eaton across the table. It showed the boy standing at a podium with silver-haired, bearded men gracing chairs in the backdrop. The banner on the podium read "Junior Science America Awards, Smithsonian Institute."

Tremont beamed with pride.

"He beat a field of eighty thousand students under nineteen. His theory, get this, shows that science has been going about the search for alternative energy all wrong these past forty years. How about that! Talk about throwing it right in their faces! And from a child that has just hit puberty-they loved it!"

Tremont tapped the picture with a finger on Matthew's chest. "There's the future, Uncle. There's the kid we can hand the baton to should anything happen to me and my father."

Nodding his head in agreement, Zebo said, "Nothing will happen as long as I've got your back. And you don't have to convince me about Matthew. Time and time again, I experienced the kid's brilliance in Maine. We've become quite close."

"I appreciate you taking time out of your sailing schedule to keep an eye on him. I really do."

"Don't mention it, I'm having a blast. It's a sportsman's wonderland up there and I've found undoubtedly the finest stash of rare wines in the world."

"Owned by the senile eccentric old innkeeper you wrote me about."

Zebo put a hand on Tremont's arm and said again, "Nothing is going to happen to you or your dad – not while I'm around. I can guarantee you that. Your dad has been waiting a long time for you to get done playing soldier. Now that you have your Rambo alter ego out of your system, you need to get up there and help him organize his little science project – frankly, he's been ready to launch CJ Energy for years. What worries him is the subsequent fallout. Regardless, you need to get him out of that damn mausoleum."

"That's my plan. But you should talk about playing Rambo. One day, you're going to have to tell me the whole story. I have Q level security clearance, so you can tell me everything," Tremont said this with a straight face, though he knew his uncle would dodge the issue.

Tremont suspected his uncle was *connected* in ways he may not even want to know. He knew Uncle Zebo had protected presidents and dignitaries, run covert operations around the world while he was a Navy Seal, and was still on the government's payroll. Protecting a couple of scientists and mentoring a wiz kid in rural Maine was perhaps a yawn for him. But even with his own commando, Special Ops, and Marine Intel training, Tremont wasn't sure anyone could protect him and his father from the potential fallout. All hell was going to break loose.

Tremont walked to the starboard side of the ship and looked out into the open sea. It was a good bet that he and his father would be soon navigating into stormy weather. Or, he thought, more than likely, a hurricane.

CHAPTER 21

August 1, 1989 8:50 a.m.

Breach

TREMONT AND HIS father spent the better part of the summer working in the lab. Every morning, and many evenings, they would hike with Popeye and Brutus through the adjacent pine forest or along the sandy beaches of the Indiana Dunes State Park. Twice they took day trips to Indianapolis to the Carson estate. Tremont made numerous excursions on his own to see the old Senator and the rest of the Carson clan.

Cameron had not taken a drink since Tremont arrived. By the end of July, they had completed and printed dozens of three hundred page presentations to hand out to the members of Congress and the Senate, as well as dignitaries and scientists from all over the world. Though nothing detailed the proprietary nature of CJ Energy Cells, by the time Cameron finished his presentation, there would only be one of two conclusions: either Cameron, the reclusive quantum physics genius, had truly gone mad or he had invented an alternative energy solution without peer.

Tremont paced from one baggage claim turnstile to another. He looked at his watch and then up at the departure and arrival monitors. He scanned the list: *Albany, Birmingham, Charlotte,* and down to *New York LaGuardia.* The blue blinking letters read *delayed.* He felt the knot in his stomach again. It had become more frequent the closer he got to Washington International. He had learned to trust his instincts and wondered why he let his father talk him into their splitting up. He retreated to the nearby coffee shop to wait. An hour ago, he had picked up his bags and then met with security to retrieve his compact .24-caliber handgun. Due to his high security level with the DIA he could still travel with his weapon and carry a concealed weapon on the ground but since he was currently inactive he could not carry it on the plane.

Tremont finished his *Americana* – two shots of espresso lightened with hot water – and went back to check the status of his father's flight. He muttered, "I don't know why I didn't talk him into waiting for me." He looked up at the top of the escalator to the left of the baggage turnstile to see his father. He felt a wave of relief wash over him and promised himself when they were not in the safety of Jackson's Place, he would not let his father out of his sight again. The knot was still there.

The black limousine bearing the United States Senate emblem drove Cameron and Tremont from the airport to the front of the Hart Senate Office Building. The driver walked around the front of the limo and opened the door. Tremont and his father stepped out onto the sidewalk. As the driver closed the door, there was a sharp sound like the snap of a dry stick over a knee. Tremont knew that sound all too well-a crack from a high-powered rifle. This one fired from somewhere to the left.

Tremont's father catapulted backward into his arms. A shower of blood spattered over Tremont, the limo, and the driver. A second bullet shattered a window inches from Tremont's head as he lay against the vehicle for support.

Tremont and the driver pulled the elderly Jackson to the back of the car as a third bullet found a target; the driver spun as he fell to the ground. Cars screeched to a stop, people screamed, and sirens approached from all directions, but Tremont could only feel his father's limp body. A fourth and fifth bullet smashed into the limo. Tremont snapped out of his shock. While bullets kicked up pieces of pavement at his heels, he grabbed his father under his arms and pulled him across two lanes of stalled traffic, the wide green median of Constitution Avenue, another two lanes, and behind a large oak tree.

As he settled his father to the ground, he heard an explosion. Tremont lay across his father's body as shrapnel from the limo hit the tree. He peered around the tree to see a smoking inferno. The sniper must have hit the gas tank. Tremont recognized the art of an equally trained professional. As he turned back to attend to his father, a bullet careened off the tree where his face had been one second before. This sniper was either intent on finishing his mission or toying with him. He could not imagine how he got away carrying his father when he noticed another splotch of blood below his father's right collarbone. The sniper had landed a shot when he was crossing the street, and his father had taken the bullet perhaps intended for him. He tore off his shirt and white undershirt to put pressure on the two wounds, though he knew there was little hope.

Even with hundreds of Washington's finest security and police blanketing the area, he was sure the sniper was not going to leave his post. The mission, Tremont realized, was to be sure his dad was dead and perhaps himself as well. Tremont held his father's bloody body. "You're going to make it, Dad. You're too tough to let this get you down. Hang in there," he whispered in his father's ear. He pressed his shirts into the wounds in his father's chest and back, trying to stem the blood flow. The more he tried, the more he knew the wounds were fatal. His father only had moments to live.

Tremont allowed the tears to stream down his cheeks. His chest convulsed and his throat constricted as he forced back the sobs. He kept his hands pressed against his father's wounds. This can't be happening, he thought.

"Hold it right there!" a voice shouted from one side and then another from the opposite direction. Tremont fell out of his trance. Two DC cops were crouched and aiming their standard issue .38-caliber revolvers at Tremont's head. He had no doubt they would fire with the least provocation.

Tremont said in a raspy voice, "My father is dying." Then again just above a whisper, "My father is dying." One of the policemen lowered his handgun and walked up to Tremont, while the other kept his .38 in ready position.

The graying sergeant spoke to Tremont. "It's okay, son, we'll take care of your father." He said as two medical technicians raced toward them. "EMTs just arrived." He took Tremont's forearm and helped him to his feet. His father's blood dripped down his cheek and neck. "Are you hit?"

"I might as well have been." He heard an unrecognizable hollow voice resonate from his own mouth. The two EMTs went to work on Cameron

Jackson, but after a moment, the young woman EMT, who Tremont imagined had been the team trainer at her high school only a year or two before, looked into Tremont's eyes and mouthed the words "I'm sorry." He found himself following the policeman toward dozens of squad cars with lights blinking red and blue, then abruptly went back to his father, put a hand to his dad's pale cheek, and made his pledge: "Dad, you have my word, I won't give up until I find out who did this. One way or another, I will make sure your work wasn't in vain."

The young paramedic fell back on her butt when Cameron lurched and grabbed Tremont by the arm. Cameron hoarsely sucked in what must have been a painful breath of air, "Show them they can't scare off a Jackson." He coughed and a trickle of blood seeped out of the side of his mouth. Tremont laid his hand across his father's forehead and moved it downward to close his father's eyes.

The male EMT checked Cameron's pulse and said, "Time of death, eight fifty-three AM." The female wrote some notes on a clipboard and avoided Tremont's eyes.

The gray haired officer now kneeling at Tremont's side said, "I'm sorry, young man. I know it's difficult, but I'd like to see what you know about the shooter. He could still be in the vicinity."

Tremont "Cracker Jack" Jackson walked toward the frantic activity around the smoldering skeleton of the stretch limo. He looked up, covering his eyes from the sun, in the direction he heard the rifle crack before the first bullet hit his father. "The shots originated from there." As he said it, he caught a glimmer of something out of place and then movement. Breaking into a sprint, he shouted, "Son of a bitch, he's still up there!" The policemen took up his trail in pursuit.

CHAPTER 22

August 1, 1989 9:04 a.m.

Face

TREMONT SLIPPED ON a shirt given to him by the old cop and pushed the elevator button but could not wait. He swung open the door to the steps while the gray-haired officer, Sergeant Higgins, radioed to have all exits blocked. He stood guard in front of the only two elevators in the building. Tremont's lanky legs took the stairs two and three at a time, climbing the nine floors in minutes. He got to the door to the roof only to find it locked. He pulled a fire extinguisher off the wall and began to smash it against the door handle.

While he labored, his mind raced on. Something about this assassin's style seemed familiar, choosing the roof and the angle. Only a qualified marksman with sniper training using a high-powered rifle with a thermal or electro-optical site and ballistic computer would even consider trying at this distance, let alone be so accurate.

The door gave way as if someone opened it from the other side, and he burst onto the white-pebbled roof. His suspicions were correct, but even as he pulled his gun and aimed it, he couldn't believe his eyes. "You?"

"Me, bro. Sorry about your dad," he said with that familiar sarcastic menace to his voice.

Tremont's mind raced back over the years of watching a man's metamorphosis from a decent human being, to a demonic animal giving little value to life. But he never imagined *this.*

"Well, Nancy, you gonna shoot or just stand there with your jaw on the floor?" Sean leaned against the three-foot roof wall with an unlit cigarette hanging from his lips, his arms crossed, and one leg over the other as if he were taking a smoking break in an office courtyard.

Through a blinding hate and excruciating pain tearing at his heart and soul, Tremont still hesitated. Sweat dripped in and burned his eyes. He knew on the modified hair trigger only the pressure of a fly on paper stood between Sean living or dying. He would place a double tap to Sean's heart, and it would be over. Hatred, anguish, and years of training screamed at his brain not to hesitate, *take the shot,* as he squinted against the morning sun and watched Sean light a cigarette with indifference. And he would have pulled the trigger, except a smidgen of reason seeped through the red blur in front of his eyes. If he killed Sean, he would not know who hired him. There was something else, he thought, how could this crazed animal be so confident I wouldn't pull the trigger after he shot my father? He would kill him, sooner rather than later, but right now he needed information.

Sean put two fingers to his cigarette, taking a long drag before flicking it over the side. He blew out a long line of smoke and, as if by magic, had a handgun pointed at Tremont. "I love a Mexican standoff, don't you? Why do you suppose they call it that? I mean, do you really think the Mexicans invented it? You're the Bible scholar. Don't you think it would've been Cain and Abel? I guess not, since one of them got himself killed."

Tremont let Sean talk but held his .24-caliber Glock steady in spite of the hurricane raging within his body and the lightning flashing in his brain.

"Where did you get that little pea-shooter? .24-caliber? Come on, Nancy. Just like the old west, a couple of buddies at the OK Coral or the U.S. Senate. Close enough. How about we both lower our guns? We'll count to three, and the fastest draw wins."

"Why?"

"To see who's fastest."

"No. Why would you shoot my father? For who? What price could they have paid you worth shooting my father*?"* Tremont's gun hand shook ever so slightly, now the only indication of his rage.

"Seven digits, baby. Five million. Half in advance. I'm a rich man, Tree; rich and crazy, so they say." He made motorboat sounds with his lips and rolled his eyes. "What a great combination. Did you know those sons-a-bitches at DIA wanted to let me go on a Section Eight? After all I did for our country? But I had too much shit on them, so how about this: I'm still on government payroll and working as an independent contractor on the side. Quite a gig, huh?"

So that's it, Tremont thought. "What did you do that finally woke the brass up to rein you in?"

"It was you, Tree. In the end, you almost brought me down. Your final report detailing our last mission together, and that damn Little John Imbrognio getting himself all shot to hell. Did you know that giant's uncle was an Alabama congressman? Who'd a thunk it?"

"This is all about revenge?" He had heard on the radio in the limo that morning that a sniper shot Congressman Imbrognio while on the campaign trail. The reporter called the incident *racially motivated.*

"Don't you wish it was that easy, bro? It's about money; the revenge part was a bonus. I'll bet you think I missed your ass. I could have taken you out along with your old man. You weren't in the contract."

Tremont could feel his pulse like the beat of a bass drum through his finger on the trigger. But not yet. Not yet. "Who, Sean? Who's paying you?"

"Sorry, ol' pal, can't tell you that, or it would negate my contract. I'd rather you be wondering while you try to track us down. You're a whole lot smarter than all of us. My money's on you."

He's too confident, Tremont thought. Sean could have been long gone from here by now. So far Sean gambled correctly that Tremont would not immediately shoot where nearly any other man would have under the circumstances. There's something more he wanted to say.

"What's your game, Sean?"

"The game. Now you're on target, buddy. Now *you* are on target. You've been playing a game, and my little brother has been a playing piece for you. Don't look so surprised; do you think I'm an idiot? Don't you know that's why they call us intelligence officers? So now the game board and rules have changed. Matthew is off the board, or your big shot Senator grandfather will be the next to take a fall outside the Senate. Then, my employers or I will take out the rest of your family, one by one. Am I being clear so far? By the way, if you or the men in blue swarming this building take me out now or anytime in the near future, the whole sequence will speed up like fast forward on a VCR. Keeping me alive keeps the Senator and the rest of the Kit Carson clan alive. *Capisca*?"

The insane picture was becoming crystal clear. Today's hit was about money, jealousy, and revenge through the clouded reasoning of a militant psychopath assassin. Tremont lowered his Glock handgun. He would pick his time and place when he knew his family was safe.

"It's your game, Sean. What's the next move?"

Sean lowered his gun as well and tucked it in a shoulder holster. He picked up the rifle that Tremont recognized immediately: a Barrett M82 Sniper rifle, accurate to 1,800 meters with a margin of error less than the twelve inches. Still, at this distance only a sniper with Sean's skill could have picked off his father and the hapless limo driver with one shot each. He could see how he destroyed the limo; the rifle could pierce an inch and a half of armor plating.

Sean cradled the gun and smiled at Tremont. "I don't suppose a hug is in order? No? I didn't think so. I'm sorry I had to take out your dad. Let's hope we don't have to continue taking out the rest of the Carsons and Jacksons . . . whoa, wait a minute, there are no more Jacksons, are there? You're the last of the Mohicans, man.

"I need you to do one thing for me," Sean said, "a favor between old friends. I'm sure your new pals in blue have all the entrances guarded. Remember, it doesn't matter who kills me, the result for you will be the same." He swung the thirty-pound Barrett to his shoulder and pointed toward the Senate office building. He mimicked the sound of the gun firing off its semi-automatic rounds. He knelt and expertly disassembled the Barrett rifle.

"Do you really think you can get off this roof?"

Sean began whistling while carefully placing each piece of the rifle in a plastic case. He then slid the case into a laundry bag.

"These stairs and the rear entrance will be clear in five minutes," Tremont said, as he opened the steel door. He faced his old friend turned psychotic killer. "This is not over, Sean."

"If it were over, Nancy, what kind of game would that be? I look forward to round two."

CHAPTER 23

August 7, 1989

Destroy

EXCEPT FOR THE grave-crew shoveling black Indiana soil upon the hand carved redwood casket, Tremont stood alone in the warm rain. Though his grandmother insisted he take her large black umbrella, he left it unopened and leaned on it with both hands.

While the rest of the crew loaded equipment in the back of a pickup, a man no older than Tremont navigated a small Bobcat loader, pushing the remaining dirt into the slough. He saluted Tremont with a tip of his soaked Indiana University cap and drove the Bobcat up a ramp onto a flatbed truck.

Tremont knelt between the nearly identical gravestones of Karen and Cameron Jackson. He arranged the fresh cut flowers on his mother's grave and placed a handful on his fathers. And he prayed.

Three hours later Tremont checked the pulse on both Popeye and Brutus. He breathed a sigh of relief and pulled out the tiny tranquilizer darts imbedded in their necks. The front door stood ajar. He reached behind his back and pulled a 9mm Glock from his belt holster, releasing the safety. He held it loosely at his side. After a cursory search of the main floor and the bedrooms upstairs, he went to the charred remains of the basement lab door hanging half on the hinges. They would have had to use sophisticated explosives to blow the door; it was nearly impregnable. He felt the warm edges around the titanium door hinges, indicating the bastards were not long gone. Tremont rubbed together his index finger and thumb, and grunted as he felt the clay composite used to centralize the C-4 explosive inward toward the bolt. He held his 9mm Glock in ready position, along side his cheek. He flicked the light-switch, the stairwell illuminated with an incandescent glow. He stepped soundlessly to the basement floor. He set the safety on and slipped the Glock in the belt behind his back.

The lab looked like a tornado had touched down. Most of the PCs were still in place, but the hard drives were missing. He looked in a few of the opened drawers – empty. He scanned the shelves along the perimeter of the three-thousand-square-foot room once filled with volumes of alternative energy textbooks and research. Now, empty.

Stepping to the middle of the room, he shoved one lab table about four feet. He did the same to three more tables, which came together with the first in the center of the room. He knelt down and opened the cover to what appeared to be an outlet. Stepping to the side, he gripped a handle on the outlet and pulled upward. The floor came with him, and a trapdoor revealed another set of steps, which he descended to a nearly identical room.

Unlike the one above it, this one buzzed with computer activity. "Hello, darlings. Did you miss me? I'm sorry to say Dad's not coming back, and this will be my last trip, though I'll be taking a part of you with me." Tremont took four duffel bags out of a footlocker. He began systematically stripping the room in similar fashion to what he imagined occurred earlier on the upper floor. "That was ingenious, Dad." He pondered his father's foresight. "I used to wonder if you were going a bit overboard." As he worked, he tried to fight off the images of spending unending hours down here with his father. For both of them it was what others would call an entertainment room. It was their playroom.

He retrieved manuals, hard drives and research papers. He collected some personal items, such as trophies, a large worn box of Cracker Jack given to him by his grandfather. In a manila envelope, he placed pictures of him and his father on various outings on the lake, around the Indiana Dunes State Park grounds, or on the Jackson's Place property, and one cherished picture of his mother and father.

He came upon a row of locked cabinets and realized he had never seen his father open them. He found the keys taped under one corner. He unlocked the first cabinet and lifted out stacks of videos, each bound with a single page of writing. He set them on the table and pulled up a stool. He read the dated letters in sequential starting with 1958, the year before his birth. The last came two weeks ago. He could only imagine what was on the videos, but judging by the letters, they were visual proof that the writer could back up his threats.

Confused and angry, Tremont decided he would delve into this new evidence once he was settled in one of his uncle's safe houses. Since he could no longer feel secure here at Jackson's Place, his mission was to collect his father's work, to find a safe haven, a base of operation, where he could coordinate the investigation to find his father's murderers, to finish his father's work, and to prepare his successor. He stopped for a moment. Was he being too presumptuous? Matthew might choose not to work with him, or Sean could stand in the way. All would be lost. He shook off the thought. Would a horse refuse water?

A clear plastic door opened when he pushed a button on the far wall, and he placed the bags on the dumbwaiter. He closed the door but did not send it; he would wait until he was upstairs to be sure there were no further threats.

A metal on metal noise startled Tremont. "Uncle Z?"

Someone said, "Well, I'll be damned."

Before he could get hold of his Glock, he found himself covered by a handgun. Either he'd missed something on the compound security system or the intruder was already inside when he got here. How could I be so stupid? he thought.

The man standing at the base of the steps was less than six foot with short-cropped sandy brown hair and a handsome square-jawed face with a significant cleft in his chin, wearing an un-tucked and wrinkled Government Express Mail shirt. Tremont didn't recognize the intruder, but had a feeling he would get the full picture in no time.

"I knew there had to be a place somewhere that your old man would escape to; one minute, I'm listening to him whistling classical tunes, and then the next, nothing. Then I don't hear him again for hours. He taught me a lot about classical music. I used to think he was passing code through the music, so I logged every album he played – gotta love that he still played vinyl – Mozart, Bach, Beethoven, Schubert."

Tremont paid close attention to how the intruder was holding his gun, loosely crossed over his left bicep with his body turned just enough to fire a fatal shot. *Professionally trained.* "So Mr . . . ."

"Lomax. But call me John. I feel like family."

"You've been assigned to watch my father for how long?"

"Well, I don't know if you would call it assigned, but if you mean how long have I been staked out here at Jackson's Place, eight years – off and on."

"U.S. government paid. Private contractor. CIA-trained," Tremont observed matter of fact and looked at Lomax to see if his eyes gave away the truth, but it wasn't necessary.

"You're young, but I'm impressed. It's amazing what you can learn with a few years of DIA training and in-country experience. You got two out of three right though. If I had not had the patience of Job, you would have gotten away clean. You had quite a few admirers waiting for your return; the last left Monday after ransacking the first sub-floor lab." He paused. "Two labs. A decoy. That was genius. I think everyone knew everyone else was here, except for me – nobody knows about me," he said with a grin. "Some of those guys fit your description perfectly: government contracted, CIA – well, Secret Service to be exact. The Saudi's contracted another. And the *sons a bitches* that got here first came in from the water. They were topnotch, Seal trained. They left their C4 calling cards."

"And you?"

Lomax avoided the question. "You know what would have been fun?" He didn't wait for an answer; as he seemed to enjoy hearing himself talk. "If they came into the compound all at the same time; man, there would have been fireworks. His eyes roved around the room. "So this is where the future of energy was developed." He looked past Tremont into the dumbwaiter. "I take it everything of importance is in those duffel bags?"

"Naw. That's just my laundry. I haven't had the chance to do wash since returning from overseas."

"Iraq on the Turkish border. I understand you and your buddy Eaton did some major damage over there training the Kurds to infiltrate terrorist camps. Good work, kid-and that's close enough," he warned, as Tremont inched closer. "I was teaching hand-to-hand combat before you were playing middle school basketball. Besides, even with that reach, I'd blow your head off before you began to press."

If Lomax knew Sean, he didn't make it apparent, but like himself, this man was trained in the art of deception. Tremont decided Lomax was not a suspect in his father's death. Having been creeping toward Lomax, an object on the lab table to his left caught Tremont's attention.

"I have to say, you do seem to have the upper hand, John. So you won't mind telling me a few things, like who hired my father's killer?" Tremont winced visibly at the thought of that day and his face-to-face altercation with Sean. He knew he would pull the trigger the next time he saw Sean. First, he had to know who hired him.

"If I knew, I would tell you. I rather liked your ol' man. It wasn't my employer – in comparison, they're the good guys." And then, barely above a whisper "they don't harm innocent mothers-to-be . . ."

"What did you say?"

"They wouldn't have considered taking out the genius behind the product, unless – "

Tremont finished his sentence. "Unless they knew they had all of the research."

Lomax raised his eyebrows, cocked his head sideways, and said, "That's right. The guy who shot your father had some other objective. Or he was going after you."

"No, if he wanted to hit me, I'd be dead."

"That is curious. If it were me, I'd have taken you out. Eliminate future threats: basic sniper protocol."

As Lomax shifted his weight, his gun lowered slightly. Tremont knew he had a split second opportunity. His right hand shot out, grabbed the basketball trophy, and launched it with such force and speed that Lomax didn't have time to blink. The base of the three-pound trophy hit Lomax square on the left temple, knocking him unconscious before he hit the floor. Tremont stepped over his body and picked up the gun, a New Hampshire made SIG-Sauer model designed for the military and law enforcement. Then he checked the carotid artery for a pulse. Satisfied with a sign of life, he checked him for identification and as he expected he found nothing but a Government Express Mail nametag stating his name was John Lomax. He dragged Lomax's two hundred pound frame, and lifted him into the dumbwaiter like one of the duffel bags, but full of wet sand.

Knowing there was a chance Lomax wasn't alone or that other interested parties might still be lurking on the Jackson property, Tremont saluted the lab one last time and vaulted up the stairwell in four quick steps. He checked the security system, puzzled as to why it didn't activate when Lomax approached the property or alert him that he wasn't alone. There were many fail-safe's from the front gate, along the driveway, and around the fencing, as well as triggers all the way to the porch surrounding the whole ranch. The first team into the compound had to have triggered alarms that would have alerted private security companies in Chicago and Indianapolis as well as his uncle's private firm in Atlanta. He figured they had covered all of those contingencies, which meant they were better than good.

The system was in good working order, and nothing larger than a raccoon appeared to be within a mile of Jackson's Place. Tremont went to the kitchen and pulled the large stainless steel Artic freezer away from the wall, revealing the extra large dumbwaiter. He opened a box on the adjacent wall revealing a lighted keyboard. He punched in 5-2-2-5 (J-A-C-K) and pushed the large red button on the dumbwaiter. The machine screeched and whined under the weight but soon halted on the main floor. He looked through the Plexiglas to note Lomax was still slumped over the top duffel bag. He opened the door with Lomax's .45-caliber SIG in ready position. He intended to put some distance between himself and the dumbwaiter, but before he could, Lomax sprung like a cheetah throwing Tremont against the butcher-block table. He tried to roll free, but Lomax had him in a bear hug. Instead, he kicked out Lomax's feet, and they both crashed to the floor. Tremont brought a knee up into Lomax's groin, who let out a howl and released his grip. Tremont dove for the .45 SIG just as Lomax recovered and pounced on top of him. With the advantage of a seven-foot wingspan and a little luck, Tremont swung the butt of the handgun, striking Lomax with a bone-crushing blow in the same spot as the last. Lomax went slack once again. Tremont stood over the stainless steel sink gasping for air. He turned on the cold water and splashed his face while keeping his body turned at enough of an angle to ensure Lomax was out for the count this time.

Surprised Lomax was still breathing, he took out two extension cords from the utility closet and bound Lomax's hands behind his back, then tied his legs to his hands. He dragged him out onto the porch where Brutus had his eyes open and was whining quietly. Popeye was still out cold. He surveyed the property before returning to the kitchen to retrieve the duffel bags. When everything was on the porch, Brutus was up on his forelegs. He licked Tremont's hand and growled when he turned his head and saw Lomax.

"Keep an eye on your friend here will you, boy?" He knelt down and scratched behind Popeye's ears and he stirred. "Time to wake up, boy."

He went back to his father's wall of security in the rich mahogany walled study. He opened a cabinet and felt for a key taped to the upside of a drawer of his father's antique roll top desk. He picked up a business card that lay on top of some papers. He thought of the strange unshaven disheveled man who would come to visit with three or four technicians whenever Dad was adding a new high tech system to the property. He was glad Flannigan was at the funeral and told him so.

He switched on the server power button, and a plasma screen lit up. It took him twenty minutes or more to type his way into the security program. After entering his username, password, and answers to a number of random questions, he typed "Jules Verne Is Dead" and touched the enter key. The screen went black. Tremont thought he made a typographical error, but the server was still humming, so he waited. And waited. Finally, a pop-up screen opened, giving him instructions. Tremont stared at the screen. He felt a fullness in his throat. He opened another drawer he knew held a few of his father's treasures. Right on top was the colorful ceramic flask given to his father by Wolfgang Pauli. It was rarely out of his father's possession so Tremont couldn't imagine why he didn't have it in DC. The drawer revealed letters and keepsakes from his parents' wedding and even the architectural drawings for Jackson's Place. He carefully placed the flask and other personal items in a black satchel. He held a picture of him and his father at the NCAA Final-Four basketball championship and then a picture of his grandparents here at Jackson's place – the only time they ever visited the compound, though not by choice. He took one last look around. So many memories, dreams that his father and mother had for a future here, happy summers with his father working on one invention or another, afternoons on the beach with Popeye and Brutus, and all the plans he and his father had to bring the future of energy to the world. He pressed his face into his palms and took a deep breath. "I let you down, Dad."

He returned to the den, moved the computer mouse and clicked the arrow over the word YES.

Outside Tremont looked at his prize Mustang and realized, there was no way he could pack everything and the pups. For a split second, he thought of leaving Lomax. He sighed. Tremont learned to make quick decisions, especially when a choice was clear. He loaded his priceless cargo and Lomax's comatose, bound body into the back of his father's burgundy GMC Jimmy. He ran his hand over the fine curves of his brand new black GLX Mustang before closing it in the garage. He stood out front and took a long look at the only real home he had ever known, and then walked back to the porch. He gave a push to the two rocking chairs. He stood unsteadily on one and unlatched the large sign his mother had made a quarter of a century before. "Jackson's Place."

He tried to imagine his mother and father rocking in their old age while he sat on the steps with one arm around Popeye and the other around Brutus, but the picture didn't come. The rocking chairs were empty – and so was his heart.

He opened the back door and whistled. The dogs didn't budge from the porch. Tremont understood. He felt physical pain at the sight. "He's not coming back, boys. It's just you and me. Let's go." They whined, seeming to understand, and trotted over to the Jimmy, jumped into the back seat, and lay down. Tremont slid into the driver's seat and sped out of the compound. He knew time was wasting, and every highway patrolman in Indiana would be scouring a two hundred mile radius beginning in – he looked at his watch – twenty-one minutes.

Once he was safely out of the gate and fifteen miles south down I-65, he pulled over onto the shoulder. He looked at his watch. *Twenty seconds.* He knew he should keep going, but –

He stood on the running board with his eyes drawn north. *Five seconds.* The sun had just set, and the sky to his north was dark save an orange hue bouncing off whisks of clouds like steamers at a New Year's parade; then he saw an enormous white flash sweeping across the Lake Michigan horizon. One, two, and three bursts before the sound of each explosion reached him. The site and the sounds were similar to what he had grown accustomed to overseas. Except this time, it was quite personal. Jackson's Place was history. This time there were no tears. Today's event launched an alternative plan he had been formulating for years, but *hoped* would not be necessary. A key player was a young genius from Millinocket, Maine, who he wished was about ten years older. "But, there's plenty of time now, eh, boys?" he said to the dogs.

He walked to the back of the SUV and lifted Lomax out. He carried him into the woods next to the highway and laid him upright against an oak. Tremont expertly snapped open an army butterfly knife.

His immediate plan was to move between his Uncle's safe-house apartments around the south Atlantic and prepare to reveal CJ Energy when the attention died down. He bypassed Indianapolis, feeling a wave of regret that he could not stop and see his grandparents and other relatives and friends. He knew Sean was not bluffing; anyone he was close to, or confided in, would be a potential target.

He thought of excerpts from his father's notes and journals. It was clear now the threats, perhaps by Sean's employers, started before his birth. His mother's death had indeed been murder. During labor, her heart stopped unexpectedly and the doctors were unable to revive her, but they were able to perform an emergency caesarean. No wonder his father drank himself to sleep every night, Tremont thought bitterly. He must have felt helpless to avenge her death especially with the threat constantly looming that his only son would be next. There was no medical explanation for her demise. No poison showed up in the autopsy. He slammed both hands on the steering wheel waking the dogs. "It's okay, boys." But it wasn't okay. His father protected him from the facts, and he had been living in an illusion all of his years.

Persuaded by Senator Carson, the police begrudgingly opened a file in homicide though there was little proof and no motive that they would understand. But after only a few months, without further evidence, her death was filed as a cold case. Tremont felt sure that whoever employed Sean was responsible for both of his parents' deaths.

He looked at his white knuckles on the steering wheel and took a deep breath, stretching out his fingers. Somehow, he had to keep a clear mind; there was much to do. The name Flannigan came to mind again. The journals referred to the FBI agent. Once he settled in a safe place, he would contact Flannigan, as he might be the only man who could fill in some of the blanks.

Tremont and his dogs sped down I-65 toward Louisville on his eighteen-hour drive from Indianapolis to Miami where he would meet his uncle and choose the best place to set up shop and plan his next move.

Part Four

Perpetual Convergence

CHAPTER 24

November 11, 1994

Purpose

THINKING TODAY WOULD be like any other, Flannigan arrived before sunrise at the J. Edgar Hoover FBI Headquarters on Pennsylvania Avenue. He went through security checkpoints as he had thousands of times over his thirty-year Bureau career. Flannigan wore an old brown tweed coat, a faded white shirt, and thin black tie. He could have passed for a homeless man on the streets of DC.

To the security staff that greeted him at the front gate, lobby, elevators, and the sixth floor as he trudged to his office, he was as much a permanent fixture as the pillars holding up the building. Flannigan didn't think of himself that way. Though he had the third highest position in the Bureau and seniority in every way you can have it, he was counting down the days to an overdue retirement. Tenure was the only thing that saved him each time he went against the system, as he has done a dozen times since taking on the Jackson case three decades past.

He had solved or closed every file he had ever worked on for the Bureau. Except that one. Entering his fourteen by twelve corner office, he hung up his frayed sport coat, flung his leather shoulder bag onto the chair, and went to start coffee in the break room.

When he got back, a large man perhaps a few years his senior dressed in a black Sunday-going-to-meeting attire was sitting in Flannigan's chair flipping through a stack of his files. Flannigan didn't try to stop him. Instead, he stepped out of the office. When he returned, he had the whole coffee pot. "How the hell did you get in here? I thought the Director put a restraining order on you," Flannigan said with mocked anger.

"Hello, Patrick. Nice to see you too." They both laughed. "He did get a restraining order, but I think that expired a few years back; and believe me, he hasn't forgotten our last altercation after Cameron was shot, so I won't be here long. I'm sure he can come up with a few new allegations to get my black ass thrown back in jail."

Flannigan took an extra coffee cup off the filing cabinet and blew into it to clear out the dust. He put the steaming cup of coffee in front of his friend and took a seat. They caught up on family, friends, lost loves, and divorces. They reminisced about their tour together in Korea where they were both Marine intelligence recon and barely survived the Chosin Reservoir battle, caught in subzero temperatures. Their small force had overcome six brigades of Chinese. A few years later as a rookie FBI agent, Flannigan had received his first call from a paranoid scientist in Indiana with a crazy conspiracy theory.

Flannigan looked at the clock. The Director would be in soon. "What's on your mind, Colin?"

His friend leaned toward him, his long thick arms enfolding the files. "You haven't given up on the Jackson affair." Flannigan did not reply. "You know, this obsession of yours got me booted out of here, and I'm surprised it hasn't buried you yet. You haven't taken my advice, so I don't know why you would now . . ."

Flannigan sat back in his chair.

Colin went on. "Your boy is back in Miami and attracting a lot of attention." He reached into the pocket of his black suit coat and passed over a piece of paper with an address. "I'm not the only one who knows his whereabouts. There's a good chance of a hit going down sooner rather than later."

Flannigan stared at the address for a minute. "Thanks, Colin. I'll head down there. It's the least I can do for botching things here and letting his parents get killed." He waved off Colin's objection. "Maybe I can protect his ass."

"You think the Director will let you do that? Officially?"

"Hell, no. As far as he's concerned, the file is closed and in moth balls in the Bureau morgue." The Jackson case was stored in one of a dozen FBI warehouses that held evidence going back before Hoover and Roosevelt. "But Cerraro has a case he's been asking me to help with, something to do with another fresh ring of cocaine smugglers working out of Miami. I can use that as cover."

"I don't want to know."

"So how do you like being a preacher? In a million years, I . . ."

Colin got up and stretched. "Yeah, I know, but God can work through the most broken and ugly vessels. It's my calling, Patrick. When are you going to come over and visit my church, or for that matter, any church?"

"I really don't want your pretty little church in the projects getting hit by lightning on my account."

They shook hands, and Colin pulled Patrick in close for a hug. Colin cussed when he pulled away to see the Director of the FBI heading their way. "Oh, I almost forgot. It's just a hunch. If you go down there, keep an eye out for a college kid named Matthew."

Flannigan turned to see the Director bearing down on them. "What's the scoop on this kid?"

"I'm not sure how he fits in, but I saw the name Eaton on one of your file tabs. The kid is some sort of energy savant, a protégé of Jackson. The kicker is his last name is Eaton." He looked down at his notes and gave Flannigan a description. And there's one more thing . . ."

"What the hell are you doing here, Preacher? How did you get past security? Heads are going to roll, damn-it," John Harrington yelled from across the room. His face was red, and his eyes wide with fury.

They both ignored Harrington. Flannigan asked Colin, "What else?"

"It seems an old friend of ours could be connected to the Jackson's somehow. He now calls himself Estebanez."

"Estebanez?" Flannigan wrinkled his brow.

"Yeah, why?"

"That was the name of an agent who was poisoned by the KGB while he was undercover in Rome."

"This Estebanez may have been involved in mentoring this Eaton for the past ten years, maybe longer. That's about all I know. I put his name on the back of the address in Miami."

"Are you two just going to stand there and ignore me?" Harrington turned to a nearby phone in an administrator's cubicle. "Security, get your asses up to the sixth floor and escort *Pastor* Jester," he added an extra dose of sarcasm, "out of here, and put everyone who allowed him through the doors on report." He raised his voice even louder. "Or I'll have every one of you on pre-school, cross-walk duty before the week is out!"

The men in the room still ignored the Director. Flannigan looked at the Miami address again and turned over the paper where there were only four letters. "Well, I'll be damned. I thought the SAVAMA," Iran's Ministry of Intelligence and Security, "killed him on a black-ops mission in the late seventies – "

"My contact at the Agency says that when he resurfaced, they ran him through an intensive debriefing. All indications are that he is truly retired. His true identity and whereabouts are classified for his own safety."

"But you found out."

"I'm good. When he's not in Maine, he's on a sailboat the size of a small country. You might also remember that he had a proclivity for rare wines."

Flannigan grinned, "As I remember, he used to stay a little too long in a target's home to study the stock."

"Study?"

"Okay. Study, and abscond."

"He has been seen at Sotheby's in London selling some doozies for as much as fifty big ones," Colin said, and Flannigan whistled.

Colin continued, "My guy at the Agency says Estebanez flew here on a charter jet the same day Dr. Jackson was killed by that sniper."

Flannigan raised his voice, "And you punched out Harrington for taking us off the case and canceling the Jackson's security that day. Man that was a great punch. Ali style, I swear." Flannigan and the preacher savored the recap at Harrington's expense.

"Let me see that paper, Flannigan!" The Director reached for the paper, and Flannigan put it in his mouth. The two chums laughed uncontrollably. "Sorry, boss. I didn't have my donuts yet," he mumbled. "Can I pour you a cup of coffee?"

Two security guards came running off the elevator in a panic. They stuttered and sputtered about not wanting to put the legendary Colin Jester, a decorated war hero and one of the Bureau's first and most respected African American agents, under arrest but also not wanting to infuriate the Director any more than he already was. Harrington threw his hands in the air and stormed to his office, muttering about Patrick Flannigan being the death of him.

The pastor put his arms around the shoulders of the two six-foot guards like they were small children. As they walked toward the elevator, he asked, "Have you boys accepted Jesus Christ as your personal Savior?"

Flannigan watched his buddy go and took the soaked piece of paper out of his mouth. He had already memorized the address, but he could not help wondering about the connection between one of the CIA's most mysterious covert agents and Cameron Jackson. He remembered a friend of Cameron, he thought, who sent Cameron expensive gifts from around the world and helped with security.

He went back into his office to plan his trip to visit Cameron's elusive son. Whether Tremont liked it or not, Flannigan was going to save him from himself.

He sat at his desk and rang Juan Cerraro's office on the fifth floor. "Juan. Would you and your team meet me in the seventh floor conference room at nine? Thanks, buddy. I have a lead that might help you, and if it's okay with you, I'm going to attach myself to your detail." His office manager, who also should have retired a decade ago, entered to put the *Washington Post* on his desk and clear a space for some fresh flowers she had cut from her greenhouse garden, as she had at least once a week for the last thirty years.

"Mildred, could you set up a flight to Miami sometime late this afternoon? And make me a reservation at the San Juan Hotel."

"You look like hell, Patrick." Without another word, she went to her desk.

Flannigan organized the thick worn files the Pastor had spread out on the desk; he reviewed each one as he had a million times before. The labels read:

Tremont C. Jackson
Senator Carson
Cameron T. Jackson
Senate Office Building August 1, 1989
Sean Eaton
Domenick DelGercio
OPEC-Saudi-bin Laden bin Taliffan
John Lomax
Solar & Fuel Cells

He made a new file and labeled it with two pseudonyms, then pushed the page button on his phone. "Mildred, will you do a complete search through all agencies and operations combining the names Zebo and Estebanez?" He spelled both. "And look up Sean Eaton's family in Maine. See if he has any siblings and print out anything you can find." He took out a few fresh manila files and wrote on one, *Miami Beach 94/95,* and on the other *kid brother of Eaton?*

He leaned back in his chair and looked at the ceiling. He thought about what his old partner had been saying to him about church, faith – When did he stop believing? Maybe it was after everything he prayed for went to hell in a hand basket. He thought he had found God in a foxhole while all his buddies were being picked off one by one by the Chinese. But that didn't last long. When he got home, he began blaming God for Korea, his first of four divorces, and many other things. "If you're up there," he said toward the ceiling fan, "let's work together this time to keep the last of the Jacksons alive, then I'll retire. Or die." He stood and poured a cold coffee. "Same difference."

He wished Tremont trusted him more, though he could understand why he didn't. Cameron's son probably blamed him for not doing enough to prevent his mother's and his father's deaths. He would be right.

The call light blinked. He turned in his chair and pushed the green button next to the word Merlin. Mildred said, "The Director would like to see you in his office." Flannigan cussed again and tucked all the files back in a brown and white corrugated file box.

CHAPTER 25

March 17, 1995 1:15 a.m.

Converge

"WE HAVE TO help in any way we can," Maria said empha-tically. "Matthew can help you carry on the research, and I can organize a grass roots campaign!"

Matthew thought Cracker Jack's wide grin meant he was humoring Maria and said, "Maria has an overzealous passion for righteousness, punishing the evildoers, and saving the planet; that and studying the criminal mind keeps her preoccupied."

"What's wrong with that?" Maria challenged.

Matthew raised his hands in self-defense and changed the subject. "What does the FBI or more specifically, what does our government want you to do?"

"The FBI, more particularly an agent by the name of Flannigan, is trying to convince me I'll be safer and the world will benefit if I would put all of the technology under the protection of the U.S. government," Cracker Jack said. "Of course, I'm not buying it. They actually believe they can protect me when they have not been successful in the past. My father thought that if we could get it in front of WCASE – "

"The World Council on Alternative Sources of Energy," Matthew interrupted.

"Right." His facial features darkened for a moment and then with a short shake of his head, the smile returned. "Anyhow, to bring things up to date, after the *last time* my Miami apartment was ransacked, the FBI arrested me on some trumped-up charges having to do with national security. They said it was for my own protection, but I've been a prisoner in this building. Instead of protecting me, they're raising my profile and putting us in danger. My every move is monitored, and there've been attempts on my life."

"Someone has tried to kill you?" Maria asked.

"Kidnap, more than likely; but once, I almost suffocated in the back of a limo before the FBI got me out. I would say I owe them that, but if they had not detained me, I wouldn't have been in that damn trunk! Another time they had me handcuffed in a speedboat. The coast guard opened fire on the boat, and I was hit in the shoulder, fell overboard, and nearly drowned before they fished me out. Everyone on the boat was killed."

"Who were they?" Matthew asked.

"My limo ride was courtesy of the Chinese, but now I'm quite certain they were hired by someone else. My uncle – ," Cracker Jack put his fist to his mouth and coughed.

Matthew took a mental note to ask about an *uncle* sometime later.

Cracker Jack continued, "We have been keeping surveillance on Hafiz-OPEC Saumba Shokran, a Middle Eastern terrorist group that uses OPEC as a cover. The CIA believes their mission is to eradicate any threat to their destiny."

"Which is death to the infidels and world domination by Islamic fanaticism, right?" Maria asked.

"That's the fundamental premise. Anyhow, when the FBI followed the money paid to the Chinese abductors, it led to an Austrian bank. The same bank used by OPEC and the current leader of Hafiz-OPEC Saumba Shokran: Bahir bin Tallifan."

"I've heard of him. He's related somehow to the bin Laden family," Matthew said.

"The patriarchs, now both dead, were first cousins and together built the Saudi infrastructure," Cracker Jack noted.

"The second group was Columbian," Cracker Jack said. "Again, just thugs paid to capture me. In the early years, my father felt the culprits were those heavily invested in the oil industry. Once he announced he had completed his work, every roach in the world came out of the woodwork. Still, we believe someone in the oil industry was behind – ," He pursed his lips and said, "I'm getting ahead of my story."

Matthew was about to say *behind what,* when Maria asked, "Where is the protection they promised!"

"I have to admit, I made it hard for the FBI to help me. Nobody knew where I was. I wanted it that way. With the urging of – ," he chose his words carefully, " – a friend, I came to Miami. I don't know how they knew I was here."

"No offense, but you do stand out in a crowd."

"I know, Barry Manilow, right?" Cracker Jack said.

"Larry Bird," Matthew interjected.

They laughed and Maria asked, "Have you tried appealing to the press?"

Matthew answered for Cracker Jack. "If he goes to the press, then he's just advertising for more trouble."

Cracker Jack nodded and then said, "One FBI agent kept a close eye on my dad for three decades," and then with a touch of anger, "but his success rate left much to be desired.

Until he cornered me here *for my own good,* I figured I stood a better chance of survival on my own."

Matthew was in awe. He was sitting with the son of one of the greatest scientists of this century. He thought of his energy projects for school, the Smithsonian science awards, and now the focus of his college disciplines at UMaine and MIT. He always believed he could make a difference. Now he was sitting with the man who could make a colossal global impact.

Maria exploded. "They can't do any of this. This is not China! I'll go to Washington for you. We'll . . . we'll . . . I'll stage a protest!"

Cracker Jack and Matthew made eye contact and smiled. Matthew asked, "Have you been formally charged?"

"Yes, with no evidence, no lawyers, no trial. They really should put their attentions on protecting America from real threats, like Al-Qaeda."

"They simply cannot do this. This is America!" Maria raised her voice, and all eyes in the diner were turning their direction. Matthew tried to put a hand on her arm, and she shook it off.

"Yes, it's America," Cracker Jack said, "but outside of the FBI there are factions in our government and power brokers that think they can force the outcome of our society by controlling business rather than letting the free enterprise system work. Low-cost energy is a threat."

"This sounds like a conspiracy," Maria grumbled.

"A conspiracy is covert. These powerful people do their worse right out in the open, yet much happens behind the scenes to shape policy and the economy. Look how our government successfully slowed IBM's growth through monopolization legislation in the '70s. The next thing you know, if the balance of power changes in Congress and the Senate, they'll be trying to break up Microsoft or Apple."

"That'd be crazy," Matthew said, "those two companies brought us out of the dark ages."

Maria composed herself. Matthew thought she was especially pretty when her Spanish eyes were ablazed. There was a red hue to her olive skin when her Latin personality was on fire. He tuned back into the conversation.

Cracker Jack asked, "Did you know that every two years technology advances more than the previous ten years combined?"

"The technological revolution!" Matthew replied. "Someday I want to use high technology to help change our antiquated energy systems. Or, like your father, develop new waves of alternative energy."

"I know . . . I mean, I can tell."

Matthew noticed Cracker Jack's mid-sentence correction. "I've been studying the biotech industry and have started a few lab experiments trying to incorporate biotech advances with natural energy. Have you heard of nano-technology?" Encouraged by Cracker Jack's smile and silence, he continued, "It's the buzzword for the miniaturization of technology to the point of atoms and neutrons. Maybe it'll be my focus through undergraduate and perhaps on to MIT for a PhD. What I propose is to miniaturize current formats like solar energy cells. And then, like your father wrote, capture and store the energy."

Cracker Jack looked like a father whose son had ridden a two-wheeler around the block for the first time. "If you only knew how close you are to what is already possible. You're young. By the time you finish graduate school, technology will be advancing so fast that what you buy today will be obsolete in six months. Dell, for example, decided that if he could make the computer the same day the consumer ordered it, he could keep the consumer within months of new technology. Before Dell, the consumer usually received obsolete equipment. Remember that example. One day it may be your saving grace when you need to get to the market before your competitors can shut *you* down," he hesitated, "like they did to my father."

"I would have been honored to have met your father. And I could probably die happy if I could visit his lab," Matthew said assuming the lab was still at Jackson's Place. He noticed Cracker Jack wince.

"How did your father die?" Maria asked.

"His father died in an accident," Matthew said.

Maria caught her breath and said to Cracker Jack, "I'm so sorry."

"Thank you," Cracker Jack said, clearly uncomfortable.

Matthew said, "It was just before he was to present a major breakthrough to a Congressional sub-committee on energy. Isn't that right?"

"Almost right; as I said, the presentation was to the WCASE, but his death was no accident. He was murdered," Cracker Jack said, sitting back and looking up at the ceiling. The pain of his father's loss was evident.

Maria touched Cracker Jack's hand. "Murdered? That's terrible. How do you know?"

"I was there. I held him in my arms as he died. He was assassinated."

"But why?" Maria asked.

"Fear, jealousy, greed, hate. Pick one or all of them. Whoever – ," he paused, looked away and took a deep breath, " – whoever ordered the hit was afraid of the impact my father's discoveries would have on their industries. Those who wanted to steal his inventions would not have killed him. Trust me, they're still trying to obtain his research."

"But who would have resorted to murder?" Matthew asked.

Cracker Jack's normal congenial demeanor darkened. "Before I die, I will find out."

Matthew got a renewed and distinct feeling that Cracker Jack could be a dangerous person given provocation, and he certainly had reason for revenge. But their new friend was holding something back. He said, "Did they catch the shooter?"

"No, but I know who he is."

"Then why isn't he in prison?" Maria asked.

"It's complicated. But I need him alive in order to find who hired him. Otherwise, he would already be dead."

Matthew thought Cracker Jack was looking at him strangely. "Surely the FBI or the DC police have made some progress."

"None," Cracker Jack said acidly. Matthew suspected there was a whole lot more to this part of the story.

Maria asked, "What have you done so far to find his killers?"

"I hired an international private investigation firm. They've been working tirelessly the last six years. I have an uncle who's obsessed with helping me finish what my father started and to find his killers. He's very capable. That way, I've been able to focus on finishing my father's work."

"How much progress have you made?" Asked Maria.

"After he was murdered, I disappeared and moved between the Galapagos Islands and a place on the west coast of Scotland. My friends call it the ends of the earth," he said with a distant look. "I worked twenty-four hours a day and seven days a week. It was more than an obsession; it was an escape after losing my father, my best friend."

"That must have been horrible," Maria said.

"It's amazing what can be started in a garage, or in your father's case, a basement, eh?" said a voice behind Cracker Jack.

The man's hair was black and slicked back. He wore charcoal black pants, a white button-down shirt, and a thin black tie. Matthew thought he looked like the Mormon bicycle riders that ventured into his town every few months on their required mission. How long had he been standing there?

"Don't you think you've said enough to these kids?" the man asked. They really should get home to Mom."

Cracker Jack didn't turn around. "Pay no attention to the man behind the curtain."

Maria and Matthew chuckled nervously.

"I got a call from Flannigan in Washington. He'll be here tomorrow, something about moving you to a secure location near DC so he can keep a closer eye on you," the man said with a yawn and a wide stretch of his arms. "I truly don't know what it is about you and your family that keeps that man going. He should have retired years ago. I should be chasing down drug runners, not babysitting you, but that's not my call. Things are quiet, but the word is someone may be here in South

Beach so keep your head down. I'm going to catch forty winks," he said, and then indicating two other agents, "Ricardo and Hector are watching from the street."

"What would I do without my babysitters?" Cracker Jack asked.

The man put his thick black-rimmed glasses on his face, folded his newspaper, and walked out of the diner.

"That was weird," Maria said. "FBI?"

"This is incredible!" Matthew exclaimed. "Everything you are saying seems more like a cross between a spy novel and science fiction."

"Jules Verne meets Tom Clancy," Maria noted.

"Funny you should say Jules Verne," Cracker Jack said and then continued as if there had been no interruption. "Is it hard for you to believe that this stored energy technology is already possible?"

"I'm too tired to think straight," Matthew said rubbing his eyes.

"When Stephen Jobs talked about personal computers in every home and every classroom in the late 1970's, do you think anyone believed him? At that time, computers took up complete New York City blocks to do what a few hundred megabytes of storage space, memory and RAM can do today.

"My father was on a parallel path with the likes of IBM and Intel. Only he captured and miniaturized energy instead of information. When the time comes, your best bet for quick market penetration might be linking my Dad's invention with the computer industry."

"My best bet?" Matthew queried.

Maria seemed to miss the point, "And why would anyone want to stop your father, stop you?" Maria asked, "The benefits are mind-boggling. Just the conservation benefits of low cost alternative energy would make it worth our government giving you its full support. Not to mention the reduction in greenhouse gasses!"

"I'm all for the reduction in pollutants, even if the concept of global warming *is* a conspiracy theory," Matthew chided and ducked a punch.

Cracker Jack didn't join the debate and his words were sharp. "To answer your first question, they're scared. Don't get me wrong, I'm patriotic, I spent many years serving my country. But remember this, the last thing you want is to have the government subsidizing even one penny of your private enterprise. If they do, they'll own you."

Cracker Jack was prepping him for something, Matthew thought perplexed, feeding him deliberate clues to a puzzle. Matthew had always enjoyed dumbfounding his teachers. Once, he was ushered to the Principal's office, accused of plagiarizing his work. He received a failing grade. The joke was on the teacher when the next summer the very same work showed up in the *New England Journal of Science,* with Matthew's name on it. The teacher had still refused to change his grade. That game of *stump the teacher* cost him, he thought.

"I'm not saying our core government officials are behind a conspiracy. Hell, I don't think they have a clue as to the extent of our technology or how close we are to rolling it out. As I've said, my father always worried his work would fall into the wrong hands. One organization could hold the rest of the world hostage by controlling the supply and demand of the cheapest energy source on the planet. The same way the oil cartels control price on the world market. Did you know OPEC accounts for forty-three percent of the total crude oil produced in the world, with the U.S. and Russia at nine percent each?"

"The U.S. consumes more than a quarter of all production. We waste more than our fair share," Maria interjected.

Cracker Jack smiled, "Spoken like a true environmentalist."

"I don't know if that is a compliment or a jab, sir," Maria said with her left eye closing slightly and her lips pursing.

Cracker Jack winked. "They accused my father of the same thing, so you are in good company."

Matthew said, "If one company or country that had a less costly energy source easily transferred into any final use product, economic power could shift dramatically."

"For anyone else to compete, it would take years of reverse engineering to replicate the three-three formula my father has developed," Cracker Jack said.

"Three-three?" Matthew asked.

"It's the final piece to the puzzle, the prize inside the Cracker Jack box." Cracker Jack winked and smiled.

"So, whoever controls your father's formulas could have a monopoly," Maria said, looking proud to be keeping up with her companions.

"Correct. You can see why you have to remember that security is paramount."

There he goes again, Matthew thought, that's enough! "Throughout our conversations you've made reference to Maria and I being somehow connected to you. Or am I imagining that?"

"I don't believe any encounter is chance."

Maria asked, "Cracker Jack, why are you avoiding that question?"

He parried again. "I believe, and my father was convinced, that all hell could break loose in our emerging world economy, and CJ Energy in the wrong hands could result in a myriad of economic and political power struggles, perhaps leading to world war. It may be hard to believe I'm sitting on an invention with that compelling effect, but for argument's sake, let's say that I am. The potential chaos isn't too hard to imagine, is it?"

"No, not at all. It would be like one person or government controlling air and water," Matthew said.

"We've created a world dependent on power. And that power is destroying the ozone layer and as Maria said, perhaps causing global warming."

"That's what I've been saying! Most people don't believe it or are ambivalent," Maria said passionately.

"Please don't encourage her," Matthew said, and caught her fist before her knuckles added more color and pain to his bruised arm.

"My father warned politicians of the environmental ramifications as far back as the fifties and more recently that our electrical grids are strained far in excess of their capacity. That one glitch in one spot could shut down a whole region at one time. It would be chaos."

"I never thought of that," Maria said. "Have they listened?"

"Oh, they listen, but like most obvious warnings, it will take an incident for them to shell out the money to fix the electrical infrastructure. It's the same for the terrorist threat. I call it the stoplight syndrome."

"What's that?" Maria asked.

"A municipality will not put in a stoplight until one of two things happens. Either the traffic reaches a certain volume, or there are a certain number of fatal accidents. It's the same with our water infrastructure. The EPA has warned cities like Newark that they need to invest in fixing their water supply infrastructure because drinking water has reached dangerous contamination levels that no amount of chlorine can overcome. Because of monetary objections from the city and state, the EPA extended their deadline by twenty years. So when do you think the stoplight will be put in?"

"When people get sick and die," Maria said.

"Exactly."

They all shook their heads while stirring their coffee.

"*Imagine* with me, kids. Once we go public with CJ Energy cells . . ." Someone out on the sidewalk distracted Cracker Jack.

Two men walked into the diner, but Cracker Jack didn't turn around to look.

Matthew recognized the Middle Eastern men. One had intentionally bumped into him earlier out on the sidewalk. Matthew had noticed that the two got into the vintage red and white Ford Thunder-Bird he had been admiring. But, instead of driving away, they sat there across from the Shell station.

Before going to their table, one of the Middle Eastern men stopped for a moment and gave Matthew what he could only described as an evil stare, and then took a shot at him with his thumb and index finger. They then chose a table at the far end of the diner.

"What was that all about?" Maria whispered.

"I don't know," Matthew said, "maybe he thinks I ran into him out on the sidewalk. It was the other way around."

"I think it's more than that," Cracker Jack said.

One of the FBI agents followed the two Middle Easterners into the diner, and took a seat by the door.

"Are there patents on your father's work?"

"Hundreds, some of them going back thirty-five years. The premise today is the same as he spelled out in *Capturing the Sun.* Capture energy in an object and then create a conducive environment – "

"To recharge," Maria interjected.

"Perpetually," Matthew said.

"Eventually."

"Possible?"

"Not only possible, but we've done it over and over in our labs. That's the magic, kids. Unfortunately, that's what people will kill for."

Cracker Jack glanced at the ancient Coca-Cola clock on the wall, and then to the men at the far end of the diner. "We'd better get going soon." He stood and stretched, and then took his seat again. "Marcos should have the rig ready."

Matthew wasn't sure he would be able to stand. He kept repeating to himself: *perpetual energy, perpetual energy, perpetual energy*. He believed it was possible, but to be sitting with the son of the man who claimed to have achieved this miracle of science was beyond his dreams. "A new energy source is one thing, but a perpetual source is quite another."

"That is what everyone had been telling my father for a very long time."

Maria said, "Were you always interested in science, and I was curious about your nickname, how did you get it?"

"Jackson's Place was to the north on Lake Michigan, and though he preferred working there, he wanted me to grow up like a normal kid. He kept a house and small lab in Indianapolis, when he had to be up at the lake, I would stay at my grandparents. As I got older, we spent more time up at Jackson's Place where his science and computer lab rivaled many major universities.

"It didn't take long to see that I loved the challenge of experimenting on what most kids would find extremely boring."

"It must run in the genes," Maria said.

"His lab was to me what Disney was to other kids. I had the most expansive erector set, test tube labs, and electronic kits."

"But where did your nickname come from?" Maria persisted.

"Grandfather Jackson. He was the first to call me Cracker Jack. He died when I was seven. Grandma died first and Grandpa died of a broken heart a year later. Anyhow, the name stuck, Dad named his work after me, *Cracker Jack Energy Cells.* He didn't tell me much about it at first. I guess he figured I'd be safer the less I knew. But when I was older, I perused his notebooks while he was out, and I had a pretty good working knowledge of his energy collection and containment concept by the time I graduated high school."

After a heavy silence, the three got up to go. Cracker Jack paid the bill and leaned way down to kiss Ronda. He brushed his hand along her oval face and whispered farewell in her ear. Maria translated his Spanish to Matthew though he understood enough to get the gist of the conversation. "I wonder what the story is behind their relationship and why this was farewell?" she asked rhetorically.

At the door Cracker Jack said, "I'm staking a lot on you kids. This may be the last time I'll be able to see you for a while."

"Where will you go?" Maria asked.

"Most likely I'll return to an island off the coast of Scotland. When I'm sure it's safe, I'll contact you with the location."

Cracker Jack glanced over his shoulder and an aggravated look crossed his face. Another man was walking toward the diner in front of Marcos. Marcos looked in the window, tapped his wrist, and then raised his hands palm up impatiently.

While they waited for Cracker Jack, Ronda broke into conversation with Maria. Matthew could pick up much of what she said despite her accent and the vacillation between English and Spanish. Apparently, Cracker Jack had intervened when a couple of Latin gang members tried to hold up the diner a few months ago. She said there were four of them and that Cracker Jack casually asked the *matones* to leave. "One swung a stiletto and, like Zorro, he took the knife away – like a child's toy. Everyone in Miami Beach heard about this, and loved him. He's a mystery with the locals. There's even a rumor that he is some kind of mafia boss. He's a very good man," Ronda said, a tear trickling down her cheek. She wiped it off and turned away.

Matthew leaned up against a lamppost and watched Marcos pace up and down the sidewalk. "What is the hurry, Marcos?" he did not reply. Instead, he poked his head in the door.

Cracker Jack returned moments later with the same easy gait and warm smile. If anything was amiss, his demeanor did not betray it.

"Like I said, the FBI has been keeping a tight hold on me. Apparently, they believe there is another eminent threat on my life.

The FBI's intelligence, an oxymoron mind you, points to the Arab concern we spoke of earlier targeting me sometime this week." All three reflexively glanced at the two dark Middle Eastern men at the other end of the diner.

"I'm placing you two in danger, so we need to part ways for now. You go with Marcos. He'll get you to your Uncle Carl's house, and I'll get back to you as soon as I can. Fate is at work here."

Marcos appeared next to them in the doorway. "*Si,* fate," Marcos mimicked, "*Si Dios quiere.*"

Matthew frowned, "Did you say 'Carl'? I never said my uncle's name."

"Perhaps Maria did?"

Matthew looked at Maria, "Perhaps."

"It's not right that I ask you to help me. But I have to assume that you will."

Matthew pressed for answers as to how Cracker Jack had known he was coming south. Though it seemed preposterous, he suspected someone engineered them ending up on the same block! But Cracker Jack smiled and turned away.

Matthew kicked at the sand. Once he got some sleep he could sort through the puzzle and heck, there was plenty of time, wasn't there? Matthew saw Cracker Jack hand a set of keys and an envelope to Marcos and say, "Put everything in there now."

"¿Todo?" Marcos asked incredulously.

"Everything." Cracker Jack said sternly.

"Absolutamente, mi amigo. ¡Tenga cuidado!"

Watching Cracker Jack and the G-Men exit through the mostly glass door, Matthew leaned back up against the lamppost. If he smoked, he thought wryly, this is when he would want to light up. His uncle had called from out of the blue and suggested Miami. They hadn't spoken in years, since he never came to see Matthew's father. Maybe there's some connection, he thought. It was my idea, wasn't it?

Maria hugged Ronda goodbye, and then stood by Matthew to wait for Cracker Jack. "I feel like we're in a James Bond movie," Maria said.

"I was thinking *Casablanca*," Matthew quipped. Maria looked at him quizzically.

Cracker Jack joined them in a few minutes. Matthew noticed a marked change in his demeanor and his eyes were darting back and forth. Cracker Jack did in fact light up a cigarette and leaned against the stucco wall of the diner a few feet from Matthew.

"See?" Matthew said, "Casablanca."

"I wish I could say I'm sorry to get you into all of this. I'll bet you wish I just gave you that big box of Cracker Jacks and helped fix the VW bug."

"Bus," said Maria and Matthew in unison.

"Look," Matthew said, "Maria and I will talk this over. If we can help you, we will, though I can't imagine how. Is there somewhere I can call you when we get back to Maine?"

"I'll call you," Cracker Jack said. They all turned to see Marcos yelling from the wrecker down by the Shell station with the bus in tow.

"¡Vamos! We really must go, *amigos!"* Marcos yelled. Cracker Jack was on the sidewalk next to Matthew and Maria. Matthew thought Marcos seemed . . . frantic.

They walked toward the Shell station when Maria blurted out what Matthew had been thinking. "We came here by accident. A few days ago, we weren't even planning to come to Florida. It was a spur of the moment thing. How do you know us?"

Cracker Jack looked left and right and ignored her question completely. Matthew noted that his nonchalant demeanor had changed. He appeared to be nervous, poised like a cat ready to pounce.

"I don't have much time. I'll get in touch with you. You're going to have to trust me. Bottom line, Matthew, I want you to take the project forward."

Matthew felt like the sky fell on him.

"You'll have to protect yourself six ways to Sunday. Finish what we started."

Matthew now knew what the product was and how he fit in. But he wanted to know why. He felt inclined to object, though secretly he was excited to be involved. "I'm flattered, but I'm just a freshman in college. I can't see how I can help in any great way, though it would be one hell of a cooperative project." Matthew kicked at the sand next to the sidewalk in a poor show of humbleness.

Maria grabbed his arm. "Matthew, we have to help if we can."

"I don't think you know what you're saying, Maria. If these people can get to Cracker Jack, what makes you think they won't track us down?" Matthew realized again that she was in his charge. Her father had protected her all these years, and now, at least on this trip, it was his responsibility. "We'll help you of course, but you have to level with us."

"I know you, Matthew, I trust you, and believe in you." Cracker Jack put a hand on Matthew's shoulder. He sighed and said, "I've read the studies you did on energy management and alternative energy. Your hypotheses, theories, postulates, and even your conclusions were visionary. If I hadn't known it was your work, I would've thought my father wrote the papers. There's no other kid – high school, college, or graduate school level – in the country that scores higher in math and science than you. Even if you set all that aside, Matthew, we've studied your character, and we need to entrust CJ Energy to you."

"Who's we?"

"My father would want me to pass the torch to someone with unquestionable integrity, brought up with solid ethics and not infected by greed. Who better than an idealistic, eighteen-year-old genius?"

Matthew kicked at the sand again. Matthew never thought of himself as a genius. Things came easy to him, like a natural artist puts on paper what he sees while others struggle with stick figures.

"He's kind of modest," Maria said and tweaked Matthew in the side.

"Also a good trait; I can see you have something in you, Matthew, a sense of adventure and enough moxie to go all the way with something you believe in. Hell, you packed up and drove 1800 miles just for the heck of it, right?"

"Why do I think maybe we didn't get to this place on our own?" Maria interjected as they approached the corner across from the Shell station.

"I had no choice. I need your help. Trust no one but your closest friends. If you let this out of the bag too soon, everything could be lost, and you could put all those around you in mortal danger. I told the FBI your parents are old friends. I think they bought it. I don't want them or anyone else to start trailing you. The idea is that you will be able to move the project forward without Big Brother government looking over your shoulder."

Matthew sat down hard on the curb. He felt a little dizzy. The excitement, the danger, and the potential for his future was intoxicating but at the same time his calculating mind was screaming, this does not compute!

"¡Vamos!" Marcos yelled from the wrecker.

Matthew began to fire off one question after another to Cracker Jack, who seemed to hold little back. Marcos cussed in Spanish and laid his head on his arms over the steering wheel. Earlier, Matthew felt like he was being interviewed as a possible protégé candidate. Now he was receiving his first hours of training.

Matthew looked back to the diner and noticed both of the FBI agents had moved out onto the sidewalk. They were not as laid back as they had been inside. They looked up and down the street. From the shadows of an alley across the street between the buildings, two other men seemed to appear out of nowhere. Matthew noted that they were out of the view of the FBI in front of the diner.

Maria said, "Do you see those guys in the dark suits? Now *those* guys look like FBI agents."

The one man looked like a pool stick with a cue ball on top. He seemed to be talking into his wrist. The other man was short, stocky, and clean-shaven with a full head of black hair and a wide face. They seemed nervous and agitated. The streets had become eerily silent with only an occasional drunk stumbling out of one of the strip bars around the corner.

If he saw them, Cracker Jack didn't let on and continued with Matthew's CJ Energy crash course. "One day you'll be ready to bring in your own mastermind group of techies and management, but until then, I or someone close to me will let you know when it's safe to go to market. Everything you do has to remain confidential. You'll have to be able to avoid direct questions from other scientists, the media, and," he said, with one long, boney finger pointed back in the direction of the diner, "especially government officials."

Then he put one hand on Matthew's shoulder and one on Maria's. "We'll talk soon, kids." He walked back toward the diner, leaving Maria and Matthew a little dumfounded and with a lot more questions.

"A few hours ago, all I had to worry about was where I was going to buy a new bathing suit," Maria said. Marcos slammed the door of the wrecker and joined them on the corner.

Matthew stood and nudged Maria to look across the street. One of the first two men in the alley across the street reached under his black suit coat, behind his back, and then held something shiny at his side. Matthew almost yelled a warning to Cracker Jack, but Marcos grabbed his arm and pulled him forward. He grabbed Maria's hand and pulled her along behind Marcos. Like a hand-in-hand chain of pre-school children, they sprinted caddy-corner across the intersection to the wrecker and VW Bus at the Shell station.

Marcos ushered Matthew and Maria into the passenger side of the idling truck. He ran around to the driver's side, jumped his slight body in like a gymnast, slammed the door, and pulled forward before stopping between the set of gas pumps. Matthew looked toward the diner and noticed one agent holding his gun with both hands high alongside his cheek while looking around the far side of the building. The shorter guy also had his gun drawn in one hand and the other reaching up to take Cracker Jack by the arm to lead him away. Cracker Jack threw his arm up out of the shorter man's grip. Matthew could not hear their conversation, but thought they were trying to get him off the street.

Marcos snapped the manual transmission on the steering wheel hard into first gear. It ground and grumbled and protested until it finally caught the latch in the gear, and the big truck lurched forward. He turned back onto the street in the direction of the diner.

Marcos was leaning over the steering wheel to have a better view of both sides of the street. Matthew noticed Cue Ball and his partner had disappeared.

"Something is definitely not right," Marcos observed.

CHAPTER 26

March 17, 1995 2:00 a.m.

Flee

IT WAS HARD for Matthew and Maria to believe that until today their greatest concerns had been college midterms and a car breakdown so far from home. In a few short hours, their lives had spun out of control with more danger and uncertainty than they could have ever imagined. Matthew thought of Cracker Jack back in front of the diner, dead or dying. His sense of goodness and integrity screamed about leaving Cracker Jack behind. He closed his eyes and rubbed his temples. His sense of responsibility to get Maria as far away from danger as possible was screaming louder.

Then there was Marcos. He felt sure he was witnessing a professional who had seen his share of action. On the other hand, it was clear Marcos was taking the whole episode very hard. He did not look well and was muttering something under his breath in Spanish, followed by *si Dios quiere*. His eyes filled with tears.

The trio was twenty miles south of Miami before anyone spoke again.

Maria leaned over to Matthew and whispered, "He is saying, 'We told him it was time to leave Miami, we told him, I told him.' Then he said something about having to call his uncle."

"It sounds like they were very close and who is 'we'?" Matthew was getting irritated, as he knew Marcos was as fluent in English as he was.

Maria spoke to Marcos in a comforting voice. She had always had a special way with people who were hurting. Matthew closed his eyes and listened. He remembered spending time with Maria when she worked with kids at an orphanage near Millinocket. The kids loved her, and she knew how to get through to them when nobody else could. She often visited elderly folks that had stopped coming to her father's restaurant, which led many times to the hospital or nursing home. Many people in town said she should become an MD or a nurse, but those who knew her well, knew she was more interested in the mind than the body. Matthew had no doubt that she would one day be Dr. Maria Teresa Bierzo Valdeorras, PhD, a brilliant psychiatrist. Matthew chuckled. She had made him learn her full name and wanted him to know her family history all the way back to the beginning of time. The only part she skipped was when it related to her mother. More than a decade later it was obviously too painful.

Matthew was unable to follow the conversation when it slipped into a more informal Spanish. He was impressed at how quickly Maria had recovered. But he wasn't surprised.

"He's a little too shook up to speak English," Maria explained. "Apparently he and Cracker Jack became strong friends while Cracker Jack was under the FBI's custody. Cracker Jack could move freely in South Beach but could not go off the peninsula. Marcos became his man for hire and would make the trips for him, passing messages to contacts and getting him the things he needed for his research."

"Marcos, I'm sorry, man." Matthew said. He still could not shake the feeling Marcos was hiding something . . . many things.

"*Gracias*," Marcos said.

"I just met Cracker Jack, and I feel a great loss."

Marcos said, "I was afraid of that. *Perdon, por favor*." He wiped his eyes. "*Era mi amigo muy bueno*."

"Shouldn't we call the police or the FBI or someone?" Maria said, reaching into her purse for a tissue.

"*No, senora. No deblamos.* He would not want you to, *como se dice, interfiera.* You must trust me. He told me *instrucciones muy especificas*."

"You warned him, I heard you. So you knew something like this might happen?" Matthew said.

"Si." Marcos grew quiet again.

He drove into the parking lot of a roadside restaurant and gas station. Matthew went into the restroom and threw cold water on his face. He looked in the mirror and swore it was a different person looking back. His face was drawn and serious. I think I aged ten years tonight, he thought.

They met at the table near the back wall. Matthew reached up and twisted the bulb off on the hanging lamp over the table. He looked up at the wall clock and noted it was after two in the morning. Maria looked at him inquisitively.

"Something my brother taught me. Sit in a dark corner with your back against the wall. Do you realize that everything has happened in less than three hours?"

"I know what you mean. It seems like a week's gone by," Maria said.

From where they sat, they could see the Shell wrecker and the VW bus. "I wouldn't be surprised if we were followed." Matthew looked around to be sure he knew where the kitchen and the back entrance were located for a potential escape route.

After eating a light snack and draining a pot of thick coffee, they went outside to inspect their VW Bus, which was hanging off the back of the wrecker like a torn shirt on a clothesline. Matthew noticed all the bullet holes, one narrowly missing the gas tank. Miraculously not one window was broken. He was sure that when the window in the back of the wrecker was shot out, he wouldn't have a single window untouched in the bus. Matthew climbed up into the driver's seat to get his knapsack and inspect the interior. He noticed the back seat was folded down and the pile of their belongings, he had covered with old moving blankets, seemed to have grown. Before he crawled into the back to investigate he turned to the glove compartment to get his driver's license and found a large manila envelope folded and stuffed in place.

Matthew sat back and opened the envelope. His eyes widened and jaw dropped. Inside were five rubber-banded stacks of twenty and fifty dollar bills. There was something else. He reached to the bottom of the envelope and pulled out a leather-bound checkbook. The first line showed a deposit of one hundred thousand dollars. The opening date was January 02 1990 under the name of Matthew Thaddeus Eaton with the Bank of Boston.

Five years ago, Matthew thought.

Tremont Jackson signed the deposit slip.

Maria pulled herself up next to Matthew and looked over his shoulder. "Matthew! That's a lot of money! Where did you get it?"

Nonchalantly, Matthew replied, "You thought I was holding out on you."

She punched him in the shoulder. "Stop it. What's going on?"

"It was in the glove compartment. We'll have to ask Marcos what he knows about this. I'm guessing plenty."

She took the checkbook from Matthew's hand. As it fell to her lap, she cried out, "One hundred thousand dollars!" She unfolded a letter clipped to the front inside cover. "It's a joint account with someone named Tremont Jackson. Was that Cracker Jack's name?" Matthew nodded, thinking that something other than his famous father rang familiar about that name. She read farther down the page, "All you have to do is sign next to Tremont's name and you have full rights and privileges to the account. I don't understand."

"Nor do I."

Attached to the bank account letter was a handwritten sticky note. Maria read it aloud.

> Matthew: Please take this cash to fix the VW, for traveling money, and to take care of my stuff until we can get together to discuss the future.

Maria looked up at Matthew. They were both quite sure they would not be seeing the affable Mr. Jackson again. She continued to read:

> The account is insurance in case something goes wrong here in Miami. In that case, my people will be in touch when this runs out. Best wishes. CJ

My people? Matthew thought. "I don't feel right taking his money; though this is probably not the time to try to figure all this out." Matthew stuffed the envelope of money in his shirt and the checkbook in his back jeans pocket.

"I wonder what he meant about taking care of his stuff." Maria said as they climbed down from the VW Bus.

Matthew looked toward the truck stop diner and saw Marcos on the payphone having a very animated conversation with someone. After he set the receiver on the hook, he placed both hands on the side of the booth and lowered his head. He then picked up the receiver and made another call.

Matthew heard a raspy voice behind him say, “You’re a perky thing. Now why don’t you follow old Bubba and check out my Peterbilt deluxe sleeper cab?” Matthew turned to find a hairy bull of a man in overalls with no shirt and his face within an inch of Maria’s. Matthew took four quick strides and tapped the man on the shoulder.

“Beat it, buster, I’m busy,” Bubba the trucker said.

Matthew pulled on the bull’s shoulder. The man spun and swung. Matthew ducked but not before a large fist glanced off the side of his head. He heard Maria scream and saw flashing lights in front of his eyes. Just as he thought he was going to fall, he felt someone holding him up.

Marcos said, “You okay?” Matthew nodded.

Marcos stepped past Matthew and as if in one motion reached down, pulled his pant leg up and retrieved a gun attached to a holster next to his ankle. In a moment, he had slammed the much larger man against the side of the bus with the barrel of the gun pressed firmly under his chin. Marcos said calmly, “Matthew, take Maria over to the wrecker, Joe redneck and I will have a little talk.”

Matthew took Maria’s hand and led her to the passenger side of the wrecker. “I’ll go make sure Marcos doesn’t need any help.”

“Matthew, I don’t think he needs a bit of help, stay here. Please?”

Matthew felt a little embarrassed that Bubba had gotten the best of him, but he saw her point.

A moment later, Marcos pulled himself into the wrecker.

“Thank you, Marcos,” Maria said as they cruised out of the parking lot and back onto the highway.

“Yeah, thanks Marcos,” Matthew said, “He caught me off guard – ”

“No problem,” Marcos said.

The three of them were quiet for a while as Marcos picked up speed. Matthew knew it! Marcos was more than a gas station attendant and casual friend of Cracker Jack’s, that’s for sure. He reached in his pocket for the silver pill case. He hoped that Marcos would curb his led foot so they would make it to Uncle Carl’s house in one piece and he said so.

“It’s okay, *amigo. No problemo.* I am the next best thing to a professional driver.” Just hold on, and we get to casa de Carl *del tio muy rapido*!” All of a sudden, Marcos was very talkative, as if the action at the truck stop had energized him. “You know, chicos, I always wanted to be a race car driver like Mario Andretti.”

"I can see that. Marcos, you know, you can cut the Cuban fresh off the boat act if you want to."

Marcos ignored him. "I decided that cars are not fast enough so now I fly jet aircraft."

Matthew knew from the increasing pain caused by Maria's long fingernails digging into his forearm, that she was not enjoying the ride. He was afraid to close his eyes to let the pill take effect, though he needed to.

Maria gasped, "Marcos, there's a stop sign ahead." She repeated it again in Spanish.

The speedometer was pushing over 70 mph. Marcos was going on about movies that inspired him like *Days of Thunder* and *Top Gun* when he slammed on the brakes and swung the wheel a 90-degree turn. The VW Bus nearly launched from the back of the wrecker.

Marcos exclaimed in clear unaccented English, "Why didn't you tell me about that stop sign?"

Marcos talked about his life in Cuba before being the only survivor when his family tried to escape from Cuba on a small sailboat. He had been nine years old at the time. Somehow, Matthew thought this part was factual. An American sailed into the port of Havana to purchase cigars and other goods to sell through the black market in Miami. The Cuban authorities greet Americans with open arms as long as they were spending lots of money. "My father was an affluent merchant in Cuba."

"Is your last name Estebanez?" Matthew queried.

"Estefan, Estefan." He looked irritated but didn't miss a beat and explained that his father, Jose Estefan, had fallen out of grace with Fidel Castro by voicing his opinion one too many times in public. My father heard a rumored that Castro was going to confiscate all of his bank accounts, so he transferred all of his money one day and escaped the next with as much as he could carry.

"So, he died in the storm."

"*Si signora*, along with *mia madre*, brother and two sisters. I was saved by the Coast Guard and adopted by family."

Matthew again thought the story credible but he was sure Marcos was holding a lot of information back. Well, why shouldn't he? He had only known him and Maria for a few hours. Still, his brother often said that there's a lot of truth in misinformation. Finally, now that Marcos was finished playing Daytona 500, Matthew closed his eyes and fell fast asleep.

CHAPTER 27

March 17, 1995 3:00 A.M.

Arrive

MARIA, MATTHEW, AND Marcos pulled up in front of Uncle Carl's house. Though it was in the middle of the night, Carl Eaton was standing at the corner of what looked like two large garages – one attached to the house and an even larger one off to the right. There were late model and specialty cars everywhere. Marcos backed the tattered VW bus into the driveway, and the three exhausted travelers stepped out. Carl shook Matthew's hand and then pulled him in for a guy hug, shoulder to shoulder. After a brief introduction, Matthew and Marcos retreated into the street where Matthew insisted that Marcos accept two crisp one hundred dollar bills from the $5000 cash that Cracker Jack must have put in the bus. He decided not to discuss the money with Marcos. But he did ask, "Marcos, can you tell me more about what happened back in Miami Beach?"

"I wish I could, Matthew." For a moment, he dropped the language charade. "But I have to go back and find out for myself."

"Will you call me?"

"Sure." They exchanged phone numbers.

"Are you going to go to the police when you get back?"

"Maybe."

Once again, Marcos' evasiveness bothered Matthew. He was sure Marcos could indeed fill in the blanks – but they seemed to have come to some unspoken understanding. Matthew could keep asking, and Marcos would keep avoiding, so, he gave up.

Maria ran down the driveway as Marcos was stepping up into the wrecker. She threw her arms around his neck and kissed him on the cheek. "I want to thank you for protecting us and for the Six Flags roller coaster ride."

Marcos smiled and whispered something in Spanish to Maria and then turned and hugged Matthew like a brother.

"You two could make a grown man cry," he said in perfect English. "You're very brave kids. I'll leave you with your uncle. Be careful on your trip back to Maine, and we'll be in touch."

As the wrecker drove down the road, Matthew looked at the number Marcos had scrawled on the back of the gas receipt. It was the same number as on the side of the wrecker.

They gave Carl a short version of their exhausting trip, having previously decided to leave out the shootings, and their harrowing escape. Carl inspected the holes in the bus, but strangely, he didn't ask any questions. When they were alone, Maria asked, "Did you notice that Marcos seemed to know your uncle?"

"I did. And even though I hadn't had a chance to call and let him know when we would be here, he was in the driveway at three in the morning. I'll tell him the rest of the story later and see what he knows. I know we're tired, but I feel a conspiracy theory blooming." He laughed. Matthew didn't want to alarm Maria any more than she already was. She had already been through so much. They all had. But there had been too much coincidence, and he didn't like the feeling that Cracker Jack, Marcos, and now maybe even his uncle were in on something. And then there was the strange meeting with Estebanez at South of the Border. And the checking account was opened six years ago. He rubbed his chin and said aloud, "Damn."

"What?" Maria and Carl said at the same time.

"Nothing. Um, I forgot to do something. I'll be right back."

Matthew opened the passenger door of the VW and looked under the seat. Maria came over and quietly asked what he was looking for. He held up an express mail envelope.

"I completely forgot that you were supposed to deliver the envelope," Maria said. "But you can't be expected to remember everything after all that's happened."

"I know, but Esteb – I mean, I think it was really important."

"We can drop it off on the way back home, don't you think?"

"I suppose."

After Maria retrieved her overnight bag from the front seat and turned back toward the house, Matthew tore open the envelope. He gazed at the empty envelope with a new understanding. He was facing the street and glanced up to see the gray Cadillac down the street. He leapt into a trot toward the car and tried the driver's side door. It would not open so he hit his palm against the tinted window. The man inside sat up and smiled at him. He saluted with three fingers to his forehead, the big engine roared to life and he pulled away.

Steaming with rage and adrenalin, Matthew picked up a rock and hurled it at the diminishing taillights. He continued, chasing and hurling random missiles, until the car vanished and the tears of frustration and the realization of all that happened in the last few hours closed in around him. Maria called from the house and Matthew struggled to regain his composure and turned back toward the house.

Matthew's Aunt Carol and their two boys, Bobby and Kenneth, were fast asleep. Carl picked up the near comatose Kenneth and put him in the spare double bed in Bobby's room. Maria slept in Kenneth's room, and Matthew took the couch.

After Carl went into his room, Maria came out to the couch. She sat on the floor and put her head against Matthew's hip. "You okay?"

"I suppose. I guess we can worry about all the details later. I just can't get out of my mind the pictures of Cracker Jack and the FBI agents hitting the ground covered in blood."

"I'm glad I didn't see that."

"I wonder if I could have done anything to help him. My mind is saying no, but my heart is saying that I should have tried."

"Even Marcos seemed powerless to do anything, and he has so much more history with him than we do." She kissed him and crawled onto the couch. Matthew folded one arm to cradle her head and reached the other around her waist, holding her tight against him.

A few hours later, they awoke to the smell of bacon and eggs. Maria opened her eyes and found herself staring into the big blue eyes of what must have been the younger brother. She sat up embarrassed and ruffled her hair. "Well, hello. You must be Kenneth." She stuck her right hand out. "I'm Maria." Kenneth let out a high-pitched giggle and ran into the kitchen.

Matthew stirred, stretched, and sat up. "Trying to give the little one some education?"

"I didn't mean to fall asleep. What must your uncle think of me?"

"That you're some black haired hussy from the back woods of Maine that has taken advantage of his poor, defenseless nephew." He put his arms around her and hugged her tight.

She pulled away with a laugh and said, "I think I saw a big bottle of Scope in the bathroom, mister."

The other brother lumbered into the great room while Matthew put on his shirt and socks. "So you're my genius cousin?" the kid asked.

"What kind of genius breaks down in Miami Beach and has to be towed all the way to your house?"

"I saw your bus. 1968, right?"

"1967 actually, but good observation. Are you sure you're only nine?" Matthew hoped he wouldn't ask about the bullet holes. He didn't.

After a shower and brushing his teeth with his finger, followed by some mouthwash, Matthew joined Maria and the Florida Eatons in the kitchen.

Though he had consumed a lot of food since midnight, Matthew ate like it was his last meal. Aunt Carol said, "I see the Eaton appetite is hereditary. I'll bet it has something to do with your father putting work gloves and a chainsaw in your crib instead of a baseball and glove." Everyone laughed because of the truth in the statement.

Maria was satisfied with an English muffin. "We've had two breakfasts in the last eight hours. But you're right about the Eaton's. Matthew could eat breakfast three times a day."

"You two act like a married couple," Carol quipped.

Maria could not hide her surprise. "I'm only seventeen."

Carl said, "Carol and I were only eighteen when we got hitched." Both Matthew and Maria concentrated on their food and orange juice.

After breakfast, Uncle Carl and Matthew went out to assess the damage on the VW Bus. Carl was quite the mechanic, and his three-car garage was set up like an auto shop. In the yard were various vintage cars in different stages of repair. He proudly showed off a blue 1958 Biscayne, a lime 1960 Dodge Pioneer, and a red 1952 Packard.

"I can see where Bobby gets his affinity for cars."

"It's a bad habit I picked up in Maine. Who do you think was my mentor?"

"Ha! Mr. Johnson? He taught Sean and I everything we know about engines. How about that? I didn't know he was that old."

"Hey. Thanks a lot." Carl put his fists up in a mock fighting stance.

Matthew ducked a shadow punch and put his fists up as well.

"Quick reflexes."

While they examined the bus, Matthew asked Carl about his past. Matthew always wondered if his father drove him away from the family business. He was beginning to feel they might have a lot in common, as he wasn't keen on entering the logging business himself.

Carl went on to tell him that he left Maine to join the Air Force, met Carol on the base in Virginia, and took to flying like a bird. After the Air Force, he and Carol moved to Miami, where he stretched his entrepreneurial wings by buying the first of many commercial airplanes. So, for the last decade, he had been flying cargo to and from El Salvador, Belize, Costa Rica, Guatemala, and Honduras. He said he would still be flying had guerrilla fighters in Nicaragua not shot him down in 1990 – permanently grounding him. He continued to lease his cargo planes to other companies and bought into a hotel investment group owning properties in the Keys and Central America. He said it was risky, but he hoped the payback would be enormous.

Matthew told Carl how he remembered overhearing his father complain to his mother that this was what Carl had been saying about each one of his ventures for years. After each venture, he barely escaped with the shirt off his back.

Matthew said, "Somehow that doesn't seem like a bad thing. Mr. Estebanez – "

"Estebanez? You said that name earlier."

"He's like a tutor back in Millinocket. Anyhow, he always said that you have to make mistakes to learn, and most successful business people fail numerous times before making it to the top."

"Sounds like a smart guy."

"He is. One day I hope to take one of my energy inventions all the way to market. I don't want to invent it and let some other company gain all the benefits."

"I will say that your grandfather was the original Eaton entrepreneur," Uncle Carl said. "He built Eaton Logging and Forestry from a tiny two-man sawmill into what it is today. Your father simply took what was already there and brought it into the twentieth century."

"Mr. Estebanez says that many inventors and entrepreneurs never see the fruits of their genius . . ." A feeling of sadness washed over him. Cameron T. Jackson and Tremont Cameron Jackson were cases in point.

As if reading his mind, Carl said, "I have a feeling you'll get on your path sooner rather than later."

Matthew cocked his head and was about to share his experience with Cracker Jack, but decided to wait.

They pushed the bus up on the lift; Carl made some notes and then motioned for Matthew to follow him. Without opening the door, he climbed into a 1993 Porsche America Roadster convertible. Matthew couldn't imagine a more exciting sports car, with a white exterior and black interior – and just enough space for two and a small dog. They zipped out of the driveway and flew up Highway One to Sam's Car Cemetery. Matthew was pleased to find they had three beat-up, late model VW Buses to choose from. "We better get some Rustoleum too," Carl said, "I noticed there's quite a bit of bare metal."

While they were walking through a countless number of wrecks the size of a football field sprawled alongside I-95, Matthew decided it was time to ask his uncle about some things that have been bothering him. "Uncle Carl, why did you start calling and prompting me to come down here?"

"What? Is there a problem with me wanting to see my favorite nephew?" Carl gave Matthew a playful shove.

"No, it's just that my folks and I hadn't heard from you for years, and the timing of your calls, along with all that has happened these last few days, doesn't compute."

"Having been shot at more times than I can count, while in the air and on the ground, I understand about what happened in Miami Beach. But what else has been happening?"

"I didn't tell you about the shooting."

"You didn't have to. Your machine looks like Swiss cheese."

Matthew wasn't satisfied. His uncle answered every question with a question. Just as Cracker Jack had at first, he thought. He had learned that very technique from his mentor back in Millinocket. He changed direction. "Had you heard of Estebanez before I mentioned him today?"

"There are a lot of Estebanezs down here, Matt."

"How about one in particular?" Matthew took a picture out of his wallet of him and a handsome man in his mid-fifties, with an arm around Matthew at the Smithsonian in D.C. "Mr. E. is a wine connoisseur, loves boats, and is very interested in science, particularly energy."

Carl looked up at the sky, shook his head, and said, "No, that Estebanez doesn't look or sound familiar. I knew a Juan Estebanez once that ran imports between El Salvador and Miami until the DEA blew him out of the water."

Matthew didn't believe him. "How about Marcos?"

"The young Cuban that brought you here?"

"Yeah."

"Nope, never saw him before today."

"How about a guy named Tremont Jackson? His father Cameron was a great scientist and inventor and was killed in D.C. back in 1989."

"I think I'd remember those names, kid. But nope, didn't know the poor bastard. It sounds like your two scientists were mixed up with some pretty bad characters."

"If you can call the FBI bad characters, then I guess they were."

"The FBI?"

Matthew avoided elaborating and changed the subject back to Uncle Carl's businesses and adventures. Carl went along, either to cover his lie or because he really didn't know any of the characters in this ever unfolding drama.

The only available parts were from an earlier model, but their salesman said they would line up just fine. "Mr. Johnson would never have allowed us to put anything on an engine that wasn't from the exact model and year. He would have said we were inviting disaster."

With the larger parts wedged in between them, and barely fitting the rest in the back seat, they sped back to the house.

By midday, they had taken the engine apart and had it back together. "Mr. Johnson would be proud of us," Matthew said and then realized how condescending that sounded coming from someone his age.

"Thanks," Carl said with a large smile. "Mr. Johnson was quite a tutor. He and I spent many weekends up at the old mechanics shop my father built into that barn. Is it still there?"

"It is. That's where Sean and I put the bus back together – the first time." Matthew got up in the front seat with Carl's boys and turned the key in the ignition. After three tries, she turned over and began humming and backfiring and humming again – sounding as good as new.

"All right!" Matthew said overjoyed. He took the boys for a spin around the neighborhood. When they returned, he parked the VW next to the Porsche.

Over dinner, Matthew asked Carl what he planned to do after the hotel business. Or was this his last hurrah?

"Well, if the hotel business turns out to be a wash . . . then I don't know what I'll do next. Maybe come up there to Maine and get in the lumber business with my big brother . . . on second thought, maybe I'll join you in the high tech energy business."

"You wouldn't last one Maine winter," his wife said.

"You got that right! Maybe you can move down here after college, and I can help you start your business. Perhaps you can invent something like you did to win that Smithsonian deal. I can manage and market the product for you, and we'll make millions. That is, if your dad doesn't have you chopping down trees up in the Katahdin."

"I think he already knows that's not in my game plan. Not in Sean's either. I think that worries him."

"Don't be too sure. If Sean doesn't come back from playing soldier and I-Spy, your dad's going to be looking at you. Just like he did me."

Matthew didn't doubt what Carl was saying was absolutely true. And he didn't think Sean would ever go back to Maine, except for short visits to see his mother.

Carl seemed to read his thoughts. "Listen, kid. You be your own man. You have quite a gift, and you're right on target with the energy issues. I have a feeling you'll have your hands full. It won't be long before the folks down in Venezuela will be holding a gun up against our heads. There's a crazy man running for office again that I used to do business with – ," he hesitated, "his name's Chavez. If he gets in, we'll have ourselves another Cuba, except worse. Venezuela supplies the U.S. half of our oil. Mark my words, the sooner you think of something to invent the better, and I'm your man for international distribution."

How about perpetual energy? Matthew thought.

Carl, the boys, and Matthew gravitated back outside. "Say, that Maria's a looker and a class act. You need to hold onto her. I'll bet you get into an awful lot of fights over her."

Matthew touched the sore side of his head, compliments of Bubba. "I have to admit, sometimes it's a challenge."

"You win any of them?" Carl asked, laughing.

"I can be pretty scrappy when I want to be." They play boxed around the driveway as the boys laughed and cheered them on.

When it was time to go, Carl opened the side of the bus and placed a bag of sandwiches and snacks behind the seat. He lifted one of the heavy moving blankets and exclaimed, "What the hell is all of this, Matt? I thought you said you were packing light." He pulled out one of four large canvas duffel bags. Matthew was so shocked to see them that he didn't think to ask Carl why he would care what was in the bags.

"I don't know." He did recall seeing the burgeoning blanket covered pile of their stuff right when he found the money. But with all the excitement he never went back to investigate.

Before Matthew could protest, Carl set the first heavy duffel bag on the cement driveway and slid the zipper from top to bottom. The duffel was full of carefully organized files, books, and tapes. They squatted down beside the duffel and began to flip through dozens of files, ten large three-ring notebooks, numerous unlabeled videotapes, and stacks of letters.

While Matthew examined the files, Carl flipped through a few engineering books and magazines. As it slowly dawned on Matthew what treasures they had discovered, he extracted a leather pouch containing two metal boxes that looked like computer drives, except much smaller than the ones he was familiar with. In the same pouch were three stacks of disks, each labeled 250 meg, numbered one through twenty; they were much larger and thicker than the common 1.2 meg floppies.

"What do you think, Matt?"

Too consumed to answer, Matthew noticed a white sheet of paper attached by a rubber band around each video. He pulled one of the letters off a blank video. It made little sense, but there was no doubt the writer was threatening and perhaps blackmailing Mr. Jackson.

Carl pulled the second duffel bag from the van. Upon examination, they found similar stacks of files, dated from 1970 to 1975. Matthew looked back at the first bag, and the dates on the files ranged from 1964 to 1969. In this bag, there were more computer hard drives in a leather pouch and a box of brown leather-bound books. *Journals!* Matthew's brain accelerated. Matthew pulled one book dated October 1964 and flipped through the pages. He sat down hard on the pavement. The journals were proof that these bags contained the life work of Cameron Jackson, Cracker Jack's father, the unsung father of alternative energy.

"I don't know about you, Matt, but I think someone had to clear out the good doctor's office in a flash. There's documentation here from his years at MIT dating back to the mid-fifties. I'm no scientist, but I think you're carrying the man's life work. My guess is that your friend Cracker Jack stowed this . . ."

Matthew looked at him squarely. "I never mentioned the name Cracker Jack."

"Sure you did, Matt. Back at the junkyard."

"No, I didn't." But, he thought, maybe I did.

Matthew let it go for the moment. Instead of arguing, he thought back to Miami Beach and the times he was away from the bus.

"Do you suppose this is what they're after? The guys who were shooting at you?" Carl asked.

"I don't know. I just don't know." Matthew wondered if Marcos knew this was in the bus and if he helped Cracker Jack stow it.

While Uncle Carl was flipping through files, Matthew found more of the same in the third bag. The fourth bag held something heavy bulging out of a zipped pocket. He reached in and pulled out a black leather pouch. Snuggly tucked inside was clearly a gun, bound in an oily leather wrap.

Carl appeared to be engrossed in one of many journals, so Matthew nonchalantly walked around the far side of the bus, opened the passenger side, and placed the pouch on the seat. He wasn't sure why, but he didn't want

Carl or anyone else to see it. He glanced again at Carl before unfolding the wet leather to find a beautiful, black .45-caliber pistol. Inscribed in gold were the initials CJ on each side of the grip. He unsnapped a side pocket that held four empty magazines and two boxes of ammunition. Someone, most likely Cracker Jack, wanted to be ready for a quick defense. He folded the leather around the gun and placed it back in the black pouch. Leaning way over, he stuffed the gun and its supplies under the driver's seat. When he turned, Carl was standing behind him.

"What're you doing?" Carl asked.

"Looking for a map to plan our escape."

Carl paused longer than Matthew thought he should have and then said, "Oh, we have plenty of maps of Florida in the house. Carol will dig one out for you." As they walked back to the treasures, Carl leaned against the side of the bus and flipped through a book. "This is amazing – this journal from 1959. Did you know Jackson's wife died after childbirth? Maybe murdered. Even back then, I guess solar energy was considered a threat to big business." Carl pushed off the bus and went back to the duffel bags.

"We should get all of this back in the bus," Matthew said looking nervously toward the house. He joined Uncle Carl at the back of the bus.

"Tell me, Matt, what are your plans? I mean, you're the man for the job. I've been reading up on your experiments and research. Your mom is quite proud of you. Well, hell, we all are." Carl flipped through a worn out notebook. "This is decades of work. Look here, this entry is from April 4, 1948 about solar-heating a house."

Matthew took the small spiral notebook from Carl and read farther. He smiled. "Dr. Jackson couldn't have been ten, if that. I've read about all of these failed experiments in *Capturing the Sun*. This one was in Dover, Massachusetts. The next notable experiment was the next year in France where a man created a solar microwave – it only emanated fifty kilowatts, but it was a milestone."

Matthew heard voices coming from the house and asked Carl to help him load the duffel bags back in the bus.

"You're not going to show Maria?"

"Not yet."

Carl laughed. "It's your funeral." Just as Carl slammed the doors shut, Maria came out, followed by two clearly infatuated boys.

Leaning in close to Matthew, Carl said, "If you feel like you're in over your head, kid, you can lean on me. I've had a bit of experience with some pretty intense situations."

"I think I'm beginning to realize the complexity of the situation I've stumbled into. But no worries, you've already done too much."

"You know, I could air cargo ship these to you in Maine. We could list them as oranges and grapefruit."

Matthew watched Carl as he ran his hands over the bullet holes in the back and side of the bus.

Carl examined the bullets still lodged just inside the wheel well. He took out his pocketknife and pried one out, then flipped the bullet up and down in his hand. "Thirty-eight slug. Standard police issue. Looks like someone really didn't want you to leave Miami Beach. Like I said, Matt, you can talk to me. You can trust me, and if you want, I can arrange to have the damn bus sent up to you by truck and fly you two out of Miami."

Matthew wanted to confide in his uncle and was tempted to take him up on the offers, but feeling a different kind of kinship to Cracker Jack and Cameron Jackson, he needed to handle this himself. He was also struggling with the commitment to Cracker Jack not to mention the research to anyone. Now his Uncle Carl, who he barely knew, was privy to nearly everything in the duffel bags. Marcos should have told him what was in the bus, if he knew. "Let me stew on everything between here and Maine. I promise to give you a call when I roll back onto campus."

Matthew was excited to get back to Maine and delve into his newfound treasures. He was also frightened about the attention from some very dangerous, even murderous, foes he would be bringing, or had already brought, on himself, Maria, and others close to him.

Maria and Matthew thanked Carol and Carl. Matthew gave Carl five one hundred dollar bills from the money Cracker Jack left them. Carl tried to push it aside, but Matthew won by telling him that he couldn't use Carl's place to crash if I couldn't at least pay for the parts when he fixed his vehicle.

Carl grudgingly put the money in his pocket and said, "If you need anything, anything at all, give me a call, and if I can't solve the problem I'll find someone that can."

Matthew could not help wondering if there was a hidden meaning in that statement.

Matthew drove out of the Homestead area and back onto Highway 1, heading north. They were quiet for a while. Matthew was contemplating whether to tell Maria about the duffel bags. Just knowing about the new cargo potentially put her in danger. All day the events of the previous night had seemed like a dream – or a nightmare – when he opened the bags, reality set in. Like his brother would say, "Wake up and smell the bacon!" Cracker Jack was surely dead, and Matthew had his incredible work not four feet behind him.

"What am I going to do?" he mumbled under his breath.

"What?" Maria asked, putting her hand on his shoulder.

"I just can't believe what we've been through these last twenty-four hours. It seems surreal."

"I think we should drive back into Miami Beach and see if anyone can tell us what happened or stop in to see the police."

Matthew was considering the same thing until his discovery. "That wouldn't be a good idea. Whoever was shooting at us is bound to be looking for us. I think we better head up the highway."

CHAPTER 28

March 17, 1995 5:00 p.m.

Chase

THE WARM SALTY wind was soothing, and the bus was purring. He looked over at Maria, who had fallen asleep with her hair covering part of her face and shoulders. He thought she looked like a cat curled up on a blanket. Considering they were dodging bullets less than eighteen hours ago, things were going good. The rest of the trip should all be downhill. Matthew shook his head to clear the cobwebs of confusion he felt. Through a crazy set of circumstances, for the first time in his life, he had more than college degrees in his future. He had a vision. It was a vision passed on by true visionaries. Maria was the one who talked about fate and faith. He was more of a realist, but he had to admit, something was going on far outside of his understanding. Once he had all the facts, he felt sure he could see a logical explanation.

How did he get interested in energy? He knew he was drawing windmills and houses with solar panels in pre-school. Then there was Cameron T. Jackson's *Capturing the Sun.* He would have to ask Sean to tell him what happened to his friend from Yale that somehow obtained a personally signed copy. What was the statistical chance that he would meet the son of the one man he most wanted to be like? There was the six degrees of separation theory, but that only covered knowing someone who knows someone who knows someone else, not meeting that six degree someone directly. It all defied probability. Or did it? He chuckled thinking about the argument he and Maria had in the diner over whether it was five degrees or six. He looked over as Maria stirred.

He began running back over everything Cracker Jack said the night before. He jotted notes on a pad against the steering wheel knowing the farther he was away from that fateful night, the less he would remember. Seeing Cracker Jack and the FBI men shot and splattered with blood was the worst thing he had experienced in his young life. With the valuable, ominous, and fateful packages in the back, he knew he would not have a moment of peace until they cleared Florida, and he was sure they weren't being followed.

Matthew merged onto I-95 and saluted Cracker Jack when he passed the signs for Miami Beach. The other drivers were passing him like he was standing still. Matthew forced the bus up to its maximum sixty as a BMW honked and sped around him. "Idiot!"

"What's that?" He'd awakened Maria.

"These Floridians drive like maniacs, so I've been trying to at least keep in the flow of traffic. That grumbling is the sound of the engine that couldn't."

"No, not that," she said leaning forward and pointing high up in the sky, "I mean that." From his line of vision, Matthew couldn't see anything but a few wisps of clouds. Then it swooped down in front of him. He blinked hard, not believing his eyes. "This can't be happening. I feel like we're in an *Indiana Jones* movie." Less than a half dozen cars ahead of them, no higher than the palm trees, a WWI Sopwith Camel, a double-winged airplane complete with twin machine guns under the hump, appeared to be on a collision course with Matthew.

Maria screamed and covered her eyes with both hands as Matthew swung the wheel into a defensive maneuver and careened off the side of the highway. Too late! Something was hitting the bus, making it shudder. The windshield that survived Miami Beach shattered and glass spewed into the bus. Matthew kept control of the wheel and waited for the right moment. He could now see the pilot's wild eyes through the antique goggles – he smiled like a kid catching a goldfish. He was a dark-skinned character wearing a leather cap with chinstraps hanging loose on each side. Just as the propeller was within feet of the bus, Matthew punched the accelerator with the intention of speeding up under the Sopwith, but instead he heard a crash in the back of the bus.

Maria screamed, "What was that?"

"I can't believe it! It had to be something in the engine!" When he looked ahead, the Sopwith had disappeared just as the bus began to lose speed. "I'll be a son of a . . . how did we get out from under him?"

"I don't know. I had my head down," Maria said.

Without warning, he heard a sound like gravel kicking up on all sides of the vehicle. Matthew wished it were gravel. He saw the Sopwith in Maria's mirror. It must have circled around behind them. The plane looked unsteady, dipping its wings from left to right. More than one bullet whizzed through the bus between him and Maria and out the windowless front. It was a miracle they weren't hit, but his precious VW bus was surely going to be in shreds.

Matthew forced a number of cars off the road as the bus bounded down an exit ramp into the infamous projects area of Dade County called Liberty Square with the Sopwith seconds behind. At the bottom of the ramp, Matthew took a sharp left and cut under a bridge. Let him try to follow me here, he thought. The Sopwith Camel kept on his tail a couple feet off the road.

"He's going to follow us under the bridge!" Maria screamed.

"This guy is nuts!" Matthew floored the accelerator. The entire bus sputtered and shook but kept right on going. He came out from under the bridge with the crazy pilot right behind putting more bullets into the back of the bus. He turned right onto the first road, between a McDonald's and a BP. Matthew noticed many buildings, homes, and a line of palm trees off to the left. He thought he might be able to lose the plane. He also noticed a small ravine between neighborhoods, so he took a chance the bus's low frame would make it and shot through the field and down into the ravine. It was dry, and they bounced out like a super ball. They sped through some wire fencing, dragging it with them for a hundred yards with wooden posts and wire smacking up against both sides of the bus, then across a field, and finally onto a narrow dirt road. Matthew pulled over to the side and stopped to let the dust settle.

Matthew looked over to Maria as she shook glass from her hair and he said, "Well, you wanted to add a little excitement to our spring break. I was thinking we could stop in Orlando and swim with the sharks at Sea World for an encore."

Maria did not seem to be amused. "You can swim with dolphins, not sharks," she grumbled.

Matthew stopped again to survey their situation. They were right in the middle of a palm tree-lined road, giving them complete cover.

"He's not there. I think you lost him, Matt – " then she cried out.

"What? Do you see him?"

"No! It's your head."

Matthew touched his head and retrieved a handful of blood. "I thought sweat was dripping in my eyes."

Maria dug into his overnight bag, which lay on the top of the green blankets in the back. Matthew kept the bus moving forward. "No, not that one. If you have to, use the Boston College crew shirt."

"You've got to be kidding. You're bleeding! And you're concerned about soiling one of your precious t-shirts?" Not finding the Boston shirt, she pulled out another one, which Matthew begrudgingly approved: Harvard Rugby, Ivy League Champions 1979.

"Sean never liked that shirt. Plus, the blood will make a good story."

Maria tried to dab at the wound, and Matthew winced. He turned down one and then another road until he was lost. The thermostat was blinking red, and the engine was sputtering. He looked down a sandy, dead end street. There were a dozen disheveled houses, most of which looked abandoned with grassy front yards and no cars in the driveway. His mind spun to come up with a plan. A sleepy German shepherd sitting on the front steps of a one story, sun-bleached house caught his eye. Matthew turned into the driveway under the palm tree cover. The house was in good condition, though the grass in the front yard was two feet high, and numerous newspapers were scattered by the mailbox. But for the dog, it could be a perfect hideout.

"Maria, see if you can open the garage door." She lifted it with ease, Matthew drove in, and they closed the door.

"We've been chased and shot at twice," Maria said. "I think someone is more than just upset about our relationship with Cracker Jack. What do *you* think? What should we do?"

Matthew closed the garage door. He didn't know what to say.

"Okay, genius, what's next?" she said, more softly.

"Let's first see if we can stay the night here." Matthew went into the house. The first room was the kitchen. He lifted the receiver of the wall phone and checked for a dial tone. Dead. Who would he call anyhow, he thought. Maybe Carl? Certainly not his father.

He ran a finger through the thick dust on the counter. There were dishes still piled in the sink. Off to the right were two tables, with test tubes, Bunsen Burners, and other items commonly used in research labs. He peered through the swinging door to the next room. The large room had children's toys strewn about and Disney videos stacked in front of the television.

Matthew tried the sink in the kitchen. The pipes groaned and growled as a stream of rusty water chugged and sputtered out of the faucet. It reminded him of the polluted Millinocket Stream below the Great Northern Paper Mill. He let the faucet run as he tried the lights. Nothing. He went back to the garage and lit the pilot on the water heater. He was surprised that the utility companies had shut off the phone and electricity but not the gas. He imagined one CJ Energy Cell running everything in this house, and smiled. He retrieved a bag of snacks from the bus and closed the door. He was halfway to the door when on second thought, he returned to retrieve the oily leather pouch he had stowed under the seat of the bus. He loaded fourteen rounds into a magazine, snapped it into place and double checked the safety. His brother had taught him to remove the rounds daily so they would not compress. He decided he would keep at least one magazine loaded and ready until they were safely home.

In the kitchen, the water had cleared.

He could hear Maria exploring farther into the house. "The water should be hot in an hour or so." He met her in the hallway where she was rummaging through a small closet. Holding gauze, tape, peroxide, she led him into the bathroom.

"Sit."

Matthew obeyed, perching on the edge of the tub. When she was done, Matthew looked in the mirror. "I think I liked it better with the dried blood."

He took blankets and towels out of the linen closet and pillows out of one of the bedrooms. Judging by the stuffed Barney, the dinosaur on the floor, and Berenstain Bears books scattered about, the child was barely school age. In the great room, he laid a sheet and blanket across the dusty couch, put new covers on a couple pillows. Then he went into the bathroom to check the shower. Still not hot. When he got back to the couch, he found Maria fast asleep on top of the blanket. He covered her with a thin wool blanket before curling up with another on the floor to rest a few minutes.

He woke hours later to sounds at the front door. It was dark outside. He slipped Jackson's CJ engraved gun from under his pillow. He crawled to the window beside the door and looked out. He chuckled, "Oh, it's you." He opened the door to find the German shepherd staring at him. The dog pushed her way into the house and ran into the kitchen. Matthew followed her and knelt down. Though she had a thick coat, Matthew could feel her ribs against her skin.

"Someone left you when they left the house, didn't they?" Matthew's heart ached when he imagined this dog sitting on the front steps day after day waiting for her masters to return. The mostly black dog had shocks of white on her feet, tail, under her chin, and two puffs just above her eyes turned in just enough to give her a sad look. She wagged her tail and licked his face. "Hey, girl, I don't know where that tongue has been. Knock it off." Matthew retrieved some beef jerky and a dozen mini-blueberry muffins from the snack bag and made that dog's night. He put a bowl of water on the floor, and she lapped it up with gusto. After the thirty seconds it took to consume her first square meal in who knows how long, the dog pushed past Matthew and lay down next to the couch. "You do know your way around this house, don't you, girl?" He thought about what to call her and remembered how his mother always said not to name an animal because, as soon as you do, she's yours.

Finding the shower warm, Matthew woke Maria. She was nose to nose with the dog, sad eyes staring back at her. She scratched behind the mutt's ears, and that's all it took to form a bond.

"I see you have a new friend. What is his name?"

"It's a her, and against my mothers' sound advice, I was thinking of calling her Solidad."

"Solidad is nice. But she doesn't look like a Solidad."

"What would you suggest?"

"What is it they call South Beach?"

"SoBe? I don't know if she looks like a SoBe. Maybe a SoHo. Well, we shouldn't name her anyhow, don't you think?"

Matthew looked into the shepherd's sad brown eyes and thought of his last two dogs, Mr. Pibbs, a chow and pitt bull mix, which really belonged to his brother Sean, and then his beloved bearded collie, Nuke. When he had to put Nuke down after a long painful bout with cancer, just before leaving for UMaine, he swore he would never have a dog again. But he knew he would. He could not imagine a pain worst than losing his pal, they did everything together.

After a long, hot shower, Matthew went out to check the engine. He made some adjustments but the engine continued to sputter and backfire. He rummaged through the homeowners tools and smiled when he found the item. What life would be like without duct tape, he thought.

"You know," he said to the dog that seemed attached to his leg as he walked around the garage, "your master has left quite a collection of tools. It just doesn't make any sense. At least where I'm from, a guy wouldn't leave his tools and his dog." SoBe barked her agreement.

The engine was running but shaking like it might come unhinged from the engine block. "I'll have to get replacement parts right away, or she won't make it another couple hundred miles."

Maria had stepped into the garage. "Why don't we go back to Miami and fly home?"

"I thought about that, but . . ." Matthew was thinking of the priceless work in the bus that Maria still knew nothing about. "But I really want to get the old bus back to Maine and put it back together. I've kind of gotten attached to it."

Maria rolled her eyes and said, "I know how you are with your toys, but this is serious, Matthew."

He did feel a little guilty not telling her about the exciting, and dangerous, cargo but wanted time to think it all through. He didn't have much of a chance to do that.

They decided to get up the highway under the cover of early morning darkness. "I sure hope we find a mechanic shop or junkyard in the next town." Matthew began to close the side door to the bus when the shepherd bounded down the steps and, from five feet away, jumped high in the air to land in the center of the bus. SoBe immediately lay down on top of one of the blanket-covered duffel bags. She raised her eyebrows at Maria, and cocked her head as if to say *please.*

Maria's left eye narrowed as she pursed her lips. "Now you're in trouble, mister." Then she laughed and climbed into the passenger seat. "You and SoBe were meant for each other. But don't look to me to take care of her while you're in school. You can't keep her in the dorm, and I don't think your dad will be too pleased to have another dog at their house."

Matthew figured he would cross all those bridges when he came to them. He wrapped the loose parts with more duct tape, and the three travelers drove out of their weathered sanctuary. After more than a few dead ends, they came out on Highway 7 and drove up the road into a small sun-baked town called Carol City. The sun was rising as they pulled into Paulo's Garage and Auto Junkyard. Matthew stopped in front and opened his punctured back hatch.

A dark, short middle-aged man with a full head of oily black hair came up beside Matthew. The name tag on his blue grease-covered jumpsuit said Paulo. Without exchanging more than an *hola*, he began tinkering with the little engine. He reached in, picked out two very large slugs, and stared pointedly at Matthew. Matthew could only shrug his shoulders. Paulo walked into his shop. Matthew considered jumping back in the bus and hightailing it up the highway, but he didn't think they would get very far. He might as well put his faith in this mechanic; after all, they had not done anything wrong. Quite the contrary, they were the victims. But, he reasoned, he did not want to have to explain the Jackson files to the authorities. Surely, they would confiscate them, then where would he be. In answer to a prayer, Paulo came out and motioned for Matthew to drive the bus into the mechanic bay. Matthew exhaled a long breath.

Maria went inside the adjacent grocery and bought two colas, a bottle of water, rope, dog chow, and two dog dishes. Sensing lunch, SoBe leapt out of the bus and followed her around the corner of the building. Maria nearly stumbled over a very large dog who looked more like an old man than an old man. Not knowing SoBe's disposition with other canines, she tried to reverse directions, but it was too late. SoBe came around the corner, nearly knocking Maria over. As soon as SoBe saw the junkyard dog, her ears lowered, she bared her teeth, and she let out a deep and menacing growl while positioning herself between Maria and the beast. "Easy now, SoBe," Maria said. The oversized brown and white hushpuppy dog with big, floppy ears barely twitched. His sad eyes opened and looked up at the two intruders disturbing his slumber. SoBe stopped growling and cocked her head, her ears went up, and she trotted over for a sniff.

Her heart still racing, Maria said, "Well, isn't he something? I don't think a hurricane could upset this old boy, huh, SoBe?" She filled up one of the dog dishes with water and the other with kibble. While she was at it, she filled up the hushpuppy's dish too. SoBe consumed the bowl of food in no time, but the junkyard dog just closed his eyes.

Though Matthew knew that he could fix the bus himself with the right tools, he was glad for the help and the facilities. Besides, Matthew thought, I still have over four thousand dollars cash in the van for emergencies. He wondered if Cracker Jack anticipated Matthew dealing with events of this magnitude. Then again, he had a bank account to deal with in Boston containing six digits. He tried to imagine how he would use all that money. Prototypes came to mind.

With the help of Paulo, they found the parts the bus needed. Matthew knew the parts were not an exact match and Paulo had to force a few bolts to fit; but under the circumstances, he was in no position to argue. Matthew understood most of what the junkyard owner told Maria in Spanish – that he thought the VW bus would make it for a while, but the vibration might cause some of the bolts to loosen, so check it often.

Right now, Matthew just wanted to get back on the road. He loved an adventure, but this was getting more bizarre and dangerous by the hour. He caught Paulo staring while running his hand over the many holes.

"*Se parece el queso suizo, no*?" Matthew said, shrugging. Paulo shook his head confused and turned to Maria. She laughed and said something to Paulo that Matthew could not pick up. Paulo nodded, and then replied in quick Spanish.

"What did you say, and what did he say?"

"I said you're trying real hard with your Spanish. And he told me he has a guy that could replace the windshield in a couple hours."

Matthew stared at Paulo again, trying to ascertain if he had called the police. Maria took Matthew aside and said she didn't think so. Paulo appeared to be from the old Cuban school that taught you to mind your own business and charge double the price.

"Speaking of price, *cuanto dinero estima*?" Matthew asked. He knew he could not go wrong with that question, as it was one of the slides in his seventh grade Spanish class. Paulo took out a calculator. "*Quinientos dolares, quizas, quizas mas.*" Matthew paid him in advance and told Maria to tell him if it's more, they would settle up before they left. Maria also asked if there was somewhere close to eat, and they walked to the recommended Huddle House for breakfast.

By the time they got back from consuming some excellent Spanish omelets, the bus had a brand new windshield and though the engine sounded good, the back was a bit shaky. Where Paulo's contact found a 1967 VW bus windshield on short notice, they could not figure. And they were not inclined to ask.

"He says we don't owe him any more for the work," Maria said. In any case, Matthew gave Paulo another fifty dollars. That brought the first smile of the day to the little Cuban man's sun-baked face, revealing a few gold-crowned teeth. "*Bueno, senor, bueno. Vayan con cuidado. Dallo con Dios.*"

"May God grant you safe travel," Maria translated.

"I got that," Matthew said, with a little irritation.

Matthew shook Paulo's hand, and the little man hugged Maria like a daughter. She had that effect on men, Spanish or not, old or young. Matthew was thinking how glad he was that he had gone with his instincts and trusted the mechanic – when he heard a car drive up. He turned to see the white sedan with SHERIFF stenciled in bright gold letters blocking the VW bus. SoBe sat up in the front seat with her paws on the door and growled ever so quietly. A middle-aged deputy wearing a smartly pressed tan uniform emerged from the Sheriff's car and spoke to Paulo. Matthew could feel his eyes darting back to them. "Maybe we misjudged Paulo," Matthew whispered out of the side of his mouth.

"I don't think so."

The deputy approached Matthew. "Paulo speaks very highly of you two, but I gotta tell ya, kid, it looks like your old hippie van was on a tour of Vietnam. What's your explanation for all these holes?"

Matthew didn't think he would buy *Oh, we must have been sprayed with gravel from a passing truck,* so he tried another angle.

"They were all there when we got the bus off of an old farmer in Maine. I think his son used it for target practice."

The floppy-eared dog passed by at an inopportune time as the deputy turned and spat a big wad of chew that hit the junkyard dog in the butt. Without even a howl, he lumbered back to the side of the building. Matthew thought of a Clint Eastwood western and assumed this was a ritual of sorts between the dog and Deputy. He looked at the officer's name tag – Alonso.

"Not a chance, young man. Those bullet holes are recent from their looks. Fresh Rustoleum – you missed a few – no rust around the exposed metal," he said as he ran a finger into one and then another. "And how about the shattered windshield that old Paulo replaced? And, I'm sure there's a logical explanation for that bandage on your head?" Paulo leaned against the outside garage wall smoking and seeming not to be paying attention to the discussion.

Matthew leaned hard against the bus. He thought he would try the truth. "Well, you're not going to believe this . . ."

"Anything would be better than that last story," the deputy said as he tucked his thumbs into his holster belt.

"The bullets came from a very old double set machine gun under the camel hump of a Sopwith." As Matthew said it, he could barely believe it himself. Matthew told him the rest of the story, and luckily, Alonso was not laughing or taking out his handcuffs.

Deputy Alonso opened the door to the bus seeming to be looking for something. SoBe barked and bared her teeth. Alonso laughed but stepped back just the same. Matthew leaned in past him and gave SoBe a friendly nudge.

Alonso chuckled. "I know this dog. She's from a bad neighborhood out in the county. She doesn't like me too much. It's good that you're taking her with you. She's been hanging around that old house since we put the owners in jail."

"In jail?" Maria asked.

"Yeah, there was a methamphetamine lab at the house. Nasty drug. Anyone can cook it. The Hernandez's are a young couple with three kids all under the age of five."

"What about the kids?" Maria asked.

"Social services, I'm afraid."

"I thought it was a bit unusual that the kitchen looked like my school chemistry lab," Matthew interjected.

"We'd been watching the house, hell, the whole neighborhood for quite some time. You could not have picked a town in all of Dade County with more crime." He looked at Paulo and said, "Except maybe here in Carol City. One of the guys down at the department was supposed to send the dog catcher, so you saved him a trip." He reached in to pet SoBe, who barred her teeth and growled. Alonso pulled his hand back and continued to look around the door frame. He felt along tears in the side of the seat.

Matthew was about to protest, worried that he might find the smaller caliber slugs from the Miami Beach affair, or worse – Jackson's .45 automatic.

The deputy dug his pocketknife into the seat and pulled out two slugs. "Looks like you escaped the grim reaper by inches. Yep, we dug this same caliber out of other cars along the highway. The slugs are from a Vickers 303 Machine

Gun manufactured about 1910, which was about the time the Sopwith Aviation Company launched. I just looked this up yesterday at the library. Aviation is sort of a thing for me. Did you know they made over 2,000 planes for Britain? That was quite a flying machine. Could spin and turn on a dime."

"That's how he got back on my tail so fast," Matthew said. "So you believe me?"

"I gotta tell ya, had I had not seen that relic myself and then you came along and told me the story, I would have locked you up and thrown away the key," he said, smiling and rubbing his chin. "We were following the Sopwith as it chased you down. Then we lost you south of the crack house. We followed the nut after he flew under the bridge, which was either good flying or pure damn luck. We chased him about fifty miles up the coast, and then he disappeared." He frowned. "All toll he caused four accidents and one fatality . . ."

Maria gasped, "Oh no!"

The deputy continued. "Three of the injured and the deceased were hit by this same caliber of bullet. It's amazing the others, and you, weren't killed. This bullet could put a hole the size of an orange into a man. From the looks of your Volkswagen bug . . ."

"Bus."

"Right, bus. Anyhow, there must be ten rounds or more in your bus and you weren't hit. Someone upstairs is looking out for you."

Matthew held his breath as Alonso walked around the bus; he knew what was coming next.

"Strange. Anything else you want to tell me?"

Matthew politely declined and filled out a police report while the deputy talked in Spanish to Maria and Paulo. Their laughter irritated Matthew because when they spoke in a quick slanged Spanish he couldn't follow the conversation. The men seemed to be quite enamored with Maria. *But who isn't,* he thought.

The deputy said he would be in contact. Matthew was amazed he didn't ask to search the bus. He must have come to the correct conclusion that they were simply innocent victims of a lunatic who thought he was a WWI flying ace. "Any ideas about who would own a rare plane like that?" Matthew asked.

"I hate to speculate, but we narrowed it down to three possibilities in southern Florida. Two are museums, and I know that neither one would have a plane that was sky worthy."

"And the third?"

"I'll drop you a line in a week or so to let you know how that one checks out. Like most of this mess, it makes no sense. I figure you were in the wrong place at the wrong time, but if my hunch is right, then we may need you kids to come back down here as witnesses."

Once back on the road, Maria said, "You know, that psycho was trying to kill us, and someone else was killed. Why? Because we saw what happened to Cracker Jack?"

"I don't know, I just don't know, but . . . ," Matthew didn't continue. He wished Alonso had told him the name of his suspect.

CHAPTER 29

March 18, 1995 6:00 p.m.

Corner

MATTHEW KNEW, DESPITE his cargo, that he needed to focus his attention on getting Maria back to Maine safe and sound. He now knew he should have accepted his uncle's offer to fly them and the cargo back to Boston. He looked over as she shook her pretty head to rearrange her hair. She often complained it took all day for her hair to dry on its own. They were an hour north of Carol City and the highway became more congested with other spring breakers heading back north.

"What were you going to say earlier, Matthew? You keep starting thoughts, and then you stop. I can always tell when you're keeping something from me. You've been evasive since your uncle's house."

Matthew didn't answer, and thankfully she let it go. He was already protective, maybe obsessed with what was placed in his care by Cracker Jack or his friend Marcos, who Matthew was sure was more than a Shell station employee. Matthew felt a heavy but *not* unwelcome weight on his shoulders. What really bothered him was keeping something so big from Maria. They had been each other's confidantes for many years with a trust that far exceeded friendship. His father said that through life you will be able to count your true friends on one hand. No matter what happened, Maria would be there for me, he thought. Besides family and Floyd, his good friend the decathlete back at UMaine, how many people fit that mold? Cracker Jack wanted him to keep his research secret, to bring in a small mastermind group of his closest confidants. On the other hand, the more Maria knew the more she would be in danger. He decided it wasn't fair not to give her the choice of being more involved.

"Penny for your thoughts?" Maria asked.

"What?"

"I know you're worried. We're in this together, and we'll be just fine."

Matthew smiled. He saw a sign for Daytona – 30 miles – and a rest area. "Let's check on the Doublemint twins." He pulled into the rest area and parked between two tractor-trailers. Maria went to the restroom while he dialed from a payphone and listened to Donna's aunt for a few minutes. He slammed the phone down. As he stormed back to the bus, he nearly ran into two Middle Eastern men. Something about the way they looked at him that made his skin crawl. He looked over his shoulder after a dozen steps; one man was leaning against a pole while the other talked on the phone. They were both staring at him. He realized he was now racial profiling because of the men he saw in Miami Beach. He didn't think these were the men, but maybe they were. Maybe they were only staring at him because he had nearly run one of them over in his angry haste. He looked around; there were plenty of travelers and two highway patrol cars. He then saw two black SUV Suburbans parked not ten feet from the entrance to the bathrooms. There were at least six men standing around the vehicles. Then two more came out of the building. Their swagger, and the way they studied the perimeter as if they were on guard, reminded him of the FBI agents; and, reminded him of the men that turned out not to be FBI.

Matthew took a few steps toward the restrooms when he saw Maria come out. He went back to the bus and sat on the edge in front of the cargo.

Maria chuckled and said, "You and SoBe look like two cats that swallowed the canaries."

Matthew kept an eye on the men by the SUV. He was sure a few of them were looking at him. He said, "I have something to show you." He considered waiting until later but then thought what the heck. He indicated the uncovered duffel bags with a ceremonious wave of his hand.

"Where on earth did those things come from?"

"From Cracker Jack. He must've had Marcos put them in the bus while we were in the diner."

Her hands were on her hips. "How long have you known these were here?" Not waiting for an answer, she added, "And when did you plan to let me in on the big secret?"

"At mile marker 126."

"Smart ass. What's in them?"

"Let's get back on the road, and I'll give you all the details," Matthew said hopefully.

He shut the door and she reluctantly got into the bus. As they drove out of the parking lot, he filled her in on the few things she didn't know since leaving Miami Beach.

"So really, Marcos, you, me, and your Uncle Carl are the only ones who know anything about these?"

"And perhaps whoever is trying to kill us."

She crawled into the back and unzipped the bag closest to her. She inspected the contents carefully and then moved to the next and the next. She commented to herself on the findings in Spanish and English. Matthew went through each item with her, explaining to the best of his knowledge its importance. He drove in silence for quite some time while Maria scanned through a few of the journals and diaries. He was glad he had put the pouch holding the gun under the seat.

"This really changes things, doesn't it?" she asked as she organized the bags with care and covered them again with blankets. SoBe crawled up on top of the blankets and lay with his head on his paws. "Why didn't you tell me?"

"I'm sorry. I wasn't thinking right. I thought the less you knew, the safer you would be. Now I'm seeing bad guys at every corner. All of this has put you in jeopardy. You could have been killed. Twice. Maybe we should turn it in to the authorities." He was fishing for her reaction. She returned to her seat but still didn't look directly at him. She must be mad. "You know, this could be the chance of a lifetime. I could live the rest of my life and never come across something with such global and universal power, something that can have a positive affect on every aspect of humanity, to be part of history and an important part of the future. I want to make a definitive mark. The Jacksons have given me that opportunity."

Maria said something in Spanish about the importance of honesty. She crossed her arms. "You're really thinking of moving forward with his research, aren't you?"

"Yes."

He looked up at her expectantly. She surprised him with a disarming smile. She could not look more beautiful. He vowed he would not keep anything from her ever again.

"Good!" She threw her arms around his neck as he struggled to keep the bus on the road. "Let's get back to Maine so you can get to work on saving the world!"

Her approval and support was essential and clinched the decision in his mind. He would protect the Jacksons work against all odds. He scanned his mirrors for the Middle Easterners, then slowed down to see if anyone was following. Nothing. He had a feeling the paranoia had just begun.

"What about Donna and Darma?"

"I spoke to the aunt – she was pretty damn rude to say the least. She bought them plane tickets and said that if I wanted any money from them or her to sue her."

"You have got to be kidding!" she then said something in Spanish that was anything but complimentary about the twin blondes.

As they headed up the highway, Maria said. "I was so upset about Cracker Jack that it overshadowed how excited I was about his inventions and how they fit you so perfectly. I was disappointed you wouldn't be able to work with him. Now in a macabre sort of way, you can. I've always known you're a genius, but to have someone like Tremont Jackson entrust all this to you, well, it's beyond amazing. What a strange twist of fate!"

"Perhaps it wasn't a coincidence that we met him," Matthew said, frowning.

"Somehow God picked you to receive all of Cameron Jackson's research and carry on where he left off. I could not be prouder. I just love you!"

Matthew blushed and nearly ran off the road as she kissed him. When he recovered, he said, "I don't know about all of this being divine providence. I feel we've been manipulated into these events. Granted, it seems impossible, especially since we made a last minute decision to head south." He didn't mention his suspicions about Estebanez and his Uncle Carl. "Well, no matter how this all came about, I can't wait to dig in back at UMaine. I don't know how I'll go to class or do anything else."

"You'll manage. Next year I'll be there to help you. I'll be your lab assistant," she offered.

"Lab rat more than likely," he said, and she rewarded him with a solid knuckle in the shoulder.

"And this summer you can work twenty-four-seven on the research."

Matthew sobered a bit and said, "What about the danger? You heard Deputy Alonso. It's a miracle we're alive."

Maria stretched her arms. "We're alive because it's our destiny."

It was after midnight, the traffic was light and there was no sign of black SUVs or T-Birds as their conversation turned more intimate. Once again, it seemed that they had aged a decade over the last few days, and now they looked at the future in a whole new light. Matthew told her he liked how she viewed their destiny together. That she was the most amazing girl in the world.

"I've known we were meant to be together since we connected at Willow Run," she said.

That revelation struck a chord in Matthew. She rarely mentioned that day and never talked about her mother's death. They remained quiet, deep in their own thoughts.

Maria broke the silence, "I've always felt like a dimwit around you."

"I don't know why. I can talk to you about my research, and you actually listen. When I'm boring everyone else with my inventions, you stay with me even on the most challenging hypotheses."

"I fake it."

Matthew looked at her with raised eyebrows.

"That's all I fake." They both laughed.

"Not to mention you make me laugh, and you motivate me when I'm feeling down," he added.

"If you're about to ask me to marry you, the answer is probably, but you'll have to ask Papa first."

"If we marry before you're thirty, we would have to elope and live on the other side of the world. At least until we produce grandchildren."

"This is true," she said, hugging her knees to her chest. "You understand my father well. But do you really think he would let me out of the house with his blessing – even at thirty?"

Maria became more serious; he could tell she liked talking about their future together. "You're the only one that understands my interest in criminology and forensics. I'm not that great in science and math, but you've really helped me get through it. I'm really going to need you when I hit organic chem."

"Ah, now I see the reason you keep me around. I have organic chem next semester. Who's going to help me?"

"You could teach the class."

"So you've decided on forensics then."

"At least for now."

"You really will be a lab rat. I read that the University won a grant to underwrite a molecular forensics lab and I heard they'll complete it by the time you start in the fall.

"I know. Otherwise I would have to go to Cal State." She looked for a reaction and smiled when he displayed a shocked expression.

"I'll focus my undergraduate studies on criminal psychology and minor in forensic science. I guess I'm not really interested in the medical angle as much as the way forensic investigation relates to the criminal mind."

Matthew grinned.

"What?"

"Nothing."

While paying for gas in Jacksonville, Matthew caught the eye of a large man in a black suit coming out of the restroom. Matthew felt sure he was the one following them in the black SUV. Again, he recognized the distinct mannerism that was similar to the men in Miami Beach, Cue Ball and his partner in particular, who he believed shot Cracker Jack. The man seemed to pick up his pace as Matthew walked toward the bus. As he drove the VW out of the parking lot, he could see the man at a run in the rear view mirror. Matthew knew he was heading toward a black Suburban, one of *the* black Suburbans. Matthew didn't mention it to Maria, as they both had just begun to relax. He would keep watching his rear view mirror. As he pulled out into traffic on I-95, he saw *the* T-Bird pulled over on the side of the road. "What's the chance of that?"

"What?"

"Look at that car."

"Another old car. So what?"

"Not just any old car. Do you remember when we first broke down, and I mentioned a mint condition white T-Bird with a red roof that I'd seen in South Carolina?"

"Was that before or after your temper tantrum?"

His grumble attested to how he felt about her bringing up the embarrassing memory of his temporary insanity on the beach. This was only second to how he felt about Bubba besting him at the truckstop. "After. Just before we met Cracker Jack. Anyhow, that's the car. The very same car."

"What makes you think so?"

"It's a guy thing. But trust me, it's the same. Plus, the Arab leaning up against it looks like one of the same guys I saw in the diner."

"You shouldn't stereotype. You can't be sure he's Arab."

"He's Arab. And they're following us. I'm sure of it."

He watched the T-Bird in his rear view mirror. He got a look at one of the two men. It *was* one of the Middle Eastern men from the diner in Miami Beach. The T-Bird pulled into traffic a few cars behind them. Farther back, he could see the black Suburban. He cussed under his breath.

Maria studied the map. "We can be back in Boston by three tomorrow if we drive all night."

"Let's shoot for that. I know we could use the rest, but I'll feel a lot better when we cross the Maine state line."

They drove out of Jacksonville and into Georgia. He was extra careful to keep the speed down so as not to attract attention. He also was not sure the makeshift jerry-rigged engine patch would hold. As instructed by Paulo, Matthew had tightened the loose bolts at the rest stop.

Deputy Alanso's last words rang in Matthew's head: "You two kids must have angels watching over you." Matthew said a quiet prayer. Lord, keep those angels close by for another day, and we'll be home free.

"It can't be," Matthew muttered half to himself as the blue and white lights came after them like a bat out of hell. He shook his head in disgust as he looked up and recognized the large green sign. He hit both hands hard on the steering wheel, waking Maria.

"What is it?"

"Brunswick-freaking-Georgia! This is the same damn area we were stopped on the way down!"

"What's the chance of that?" Maria looked at her watch. "It's about the same time too. Wouldn't it be funny if it was – what did you call him?"

"Boss Hog." He maneuvered the shot-up old VW bus over to the side of the highway. "And no, that would not be funny." The police car pulled in behind him. In the mirror, he could see bright lights and the blur of a short, wide cop writing down his license plate number. The officer ran his hand along the side of the bus as he approached the driver.

"I don't believe it!" Matthew exclaimed, "It's a *Dukes of Hazard* rerun."

"No possible way," Maria said, looking out through the back of the bus. "Maybe this is fate too? Maybe you should tell him about the guys following us?"

"Like he would believe me? I should have taken back roads."

Boss Hog first looked into the back seat, then over at Maria who waved half heartily, and then he leaned in the driver's side window. The familiar chewing tobacco odor surrounded Matthew's head, and like before, he felt nauseated.

"Well, well, well. If it ain't my hippies on their way back to Woodstock. Where's them twins and where did-ja get the dog?"

"They decided to fly back, and SoBe was a stray."

"Can't say I blame them. And ya can never go wrong with a good hound dog." Strangely, SoBe lay with her head on her paws without even a growl. "Sounds like the twins got themselves some sense along with a sunburn on their lily white skin." He turned and spat. "You didn't pick up a load of mari-ju-ana for all of your college buddies, did-ja?"

"No, sir." Matthew wanted to say that he had seen on *60 Minutes* where the poor Georgia cotton and tobacco farmers, he felt sure were Boss Hog's kin, had gone into that business. But he decided against it.

Hog looked over Matthew's shoulder. Matthew held his breath. Hog said, "Whacha got under them there blankets?"

Matthew had already planned a reply, "Just our luggage and some research materials for school." As he said it, he didn't think it was very convincing. His brother had said that Matthew might as well tell the truth because he couldn't lie if his life depended on it. It was true, he thought, as if there was something wrong with that.

"Mind if I take a look?" Boss Hog asked. He walked around to the other side of the bus and without waiting for an answer opened the side door.

Matthew turned and watched him as Boss Hog said a few dog-talk things to SoBe and scratched behind his ears. Then, much to Matthew's surprise, Sobe slid off the top of the blankets.

Boss Hog threw back the blankets and unzipped a couple of the duffel bags. "Looks like study materials all right. What did you say you were studying in school?"

"Physics, quantum physics."

As if Matthew had said hunting and fishing, Boss Hog said, "That's good, that's good," and closed the side door walking back around to the drivers side window.

"What've you done to your head?"

Matthew touched the scratches where earlier Maria had removed the dressing and covered the area with an antibacterial. "It's nothing. Just something I ran into down in Miami."

"Shaw kid. And I'm Santa Claus."

Matthew heard Maria say under her breath that he sure had the belly for it; all he needed was the beard and the suit. Matthew gave her a reproachful look to hide his desire to laugh aloud. Whether the deputy heard, he could not tell.

"Step out of the van, young fella. I want ya to take a look at something with me."

Matthew followed the Sheriff's deputy around the bus as he pointed out bullet holes one by one. "Now you want to explain to me what happened here and to your head?"

Matthew considered his answer carefully. "We literally drove through two shootouts and were innocent bystanders."

"I would say that's one of the wildest turkey tales I've heard in a long time." He wiped a drip of chew from his face. "But I reckon it could be true. You have the bullet holes to prove it, and from what I understand, there's a pile of crazy folks with guns down there. Bunch a Cubies runnin' them Eyetalians and Jews back to New York."

"I appreciate your believing me, Sheriff."

The deputy seemed to like being called Sheriff. He hoisted his belt, which was to no avail as his large paunch pushed it right back under where it disappeared again. "Well, son, truth be known, a fella with the Florida highway patrol sent a bulletin explaining the whole thing – your van and license plate were listed. I was watching for ya. There's something on the news about the shootout at Miami Beach, probably had somethin' to do with drug runners."

"Did it say anything about anyone being killed?"

"I don't remember nothin' about any fatalities on that report. As to the larger holes in your van . . ."

Matthew held his breath.

" . . . It seems a nutcase in a World War One plane sent a bunch a folks to the hospital, and on *that* report it said one gal was killed." The deputy opened the door for Matthew. "I can't see how the two situations are related. You?"

"Yes, sir, I mean no, sir. Just unlucky, I suppose."

"Like runnin' into me twice in one trip?" he asked rhetorically, laughed, and then wiped spit from his chin. "So get on in your hippie van and get yourself back to the safety of your college dorm." The deputy walked away muttering, "Damndest thing I've seen in a month of Sundays."

When he got to his cruiser, he turned back with his thumb pointing over his shoulder and said, "You know those folks?"

Matthew looked past the deputy. Pulled off on the side of the highway, down about half the length of a football field, was a black Suburban. "No, but if you don't mind, could you check on them? They've been driving erratically."

"What did you tell him?" Maria asked when he got back in the bus.

"Pretty much the truth."

"Be that a lesson to ya, whipper-snapper," she said, with a twang.

As Matthew pulled back out onto I-95 heading north, the black Suburban pulled out as well. Matthew watched in his rear view mirror as the deputy immediately flagged the Suburban down and motioned for him to pull over. Matthew smiled, but the joy was short-lived, he noticed another car.

"There it is again."

"What?"

"The T-Bird."

Once in South Carolina, near Charleston, the traffic thinned, and he did not see either vehicle. But when they drove into the massive parking lot of South of the Border, Matthew noticed a black Suburban pulled in four cars behind him and parked on the other side of the lot. He scanned his mirrors looking east and west, but the white T-Bird and the second Suburban were not in sight. The bus had enough gas to make it another hundred miles or more. But just as he began to turn the ignition, he saw him. "Sit tight, Maria, and keep the doors locked. I'll be right back."

"What is it?" When he didn't answer, she yelled at the closed window, "Be careful!"

Matthew approached the man who had waved to him at the side of the building. An awful lot of things are repeating themselves on this trip, Matthew thought, shaking his head. As he approached Estebanez, Matthew put both hands palm up in front of him and said, "You have a lot of splainin' to do, Lucy."

"You're going to have to trust me, kid. We've been keeping an eye on you and . . ."

"We?" Matthew asked. "I feel like my whole life has been scripted!"

Estebanez gave Matthew that familiar warm Dutch uncle smile and said, "We only have a few minutes. If you don't hear from me for a while, just know we'll be there when you need us for support, money, or whatever you need to move the project forward."

"I knew you were mixed up in all of this. How are you connected to the Jacksons? Are you related to Marcos? Is my uncle in on this too?"

"All in good time, son. We'll come to you. When you need us."

"We've nearly been killed! Twice. Why should I trust you?"

"You've been able to trust me all these years. You know the product is priceless and right up your alley. Your parents trust me. And how could you not trust this face?"

Matthew cocked his head and raised his eyebrows.

"Well, at least your mother does. If for no other reason, I know you would do it for the Jacksons. And think about it, it's me or them, kid." He nodded his head toward the black Suburban.

"Do you know who they are?"

"Just a suspicion as to who they work for. We know some of the guys in the SUVs . . ."

"So there's more than one?"

"They are former US, British, and Soviet intelligence officers."

"You've got to be kidding."

"I wish I were. Who exactly is in the T-Bird remains to be seen. But I suspect that they are linked to a terrorist by the name of bin Taliffan."

"Terrorist! Terrorists?"

"The worst kind – he's a terrorist with money and power. Taliffan is the leader of an influential organization that has loosely attached itself to OPEC called Hafiz-OPEC Saumba Shokran. OPEC denies any connection. The fact that the terrorists meet in the basement of 93 Obere Donaustrasse Street, seems to escape them."

Matthew was doing his best to connect the dots as Estebanez threw in more pieces to the puzzle.

"You also have admirers in more than one U.S. government division . . ."

"Great."

"You won't have to worry about them. Their primary concern is for your safety, but only because they believe you have Dr. Jackson's research. They want to keep the prize and reap the long-term benefits. If you're contacted by anyone, especially an investigator named Flannigan, he's safe enough but don't tell him anything. The less they know, the better."

"Who do you work for?"

"Someone making sure you're successful and nobody stands in your way."

"Who?"

"Sorry, that's all I can tell you, kid."

"That's not fair, Mr. E."

"When the time is right, Matthew, I will fill in all the details. Until then, you need to trust me."

"Not good enough."

Estebanez stared into Matthew's eyes for a long moment then said quietly, "Everything you and I – and others – have worked on these last years boil down to what we do now. Matthew, this is one of the few things I've done in my life where I have a very personal stake in its outcome. Frankly, I'm doing a lousy job." He rubbed his tired eyes and cleared his throat.

Matthew heard the doors of the Suburban slam and then saw four men heading in their direction. Estebanez took Matthew by the elbow and led him around the building just as sirens sounded and half a dozen state patrol cars rushed into the parking lot to block the path of the men.

Matthew choked out, "How did . . . I mean, where did they . . . ?"

Estebanez took Matthew's arm firmly and said, "You better get going. We'll be in touch." When Matthew resisted, Estebanez gave him a slight push, once and then again, and said, "Look, get the hell out of here before it's too late!"

Matthew made his way back to the bus the long way around the buildings. Maria was not there and SoBe was pawing at the window. He stood on the edge of panic for a moment. Then Maria came running up behind him. Matthew had the bus in gear before she closed her door.

"I heard the police sirens and came looking for you. I couldn't find you! When police cars were racing into the parking lot, I got so scared. Where were you?"

"I'll tell you in a minute, we've got to get out of here!"

When they were a dozen or more miles up the road and Matthew didn't see a single car in his mirrors, he said, "You're not going to believe who was there."

"Mr. Estebanez?" she guessed.

"I don't know what he knows, and I really don't know where he stands on all of this. I think we can trust him. Up to a point, that is."

"What do you mean?"

"It's confusing. But just as the goons from the SUV were about to approach us, the cavalry shows up. I shouldn't have left you alone."

"It's not that. I thought something had happened to you." He heard tears in her voice. "Why do you think the police went after them?"

"Maybe our old friend Boss Hog checked them out after he let them go. Or maybe Mr. E choreographed the impeccable timing. We're not completely in the clear. The T-bird is still behind us."

"I guess you were right about the Arabs."

Matthew laughed. "So now they're Arabs, Miss Politically-correct."

"This is getting complicated," Maria said. "Let's argue about the semantics later."

A few miles later, looking in the mirror and cussing, Matthew gave up on the idea of trying to lose the T-Bird. Once again, he regretted not taking advantage of Uncle Carl's offer to ship them and the cargo back to Maine. After all, Cracker Jack had given him the means to pay for it! Idiot, he thought, idiot.

The bus was running hot pushing sixty so he cut her back to fifty. "Our best defense will be trying to stay in busy traffic and crowded gas stations." He looked at the desolate tree-lined highway ahead and then again in the rear view mirror at the empty road behind.

CHAPTER 30

March 19, 1995

Target

WHILE MATTHEW AND Maria ventured through the Carolinas, it was early morning in Vienna, Austria.

The organization most westerners believed to be a front for terrorism, called Hafiz-OPEC Saumba Shokran, meaning *Protectors of OPEC Stability and Longevity,* convened in the basement of the heavily guarded OPEC building.

Their meeting was underway when two formidable Cobra soldiers escorted Senator Wayne Green and former FBI agent John Lomax into the room. Lomax and the Senator took their usual seats near the door.

The dynamics of the once secret group had changed dramatically over the years. Lomax knew that though he himself was serving in Vietnam, the Senator, then the CEO of one of the major American oil companies had attended these meetings as far back as the middle sixties. Back then Hafiz-OPEC's half dozen members were visionaries – elder statesmen and oil industry leaders. The seventies invited a conflict of ideals, but under the leadership of the moderate then assistant secretary general of OPEC, Sheik Mohammed bin Bandar, it remained focused on business, diplomacy, and politics.

Lomax had spent ten years after Vietnam as a field agent for the FBI and then with the Secret Service served on the presidential detail for five years. It was during his tenure with President Reagan that he met Senator Green of Texas. He then left the Secret Service and for the last decade his paychecks have come from a bank account called The Fund which he knew originated from the group simply known as The Seven Sisters, the seven leading USA-owned petroleum companies.

Following the apparent assassination of the moderate leader of Hafiz-OPEC, Sheik Mohammed bin Bandar, the new self-appointed leadership by the bin Taliffan brothers catered toward radical Islamic fundamentalism. A document purported to have been smuggled out of 93 Obere Donaustrasse Street in 1990 and sold to a British news agency allegedly revealed much about the elite Islamic society and indicted many prominent Middle Eastern families. One paragraph stated their mission: *To assure Islamic world dominance and the destruction of western ideals and infrastructure.* The non-Muslim OPEC members were not pleased, especially Venezuela, the country that initiated the cartel in 1960. Publicly, OPEC and their Arab membership governments, as well as the royal Saudi family, denounced any involvement with the extremist behavior.

Lomax looked around the room and noted that the current membership was half the age of their predecessors and he knew they were hand picked by the now deceased Omar bin Taliffan. Many believed the eldest bin Taliffan brother's death was an assassination ordered by either the CIA or British MI6. Others believed the OPEC leadership ordered the assassination. Either way, Lomax mused, it led to Omar being succeeded by his extreme younger brother Bahir bin Taliffan. Increasingly, those who disagreed with either bin Taliffan met with some unfortunate accident.

Lomax glanced down at a familiar face to Bahir's left, Osama bin Laden. After Omar's death, bin Laden swore revenge against the Western infidels. But, Lomax thought ruefully, bin Laden was always swearing revenge against the West.

When Bahir bin Taliffan, now the patriarch of the bin Taliffan Construction Empire, took over as self-proclaimed chairman of the radical group, he made it no secret that his dead brother's economic goals were also his. Lomax was at that first meeting. Bahir said that he would see the Hafiz-OPEC Saumba Shokran charter upheld as the group continued to do what OPEC could not due in part to a fragmented membership including African and South American countries. His objective along with the death of Americans and other westerners was to protect Middle Eastern energy dominance.

Lomax noted a subtle and contradictory difference among the Haviz-OPEC representatives. Today only bin Laden was dressed in traditional Arab robes. Lomax knew that like their leader, most were educated in American or British colleges and their clothing reflected a contemporary style.

Senator Green fiddled impatiently with a pen and began to push his chair back. Lomax put a hand on his shoulder, and whispered, "You don't want to interrupt Bahir bin Taliffan while he's in private conversation with bin Laden. Be patient." The Senator gave Lomax an angry look but took his seat and kept quiet.

Lomax had a passable understanding of Farsi and Arabic and listened as the young men discussed the fate of Tremont Jackson and the energy research. There was news about a possible Jackson confederate: a first-year college student.

Bahir placed his hands on the solid marble boardroom table and leaned toward the man closest to his right. "So is it done?" he asked Mahmoud, his head of security who was also one of his fifteen brothers. Their other brothers, all born in Yemen and schooled in the United States, worked in the family construction business. "And do we have the research in our possession?" Bahir asked.

Mahmoud said, "Yes, it is done. But, we were not responsible for what happened to Tremont Jackson. And unfortunately we are still not sure of the whereabouts of the research."

"Not sure?"

"We are following a lead."

"I read your report," Bahir said with a hint of anger. He stood and addressed the full boardroom. "It is preposterous that we can control the price of oil, eliminate competition, and support the largest Islamic freedom fighter networks in the world, but it took us years to locate his research. Now am I to understand that we are chasing a boy up the eastern coast of the United States? Who is he? And what is the probability he has the research?"

Lomax had read the U.S. State Departments file on Mahmoud and knew he was a very dangerous character and not easily intimidated. He was a former intelligence officer with the *Mabahith* – the Saudi secret police – and for the past decade had served as the group's full-time head of security. Mahmoud stood and walked to the far wall. The projector came to life and broadcast a recent video taken of a young man and woman talking with Tremont Jackson.

"This was about fifteen minutes before the shooting," Mahmoud said. "The young person on the left is Matthew Eaton; the young lady in the middle is Maria Valdeorras."

"How long have you known about them?"

"Once we made the connection between the Jacksons and a merchant by the name of Estebanez, we began keeping intelligence on anyone he contacted. Until this week, our suspicions were only conjectures."

"And those suspicions?"

"Through the ex-CIA agent Estebanez – "

"CIA? I thought you said he was a merchant?"

"We just learned of his CIA involvement. It appears the Jacksons were grooming young Eaton to one day work with them."

"A contingency plan?"

"It seems so."

"Ah. One of the reasons we have so many wives is to have many offspring to ensure the future of our work. Inshallah, Inshallah, if Allah wills." He looked at his two American guests. "What, you thought it was the sex?" The room erupted in laughter. "Please proceed, my brother."

Mahmoud was clearly not amused. "We followed the elusive Mr. Estebanez, or Zebo as he is better known around intelligence communities, to a small town in Maine and came upon a local private detective who was investigating Estebanez." He looked down at his notes, "Fazio, Joe Fazio. We retrieved a copy of the hard drive from his computer only to be attacked by another former agent, DelGercio."

"DelGercio? What, are we dealing with the Sicilian Mafia again?" Bahir asked with a chuckle.

"Ironically, he's a former CIA NOC. who appears to have been hired to keep an eye on the Jacksons and anyone involved with them." He turned and glared at Lomax and the Senator.

Lomax raised his hands in defense and said, "I know DelGercio. We had no idea he was also working with the American petroleum industry. I'll look into it."

Mahmoud's eyes narrowed and said, "I never said he was working with one or more of The Seven Sisters."

Lomax, also not easily intimidated, smiled, cocked an eyebrow, and shrugged.

Mahmoud continued, "It is even more interesting, Mr. Lomax, that the boy is Sean Eaton's brother." He crossed his arms with a look of satisfaction as if he were a cat that just cornered an allusive mouse.

The room grew quiet hearing the familiar name.

Now Lomax was clearly surprised. He leaned back and clasped his hands behind his Cowboys baseball cap. "Now *that* is very interesting. The plot thickens."

Senator Green, his hair gone silver and weight out of control since their last visit, leaned over and whispered to Lomax that it was time to leave.

Bahir interrupted them. "Would you two care to bring us in on your discussion? How is Sean's sibling involved in all of this? Is Sean working against us?"

Senator Green fidgeted in his seat more than usual. "I wouldn't say he's working for you or against you."

Lomax gave the Senator a long stare and wondered what the Senator knew that he didn't. Lomax said, "Sean works for Sean, your eminence."

Senator Green cleared his throat and shuffled some papers. "We'll have to investigate this further when we return to the States. I don't mind telling you this is all going outside of what my constituents and I would deem appropriate. But I'll look into it."

"There is no time," Mahmoud said. "As we speak, there is a race to retrieve the research."

"Who do we have in the U.S.?" Bahir asked.

"Our very best." This was the first time Mahmoud exhibited the hint of a grin.

"Our cousins Ahmed and Saleh? Ah, I assumed that was Ahmed charging my American Express. Tell me of their progress."

"They lost Eaton only hours ago in the Carolinas. It appears DelGercio and his team is also in pursuit along with others, perhaps the FBI."

Senator Green cussed and said, "Taliffan, this is unacceptable. If further attention should be brought to the Jacksons by something happening to these young people, the investigations by the FBI and, worse yet, the press could be detrimental to our relationship, not to mention my position in the Senate and as chairperson on the Energy Commission."

Mahmoud responded, "We will take care of it. Saleh and Ahmed are our most capable and well trained. You might remember they were the two Cobra guards you first met in '83."

"I remember, and I mean no disrespect, but there is a lot at stake here. Letting the research fall into the wrong hands is not an option," Senator Green said.

Bahir returned his attention to Mahmoud. "So you must believe that Sean's brother has the research? "You will of course do whatever it takes." He stood and stretched his imposing frame forward toward his brother. He didn't have to say, or *else.*

The videotape resumed. What came next caught everyone's attention. The camera shook, and only pavement showed on the screen. When the camera stabilized, they saw Tremont fall backwards grabbing at his chest as bright red blotches appeared and the film ended.

Someone turned the lights up and Bahir waved a dismissive hand at Lomax and the Senator. "Thank you for being here." The doors opened, and two Cobra guards stood at attention.

Senator Green did not get up. Instead, he seemed to be mustering his resolve. He finally said, "I'm afraid you have gone too far, Prince Taliffan."

John Lomax winced and kept his seat.

"We will have to reconsider our relationship," the politician continued.

Lomax put a hand on the politician's shoulder and said, "Senator," but the Senator brushed it off and began packing his yellow pad and pen into his briefcase.

The Senator raised his voice. "You have in no uncertain terms admitted to conspiring with known terrorists!" He did not dare look into bin Laden's direction. ". . . to terrorize U.S. citizens. Are you mad?" He now seemed to be talking to himself. "And to have agents in our country tracking down U.S. citizens?"

Mahmoud was now standing behind the Senator. He pulled a small gun from his robe and twisted a silencer onto the end while the politician talked.

Lomax slid his chair back and stepped away from the Senator. He knew he had two choices, he could easily disarm Mahmoud and then never leave this room alive, or let the cards fall where they may. The men closest to the assassin had already stood and moved toward the corners of the room.

The Senator appeared oblivious. Mahmoud placed the muzzle against the bottom of his neck under the occipital bone to minimize bone and blood dispersal. With his other hand, he threw a gray vinyl bag over the Senator's head and pulled the trigger. A small amount of blood splattered across the marble table in a sunburst design.

Bahir looked disgusted. "Clean up this mess." He shifted his attention. "Mr. Lomax?"

"This will be a little hard to explain. I only hope you have a plan. As for me, I wasn't here. Though I disagree with your tactics, this will not change the course for my associates or me." He paused and looked around the room. He knew his life was momentarily as fragile as a caterpillar underfoot.

Trying to appear confident, Lomax continued, "I trust our arrangement has not changed? When we obtain Jackson's research, your people will assist in financing product development, and we will share equally in the profits."

Lomax looked deep into Bahir's eyes. He seemed to be considering Lomax's fate. Lomax's mouth twisted in a grin. "In the meantime, together we will continue to control prices and maintain the demand for both oil and whatever this is that Jackson discovered. Good." Lomax adjusted his baseball cap and picked up his worn satchel. "I'll contact Sean when I get back and talk to him about the connection with his brother. I'm as perplexed as you. And I'll let you know what I can find out about DelGercio, and who he's working with. I'm concerned about the FBI closing in. They were all over Miami when all these went down."

Bahir nodded and waved a hand in dismissal.

After Lomax departed, Bahir bin Taliffan turned his back to the group. Most of them had trained in either their own country's military or an outside paramilitary camp – what the West would call terrorist training camps – and they didn't seem to be fazed by the high profile Senator's head lying in a pool of his blood on the table in front of them. Bahir asked Mahmoud, "You are sure our cousins didn't pull the trigger in Miami?"

"I am sure. Not that they would have hesitated if we had obtained the research, but no, we had nothing to do with the hit on this Jackson."

While the Cobra guards placed the Senator on a gurney and rolled him out of the room, Bahir flipped through some notes. "I had a charge on March 14 to my American Express for 131,000 Ryal. That's 35,000 U.S. dollars from a . . . Calvin's Classic Cars?"

Mahmoud stepped aside as two women wearing full black Niqab veils with only their eyes showing began cleaning up the blood. Mahmoud scrunched his face and lifted his hands palms up in resignation.

Bahir shook his head. "Ahmed."

Mahmoud said, "He felt that a vintage car would be less suspected, that he would blend in. I argued that a white, 1950s Thunderbird with a red convertible top would be easily identifiable. But you know Ahmed."

Bahir looked at his cousin Osama, shrugged his shoulders, and said, "Is this how you are training our family members in your camps, cousin?"

Osama reminded him that Ahmed schooled at Princeton. Since then, he had a propensity toward Western capitalism. His training in Austria with EKO Cobra did not help matters any. He kept a collection of automobiles at his family home in Salzburg. But, bin Laden believed their cousin Saleh would keep Ahmed focused. He had the heart and instincts of a panther.

Bahir grunted and turned his attention back to Mahmoud. "Perhaps we should back off the Eaton boy. With so many operations under way around the world, we don't need closer scrutiny in the U.S."

"We believe it's worth the risk. The limited details we have of what Jackson proposed in 1989, combined with Tremont Jackson's disappearance these last six years, only to appear suddenly under FBI protection, worries me greatly. I fear we might not have taken the connection to Zebo, or Estebanez, seriously enough. If Sean's brother or any other person has the research, we must follow through."

"I see your point. As my brother said years ago, if the Jackson research has merit and if the final product is as simple and cost-effective as described, we could all be out of business in a matter of decades. We have never had a formidable threat that we were unable to deter."

Nobody had to explain to the leader that the end of the oil industry as they knew it would be the end of the funding to achieve his brothers and his cousin's vision for Islam.

Bahir lowered his voice, and his eyes seemed to turn to fire as he presented his benediction. "My distinguished friends and allies of the holy truth, use all of your countries' resources to provide us with information regarding threats like the Jackson's. We must detect these cancers early and," he clenched his fist and thrust it toward his spellbound followers, "cut it out before it spreads. Mahmoud,

I will hold you personally responsible to finish this business with haste. Failure is not an option.

"Islam's future is secured through the control of all energy resources. Not only oil. Mark my words." He bowed slightly and said, "*Assalamu alaikum.*" Peace be upon you. Bin Laden rose beside Bahir bin Taliffan, signaling for the rest of the room to stand. Each country's representative walked one by one past the two imposing leaders bidding them peace and prosperity. Only then did Bahir bin Taliffan and Osama bin Laden leave the conference room, followed by Mahmoud and then the two Cobra soldiers.

As they stood outside the OPEC building, four ominous Austrian *Cobra* soldiers in full metal jacket flanked Bahir, Mahmoud, and bin Laden.

Bin Laden praised his cousin's achievements. He waved his hand behind him at the silver and black OPEC letters high up on the building. He lauded the importance of making the imposing OPEC institution and their holy cause one and the same. He said that one day, Islam would have economic dominance while expanding their holy martyr army's presence throughout the world, bringing their *Jihad* to the West.

Bahir reminded his cousin, "That is your objective, and you know I support you. My charge is to protect our people's holy rights and the future economy of the Middle East."

Osama reassured Bahir that he was God's divine instrument. Allah had given Islam the resources under the sand to further an earthly kingdom and to destroy the Western infidel's dominance. Bahir looked irritated and turned to Mahmoud.

"Mahmoud, my brother," Bahir began, "though it may seem like a small thing, I had a dream that this Jackson was a giant cobra coiling and then devouring everything and everybody I have known and loved. My brother Omar had the same dream the night before he was assassinated. If our cousins Saleh and Ahmed fail, we must not stop until we have control of the Jackson's mysterious creation. Can you understand that?"

Mahmoud looked at the clear blue sky. "Another of our cousins has been waiting for an assignment since we placed him and his family in Massachusetts ten years ago. I asked him to keep close to this Estebanez. I will contact him today, and unless things change, he will stay in Maine to wait for the Eaton boy to return to Orono where he attends University. He fits in well; he is an associate professor at Harvard."

Bahir smiled and said, "I miss my old alma mater. Those were good years. You must mean our cousin Ali Sharif who sends you the Jack Daniels whiskey?"

"You knew about that?" Mahmoud said, embarrassed.

Bin Laden mumbled something about the devil's drink, running his hand through his beard. In the Arabic language of their fathers, he explained that he had personally trained Ali Sharif for a mission. He had also mentored him personally, as Ali studied aviation and law. Ali would be one of the great martyrs for their cause.

They stepped away from the front of the building as an ambulance arrived. A Cobra guard pushed the gurney holding the Senator with haste to the curb. Two EMTs lifted the dead Senator into the ambulance. With sirens blaring, it departed in the opposite direction of the closest hospital.

Bahir said to bin Laden, "Ali may not wish to get involved any further with so much at stake and with so much attention already on our families throughout the United States. Many of our family members are concerned your activities will soon get them deported by having the bin Taliffan or bin Laden name."

Bin Laden contended the risk was worth the reward. He felt Ali would do what was required of him as he owed many favors for his cousins protecting his immediate family and moving them to the United States during the near collapse of the royal Saudi family.

Appearing to consider his cousin's words, Bahir said, "Then if you will, Mahmoud, please contact Ali. If Saleh and Ahmed fail to obtain the research, Ali has my – ," he lifted a hand toward bin Laden, " – our full support."

CHAPTER 31

March 19, 1995

Fail

"WHAT THE HELL happened?" Flannigan paced back and forth at the far end of the seventh floor FBI headquarters conference room. He stopped and frowned at the life-sized picture of J. Edgar Hoover who seemed to stare back at him with disgust. The balance of the Miami Beach detail sat either hunched down in their seats or leaning over the table, resigned to the crush of their recent failure. Flannigan's secretary, Mildred, sat at a table in the corner next to the window overlooking Pennsylvania Avenue.

"These kids showed up and – "

"I know the particulars. I read your report, and I've listened to your excuses for the past – "

"Hold on, Patrick," said Juan Cerraro, the leader of the original detail set up to monitor an increase in cocaine traffic through Miami ports. Cerraro had sidelined his men to moonlight as Tremont Jackson bodyguards as a favor to his friend and mentor. "The guys are still reeling from the events in Miami, so go easy." He put on his reading glasses and looked down at the file in front of him. "We know the kids are between Dillon, South Carolina and Richmond, assuming they are still headed north. That's where we lost them." He looked over his glasses at one of the men across the table and close to the door. "Stevens, who's on the list of suspects?"

"From what we've gathered at the South of the Border, those kids are up against some heavy hitters. Someone has hired professionals. These guys were in government vehicles no less."

"Could be NSA?" another agent suggested.

"No, these guys were all independent contractors, either retired government security or mercenaries. We'll have more details shortly. We've tracked as many as four black Suburban SUVs pursuing the VW bus. We got two of them, but the other two bypassed our trap and drove on after the kids."

"How did you know to set up the trap?" Flannigan asked.

"We got an anonymous call," said Stevens.

"Zebo," Flannigan said quietly.

"Could be," Cerraro agreed. "Who else, Stevens?"

"We have identified two EKO Cobras."

"Austrian antiterrorist soldiers?" Flannigan couldn't hide his incredulousness.

"There's more," Cerraro said. "These two guys are Saudi-born."

Stevens interjected, "Yemen to be exact. We had the highway patrol stop them in Florida, but their passports came up clear. They're driving a late model T-Bird and claim they're vacationing, taking a couple weeks on a tour of the east coast ending in Boston to visit family."

"Bullshit!" Flannigan yelled, "That's too much of a coincidence."

"We agree," said Cerraro, "especially since they were in Miami Beach on the seventeenth. When Alaron . . . ," he paused at the mention of one of the two agents shot and killed protecting Cracker Jack, "when Ricardo," using Alaron's first name, "checked in, he was commenting on this red and white T-Bird parked near the Executive Clubs. He said he would kill to have it in his driveway."

"Yeah," Stevens added, "you know how Ricardo is – how he was – when it came to old cars."

"Bring them in for questioning. Cobras or rattlesnakes, I'll get them to talk," Flannigan said.

"On what charge?" Cerraro asked.

"Since when do we need a legitimate charge, Juan?"

Flannigan threw back his wrinkled blazer and put his hands on his hips. Turning to the wall, he said, "If anything happens to those kids . . ."

"What about Zebo? What's he calling himself now?" Cerraro asked.

"Estebanez," Flannigan said. He didn't want to cross this bridge yet.

"Right, Estebanez. What's his status?"

Flores, one of the other agents assigned to Miami Beach, spoke up. "We lost him at South of the Border. He's a ghost. Comes and goes."

"Ghost is right. He was former CIA NOC, non-official cover. So, when Flores called over to the agency for a little help, they never heard of Zebo or Estebanez. I still don't know what the hell he's doing in the middle of this mess. We thought he was dead a long time ago," observed Cerraro.

"We have been searching and cross referencing every intelligence database and every name in the case file going back to 1960," Flores said, "We have yet to find the connection."

What Flannigan now knew about Zebo and his connection to the Jacksons was on a need-to-know basis. The team did not need to know.

Cerraro looked down the table and said, "Stevens, you're good at wiring into the CIA database. Could you maybe . . ."

Stevens raised his head off his arms folded on the table. "Got it, boss."

Flannigan wasn't concerned since Zebo's files had been purged. He ran his hands through his spindly black and silver hair and his demeanor softened. He said to Cerraro, "I'll go meet with Ricardo Alaron's and Hector Paya's wives later this morning."

Cerraro put his glasses on the table and lifted a hand. "I'll handle that, Patrick."

Ignoring his friend, Flannigan looked across the room at Mildred and asked, "Would you get me a file on both men so I can familiarize myself with their family situations?" Then looking at Cerraro, he added, "You wouldn't have had them there if it weren't for me. It's my responsibility."

Cerraro nodded and put his glasses back on. When he looked up again, he said, "The men in Dillon at the Mexican place – "

"South of the Border," Stevens offered.

"Right, South of the Border, they were former U.S., Russian, and British secret service agents. We moved them to our Charleston field office and have them detained on weapons charges, some registered, some not, but so far ballistics has not been able to link them to Miami Beach. If they were the shooters, there's no proof. We'll either have to let them go or risk this becoming an international incident."

Flannigan asked, "And the other two black SUVs?"

"The guys we have in Charleston knew nothing about them," Stevens said.

"Of course," replied Cerraro.

Flannigan began to pace again, "To summarize, on these kids' trail we have God knows how many renegade government-issued SUVs complete with trained mercenaries, and two highly trained Middle Eastern Cobra soldiers," Flannigan asked rhetorically. "We can't afford to let the press get wind of all of this. They would have a heyday," Flannigan said. "Wait twenty-four hours and let the guys in Charleston go."

Director Harrington burst into the boardroom. "What the hell is going on? Are you running a covert action behind my back again?" He waved a file like a lunatic. "I will bust you so far down you will be working at Dunkin' Donuts trying to make up for your lost pension – if I don't have you locked up instead. Two good men dead! With your name on their blood."

Flannigan charged down the thirty feet separating them reaching the Director in seconds. But Stevens, who was built like a refrigerator, pushed his chair back to block his advance, stood up, and wrapped his arms around Flannigan in a bear hug. When the Director made a quick exit while grumbling about it being the last straw, Stevens let go of his grip.

"I'm sorry, boss," Stevens said, "but I thought you were going to hit the Director."

Flannigan patted Stevens on the shoulder. "You really should have tried out for the NFL." He returned to the end of the room. "Let *me* worry about Harrington. You focus your attention on finding the kids.

"Check every hotel and all the rest stops between Dillon and DC. Unless they changed vehicles, that van can't be too hard to find. It looks like Kent State and Woodstock combined." There was no humor in his voice and nobody in the room could muster a smile if they tried. "I doubt they would leave the highway for long, and we know where they're headed."

Cerraro dismissed the rest of the team, leaving himself and Flannigan in the room alone. They both leaned back in their chairs as Flannigan offered Cerraro a cigarette. After they lit up, Cerraro said, "This is a fine mess you've gotten me into this time, Ollie."

"It sure is, Stanley." They both grinned and took long drags on their Marlboros.

"Thanks, Juan."

"No problem. I want to get all these bastards as much as you do. They've been making us look like fools for so long, we might as well be Laurel and Hardy."

"What's your take on the Austrian and Middle East connection?" Flannigan asked.

"This is really the State Department's or the CIA's area, but if these guys are in the USA, then it's our problem too. What do you know about a group that works out of the OPEC Cartel building, run by a Sheik Mohamed bin Bandar in the eighties?" Cerraro asked.

"Just what I read in the papers," he said and lit another cigarette. "My guess is they're a bunch of terrorists! As I recall, someone assassinated Bandar in Egypt. The new leader and probably the guy responsible for Bandar's hit was one of the Taliffan brothers. There's always been speculation that we took him out. Now the next oldest brother runs the show, and though he's not as extreme as his brother, he's a whole lot smarter."

"That's pretty good for what you read in the papers." Cerraro closed one file and opened another. "By the way, while I was digging around with my CIA and DOD contacts, I've found that they are more than well informed on your Cameron and Tremont Jackson, and on Matthew Eaton. They also asked me what we knew about Estebanez.

"And, you're right about the terrorist connection. They recruit wealthy young OPEC relatives sympathetic to the extreme Islamic version of *Jihad*."

"Holy war," Flannigan stated.

"Yes, in this case against the West. The group is," he struggled with the pronunciation, "Hafiz-OPEC Saumba Shokran."

"That's the name."

"Bahir's and his older brother . . ." Cerraro flicked his cigarette onto the floor and leaned in toward his old comrade. "You were right on that too, his older brother, Omar, ran the group until the Agency – hoping that would be the end of the group – took him out."

Flannigan handed him another cigarette and lit it.

"But you're wrong about Bahir. He has a chip on his shoulder engraved with the letters U, S, and A. He's been linked to at least four terrorist groups including Al-Qaeda. Get this, he used to camp in the desert as a kid with his cousin Osama."

"You don't say," Flannigan said, whistling through his teeth.

"The latest intel shows that Bahir bin Taliffan may be a mediator of sorts between the various groups using OPEC as his cover. Needless to say, with him in charge of this Hafiz Shokran group, he can be dangerous."

Flannigan asked, "What on earth does this have to do with the events of the last thirty-six hours?"

"Perhaps nothing."

"Then what the hell?"

"Or perhaps everything."

Cerraro flipped through his file, pulled out some black and white photographs, and slid them over to Flannigan. "These are the two men in the T-Bird Stevens mentioned earlier, the EKO Cobras. They passed through customs in Miami two days ago. This morning we confirmed their ties to Prince Bahir bin Taliffan. Though raised in Austria, they are first cousins. Ahmed Jobrani Maher is the smart one and his younger brother Saleh is known in the Arab world as *koshrakan* – the shadow of death. Ahmed was schooled here in the United States – Princeton of all places – along with a number of members of the bin Laden family, I might add. They are Austrian citizens, hence the ease of passage through customs. His brother Saleh's trail was harder to follow and is still a bit of a mystery. After his dishonorable discharge from the Cobras, he disappeared off the CIA's map for nearly a decade. If his name hadn't popped up on their potential Al-Qaeda list, he would have disappeared into the background." Cerraro sat on the back legs of his chair.

Flannigan put his head down for the first time since arriving at the office at 4:00 a.m. after two restless hours of sleep, a quick washcloth under the arms, and some Old English aftershave. He rubbed his temples. Thirty-five years of investigation since Karen Jackson's death was spinning through his mind. Along with the U.S. oil industry, he had always suspected members of the cartel. Who on earth had more to lose? "A couple of potential terrorists show up in Miami the day before Tremont and the two agents were shot."

"Too coincidental."

"Where the hell is the T-Bird now?"

"We lost track of it in Virginia."

"Shooters?" Flannigan asked.

"Nope. Every eyewitness identifies one Caucasian and one African American. And get this, the gal at the diner said Tremont thought they were replacement agents." He handed Flannigan descriptions and artists renderings of the suspects. One looked familiar. He lifted the picture of a wide faced, bald headed man and said, "Cue Ball."

"Alfonse D'Amato, aka Cue Ball, just finished a nickel in Leavenworth." Cerraro added, "D'Amato is suspected for mob-related hits over the last twenty years, but all we could get him on was tax evasion."

"He's top dollar," Flannigan said.

"Whoever hired him would have paid six digits per hit."

"Put out an APB on Mr. D'Amato."

"No need. Cue Ball and Clayton *the carver* Manning – "

"The Carver? The same bastard known for the gruesome way he finishes off his contract?"

"The same. Both demons have been sent back to the gates of hell. They were both crushed in their sedan while chasing the wrecker." Cerraro chuckled, "I'm not sure Satan himself would want them back."

Flannigan picked up a stack of files and walked to the door. "Let's find those kids. Or we're going to have more funerals to attend."

CHAPTER 32

March 19, 1995 3:00 a.m.

Hide

MATTHEW KNEW HE did not want to venture off the main highway, but they had to rest. He had to rest. The weary couple looked for the green highway signs that would indicate hotels, restaurants, and gas stations.

"There. Turners Crossroads in Wilson," Maria exclaimed. The first sign indicated two hotels, the next showed one restaurant and the last featured two gas stations.

"Compared to the last five exits Wilson is a booming town," Matthew observed.

Both ramshackle hotels had seen better days. Maria said, "eenie-meenie-minie-mo, let's take the one with the picture of the funny-looking man drinking that oversized cup of coffee."

"Done. At least we can get coffee and eggs before we leave."

They checked in and asked for a room in the back facing away from the highway. After parking away from the streetlights, they dragged themselves up three levels of rusty wrought iron steps and railings to their corner room. Maria immediately turned on the shower and Matthew went back outside to be sure they hadn't been followed. He and SoBe walked around the entire building twice and all he saw were multiple pairs of shiny eyes staring at him from the base of the dumpsters in front of the woods. SoBe pounced in their direction, and they scattered like leaves in the wind. Other than the night clerk and a whole lot of stray cats, they could not be more alone. He returned to the room to find Maria wrapped in a large white towel.

"You should take a shower," she said.

"I can wait."

"Take a shower."

"That bad, huh?"

"That bad."

Matthew tried to give her a bear hug and she laughed, pushing him away. He dropped his clothes at the door to the tiny bathroom. A roach ran across the floor and then another. They both were out of sight behind the toilet before he could do anything about it. If Maria had seen one, he would have surely known about it.

They crawled into bed, which surprisingly had fresh scented sheets and what appeared to be a new comforter. Matthew took Dr. Jackson's gun out of his overnight bag and placed it under his pillow, careful not to let Maria see him. Besides being infested with roaches, the place was not half bad, Matthew thought, before he was fast asleep.

They slept far longer than they intended. Maria woke first and opened the curtains. Matthew squinted to see the sun was high up in the sky and groggily rolled out of bed.

"Stay inside for a minute and let me take a look around." He waited for Maria to turn, and then retrieved the gun. Once outside, he and SoBe repeated his investigation of the night before. Minus the cats, the scene was about the same. It was Sunday, traffic was light and besides a church bell ringing off toward the town of Wilson, everything was quiet.

Matthew and Maria stepped out of the motel coffee shop: Cup O' Joe's. They had opted out of the full breakfast settling on coffee and prepackaged pastries.

"At least the cup-o-joe is hot," Maria said with a grin.

"Not hot enough to kill my taste buds. It was the blue tint to the eggs that did it for me," Matthew said.

As he backed out of the parking space on the east side, a gray U.S. government tagged sedan pulled in the west side. Two men entered the manager's office.

Amused, the man in the gray Cadillac sipped his coffee and watched the scene unfold. He observed the kids pull out of one side of the parking lot, sheltered by the building and trees, while a black government tagged Crown Victoria pulled in the other side. In minutes, the two FBI agents bolted from the coffee shop and started the engine. The man in the Cadillac cut in front of them causing the two cars to collide. He strutted over to the flustered young agents and feigned a mock tirade, calling the agents every nasty word he could think of.

He insisted the local police come to write a report and when one of the young agents showed his FBI identification, the Cadillac owner said he didn't care if he was J. Edgar Hoover's ghost!

After the city of Wilson cop finished his report, and the angry agents spun out of the parking lot, the Cadillac owner approached the pay telephone next to the coffee shop and made two calls. He went in for a refill of what he thought was damn good coffee, thick and black. He was not in a hurry, figuring it would not be hard to catch up with the cavalcade. Though he hadn't seen the two black Suburbans or the T-Bird for the past twelve hours, he figured they wouldn't be far behind. What a circus, he thought.

As soon as Matthew pulled off the highway at the North Carolina and Virginia border, he realized he had made a mistake. Construction areas dotted the desolate area. Besides a couple of trucks in the back parking lot, his was the only passenger vehicle. Not a problem, he thought, I'll just keep going. He looked in the mirror and cussed. The white T-bird had appeared behind him and it was picking up speed. Matthew tried to accelerate, but against the 292-horsepower cid V-8 engine under the T-Bird's hood, he was toast. The T-Bird swung wide around the bus and cut them off. Matthew stopped without ramming the car, though he was tempted. One of the two dark-skinned men inside smiled and waved at him. Matthew didn't know what to think, but he reached under the seat, lifted the snap on the leather pouch, and put his hand around the oily canvas holding the Jackson's gun. SoBe growled.

"What is that?" Maria asked. As Matthew unfolded the leather, she exclaimed, "Matthew, where did you get that? I'm scared."

"Trust me, I don't want to have to use it. If anything happens to me, keep your head down, jump in the driver's seat, ram the bus into their car, and go for help. Don't stay here." He didn't leave room for discussion as he left the feeble engine running and stepped away from the bus with the gun behind his back.

Both men were now out of the T-bird. The man closest to him spoke first. "Mr. Eaton, we're sorry to stop you this way, but we feared that this . . ." He seemed to be struggling for the right word. "Charade? Yes, this charade has gone on long enough. We expect you know we have been following you. We have had quite a time trying to get your attention. Fortunately, those who meant to do you harm seem to have been detained."

Matthew was perplexed. The man looked Middle Eastern but as in Miami he noticed a Germanic accent.

"We mean you no harm, Mr. Eaton. But I must ask you to allow my friend to inspect your Volkswagen, which I am sad to see has taken quite a beating since Miami. I want you to know we had nothing to do with all of that."

Matthew noted that the man really did seem to be sorry about all the damage. The other man, the driver, had been moving toward the bus on Maria's side. SoBe barked a warning. "Please stop right where you are," Matthew said. "What are you looking for?" He did not brandish the gun, not yet. The man stopped, folded his arms, and leaned on the hood. Matthew could not detect any firearms, but they could have them tucked behind their backs.

"An honest question deserves an honest answer. We believe you may have something of ours that a new acquaintance of yours may have had in his possession. We would like it back and will pay you handsomely . . . as a reward of course . . . for its safe return."

"I have no idea what you're talking about."

"Then you have nothing to fear. I imagine in your hand is a weapon?" The speaker raised his hands. "You may keep your weapon trained on me while my friend takes a look. If what we are searching for is not in your Volkswagen, we will leave you to your travels and not bother you further."

If Matthew said no, there might be a gunfight. If he agreed, he might have to turn over the duffel bags in order to get Maria out of here safely. Where is the highway patrol when you need them? he thought. He looked to the semi-trucks but could see no activity. He made his decision and moved the gun into view. "I will use it if I have to. If you'll both keep your hands raised and keep your distance, I'll show you what's in my bus. But then, I'll ask you to leave before any of us have to resort to violence," Matthew said, hoping he would be able to think of something. Or that someone would arrive in the rest area before he had to give them the cargo.

Both men kept their hands halfway up and walked to the bus's side door.

Matthew said, "Please stand up on the grass." He then motioned to Maria. He didn't want to say her name. The less these guys knew, the better. "Could you open the doors?"

"Matthew," she said in a whisper.

"Please, just do it, and hold onto SoBe."

Maria opened the doors and crawled up inside. Matthew kept his eyes on the two men, who were grinning like they were shopping for clothing at Saks. Matthew turned sideways so he could look in the van and watch the men at the same time.

SoBe broke away from Maria, and Matthew grabbed her collar just as she was about to jump from the bus at the strangers. They stepped back. Maria peeled back the blankets to reveal mesh bags of oranges and grapefruit as well as dozens of boxes of fireworks and enough roasted peanuts to feed an army.

It was all Matthew could do to keep his jaw from dropping. He glared at Maria as she was about to speak. She didn't. The two men lowered their arms and their smiles disappeared.

"Is this what you are willing to pay me a lot of money for? Fruit and fireworks?" Matthew asked, his voice cracking ever so slightly.

The first Arab craned his neck to look deeper into the bus. He started to laugh. "You really have no idea what we're looking for, do you?" he asked.

"I really don't. But whatever it is, it must be very valuable because someone has been trying to kill us thinking we have it."

"Have you seen or heard from your friend Estebanez since you left Maine?"

That caught Matthew off guard. Before he could speak someone from the semi-trucks yelled, "Hey, is everything all right? What's going on over there?"

"Is everything cool between us, Mr. Eaton?" the Arab asked.

Matthew lowered the heavy gun. "As long as we never have to see you again, sure."

"Our task is accomplished. You do not have what we are looking for."

The other Arab spoke for the fist time. "I am not convinced, Ahmed. We are being played for fools!"

"Do you wish to inspect the fruit, Saleh?" He then seemed to chastise Saleh in what Matthew thought *was* Farsi, albeit with a German accent.

"They could have disposed of the bags," Saleh said in English, glaring at Matthew.

"Perhaps, but for now, we have caused Mr. Eaton and Miss Valdeorras enough stress and worry," Ahmed said trying to take Saleh by the arm, but he shook it off and glared at Matthew. "Saleh, we must be on our way."

SoBe was pulling on her collar and growling. Matthew considered letting her go.

The men returned to their car, but Saleh mimicked a firing gun with his right hand, before closing the door.

The trucker yelled something else. Matthew set the gun inside the bus and waved. "Everything is fine, thanks." The trucker seemed uncertain and continued to stand in front of his rig. Matthew got into the bus as the T-Bird drove away.

"They knew both of our names, Matthew. And where the hell are the duffel bags, and where did all of this fruit and stuff come from?"

Matthew felt dizzy. A tremendous migraine would follow the adrenalin rush. He reached into his pocket and found nothing but change.

"Here." Maria handed him the backup silver pill case she kept in her purse. She had been carrying spares for him ever since he could remember. Matthew winced as the first ache began to radiate from his neck into his brain.

"Maybe you should lie down for a few minutes and let the medicine take effect."

"We really should get out of here. The trucker might have called the cops, and I don't want to have to explain all of this again." He swallowed the pill, thought for a moment, and then took another one, both without water. He closed his eyes as the pain spread out to different areas of his head.

"I have no idea how they knew our names. I don't have a clue." And he didn't. As he drove back out on the interstate, he remained as shocked as Maria with the cargo switch. What did come to mind was the name Estebanez.

CHAPTER 33

March 19, 1995 11:00 p.m.

Escape

THEY HADN'T SEEN the black Suburbans since South Carolina, and the Middle Eastern men in the T-Bird seemed to be off their trail. "We should have smooth sailing now," Matthew said as they cruised north on I-95 toward home. They passed through the rest of Virginia, Washington DC, Maryland, Delaware, and up the New Jersey Turnpike into New York.

Halfway across the George Washington Bridge, Matthew glanced at the fuel gauge. He cussed under his breath. "I should have filled up at the last Turnpike service center."

"Maybe we can make it to Greenwich. I'd feel a lot safer if we were past all the big cities."

"We're riding on fumes right now, and the last thing we want is to break down at night on the highway in New York City. I've heard stories."

Maria laughed. "You mean stories more bizarre than our spring break?"

"Did you see the movie *Escape from New York*?"

"No. It sounds like a real blockbuster."

"Kurt Russell and Adrienne what's-her-name with Ernest Borgnine?"

"Adrienne Barbeau? She must have been desperate."

"My brother bought our first VCR when I was nine or ten and that was the movie he picked out. My folks were out, or they would never have let me see it. Now when I think of going to New York City . . ."

"Matthew Thadius Eaton, you have a phobia, or should I say another phobia."

"I do not, and that wasn't my point." Matthew sensed he boarded the Dr. Maria track of psychoanalysis. He wanted to get off the train. At the end of the bridge, they found themselves amidst the Cross Bronx Expressway cloverleaf. Matthew mumbled, "New York City can be dangerous." He kept his eyes peeled for signs to stay on I-95. He remembered his father's colorful, if not crass, language when passing through the same junctures, especially when he missed signs or ended up on the wrong highway.

"There's a sign for Getty," Matthew said. Let's make a quick stop." He pulled off the exit for Tremont Avenue – appropriate, he thought – and landed square in the middle of a road construction site with blinding halogen lights, men working with jackhammers, and front-end loaders dumping concrete into a line of four triple axle dump trucks. He was stuck. He couldn't go back up the ramp, and as he maneuvered around the cavernous site, he noticed the ramp going back onto the highway was also blocked.

"I hate to be superstitious but did this happen in the movie?" Maria asked.

Matthew snapped back, "This is no time for humor or your armchair psychology." He regretted the comment before it was out of his mouth and said so.

Maria gave him *that* look, and this time it was not hard to discern. "Just get us out of here, Matthew."

Lights filled the rear view mirror. He turned to see a large grill with the Chevrolet symbol. *Couldn't be.* He could not go forward, he could not go left toward what appeared to be a retail center, so he made a right toward the city. He turned into the pitch black where all he could see were the seared images of the halogen lights. He rubbed his eyes and tried to focus on the street ahead.

"I don't like this, Matthew. We really should stop for directions."

The last thing he wanted to do was stop. After less than a mile, he took a left at the first major intersection. He expected he would see signs for an access road to I-95. Block after block, he seemed to be driving farther and farther into a dismal part of the city. He got excited when he pulled back onto Tremont Avenue. Then the road flipped up onto another major highway. "Good Lord," he exclaimed as he read the Bronx River Parkway sign. He pulled off the next exit to swing back around and go south.

Preoccupied with what was ahead, he had forgotten about the black Chevy truck he had seen behind at the construction site. It could have been a pickup truck, they have the same front end as a Suburban, he thought.

Bright lights reflecting in his rear view mirror caught his attention. "Damn. There it is, the black Suburban!"

"Where?"

"Behind us!"

Maria looked out the back and caught her breath. "There's two of them!"

He picked up speed. There wasn't another car in sight. At the end of the exit ramp, he could see there was an easy-on ramp on the opposite side of the bridge. He didn't bother stopping for the light and made a sharp left under the large bridge. He had a strange flashback to dodging the Sopwith Camel.

Just as he was about to enter the Bronx Parkway, one of the trucks swung wide and cut him off.

Maria screamed. "It's them! Where did they come from?"

Matthew tried to regain control without hitting the Suburban and went the only way he could – straight into the Bronx Park. "There's got to be cops around here. I've broken laws, and they have to be patrolling this park. They have to be."

Matthew heard thunder. Three seconds later, the flash of lighting lit up the park. SoBe whined and pushed her way up front and onto Maria's lap. Matthew was about to read the nearest sign just as Maria said, "Jungle World Road? We're on Jungle World Road. This can't be good." They passed over the Bronx River as the road took them deeper into the park with the two SUVs close on their tail. The narrow, winding street had intermittent lamp posts casting dim light. He didn't want to run off the road. He was hoping there was a way out at the bottom of the park. Numerous signs appeared on the left to signal a road. He turned, realizing too late that it took him away from their only escape route. The river was ahead between a sparse set of trees and picnic tables. He turned left to backtrack. Wrong again. "We're trapped!"

Matthew reached under the seat for Jackson's .45. The Suburbans flanked the bus, forcing him to stop in a cul-de-sac facing two maintenance buildings; the river ran to the right, and woods covered the left. Thunder crashed and rolled. He snapped at Maria, "Get in the back with SoBe! Don't move." Maria was about to protest when her door was jerked open, and she was pulled from the bus. Matthew yelled for SoBe to get the intruder, but the dog was way ahead of him, diving on the back of the man. Matthew heard a thud and a horrible, sick-sounding whine from SoBe. He began to raise the pistol to shoot through the back window at the man when his door swung open. Someone had him by the shoulder. He leaned toward the man, brought the gun under his left arm, and pulled the trigger. The sound reverberated through the van as Matthew and the man he shot fell together to the ground. The heavens seemed to expel all the rain they held at once. Matthew pointed the gun toward his assailant, but he lay motionless. A man came around the back of the bus with one arm around Maria's chest and the other holding a gun against her head. Matthew didn't have to think about his options. He raised his hands. Another man came up behind, took the gun, and hit him hard in the kidneys. Unable to breathe, Matthew fell to his knees.

With a pronounced New York accent, the man holding Maria said, "That's enough. There's nothing in the VW. Nothing but fruit and shit."

"Shit? What you mean *shit*, DelGercio?" Matthew's assailant yelled in a strong Russian accent over the sound of the torrential rain.

"Not literally, Klaus, you idiot." He threw something down in front of Matthew. "We'll take them with us. Hurry up."

With his foot, the Russian pushed Matthew who caught himself before his head bounced off the wet pavement. Judging by the voices farther away, there were a couple more men in the group. Matthew looked up as the Russian moved forward to pick up the binding materials. He could barely see through the sheets of rain but thought plastic or wire bound Maria's wrists.

DelGercio leaned down to check the man who Matthew shot. "Damn, kid. He was a good man. Jerry made it through two tours of Nam and a dozen missions since, only to get killed by a science major."

Matthew tried to think what Sean would do in the same circumstance; of course, Sean had a dozen years of Special Forces and intelligence training. He calculated that once tied up in an SUV, it would be the end of them. Especially since Matthew and Maria could identify at least two.

As the Russian bent to pick up the black plastic bindings, Matthew pushed his body against the man's knees, grabbed his gun wrist, and jumped to his feet. Then he brought his knee up in the man's groin. The Russian buckled but still managed to drive an elbow into Matthew's gut.

The New Yorker reappeared. Maria screamed, "He's going to shoot." Matthew, though locked in a full nelson, turned his opponent in the direction of the New Yorker just as the gun sounded. The bullet hit the Russian square in the back an inch from Matthew's clasped hands. Matthew fell into a puddle as the gun roared again. He pried the Russian's gun out of his hand and brought it up level with the New Yorker. Out of the corner of his eye, he saw Maria hit the ground as their guns went off simultaneously. Matthew knew he had shot high, well over the man's head, yet the New Yorker grabbed his shoulder and dropped his gun.

Maria had disappeared, and Matthew knew the other men would be coming around both sides of the bus. The lights of a speeding car came into view toward the entrance. It skidded sideways, hydroplaning on the wet pavement. Matthew thought stenciled on the side of the car were the words Park Ranger. The New Yorker receded into the dark and said, "Looks like your lucky day, kids." Before Matthew could move, the man called DelGercio was in the other Suburban, tires screeching. Matthew thought the Suburban would collide with the Park Rangers car, when the Suburban swerved to miss it by inches.

Matthew looked at the gun in his hand and the two men at his feet. It was all so surreal. He watched as blood and water flowed down the grade, into the gutter, and disappeared down a large grate.

Someone he couldn't see through the blurring lights was yelling at him. "Hands in the air; I've got you covered." When Matthew didn't respond, the man yelled another warning. "I am a Bronx Park Ranger. Drop your weapon, or so help me God, I will shoot. I will."

Matthew lowered his arm. Something scraped against the concrete behind him.

"Matthew, it's me. Let go of the gun." A hand was on his wrist, another on the gun. Matthew let go. "I wasn't here, Matthew. Just answer their questions. Everything will be okay. You did great. I thought I was going to lose you for a minute there. How would I explain that?"

Explain to who? Matthew thought.

"I'm sorry I didn't get here sooner. I lost you guys back at the construction site. Thank God for that tracking device."

"What tracking device?" Matthew turned to look for Estebanez, but all he saw through rain were the dark silhouettes of the maintenance buildings. He felt sick to his stomach. Maria might have been in the other SUV. With his voice cracking, he said her name.

"I'm under here. I think I'm stuck."

"Thank god!" he said, nearly sobbing.

"That I'm stuck?"

"That you're okay. Stay right there."

"Like I have any choice. Are those men dead?"

"I think so."

She muttered a Spanish prayer, and Matthew followed with one of his own for the powers that had protected them once again.

Matthew and Maria sat in separate squad cars. The rain had subsided, the air was warm, and the moon was peaking out between fast moving clouds. They remained in the cars for an hour as ambulances arrived and the park area turned into a different kind of Bronx Zoo.

Earlier, the park ranger had helped dislodge Maria while Matthew power lifted the side of the bus off its axle an inch or two. As the ranger cut Maria's bindings, he said he had worked in the park ten years and had never seen anything like this. The only time he ever pulled his weapon was to clean it or place it in the bureau drawer when he got home. When he questioned Matthew and Maria, they simply said they had become lost and got stuck in the middle of these thugs shooting it out. Matthew and Maria had quickly agreed that would be their story. Who would believe the rest of it anyhow?

Later, a fine featured, African American NYPD policewoman opened Matthew's door, took off his handcuffs, and led him over to where Maria and a man were leaning against the other patrol car. In between them was SoBe with a bloodstained bandage on her head. Matthew felt a lump in his throat.

The detective was laughing at something Maria had said. He was not quite thirty, handsome, rugged, and wearing a dark suit with a badge hanging off his lapel pocket. Matthew noticed another man who turned away when Matthew caught his eye. He would have just been another person milling around the crime scene had he not seemed out of place in the cool night air wearing knee length khaki shorts, sandals, and a Dallas Cowboys cap.

SoBe barked and pulled on the leash. When Maria saw Matthew, she ran and enveloped him in her arms. SoBe jumped on both of them nearly knocking them to the pavement. The female cop smiled and said to the detective, "I checked on the kids, and they're who they say they are – wrong place at the wrong time."

The detective said, "You two must have the worse luck of any spring break college kids in history. You have a trail of police reports all the way back to Dade County."

The female cop said, "Judging by the looks of those two corpses back there, I'd say they're *very* lucky."

All but one of their stories matched up. Matthew had said SUVs were already there and Maria that they came up afterward.

When questioned, Maria said, "I was so scared. I'm not really sure. I thought they came up behind us, but they could have been here already," Maria added.

The policewoman and detective looked at each other but accepted that explanation. They would be in contact and had both kids sign their statements. Matthew counted all the officers that might be in touch with him. If they all talked to each other, he'd be busted.

"We better get out of town before they change their minds about letting us go," he whispered to Maria.

Once they left the zoo and media circus behind, Matthew pulled into the first Getty station for gas. Maria chattered about what the detective told her regarding who they thought the men on the pavement were. The detective could not identify one of the perpetrators, but the other had a long file of military, police, and U.S. government intelligence work going back more than thirty years. But he had disappeared off the radar for the past four years when he was let go from the CIA due to an undisclosed conflict. Classified. The only other fact they were sure of: the SUV had U.S. government plates. None of the facts made any sense to the detectives – the answers were in that other SUV. The detective told Maria that these guys were mercenaries of sorts. Guns for hire.

Taking a deep breath, Maria asked, "Was that Mr. Estebanez?"

"Yeah. I'm sure he's had a part in getting us into all of this. But he showed up just in time to save our lives."

Maria laid her fingers along Matthew's cheek. "Are you going to be okay?"

"Look at you. If I didn't know better, I'd say you're getting a high from all of this."

"How could you say that?" she said without conviction.

He rubbed his sore shoulder. It only hurt slightly worse than his lower back. "I have to admit, I'm still pretty shook up."

"It'll take a while before the shock wears off. Even trained professionals go through a period of post-trauma after something like this."

Matthew shot a look at Dr. Maria.

"They believe we got caught up in the middle of some kind of illegal international deal that went bad. So you killed both of those guys. How do you feel about that?"

As if it made it a little better, Matthew said, "I didn't kill them both. I did get the guy who pulled me out of the bus, but his partner shot the second guy, the one with the Russian accent."

"The one that was holding me shot the Russian?"

"The Russian called him Gercio. No, DelGercio. He shot at me and hit the Russian. I mean he's just as dead. And then DelGercio and I were facing each other, and my shot went high, but he spun and grabbed his shoulder." Matthew was gripping the steering wheel so tight his knuckles were white.

"I'm sorry to get you into this." Matthew looked at his hands. They were shaking, so he gripped the steering wheel tighter to keep it from showing.

As they drove onto I-95 and saw the signs for New England, he opened his window and drew a long breath of fresh air.

"Let's go home."

CHAPTER 34

March 20, 1995 3:00 A.m.

Safety

STUDYING A STATE map outside of Fairfield, Connecticut, Maria suggested they exit the highway and drive back roads as much as possible. Matthew agreed, and they chose their route.

Maria dozed as Matthew navigated the tree-lined Merritt Parkway. He turned on the radio and a familiar name caught his attention. The talk show host was discussing an unpopular Senator Green from Texas who he said had a serious conflict of interest by serving on the Senate energy committee when his constituency included the powerful oil companies. Children playing along the Danube River near Nuremberg, Germany, had discovered the Senator's body, shot execution style with a bag still over his head. The host said that the Senator missed his meetings with energy officials in five European countries, none near Nuremberg. The talk show's guest speculated that his murder had to do with his controversial pro Middle East positions.

Matthew switched the channel to light jazz. The world was going crazy. Look what people were willing to do to a U.S. Senator. Even though it wasn't related to his situation, he thought, others were willing to kill over some research which most people believed was still speculative. He marveled that he and Maria, along with Estebanez, might be the only ones who knew

CJ Energy cells were a reality. He felt exhausted as he reviewed the recent incidents and their potential ramifications; all in less than one week. He was not old enough to deal with all of this. But how old do you have to be? His brother Sean had killed before he was much older. Two of his cousins were in the Gulf War and had seen some of their buddies blown to bits. His father and grandfather had seen action by the time they were his age. Though his father never talked about his Korean War experiences, Matthew knew he had been in the Special Forces and in battles where hundreds had lost their lives. He wished Sean were here to give him advice. His brother had changed since being in the military. Matthew decided not to let this situation ruin him. He would be strong – like his father and the huge oak tree on Willow Run. After all, the men who died could not have intended anything but harm to them. If Estebanez had not acted, he and Maria might be sitting, bound, in a truck on the way back to Miami. Or dead.

He was startled back to the present when Maria woke with a gasp. She turned to look out the back of the bus.

"I must have been dreaming. I hope the Bronx Park was the end of those guys. But I don't think whoever put them up to this is going to stop until they find what they're looking for. I don't want to bring all this back home."

Matthew's head was splitting. He nodded his agreement.

"You look tired. Why don't we take a break? Or I can drive, if you want."

Matthew could tell she didn't want to drive. Nor did he want her to when the folks trying to kidnap or even kill them, could cut them off at any moment. Using the back roads was a good idea, and some rest would not be a bad idea either. He pulled off into a roadside rest area where there were many vehicles, including two highway patrol cars. He pulled the VW to the other side of the lot to avoid scrutiny of the bullet-riddled bus.

Matthew took a pill and lay on a bench with his UMaine Crew cap covering his face. The battle-wounded SoBe laid at his feet. He thought he would pass out, but he felt like he couldn't sleep. A few moments later he sat up, eyes darting. The police cars were gone, but there were plenty of early morning travelers.

"That's what they call a power nap," Maria said.

"I couldn't fall asleep."

"You were asleep for nearly an hour." She handed him half a peeled orange and a drink.

He raised his eyebrows at the bottle Maria handed him. "Very funny."

"The label says it's good for you, gives you energy, and the name seemed appropriate." She bit into a piece of orange. "You look like you could use a sip of SOBE Power."

"Well, don't give it to SoBe. She has enough energy to go around." He scratched behind the dog's ears, careful to avoid her head wound. "You did good, girl. You did really good."

"If the guys in the Suburban's and the T-Bird don't have Cracker Jack's duffel bags, who does?"

"Estebanez, I hope," Matthew said.

When they got back up in the bus, she said, "You know, Estebanez looks a lot like Marcos – or the other way around."

"Why? Because he's Cuban?"

"No, seriously, just something about him."

Matthew didn't say he had the same thought as far back as meeting Marcos at the Shell station in Miami Beach. He didn't like being kept in the dark about matters affecting his and Maria's safety. And he was especially irritated that people close to him may have been orchestrating events to screw with his fate.

They arrived on the UMaine campus in Orono, Maine, before noon. School didn't start for a few days, so the way-worn travelers picked up Maria's car and drove separately to Millinocket. Matthew drove behind Maria and kept a careful watch for trouble in the mirrors.

Matthew parked the shot-up, beat-up VW bus in the barn where Sean and he had first put it together less than a year earlier. It would take more than a few engine parts to fix it up this time. They loaded much of the fruit and nuts into her car, left all the fireworks in the bus, and lashed her luggage on top of the car with bungee cords. With SoBe between them in the front seat, they headed for Matthew's house.

After hugging and kissing them both, Matthew's mother scolded him for not calling to let her know they arrived in Florida safely. Of course, she had checked with Uncle Carl and had called Maria's father more than once, but that was beside the point.

Matthew and Maria stared at each other. It was obvious his mother knew nothing about their many brushes with the law. Matthew breathed a sigh of relief.

While Matthew's mother became acquainted with SoBe, they agreed Maria should take her home. Matthew's father had made it clear, more than once, that he had better not find another dog on the property.

"I have to go over to Godello's," her father's restaurant, "and face the music. I know by now he's worried himself sick. First, he will hug and kiss me, then all that anxiety build up will result in him yelling and telling me how I'll be the death of him."

Matthew whispered to her, "I hope he is also oblivious to all we have been through."

Maria made a face and nodded. She said, "Then he'll hug and kiss me again and tell me I'm grounded for life." Matthew kissed her and hugged her himself before she and SoBe drove away.

Matthew sat at the kitchen table while his mother asked lots of questions, starting with what happened to his beautiful face. He made up a story about body surfing in the Atlantic and then gave her the abridged version of the trip. He realized there was very little he could tell her that did not reveal his encounter with Dr. Jackson's son and the events surrounding his death. His mother insisted on fixing him a sandwich though he said repeatedly he wasn't hungry, while she asked about his visit with Uncle Carl, she put the sandwich and a row of Pepperidge Farm cookies in front of him with a glass of milk.

His mother was quiet for a while as she made a project out of folding a dishtowel. She sat down next to him and said she could see a significant change in the relationship between him and Maria.

"Sweetheart, you need to get through college before thinking of having a family."

"Mom."

"Well, someone has to say it. And things happen," she said, placing her hand on his and smiling.

He had to admit it to himself. In a short time, his relationship with Maria – along with his entire view of life – had transformed into adult.

"How are your headaches, sweetheart?"

“Manageable,” he lied. In fact, he realized, they had become much more frequent and severe.

“I can set an appointment with Dr. Sacko,” she said.

He never could fool her, he thought. “I like Dr. Sacko and she’s the top neurologist in New England, but she would only tell me that I needed to try another experimental drug and frankly,” he laughed, trying to lighten up the moment, “I have enough quirks as it is and don’t need all the side effects. I’m okay, Mom, really.”

They heard his father come in the front door and go through his customary practice of throwing his work on the couch, marching across the great room to the mahogany bar, and pouring himself a glass of Scotch whisky. He walked to the kitchen, where he opened the refrigerator without noting Matthew’s presence. After removing a bottle of green olives, he turned to his wife and son.

“Hi, Pop. How are things with the mills?”

His father set his drink on the counter, put a dozen olives in a bowl, picked up both on his way to turn on the evening news. “Did you get any speeding tickets?” he asked, “because if you did, don’t expect me to pay for them or a damn lawyer to get you off.”

“It’s nice to see you too, Dad. I did have a run-in with a Georgia state trooper, but I have a feeling that ticket will never make it to Maine.” His father grunted and left the kitchen.

“I’m sorry, honey,” his mother said.

“You’re not responsible for his ways, Mom.”

“I know, but I often wish you boys knew the man I fell in love with. You might find this surprising, but he was gentle and laughed all the time.”

Matthew knew his father loved his family more than life, but he found *that* picture of his father hard to imagine. Matthew kissed his mother and went up to his room. He fell into the bed without removing his shoes.

The next morning Maria waited for her father to leave the house and then met Matthew in town to discuss where to go from here. They couldn’t talk to the authorities. Maria suggested they confide in Johnny Fazio’s father, as he had been a cop. Matthew said he trusted Joe Fazio but in the end, the less that knew, the better.

They spent the rest of the day and the following day, after Maria attended mass with her father, on the southern shore of Millinocket Lake. It was difficult for Matthew to go back to UMaine Sunday afternoon to finish the semester, especially with so many questions unanswered. But he figured the ball was in Mr. E's court.

On Monday, his second day back on campus Matthew carried a stack of empty yellow pads and a large knapsack full of books into the library. He sat in his favorite corner of the fourth floor and began to plan how he was going to attack the future. He wrote something Tremont had said: *the prize in the Cracker Jack box.*

CJ Energy Cells.
The 3/3 formula???

Miami Beach seemed like a hundred years ago, he thought sadly.

The next time he looked at the clock, four hours had passed, and he had filled two thick yellow pads with notes. He turned to his worn copy of *Capturing the Sun* and thought what a tragic waste it was to lose not just one but two Jacksons. For the next hour, he pored over a set of complicated formulas with books spread across a desk large enough for six students. He had been dozing when a tap on the shoulder startled him.

"Hello, Matty. I'm still mad at you for dumping us off in Daytona without even a goodbye kiss."

He turned to see Donna and Darma smiling – one over each shoulder. "I would have picked you girls up but – "

Donna interrupted, "I know. I'm just teasing. My aunt told me you called on your way past. Why did you leave Florida so soon? Well, never mind, I've been carrying this thing around for days." She dropped a heavy envelope on the desk and they both giggled. "Some guy paid me two hundred dollars to deliver it to you."

"What did he look like?"

"Probably close to my father's age, under six foot, fit as a fiddle with a striking cleft chin. Does he sound familiar?"

Matthew shook his head.

"He sure could have saved a few bucks by giving it to you himself, don't you think?"

Darma kissed Matthew on the cheek and whispered, "If Maria ever decides to dump you . . ."

When they were gone, he tore open the envelope. Inside were photographs, lots of photographs. There were pictures of him and Maria with Cracker Jack in Miami Beach, and later with Marcos at the truck stop, and then a few in the driveway with Uncle Carl's family. If those were not alarming enough, the next stack of eight-by-ten pictures were of him rowing in the river and walking on campus, Maria and her father at their restaurant, his mother with Estebanez in the Eaton kitchen, and many more of family and friends. There was no note. But, there didn't have to be. Someone wanted him to know *they* could get to him or loved ones anytime, anywhere. Cameron's journal notes made it clear that someone had used the same tactics on him. Matthew packed up his books and said to the empty stacks, "I wonder when the bloody horses head is going to show up in my bed."

April and May passed. He did his best to concentrate on his classes and his correspondence course with the MIT program. Nearly every morning before the sun rose, he wore out his anxiety on the river with his rowing crew. His friends often commented about how serious he had become.

At the very least, he expected to hear from one of the many authorities that had his name, address, and social security number, but by finals time in late May, he still had heard nothing. He could rationalize why he didn't hear from the policewoman or the detective in New York. What happened to them was just another of many unsolved crimes. A few times he considered calling Deputy Alonso in South Florida, but each time would decide it was better not to stir the pot. He was particularly curious about the connection he might have discovered with the rare plane and its owner. It could be a link to the rest of the criminals. Most of all, he wondered and worried about the precious cargo Cracker Jack entrusted to him that had been replaced by fruit and nuts.

He finished his semester finals and express mailed his last project to MIT. This was his last morning on the river until September; and instead of rowing, he pushed out on the choppy water in a seven-foot kayak. He thought of how he and his brother had spent many summers in kayaks and hoped Sean would soon be back from Kuwait. That's where he assumed Sean was. The last postcard had a Kuwait postmark and simply said, "Study hard, I'll see you soon." He so wanted to tell Sean about his crazy spring break adventure. There was the need to impress his older brother, but there was also the promise to keep the research a secret from everyone except Maria.

Since he returned to UMaine, he had been creating scenarios, postulates, and theories based on what little he had read in the Cameron Jackson's journals and the information Cracker Jack fed him in Miami Beach. He revised his MIT project to focus solely on quantum physics and energy storage.

Each night he sat in Fogler, the UMaine library, devouring everything he could find on the subject. And, when not competing on the river, he left in the middle of the night and drove to Cambridge, where his enthusiastic MIT professor set aside articles and books on his core subject. His professor gave him an empty classroom so he could research in peace. He bunked with a quiet quantum physics grad student, with coke bottle glasses and a proclivity for heavy metal music.

After a few weeks, he became satisfied that he could study, work in labs, and submit his research all the while skirting wide around CJ Energy Cells, a completely new and renewable energy source. Nobody would ever guess that he was preparing himself for the time when he would receive the duffel bags from Mr. E. He suddenly felt a nervous energy and thought, *if* I received them.

Matthew packed up his VW bus replacement, a dark blue Jeep Cherokee he bought off the company mechanic, Mr. Johnson; strapped his kayak on the top; and latched his mountain bike on the back. He drove north to Millinocket unsure of what he would do for the summer. Probably work for his father. And wait. He felt depressed and lost. He knew CJ Energy possessed him.

He was ready to run with what he now knew was his life's mission – carrying on the Jackson legacy.

CHAPTER 35

June 2, 1995

Riddle

MATTHEW HAD PLENTY of time to get from the UMaine campus to Maria's graduation. He didn't expect a logging truck to flip, causing hours of traffic delays.

When he finally saw the sign for Millinocket, he looked at his watch. He would never make it. He drove up to Stearns High School past the vinyl "Class of 1995 Graduation" sign. He parked and ran into the building, down the hall, and into the auditorium. The packed room seated no more than two hundred, with families lining the walls and kids sitting in the aisles. He heard a familiar voice greet the audience. Maria was at the podium ready to give the valedictorian message. She looked up, and even at a distance, Matthew could see her give him *that* look. He spotted his parents and Mr. Valdeorras sitting together in the front row and plunged through the crowd of Moms, Dads, and siblings. Maria continued her speech as Matthew took his seat.

After the graduation, most of the senior class and their families gravitated a few miles east to Godello's Spanish Restaurant where Mr. Valdeorras's staff had prepared a massive display of food and champagne, accompanied by a popular but awful local band led by one of Maria's classmates. The graduation party lasted late into the night.

At midnight, Matthew and Maria watched the last family drive away.

"Sorry I was late, there was a logging truck – "

"You made it; that's what's important. I have to help my dad finish closing up. Will you pick me up in the morning to get some breakfast and catch up on everything?"

Matthew went home to find his mother in the kitchen and his father long since in bed, snoring so loud Matthew thought the dishes in the sink were rattling. He sat down in his usual chair. His mother dried her hands and handed him a stack of mail. She pulled one envelope out and put it on top. It was addressed to him and had a return address he did not recognize: Destin, Florida. There was no postage. Matthew's heart rate doubled. "When did this come?"

He thought it was strange that his mother's face reddened. She seemed self-conscious as she returned to the dishes in the sink.

"Felix," she cleared her throat, "Mr. Estebanez, brought it by yesterday morning."

Matthew's chair fell over as he stood. "He was here? Is he still in town?" He headed for the door.

"No, honey. He said he had business to attend to, and all he left was that envelope."

Matthew tore open the envelope and sat back at the table reading. Bewildered, he looked at his mother. "What did he say? Was he here long?"

"He was here a short time," she answered, "I don't know, maybe an hour, two."

"Did you tell him I'd be home today?"

"Yes, dear, but he said he had business in Boston and couldn't wait. He said you would understand."

Matthew did *not* understand. He had enough bottled up inside his heart and head to burst, yet the man who had all the answers visited his mother instead of him and left him a one-page note bearing a riddle.

> Within this year, the mortar set, and now the treasure lies: The Clementine lunar probe launches an old bottle vertically from the moon's surface. Four hundred thirty milliseconds after launch, the bottle is exactly 2,222 millimeters from the moon's surface; and 5 seconds after release, the bottle is moving towards the moon's surface at exactly 5 meters per second. The time in milliseconds tells the cornerstone year when the object is exactly 4 meters from the

> moon's surface. Once inside, the only yarn one who spins has to sell is to tell. Your destiny lays four paces south of that which was made in the oldest of the largest in Europe by mass. You are over a barrel as the seller has lodged high prices.

Matthew could not sleep as he wrestled over the riddle. It was just like Mr. E. As he tutored Matthew, they had devised puzzles and played games. After a few years, Matthew was stumping his tutor and could unravel nearly anything Estebanez threw at him. But this latest was a doozey.

Maria and Matthew sat at Danny's Nook in the center of town enjoying biscuits, gravy, and most of all, each other's company. They held hands across the table, and after the food was gone, they studied Estebanez's riddle.

"I have the math portion figured out, but I think that was a ruse to throw me off. I don't know what his game is now, but if anyone else close to me goes berserk, I don't know what I'll do. My mother was acting weird last night when she handed me this note. She called him Felix. He never once told me his first name."

"You don't think . . ."

Matthew held up his hand. "Don't say it. I wouldn't put anything past him, especially now, but my mother would never."

"I'm not saying they did anything, but it's possible there's some chemistry between them. Mr. Estebanez can be very charming, and your mom is high class and beautiful. He's been part of your family's life for more than a decade, so . . ."

"Which parts of *don't go there* do I need to spell?"

She took a bite out of her biscuit and mumbled, "I'm just saying."

Matthew tried to shake off the idea of his mother and Mr. Felix Estebanez. He flattened out the riddle and read it aloud yet again.

"Most words in a riddle have alternate meanings," Maria said, "so let's separate each word. What else could a spinner be than someone who makes things out of yarn? Maybe it's a silk worm or a spider? And notice he indicates he doesn't have any yarn? So maybe instead of yarn, it's thread."

"Or a tale."

"A tail?"

"A yarn can be a story, or a tale."

"Oh, right," she said laughing.

They tried to dissect each word, but as the morning lapsed, the many interruptions to congratulate Maria and welcome back Matthew, and the "When are you two going to get married?" cracks from the old men soon forced them to find a quieter place. On the way out the door, they nearly ran into Joe Fazio, who had an office above the restaurant.

Joe gave them a bear hug, one in each huge arm. "I thought that was your mutt sitting by the door. A trophy from your trip to the Florida beaches, I understand. Johnny will be back from college at Miami of Ohio on Monday, and the wife insists that you two join us for a serious night of eggplant *parmagiana e molto bene*!" he said, touching his fingers to his lips and closing his eyes. Nobody loved food more than Joe. They assured him it was a date – not that he would accept anything less – and went out to Matthew's Jeep where SoBe was already sitting in the backseat.

They drove north. Matthew unlocked the double doors of the barn. Inside was the severely injured VW bus, just as they left it. He was running over every word of the memorized riddle in his mind. But Maria had other things on *her* mind, and Matthew was easily persuaded.

Later they sat on a couple bales of hay laughing at SoBe, who was fast asleep with her forepaws covering her eyes.

"I think that dog knows more than she lets on," Matthew said.

"Every time I look at her, I think of those poor kids living with drug dealer parents. And now they are in social services!"

"Maybe we should have picked them up too?"

She hit him in the shoulder. "Don't make fun of me. Can you imagine how much those children miss SoBe and how much she must miss them?"

"Maybe one day we'll go back and look for them," he said a bit more seriously.

Maria liked that idea and let him know it with a kiss. "Okay, let's get back to the riddle."

"I've got it!" Matthew cried out, jumping to his feet. It's in the cellar of the Katahdin Sporting Lodge!"

"How do you get that?" She hit her hand against her forehead. "Weaver. Mr. Weaver! The spinner is not a spinner at all, he's a weaver!"

"Exactly. Estebanez spent more time at that lodge than anywhere, and he talked about wine more than he did science. He complained about strange Dennis Weaver, but Mr. E tolerated him. They weren't friends but maybe partners in crime. I overheard Mr. E one day on the phone tell someone he was selling the bottles at Sotheby's in New York City for small fortunes."

He jumped in the Jeep, pushing SoBe out of the front seat. "While I was studying at the lodge, I overheard their arguments. Estebanez played on Weaver's eccentricities. They debated everything – the history of a particular wine, the value and year of a rare edition of Walt Whitman's *Leaves of Grass,* or Thoreau's writings about the woods of Maine. When Weaver wasn't there, Estebanez would go into the cellar on his own, which meant he either had a key or broke in because old Weaver guarded it with his life."

"You don't think Mr. E would steal wine from him, do you?"

"No, of course not." But then again, Matthew thought, what wasn't he capable of?

They drove northwest out of town on Route 11, turning on to the Golden Road just outside of Millinocket.

"The equation?" Maria asked.

"The answer is 1776. That's when the lodge was built, the date on the cornerstone, and Mr. E always said that Weaver lived in that era – in his mind."

"What about France?" Maria asked, alluding to the section of the riddle referring to the largest land mass in Europe.

"I don't know," Matthew said, but he had an idea.

They drove through the narrow pass the locals call *the dike,* between Millinocket and Ambajejus Lakes, taking Baxter Park Road ten miles toward the bottom western side of Baxter State Park.

Matthew was deep in his thoughts about what he hoped to find at the lodge, when he realized Maria had not spoken for quite a while. He turned to find she was hyperventilating. The Jeep screeched to a halt. "What is it?"

"I don't know. I mean, I know, but I," she struggled to talk, "I get these visions, they are like a dream, but my eyes are open. It started when we passed through the dike. You know it has happened before but only when we are this far north. At night after each episode I have that crazy nightmare – " Maria held her hands to her chest and choked between breaths.

This time, Matthew was experiencing a creepy feeling and said, "I think I should take you back to town. I'll bet Doc Malone would see you on short notice."

"No! I mean no, let's go ahead, it's passing as quickly as it came."

Matthew wasn't convinced.

"Really. Let's go to the lodge, it's too important."

Reluctantly Matthew turned off at the Katahdin Sporting Lodge sign and drove up the steep long gravel drive to the front of the two-hundred-year-old rustic building. Maria had never been to the lodge, and she could not hide her reaction to the stunning views of Mount Katahdin a few miles to the northwest and Millinocket Lake to the south.

SoBe bounded out and ran after a rabbit high tailing it to the woods. "SoBe!" Maria called.

"She'll come back. The exercise is good for her. Winter is the busy season for Weaver, but there's typically a lot of year-round activity here." There were four trucks and SUVs in the lot as well as a late model Jaguar that Matthew knew belonged to Weaver. "The visitors are probably hunters." People came to the lodge to fish, hike, hunt, or as a base for overnight trips deep into the Katahdin forest.

They walked up the granite steps into a massive porch and through solid oak doors hung in the late nineteenth century.

"How are you going to get into the cellar?"

"I have no idea. Maybe he'll just let us in."

Maria laughed. "Even my father has never been allowed into that Revolutionary War shrine, and he's bought more bottles of wine from Mr. Weaver than anyone."

They approached the front desk where the unmistakable Mr. Weaver had his back to them as he adjusted an autographed picture of the actor Dennis Weaver. Satisfied, he slapped his hands together and turned to his guests. He raised his eyebrows comically as he asked, "Have I ever told you about the other Dennis Weaver?"

"Yes, sir, you have," and before Weaver could ask Maria, "I've told Maria as well," Matthew said. With that small lie, he aimed to save an hour or more.

"Then I will save you the boring details. Did you know he and I are the same age? Born on June 4, 1924. I've been told I sound more like him as I get older. What do you think?"

"Absolutely, Mr. Weaver, my father was saying that very thing just the other day," he lied, knowing how much Mr. Weaver respected his father. That lie brought a big smile to the gray and leathery man.

Mr. Weaver walked along the front desk that spanned the width of the room decorated with mounted heads of big game and Native American relics along with a life-size picture of Dennis Weaver as his television drama character Sam McCloud. He reached under the picture and took out the key Matthew had seen him hide there many times. "It's about time you kids got here."

Surprised, Matthew said, "You were expecting us, Mr. Weaver?"

"I had a bet with our mutual friend Mr. Estebanez. I said it would take you a week to figure out the riddle. He said less than a day." He looked at his watch. "I figured if you got the letter after the graduation – by the way, congratulations, Miss Valdeorras – it's been less than twelve hours. You've cost me a 1947 Australian Torbreck Shiraz. A rare bottle indeed." He sighed. "Easy come, easy go."

Matthew and Maria were smiling like children about to enter the living room on Christmas morning.

"Do you realize you will be the first Eaton in over a hundred years to visit the Weaver cellars? And you, the first Valdeorras ever?" He walked to the end of the check-in desk before saying, "And the last."

"What was that, Mr. Weaver?" Matthew thought he might have heard him wrong. But when Weaver didn't respond, he shrugged it off as eccentricity.

"No photography, ladies and gentlemen, and please do not touch anything. You break it, you buy it."

Matthew wanted to ask about the Eaton who visited the cellar a hundred years ago. He was sure it was quite a story when told by the verbose Mr. Weaver, but he decided there was nothing more important than what was in that cellar.

They followed Weaver into the lodge library full of lounge chairs, small tables with chess sets ready for play, and thousands of books of which many were first editions, some preceding the American Revolution. Maria's eyes widened as Weaver pulled a nine-foot-by-four-foot false bookshelf section away from the wall to reveal a rock wall and a rounded black door with crisscrossing steel bars. It creaked and groaned under its own weight as the musty air met them. Weaver motioned for them to go ahead as he pulled the library shelves and then the medieval-like door behind him.

"It's too dark," Maria said, "I really can't see in front of me." There was a clicking sound as Weaver lit an oil lamp with a fireplace lighter. "This is pretty spooky. I love it."

At the bottom of the step was a larger door that took much of Matthew's strength to open. Even cooler, damper air rushed at them. Weaver reached past Matthew and lit another oil lamp.

The cavernous wine cellar illuminated in front of them revealed aisles of wine racks as far as they could see. They heard another click behind them. When Matthew turned, Weaver, who he thought resembled a killer out of a Hitchcock movie in the flickering lamplight, was closing the door. "I like to keep the doors closed when I'm down here. You never know what kind of character might wish to venture in to see my family treasures. Watch your step, children."

When they reached the bottom, Matthew asked, "Mr. Weaver, do you know what we are looking for?"

"I certainly do. As I said, Mr. Estebanez and I have become great friends. Go down to the end of the third aisle and turn right." They heard more clicking as another and then another lantern was lit. The room took on a dim eeriness with the lantern flames flickering off the wet walls.

"Near the oldest French wines, right?" Maria asked.

"Precisely."

They took the right turn at the end and found, stacked against the far wall, the Jackson's duffel bags. Matthew breathed a sigh of relief and reverently ran his hands over them. "I've been thinking about you guys for quite some time."

"I'd say more like obsessing over them," Maria said, laughing. Her glee ended with the sound of the creaking door. Matthew turned around expecting to see Weaver but he was gone. He walked around the corner and looked down the aisle. Getting nervous, he called out, "Mr. Weaver?" When he got to the base of the stairs, he was just in time to see the door shut and hear the key turning in the padlock. He sprinted up the lower steps yelling Weaver's name. When he got to the shelf, he tried the black iron handle. It would not budge. He pounded on the door and yelled, "Weaver, this is not funny. Please open the door." But he knew it was useless. The chance of any sound getting through the thick door, the next one, and into the library was slim to none.

Matthew rummaged through the four bags and was satisfied the contents were all intact. He dug down deep into one of the bags, breathed a sigh of relief as he felt a familiar leather pouch, and pulled out the oily rag containing the gun with the initials "CJ" on each side of the handle. Thinking back to the events at the Bronx Park confirmed that only Estebanez could have put the gun in the duffel bag.

"I sure hope you won't need that again," Maria said.

"Me too, but it's nice to know we have it. If that crazy Weaver comes through that door again, I might have to shoot and ask questions later. As far as I can tell, there's no other way out of here except up."

"Why would Weaver lock us in down here? He said he was working with Estebanez. Do you think Estebanez put him up to this? I would hate to think he's the enemy."

"Why would he go through all of this trouble when he obviously is the one that took the duffel bags out of the bus down at South of the Border? He's the only one who could have put the gun back in the bag. If he planned for Weaver to lock us down here, he wouldn't have left us a weapon."

"Then who put him up to this?"

"Maybe Weaver is working with the guys in the Bronx Park or the Arabs. He's a greedy bastard, so if someone got to him after Estebanez delivered the bags, they're either in Millinocket or on their way. I feel like we can trust Estebanez. He's gotten us out of more than one jam. If he wanted the research, he could have kept it." He stopped and lowered his head. "Then again . . ."

"What?"

"Then again, he seems to be the one that got us into this in the first place. I feel like such a damn puppet. Sometimes I feel angry, but mostly I'm confused and a bit in awe. If Estebanez wasn't one of the good guys, then why would he have groomed me all of these years for this?" He patted the duffel bag under him. "Even if he isn't who he has said he was, it's clear he's always been watching out for me."

Maria sat down beside him and put an arm around his shoulder.

"I know. I keep contradicting myself," Matthew said.

"It's clear he knows a lot about Cracker Jack and the inventions, and he devoted a decade to working with you. Even if under false pretenses."

"How's he linked to the Jacksons? The whole Weaver connection makes no sense at all. Estebanez barely tolerated the loony old man and, I think, only played along with his dementia because he liked wine and living here in Maine."

"I still think the connection between Mr. E and the Jacksons is through Marcos," Maria said. "Did you finally reach Mr. E?"

"I called all the numbers Estebanez left around town for forwarding. They were all disconnected. Then I called the Shell station in Miami Beach. I told the guy who answered I was a reporter doing a story on the shootout. Turns out, he's the owner, and has never had anyone working for him by that name, not Marcos Estebanez or Marcos Estefan or even anyone meeting his description. He did have a wrecker stolen off his lot that same night, and the employee who was supposed to be on that shift never showed up again. But the shot-up wrecker did."

They sat in silence for a while and then Maria chuckled.

"What could be funny?"

"I just had a picture in my mind of Clarice Starling stuck down in the cellar with a serial killer!"

"You, my dear, are insane, but there's not another woman in the world, besides Clarice, who I'd rather be with through everything. And you can still find humor in it. We'll get out of this mess, I promise."

She kissed him. "I know. And then you're going to get to work on saving the world."

Matthew unfolded the oily leather, loaded twelve rounds into the magazine and snapped it into Cameron Jackson's .45. He wondered how many times over the years Cameron or Tremont had held this same gun, expecting someone to come through the door.

"Knowing all you know now about the deception and the danger, then measuring it against the research with all it could offer, have you ever wished you never knew about all of this?" Maria drummed her fingers on the duffel bag under them, waiting for his answer. Matthew just smiled.

CHAPTER 36

June 3, 1995

Lost

THE NEXT DAY everyone in the town buzzed about the disappearance of their Matthew and Maria. The *Katahdin Times* moved their front-page story about a controversy over the new owners of the Great Northwestern Paper Mill property. Prior to this, the biggest story in the area was the train crash of 1979 that was heard two counties away. Today's headline read, "MISSING! Jeep Found Abandoned." The article, complete with a picture, reported a Great Northern Paper Mill employee heading south to Millinocket for the second shift had noticed a Jeep north of town, on the side of the Golden Road between Ambajejus and Millinocket Lakes. "It just seemed out of place," he told the plant security guard. The guard had called the Millinocket police, who drove north to find the Jeep parked between two of the many tall white birch trees above Ambajejus Lake beach. A Baxter State Park ranger stood waiting.

The ranger, Pete Cartier Marks, a Millinocket-born Native American of the Aroostook Micmac tribe, shook hands with Officer Franklin Dubois. "Hey, Frank, I was heading up to Baxter when I heard your call over the radio. So this here is the Eaton kid's car? It's completely cleaned out, doors open, keys still in the ignition."

"Much too clean for a teenager's car," said Officer Dubois. "I hate to think anyone would do them harm. They're like my own kids. Maybe the two went for a hike and got lost."

"That don't make much sense, Frank. Why would they park here?" Pete asked rhetorically. "And they wouldn't leave the keys!"

"Thanks, Pete. You can head to the park if you want. I'll radio Harry and get him to begin organizing a search and rescue." Colonel Harry "K-9" Williams held the top post in Maine's Department of Inland Fisheries and Wildlife. The Colonel was best known for upgrading the bureau's search and rescue equipment to high technology and drilling his wardens on techniques until they dropped. Harry came to the Bureau of Warden Services fresh out of UMaine's school of forest resources as a K-9 specialist in the early eighties.

"Naw, I think I'll hang here. I called in, and a couple of the other guys will be off soon and are gonna come down if we need them. I'll be in charge of the search on Baxter Park property for the first twenty-four hours and as you say, the warden's department will take over after that. I also called my mother and she's going to call Chief Tanner. If anyone has seen anything up here, he'll know."

"Don't start telling me this all has to do with that damn angry spirit on the mountain, Pete. I really don't have time for it."

"I know you're not a believer, Frank, but I've seen too much crazy stuff up here not to believe it. If anything happened, you can be sure Pamola had something to do with it."

Officer Dubois spat and shook his head, "Do you know Matthew?"

"I went to school with his brother Sean. He's a good friend and was a hell-of-a tight end. If something's happened to Matt, there'll be a lot of folks all over wanting to help out."

The idea of foul play began to set in as the hours went by and newspaper reporters arrived on the scene. A national newswire ran the story.

Parker Eaton arrived in a company truck. Dubois briefed him on what little he knew while they walked the four hundred yards to the Millinocket Lake shore to the east. They crossed over the Golden Road, pressed between thick rows of bushes, and then crossed over the Baxter Park Road. Stopping to rest between

The North Woods Trading Post and Big Moose Inn, Parker said, "I can't believe nobody saw anything. This is a busy time of year up here."

"Pete and I have questioned anyone who would have been in the area in the last twenty-four hours. So far . . . we have no leads."

The two men hiked down the hill through a thicket of pine trees to the shore. They stood for a long time staring out into the vast Millinocket Lake, and off toward the smaller eastern mountains.

They hiked the quarter mile back to Matthew's Jeep and then down through the white birch trees and to the Ambajejus shore below where a familiar game warden was crouched at the waters edge. He turned and they recognized Sergeant Allen Willis. The warden had a strong build, was graying at the temples under a black cap, and appeared to be in his fifties – but he could be older. He wore the bureaus traditional forest green military type fatigues with red insignia and patches above the pockets and on his shoulders.

Willis reached out and took Parker's hand and then gave Dubois a friendly nod. "Hell of a situation Parker. We'll do all we can to find the kids as quickly as possible. The colonel has made this our top priority. The chances of finding them is much higher in the first few days, so we'll waste no time."

"Thanks Al, it means a lot to me that Harry sent you."

"I was only a few miles north checking on a crazy drunk who reported being harassed by a moose. I'd have arrested *him* for harassing the moose! But this was more important."

"Do you have all three air boats at your disposal?"

"Only two, but they are on the way; Harry, I mean Colonel Williams has also dedicated all of our K-9 teams. And you know we have the best dive team in the country – " He paused and looked away from Parker's shocked expression.

The men stood on the beach and looked north toward the floatplane base. Dubois interjected, "Jean LeVasseur will have two floatplanes up in the air within the hour." To the south was a boat launch and several seasonal cottages, and off to the southwest they could see a few small islands and Jo-Mary Mountain, part of the hundred mile wilderness. "There are already a couple dozen locals out on their boats searching the shore area of all eight lakes. The off duty Baxter Park rangers are getting' them organized."

Parker sighed deeply and said, "We got a hundred thousand acres to cover and half of that is water; beyond that we have over a half million acres of wilderness."

"The weather could not be better," Warden Willis encouraged. If they're out there, we'll find 'em."

Parker's normally gruff demeanor seemed to have gone through a metamorphosis. It was clear that nothing in the world mattered but finding his son. "I know you guys will pull out all the stops. My other boy's expected in today, and all my employees will be up here within the hour to help search." He looked over at the four Baxter Park Rangers who were now huddled over maps spread out on one of their trucks. "Those rangers' giving us their spare time is sure appreciated. That looks like Pete, he knows these parts almost as good as Sean." He rubbed his forehead. "Nothing makes sense here, Frank. What do you really think? And don't give me the canned cop version."

"You're right, Parker. It's like they vanished without a trace. I called Bangor, and they're sending a forensics team to dust the Jeep. Right now, it's all we've got. Joe Fazio seems to be the last to see them at the cafe. I only hope there's a simple explanation, like when you misplace your wallet or keys. They're always somewhere close by."

"Matt's an expert woodsman. He knows the territory better than any guide twice his age."

"Do you think the dog was with them?" Dubois asked.

"What dog?"

"The kids had a shepherd mix with them in town."

"I don't know anything about a dog," Parker said, looking northwest toward the mountains. "If for some crazy reason he's out there, he can take care of himself." He noticed Phil Valdeorras approaching. "And Maria."

Sean flew in from Washington DC that morning and arrived just after ten at the crime scene, with his mother. It had been forty-eight hours since Matthew and Maria disappeared. Dozens of cars and trucks lined the one mile stretch of parallel roads flanked by the two lakes. Though he knew he was working outside the proper chain of command, Ranger Pete had called in every ATV owner and boater in the area, official or civilian. Search parties were underway on land and by water and Pete helped the agitated wardens coordinate a makeshift command center on the Ambajejus shoreline. Then he made a phone call. One that he knew could be more important than anything else. He called his mother who was Tribal Liaison to the Chief of the Aroostook Band of the Micmac Tribe.

Someone hailed Warden Willis from up on the Golden Road. "That's Warden Donnie Leighton," Willis said. He's going to set up a large tent and some tables down here." The warden jogged up the hill to meet Lieutenant Leighton.

A square-jawed, blonde young man approached Parker Eaton. "Mr. Eaton. I recognized you from pictures in Matthew's room." He shook Mr. Eaton's hand. "My name is Floyd Schmidt. Matthew and I go to school together. You could say we're best friends. I had pulled out of UMaine to head home to Fairfield when I heard the news on the radio." Parker assured him they appreciated his help.

News reporters were arriving all morning from Bangor, Boston, and Hartford. When news that college students disappear under suspicious circumstances, especially in an area where crime was non-existent and one of the kids is a celebrity, it became national news. Someone yelled, "I think that is CNN!" All eyes focused on a huge colorful van clad with large satellite dishes as it raced up the Golden Road from Millinocket.

With that and other distractions, hardly anyone noticed a short, dark-haired, burly stranger against a gray Cadillac Seville. He took notes on a flip pad and then, just as Kip Ackerman, the *New York Times* reporter, headed in his direction, got in his car and drove toward Millinocket.

Estebanez and his nephew Marcos lay on thick-cushioned lounge chairs soaking in the sun on a huge sailboat, their office and home, moored off the coast of Destin, Florida. A dark man resembling a linebacker, wearing a shoulder holster, approached to hand him a portable telephone. The man returned to his post on the port side where he stood staring toward the shore with his left hand locked on his right wrist behind his back. Across the boat stood another man of similar height and build, a cigarette hanging from his lips as he stood at attention staring at his side of the ocean.

Estebanez listened for a moment before he dropped his cigar on the deck and leapt to his feet. "Bruno, Marty, get the dinghy." Not bothering to pick up his cigar, he gave Marcos an overview while they ran mid-ship and down in the galley to change and pack an overnight bag. They both slipped extra magazines and boxes of ammunition in with their gear. Marcos and Estebanez rushed to a dinghy attached to the stern of the yacht. "Call ahead to have my plane pulled out of the hanger. We're going back to Maine."

Four hours later Estebanez's Cessna Citation V landed a hundred miles north of Millinocket at the Presque Isle Regional Airport. He considered flying into the Millinocket Regional Airport to save time, but didn't want to bring the media down on top of him.

He used the phone in the air traffic controller's office. "I'm in Maine, and I'll be down there in a few hours." He listened for a minute. "I'm not sure what to think." He listened another moment. "CNN? Already? Son of a – I'll call you as soon as I get there."

"He's upset?" Marcos asked.

"Damn right he is. I dropped the ball on this one." Estebanez put both hands on his head and ran them down his face stopping his fingers at his temples to massage in small circles. "How could I have been so stupid?"

Three stories above the wine cellar a CNN crew camped out in the lobby of the Katahdin Sporting Lodge. Stacy Stossal, Broadcasting live across the world, interviewed the proprietor.

"Yes, I knew the kids well, and it will be a terrible tragedy if they aren't found. Why, it wasn't long ago young Matthew was studying chemistry or astronomy right over there." He pointed a bony finger in the direction of the library. "Of course, I haven't seen him or Miss Valdeorras since the graduation a few days ago. Would you like to see the library? Or perhaps you would like to see my collection of Dennis Weaver memorabilia?" With that, the cameraman panned back to Stacy who, through a small receiver in her ear and a tiny microphone on her lapel, was in conversation with the Atlanta news anchor.

She put a hand to her ear and said, "Yes, John, the small mill town of Millinocket is in shock." She said into the camera. "There has been no word from the authorities that they have even the slightest lead to the disappearance of Matthew Eaton and Maria Valdeorras." She listened before replying, "That's right, John. He is the very same young man who amazed the science community as a child. His high school science teacher told me this morning that Eaton won the Smithsonian Youth Inventors award, the highest honor in the science community for youth. He won it a record five times over ten years. Matthew is currently a student at the University of Maine." She listened again. "Thank you, John. We'll be getting information to you as the story unfolds." She pulled the tiny microphone from her collar and handed it to her assistant. "Let's head back to town and get some interviews from the locals." The rest of the news crew had been standing close by awaiting directions. She dispersed her team to maximize the story's mass appeal. "Carlos? You and Sheila stop at the picnic grounds where they set up the search and rescue command center. Linda, see if you can find the paper mill employee who first reported the Jeep. If you come across the parents of either kid, call me immediately."

By now, every national news agency had a crew in town. Stacy had followed up on a lead involving the Katahdin Sporting Lodge, but it seemed to be a wild goose chase. Back in Millinocket, reporters were camped in front of the Eaton and Valdeorras households and their businesses. Godello's had been closed indefinitely as all the employees had insisted on joining in the search.

Parker and Maria's father, Phil had barely slept since their children went missing and, along with Sean, were leading separate searches north and northwest of the search party camp.

Maria shivered and looked at her watch while repositioning her head on one of the duffel bags. "It's nearly noon. It'll be three days. Papa will be sick, and I'm worried about SoBe. Who knows what that crazy old man will do to her?" She watched as Matthew pulled a dusty bottle out of a wine rack.

"How about a 1962 Chablis Grand Cru?" He stumbled on the pronunciation of Vaudesir Billaud-Simon and sat down next to her to dig out another cork with his pocketknife. "I'm worried about SoBe too." He looked at the five empty wine bottles lined up in front of them. "Want another potato?"

"I don't think I ever want to see another potato as long as I live." She sat up and held her head with both hands. "But I'll take another carrot."

"If we only had some oil, salt, pepper, foil and a camping stove, I could make us a great hiker's stew." He went over to the crates of carrots, potatoes, and onions that, along with a plentiful supply of wine, provided their sustenance. He peeled the skin off a carrot before handing it to Maria.

"Eh, what's up, doc?" she said with a wine enhanced grin.

"You're a cute carrot-eating lush, Bugs."

She took the new bottle from Matthew to wash it down. "At least we're discerning drunks." She put a hand to her temple. "Oh, my head aches. How long can we live on raw vegetables and rare wines?" She took a sip and then said, "Speaking of headaches, you haven't needed your pills since we've been down here."

"That's true. Maybe it's the damp air or the expensive wine?"

"I guess we are going to have to keep you drunk in a dungeon then. Don't worry, we can set up your energy lab and I'll allow you conjugal visits."

"Really? Can I choose anyone I want?"

Maria's mouth opened wide and she gave him that look. He knew what was coming as she punched her knuckles into his shoulder. Still, Matthew could not control his laughing, which made her all the more infuriated.

After the spar, Matthew leaned back against the cold wall and stared at one of the lamps. "I just realized something," he said. "The flames are flickering."

"So?"

"There has to be a breeze coming from somewhere."

Maria picked up the bottle and followed as he walked the outer perimeter of the cellar. Matthew touched his finger to his tongue and tested the air. He found the cool air was strongest along the floor. They walked to the far corner on the opposite side from where they had found the duffel bags. Piles of antique winemaking equipment, barrels, and crates of bottles at least six feet deep and just as high blocked the back corner. He could feel the breeze coming from between the rustic items.

"We have nothing else to occupy our time. Well, almost nothing," Maria said with a wink as she climbed unsteadily onto one of the barrels. She handed down crates and unusual iron and wood tools, and Matthew piled them up against the sidewall. When they finally cleared it all from in front of the black wall, it revealed a door identical to the one leading from the library to the cellar. A rusted padlock with a skeleton key hole on the handle hung from the latch on a steel bar spanning the width of the door. The breeze was coming from where the dirt and rock floor had eroded to reveal a four-inch space.

Matthew went back to the pile he had created where he remembered throwing an iron pole. He slid it into the padlock and leveraged one end against the rock wall. "Let's just hope the old lock has weakened from age." With his foot against the wall, he pulled on the other end with all his might. It wouldn't budge. Then he heard a heavy door creak.

"Someone's coming, Matthew."

"Hide behind the junk," he said, running to retrieve Cameron Jackson's pistol.

CHAPTER 37

June 6, 1995 11:00 a.m.

Search

ESTEBANEZ HAD ARRIVED in town with Marcos around noon on the third day after the kids disappeared. When he and Marcos got to the crime scene, they observed the Jeep and four officers with CSI printed on their jackets. They were working a large area surrounded by yellow crime tape. Evidence squares were spray-painted on the grass around the vehicle. Dozens of cars, trucks, and vans were scattered throughout the area running alongside the western lake.

Estebanez and Marcos joined the locals and law enforcement, including an FBI team led by a DC agent named Flannigan. Flannigan's shirt was partially tucked; his tie hung wrinkled just below a day or two of stubble that could grow into a full beard in a week. Estebanez recognized Flannigan. As he tried to avoid him, the agent caught his eye. Turning away to look for Kate, he noticed a man leaning against a gray Cadillac Seville. Estebanez nodded and brushed his hand along the side of his head in a salute. The other man did the same, got in his car and headed south toward Millinocket. Dependable friends willing to take a week away from their agency retirement in the Caymans to help you out in a pinch were few and far between, he thought.

"Hello, Estebanez, or is it Zebo today, or Smith?" The men stared at each other long and hard. Flannigan seemed to be considering his next words carefully. "I'm sorry for your loss. They meant a lot to me as well."

Estebanez cocked his head slightly, clearly not expecting this from the old agent.

"A word of warning." Flannigan flipped his thumb over his shoulder, "That young NYPD detective – "

"The Flannigan look alike?"

"Yeah, from one hundred years ago, and I never looked *that* good. He's asking a lot of questions about the kids. Apparently, he was on a crime scene in the Bronx Park. You know anything about that?" He paused, and when he didn't get a reaction from Estebanez, he pointed toward the shore of Ambajejus Lake. "Do you see the balding middle-aged man over by the water – the one talking to Mr. Eaton? His name is Kip Ackerman with the New York Times."

That name rang a bell, Estebanez thought.

"He says he can connect your Matthew with Cameron and Tremont Jackson and plans to write a story, once the kids are found." Flannigan held a long pause again. "If I were you, Felix Estebanez, Mr. Zebo, I would keep the press as far away from Matthew as possible."

Estebanez knew Flannigan was fishing for information. He always was. It had been hard as hell to stay out of his path these many years, but he knew Flannigan would eventually connect him with the Jacksons. Estebanez shook his head and said, "Thanks for the heads up."

Flannigan nodded and then reluctantly turned away.

Near one of the shelters, Estebanez saw Joe Fazio, Sean Eaton, and a young man with striking Aryan features. Flannigan handed his card to the young man. He was always recruiting for the Bureau, Estebanez thought wryly. He learned that the group of men had just returned from working their way north of the lakes around the base of Mount Katahdin. Estebanez had been talking to Officer Dubois, though some distance away he clearly heard the familiar baritone voice of Joe Fazio say, "What the hell is he doing here?"

Estebanez was staring at a man wearing a Dallas Cowboys cap as Sean, Floyd, and Fazio walked over to him and Marcos. Officer Dubois finished writing something in a notebook and said, "I'll let you know as soon as I know. You'll do the same?"

"Absolutely, Frank. Good to see you again," Estebanez said. Estebanez turned to Joe Fazio and smiled. "I came as soon as I could." He reached his hand out to shake, but Fazio folded his arms. Estebanez turned to Sean, who took his hand and held on longer than might be considered normal while giving Estebanez a cold-eyed stare. Fazio grunted and returned to the tent area.

Estebanez said, "It's especially good to see you again, Sean, but I wish it were under better circumstances. I hear you've had some serious tours – Iraq, Afghanistan, DC." He noted a small upturn at the side of Sean's mouth with that little bit of humor.

Sean looked hard at Estebanez, but his shoulders relaxed. "Thanks for coming," he said, "we combed the north from land, water, and sky. There're search parties out east and west of here and all over the lakes; my dad's up in a helicopter right now. He should be back soon. Mom is around here somewhere. This is Floyd Schmidt, one of Matthew's buddies from UMaine." Estebanez introduced Marcos, and then Sean retreated to the tent to let Estebanez, Floyd, and Marcos talk.

"Sean is a man of few words," Floyd observed, still flipping Flannigan's card over between his fingers. Marcos nodded in agreement.

"The type of action he's been involved in this past decade can wear on a man's psyche," Estebanez said.

"I'm in peak condition from my decathlon training," Floyd said, "and I'm telling you, I couldn't keep up with the man on the trail. It's good to meet you folks. I've heard a lot about you from Matthew."

"Likewise, Floyd. Your father is the well-known industrialist?" Estebanez remembered reading an extensive file on Floyd's father and found it interesting that he and Matthew had become chums in college. The CIA had compiled a substantial *jacket* on Wilhelm Schmidt starting with his questionable connections in Germany and his migration to the United States after WWII.

"Yes, that's right," Floyd said and then changed the subject quickly. "I hope we find him and Maria soon." Floyd went back to the shelter where Sean was filling packs with provisions for another day in the mountains.

Estebanez turned to find Kate Eaton approaching. Marcos grinned and was about to say something when Estebanez lifted a finger and gave him a warning look.

"Kate, I got here as quick as I could. This is my nephew Marcos. He has a background much like Sean's, and maybe we can help in the search."

"Thank you, Felix, it's all so bizarre, they have to find them." She struggled to hold back the tears. Regaining her composure, Kate looked at Marcos, "It's nice to meet you. I was beginning to think Felix had no family and was beamed down from an alien ship."

"Well, that still may be true."

Kate gave him a half-hearted smile and asked, "Do you mind if I talk to your uncle alone?" She took Estebanez by the arm, and they walked away from all the commotion.

"I've missed you, Kate. And Matthew."

"You disappeared after leaving that letter. I can't tell you how upset Matthew was that you came and went without seeing him."

"Things got crazy with my other businesses and . . ." He noticed something other than worry in her eyes. "What is it, Kate?"

"I have to ask you something, Felix."

"Sure."

"Do you know anything about all of this?"

"How could you even think such a thing?" Estebanez pulled away from Kate in a show of shocked indignation.

Kate seemed embarrassed. "I've never pressed you about your past, but Joe Fazio . . ."

"You don't have to say anything more. Old Colombo Joe has been on my ass for ten years. I have nothing but Matthew's best interest at heart."

"I know. Joe's only looking out for our family." She hesitated. "But this all happened immediately right after Matthew read your note."

"That was nothing but a game between Matthew and I, a word game we've been playing for years. I'm still trying to figure out the last one he gave to me to solve."

"I must admit I thought the riddle a bit strange."

Estebanez frowned. "You read it?"

"I've been reading Matthew's mail since he was in grade school." The sound of trucks arriving got their attention; she gave him a quick hug and went to greet the latest search party arriving from the north. Estebanez wanted to say something. Something that might take away her worry and stress when he noticed the arriving search party included Parker Eaton. He said to Marcos, "This would be a good time to check out the lodge and see what Weaver knows."

"You don't want to face the other man, Uncle?" He asked

"Keep your thoughts to yourself, or there'll be another missing person around here."

As they walked toward the rental car, Marcos couldn't resist. "She's close to your age. That's a first."

Marcos ducked as Estebanez tried to smack him along side the head. "You are misconstruing concern between friends for romance. Let's find young Eaton, shall we?" They pulled away as the other four-wheel drive vehicles pulled in.

Estebanez sped up Baxter Park Road northeast toward his haven these past ten years, some of the best years of his life. He looked in his rear view mirror to see a familiar Land Rover spin through the dirt and onto the road behind him. At first, he thought he should lose the tail, but he had to find Matthew and check on Jackson's research. He wondered which was more important. His professional training said the research, but his heart said the kid.

Ten minutes later, they were turning up the gravel driveway to the Katahdin Sporting Lodge.

"You trust this guy? What's his name? Dennis something?"

"Dennis Weaver. You know, like the actor?"

"Don't know him."

"McCloud?"

"Nope."

"*Seven Angry Men*?"

"Nope."

"*Gentle Ben*?"

"Never was much for television."

"Well, be careful with Weaver. Don't egg him on if he begins talking about the actor Dennis Weaver."

"Gotcha."

After a long silence Estebanez said, "What is it?"

"It's what Agent Flannigan said."

"Yeah, well every time he sticks his nose in our business someone gets hurt. I wish he would stay the hell away."

"I was there in Miami," Marcos said. "I didn't – "

"Like I said before, you did exactly what Tremont told you to do. What I told you to do. You got those kids out of there safely. As I've told you a hundred times, there was nothing else you could do. Tremont knew the risks when he came back out of seclusion."

"I know but – "

"Let's focus on the job at hand." The truth was, Estebanez blamed himself. He should have been down there, watching Marcos's and Tremont's back. Was he really slipping that much? he thought sadly.

They pulled into the parking lot in front of the lodge. Four dark-skinned hunters in full camouflage were stowing gear into their truck. They looked a bit out of place. But this was a tourist area where people came from all over the world to hunt, fish, and hike. He looked at them again. No. Too coincidental.

Estebanez was pleased to see the media staying at the lodge were away. Though not convenient to the town, the lodge was in the center of the fish and game wardens' search and rescue. He noticed an elderly couple emerge from the walkway along the cliff overlooking the valley and Mount Katahdin. Other than them and the hunters, the place was quiet.

"On second thought, why don't you stay out here? Try to stall Joe Fazio."

"The big Sicilian? No problem."

"And keep an eye on those hunters; the tall Arab has put the same bag in and out of the truck twice since we pulled in. I'll only be a few minutes."

The Land Rover sped into the parking lot and came to an abrupt halt next to Marcos. Joe Fazio struggled to get out of the vehicle. "All this hiking is more than I'm used to," he said to Marcos and then walked around him as Marcos tried to bar his path. Marcos, about one quarter Fazio's size, stepped in front of him again. "Hello. It's Joe, isn't it?"

"It is, kid. What's your uncle doing up here?"

"He thought they might have overlooked the fact that someone up here might have heard or seen something."

Fazio pushed past Marcos, who then grabbed hold of Fazio's beefy arm. "You really don't want to be touching me, kid. I snap guys your size for kindling before breakfast."

"It's just that my uncle wanted to talk to the owner alone first. Less confusing. You understand."

"I'll tell you what I understand. Your uncle is up to something and knows a whole hell of a lot more than he's saying. I'm betting he's been up to no good ever since he showed up in the region a decade ago." Fazio lifted the snap off his shoulder holster and checked the load of his older police issue model .38-caliber revolver. He was about to head up the stairs when he heard the grating sound of a magazine seated in the frame of a gun. He turned to see Marcos holding a 9mm Beretta.

Marcos smiled. "I had strict instructions, Joe. Let's wait and see what my uncle comes up with."

Before Fazio could reply, a gunshot went off inside the lodge, then another, and another. They both ran up the steps, with Marcos taking two at a time and Fazio moving fast for such a bulky guy. They stood on both sides of the huge doors. Fazio nodded to Marcos, who pulled a door open. They both kept their guns in ready position when the two of them entered the foyer.

Weaver and another man lay on the floor covered in blood. In Weaver's hand was a nineteenth century long-barrel Colt pistol from his antique collection. Blood pooled from a wound in his neck. Fazio knelt down to close Weaver's eyes before lifting his gun to waist height and disappearing around the corner.

Marcos kept his gun on the other victim while he kicked the gun out of his hand. He checked for a pulse. "Dead," he said aloud.

The sound of talk and laughter at the top of the stairs brought Fazio back into the foyer. Marcos stepped into the room and aimed his gun up the stairs. He exhaled and lifted his gun to his shoulder. "It's okay, Fazio." Three couples, oblivious to the gunshots, were on their way down the stairs. They stopped when they saw the man with the gun. "Get back to your rooms, ladies and gentlemen," Marcos said. "There's been a shooting." The couples scrambled back up the stairs.

A maid came down the hallway behind Marcos and screamed when she saw Weaver's body. Marcos told her to go back to somewhere safe.

Fazio left to check the rest of the hotel. He met up with Marcos in the lobby. "There's no sign of your uncle and the rest of the first floor is clear. Poor bastard," he said, looking at Weaver. "I'd have bet that relic would backfire."

"The gun or the old man?"

"You have a strange sense of humor, kid. If the old Colt did fire correctly, the old coot would have been lucky to hit the broad side of a barn. Where the hell is Estebanez?"

As if he heard his name, Estebanez came from the east hall of the lodge. "There's at least one more. He went out the back, and I lost him." Kneeling over the man whose pulse Marcos had checked, he whispered, "Domenick, you idiot." He laid a hand over the dead man's eyes to shut them. "*Que Dios lo tenga en la gloria,*" he whispered.

"You know him, Uncle Z?"

"I tried for a non-fatal hit. We ran together back in '74. It was our last mission before Executive Order 12333 passed. That was the last time we *legally* tried to take out Castro. Domenick DelGercio," he said, "had the highest security clearance you could reach in the CIA. Last I heard, he was NOC in Europe."

"Non-official cover," Fazio said. "Is that what you are, Estebanez? NOC? CIA operative? I figured something like that when your records came up cleaner than Mother Teresa."

Estebanez didn't answer the questions. Instead he said to Marcos, "Domenick was a good man, but he must have become a gun for hire after the Cold War went warm."

Marcos asked, "Was he the one at the Bronx Park? You put a bullet in his shoulder."

"In that case, I was *trying* to wing him before he shot the kid."

Fazio raised his .38 revolver toward Estebanez.

"Put it down, Fazio. We're the good guys," Estebanez said.

"I'm not so sure. That New York detective was talking about the kids caught in the middle of a shooting in the Bronx. You've got some explaining to do."

Estebanez looked at him strangely. "That's what Matthew always says to me. And right now, he's our priority."

"Drop the act," Fazio said. "Where are the kids, you bastard? I knew you had something to do with everything that has happened. You may have fooled the good people of Millinocket, but in Chicago, we would have run you out on a rail ten years ago."

"Joe, put down the gun," Marcos said. He had slipped behind Fazio and was aiming his 9mm at his back.

"For Matthew's sake, you're going to have to trust me," Estebanez said. "Do you really think I intended to hurt these kids? They're like my own."

Joe slightly lowered his gun. "Go on."

"It appears Weaver was holding them for ransom," Estebanez said, altering the truth somewhat. He explained to Fazio that, seconds before Weaver was shot by DelGercio, the old man confessed he was offered a sizable sum by two interested parties: DelGercio and an Arab man who did not give him a name.

"Why would people like them be interested in Matthew?"

"I haven't a clue."

"You're lying." But he went on trying to reconstruct the scene before he and Marcos had burst in. "If DelGercio shot Weaver, don't tell me Weaver shot DelGercio?"

"When I stepped into the foyer, they were arguing. Weaver had his gun on DelGercio.

"So what did they want with the kids?"

"I don't think we'll ever know," Estebanez lied. "Before Weaver tried to take a shot at Domenick, he told me all he had to do was hold the kids for a few hours so the men could ask them questions. When hours turned into days, he must have mentally shut down. The Weaver I knew was crazy and greedy but he wouldn't have hurt the kids. Weaver suffers from schizophrenia and must have been off his meds. I've seen him shut down like this a few times. Just before Dom shot him, Weaver corrected me by saying his name was McCloud, not Weaver, that Weaver was an alias, and he was undercover."

"I knew Weaver was a bit eccentric, but I had no idea he was a complete nutcase," Fazio said.

"Instead of dealing with his plan going awry, he left them wherever he left them."

"They're alive?"

"Let's hope so," Estebanez said. He didn't want Fazio going down into the cellar and told Fazio that the Middle Eastern men out front were not hunters. "If you can keep them distracted, I can look for Matthew and Maria. We need to buy some time until the cavalry arrives."

"You put in a call?"

"I called the command center and spoke to Flannigan." Estebanez lied. The last thing he needed was the FBI and the media up here.

Fazio lowered his gun. "Why don't *you* watch the Arabs and I'll look for Matthew and Maria?"

Marcos lowered his gun as well and went to the front windows.

Estebanez said, "I know this lodge and these grounds. Hopefully, I can find Matthew and Maria before someone else does. With your help."

"So help me, if you're playing me," Fazio added before taking his position, "I will hunt you down, burn your eyes out, cut your fingers off, dunk you in gasoline, light you on fire, and then I'll begin the torture."

Fazio opened the front door of the lodge and walked out whistling. He sat down in one of the rocking chairs on the front porch with his gun tucked to his side. Marcos went to guard the back doors of the lodge.

Estebanez ran to the front desk and retrieved a flashlight and matches. Back in the foyer, he peered out front. The alleged hunters were milling around the parking lot with marked professional caution. He wondered what was holding them back from storming the lodge.

When Estebanez was sure he was alone, except for the two dead bodies, he went into the library and searched along a shelf next to the false bookcase. He found the book he was looking for, a first edition of Noah Webster's *The American Spelling Book,* 1801. He figured this book had been off the shelf no more than a dozen times in the last two hundred years, and each time by him. He retrieved the duplicate key taped behind it.

He turned off the overhead lights and stood in the darkened library while he waited. Thunder rolled in the distance. He thought about the trip to New York City ten years ago when he had a locksmith friend duplicate the original key. While he waited, he had made a detour to Sotheby's where he put the first of many bottles of rare wine up for auction. He felt a little guilty, but considering all the international laws he had broken over the past years, this little venture was surely the easiest to forgive and forget. He deposited half of the money in his Swiss bank account, and the other half in what he liked to refer to as "Matthew Eaton's energy trust fund," also a Swiss account. Before his closest friend Cameron was murdered, Estebanez had promised to keep an eye on Tremont and Matthew, and to help them bring CJ Energy to fruition. He would make sure they never needed to go to the government or the public for funds. Greedy Dennis Weaver provided the perfect vessels.

As he opened the false bookshelf and unlocked the first door, he smiled at the memory of that first bottle. He chose one of five rare and old bottles from the cellar that none of the experts at Sotheby's London thought existed. He didn't tell them there were more. He sold the bottle in a private auction for over

$300,000. Soon, Estebanez had realized that Weaver long since lost track of the expansive inventory in the cellar. Over ten years, Estebanez had sold fifty-three bottles. Each Swiss account had received over five million dollars. With interest and good investing, there should be enough for Matthew to launch the greatest world-changing invention since electricity. His smile turned to a frown as he thought, if he's still alive.

He pulled the doors behind him and ran down the steps to the next door. "What the hell is this?" He lifted a heavy padlock similar to the one at the top of the stairs. He cussed and hoped the same key fit. He dropped the key in his haste, but when he finally got it in the skeleton keyhole, he breathed a sigh of relief.

He stepped into the well-lit cellar and called out, "Matthew? Maria?" He pulled his gun and walked to the far right side where he had stored the duffel bags. When he got to the back, the bags were gone and there was no sign of the kids. He felt something under his feet and bent down. It was a pile of carrot and potato shavings. Behind him, he noticed six empty wine bottles sitting in a row. Estebanez smiled.

Backtracking through the maze of ceiling high wine racks, he got to the other side and found three stacks of crates and winemaking equipment. He worked his way to a door between two tall stacks of junk. He figured he was at least twenty to thirty feet below ground level, and if he judged the position of the back left corner of the cellar, the door would lead straight to the sheer cliff with at least a hundred foot drop straight to the valley. A busted padlock similar to the other two, lay on the floor. He pushed on the door, and it budged about six inches. Dusk was settling in. He could see plenty of lush vegetation but nothing more. He put his full weight against the door, being careful not to go tumbling off the cliff if it did give way. It would not budge any farther. Something caught his attention on the old padlock. It was sticky with fresh blood.

As he retreated to the steps, he studied the floor. He found what he was looking for: splotches of blood along the wall where someone stumbled toward the stairs. The picture was becoming clearer. He ran up the steps. More blood. Before pushing the shelves out, he listened. All seemed to be quiet. He pushed out and peered into the library. He could hear Fazio talking, or more accurately, arguing. He left the door unlocked and closed the bookshelves.

He went to Weaver's body. The double tap fatal shots from Dom's gun that went through Weaver's heart would have killed him instantly. He looked at Weaver's hands. One was covered in dry blood that came from a wound high up on his shoulder. His blue blazer revealed a tear where a bullet had grazed his arm. The blood had flowed down his arm where it pooled and dripped from his hand.

"What have you done, Weaver?" he hissed. "Marcos!"

Marcos came around the corner. "One of the Arabs was out back. I didn't see a gun on him. When he saw me, he smiled and waved. But he's been posted back there. No doubt. What did you find in the wine cellar?"

"Nada. But the kids were down there. I want to look out back and to the left toward the valley. Either someone took them out of the cellar, or they went over the cliff. It's a straight drop to the bottom."

"The research?"

"Gone."

"That can't be good."

Marcos moved to the window and Estebanez to the door. With a glance to the sky, Marcos said, "Looks like quite a storm is coming in fast."

One of the hunters appeared aggravated with Fazio. "Look, Capone, I see that you don't have any official credentials. You are what, a private eye? So I think you will let us in the lodge, yes?"

"Don't think so, Saddam," Fazio replied.

Marcos whispered to Estebanez, "I can see one at the right of the porch. Can't see to the left. There's one in the back and there's one by the truck. That leaves one Arab and DelGercio's man unaccounted for."

Tucking his gun out of sight, Estebanez stepped outside beside Fazio. "We got a problem here, Joe?"

Thunder cracked, and a light rain began to fall. "I don't think these guys are hunting rabbit or elk."

"What is your business up here, sir?" Estebanez asked, though he immediately recognized him. The family resemblance was uncanny.

The Arab relaxed his shoulders. "We do not want any problems, Mr. Estebanez. We are simply vacationing in this beautiful land and concerned about the shots we heard inside the lodge. Perhaps my dark skin has intimidated your friend here, but I assure you, we mean no harm. We would like to check in and dine."

Estebanez reasoned, if they had the research, they would already be gone. Weaver must have thought he could benefit from a bidding war between Dom and these men, whom he was sure were associated with the oil cartels. He decided on a new course of action. "Might I ask your name? Your real name?"

Without hesitation, the man puffed up his chest and said, "I am Prince Ali Sharif bin Taliffan."

"I'm familiar with your family. Particularly your brother."

"Cousin."

"Cousin. Yes. Well, Mr. bin Taliffan, here's the situation. I believe you had business with Dennis Weaver, the proprietor of the lodge. He's dead." Bin Taliffan didn't flinch. Not even a blink. "From the way I see it, old Weaver was playing you against another interested party, things got tense, and the result is two dead bodies in the foyer."

Bin Taliffan's smile disappeared. "If you will permit me, I would like to see this for myself."

Fazio was about to object. Estebanez raised a hand to cut him off and opened the door for bin Taliffan. He signaled Fazio to continue keeping guard outside. Looking confused and miffed, Fazio settled into the rocking chair. "If you guys are game hunters, I'm the Sultan of Arabia," he said loud enough for the others to hear.

Inside, Ali bin Taliffan looked over at Marcos, who was watching him. "I don't suppose there's a price I could offer you and your nephew that would persuade you to turn over the merchandise Mr. Weaver was holding for us?"

"I don't know what merchandise you're referring to, Prince Ali. By the way, how is your Harvard Crimson Rowing team doing? I understand you led quite a crew there."

"You went to Harvard?" Marcos perked up. "Man, we educate all of our competition, don't we? You go back to your oil fields and double the per barrel prices with economic models you learned from a professor from India."

Bin Taliffan's eyes narrowed. "I don't think you have room to talk. I believe this country has been very good to Cuban dissidents." He revealed an expensive smile.

Marcos pushed away from the wall to respond, but his uncle gave him a stern look. He leaned back against the wall, but crossed his arms in such a way that his 9mm gun was more visible.

Bin Taliffan spoke up. "Let us not dance around the subject. My sponsors are willing to offer you a seven-digit sum, negotiable."

"Whatever you're looking for must be very valuable, Ali. But I can't help you. You've seen that your source for whatever you're looking for has expired. I would suggest that before this place is swarming with police, FBI, and media, you and your countrymen head back to Austria and let your cousin know whatever he's looking for, if it did exist, has been destroyed."

"And what assurance do I have of that, Mr. Estebanez?"

"My word."

"The word of an international spy?"

"You flatter me, Ali. I am but a teacher and mild-mannered rare wine and sailboat merchant," Estebanez said.

Marcos could not stifle a snicker.

"Where on earth would you get such an idea?" Estebanez asked, as he escorted the Prince out the door just as sirens sounded in the distance.

Ali stopped and turned; his eyes appeared to change color as they burned into Estebanez. "We will meet again."

"Fabulous. I'll bring my catalogs to the meeting. We can talk about the right two-hundred-foot, seven-mast schooner for you. But if you or members of Hafiz-OPEC Saumba Shokran – " Estebanez stopped long enough to revel in the surprise on Prince Ali's face, " – if anyone comes anywhere near Millinocket, Maine, again, I will know it." He pointed to a totem pole on the porch. "And I will personally send you and your cousin to what the natives here call *the happy hunting ground*."

On the porch, bin Taliffan pinched Fazio's cheek. He pulled away in time to miss a reflexive swing from the angry detective. Ali backed down the steps and looked up into the thickening black clouds and then back down to Fazio. "By the way, Capone, there is no Sultan of Arabia. But if there were, you could not shine the rubies on his robe."

Thunder crashed and the rain began to fall. Fazio stood and lifted his revolver. Estebanez put his hand on the cold steel. "Let's turn our attention to finding the kids."

The alleged hunters retreated to their dual cab pick-up truck and headed down the driveway as the rain began to fall and a cavalcade of vehicles roared into the parking lot past them.

CHAPTER 38

June 6, 1995 9:00 P.m.

Storm

A LIGHT RAIN began to fall on the weary family and friends as they retreated to a tent. They sat at long foldout tables while Parker, Sean, and Floyd scanned a topographical map with two game wardens. Sean marked off all the areas combed by the three search parties and took out a yellow highlighter to mark unsearched areas.

"Hello, big brother."

Everyone turned their heads to see the newcomer, a younger but taller likeness to Parker Eaton.

Kate threw her arms around him, "Carl! It's all so terrible. I'm so glad you are here."

Parker walked over to his brother. "What brings you to Maine, Carl?"

"Why, Matthew, of course."

"How did you know about this mess?" Parker asked sharply.

Carl hesitated, "I heard it on the radio and then saw Matthew on CNN, it's all over the news clear down in Miami." Changing the subject, he said, "You look good in spite of the situation."

Parker stared at his prodigal brother a minute longer then returned to studying the map. Sean got up and gave Carl an unexpected hug, introduced

Floyd and went back to the mapping process. Carl made his way around the group shaking hands and introducing himself.

Maria's father stood away from the group looking west into the darkening sky. He didn't turn when Kate approached him but said, "That storm is coming quick. Yesterday they were predicting clear skies all week. Pete says it's a bad omen, that the mountain is angry. I never did understand any of that. I just know, if they're out there – ," he choked back his tears. "Nothing makes sense, Kate. If I lost Maria – "

Kate put a hand on his shoulder. "We'll find them soon, Phil. I would know in my heart if anything happened to Matthew."

"Yes. Salina always knew . . . even before Maria would catch a cold." Kate gave him a hug, and they retreated farther into the shelter as the wind and rain picked up.

They all had decided to stay in the camp to wait for Fazio, who had left to follow what he called a long shot lead. An hour later, the core family group decided to stay put even after a call came in that guests were reporting that there was trouble at the Katahdin Sporting Lodge. Word spread quickly and more than three quarters of the beleaguered command center camp emptied out.

"Vultures!" Parker Eaton said of the media crews. "They smell blood, and they're off on another trail. Good riddance to them." Sean folded the maps. He and Floyd began to pack some water and food into backpacks. "Where the hell do you think you're going?" Parker barked, but it was clear he was trying to hide his mounting anxiety. He seemed to have aged ten years in the last three days.

Floyd replied, "Mr. Eaton, we were studying the map, and there's one area on the north side of what's it called something Jesus?"

"Ambajejus," Parker corrected.

"Right, so there's this area both search crews missed. It's pretty rough ground, but we thought the two of us could handle it better than a large group."

"Well, take the mule," Parker said, handing Floyd the keys to the mammoth six-wheel company truck that sat at the park entrance. Thunder cracked and it began to rain.

Pete, came running down the hill from between rows of white birch trees with a soaking wet shepherd at his heels. Two much larger German Shepherds from the

K-9 unit rushed over teeth barred to the canine intruder – with their game warden partners in tow. "Mr. Eaton," Pete said breathless, "Pamola may be changing his mind," referencing the legendary spirit who lived at the Peak of Mount Mountain, "I think you'll want to come across the street." He was holding a pair of binoculars. "We had all boats accounted for when this dog comes out of nowhere," he leaned over to catch his breath, "and I saw a speck, a reflection way out on the lake."

Kate ran to the dog and went to her knees throwing her arms around her neck, "SoBe! Where are they, girl? Where are they?"

"Kate, do you know this dog?" Parker asked incredulously.

"She's Matthew's . . . and Maria's!

"Matthew doesn't have a dog," Parker said.

Sean grabbed Pete by the shirt, "Spit it out, Pete. Spit it out."

"Well, after the dog came out of the water I looked out on the lake. I thought there could be a fisherman out there that maybe pushed off from another dock, but that didn't make much sense since it's getting dark and he had no running lights. By law, they gotta have running lights." Everyone in camp had gravitated to the out-of-breath ranger. "I ran to my truck and got my infrared binocs, and I got to tell you . . ." He stopped and bent over, hands on his knees, to take a breath. "I knew Pamola was behind all of this, my mother said he took its prisoners," referring to Matthew and Maria, "to Alomkik, but, then a few hours ago Chief Tanner said he saw in a vision that they were on the water, I knew – "

Sean still had Pete by the arm and shook him. "Damn it, Pete, we know all about the God of Thunder! Why is everything such a production for you? What is it, man?"

"It's Matthew and Maria! I'd bet my life on it." As the rain intensified, SoBe barked, ran ahead, and the group pushed Pete up across the dike to the other lakeshore.

When they reached the water's edge, the wind and rain made the sky darker than it would normally be at dusk. It was impossible to see anything with the moon behind clouds.

"Everyone quiet down for a minute," Parker yelled. "Listen."

They heard the faint sound of a small motor. Parker snatched the infrared binoculars from Pete, knocking the green cap off his head. No one breathed. "I see them! By God, it's them!"

Sean took the glasses from his father for a look. "I'll be damned."

There was a collective cheer from the group. "They must be a couple miles out," Parker said. "Pete, what the hell are you waiting for? Let's get in a boat and go get them." He looked around and could not see Pete.

Sean put down the binoculars. "There's a slight problem, Dad." It was the first time in a long time Sean had referred to him as anything other than sir or something with an obscenity attached to it.

"What, son? What?"

"I've never seen waves like that on any of the lakes. They're kicking that little boat around like a styrofoam cup. We better get to them soon, or they'll be taking a swim."

"Nobody's better on the water than Matthew," Kate said, but her usual confidence wasn't there.

Thunder pounded across the lake followed by bolts of lightening that seemed to stretch from heaven to the water. In the brief light, the group could see the small craft, about the size of a quarter, lift above the waves and then disappear.

"Let's go!" Pete was yelling from a dock a few yards south on the shoreline. He stood waving on the back of a boat tied up to a tree a few hundred feet away. Thunder muted the outboard motors when the Eatons, Floyd, and Maria's father climbed in the boat and they bounced out into the choppy water. "I've radioed to the Wardens and Rangers. We should have help out here soon. Hopefully, we won't need it." Pete flipped on a searchlight as the clouds released a fierce rage of stinging rain upon their heads. Navigation became impossible.

"Why are you slowing down, Pete?" Kate yelled over the sound of the rain and the boats' motors.

"I don't want to flip us, and if I can't see them, I don't want to run them down."

Sean stood at the helm with the binoculars and looked right and left. There was no sign of Matthew and Maria.

"They couldn't have just disappeared, could they?" Floyd asked as he strained to see through sheets of rain.

"If they went over . . . ," Pete began as they crept along near idle.

"I see the boat!" Kate yelled and pointed. Pete turned the spotlight on the craft, which was no bigger than a rowboat, floating upside down. The tiny five horsepower motor still puttered and spurted in agony.

Without a word, Sean handed the binoculars to his father and tore off his clothes. In seconds, he was down to his skivvies and off the boat. Pete guided the cruiser in the direction of Sean and the rowboat, which had disappeared. He pulled the spotlight off the rack to shine it in slow arcs.

Sean dropped out of view. Suddenly, Sean and another head popped out of the water a few yards starboard. Parker, who already had a red and white ring buoy in one hand and the rope in the other, threw the buoy at least twenty feet to land over Sean's left shoulder. Sean grabbed hold of the rope, and Phil and Parker pulled until Sean had the round buoy hooked over his arm. The two fathers braced themselves. When Sean and Maria were a few feet away, Phil let out a Spanish laden burst of relief. Sean had Maria against the side of his body with her shoulder tucked under the arm he had around her waist. He scissor kicked until he was reaching for the ladder on the side of the boat with his free hand. But each time he reached for the ladder, a wave knocked him against the boat and he lost his grip. Pete and Floyd jumped in to steady the unconscious Maria as the two fathers reached under her arms and pulled her onto the boat. They laid her on her back. Kate checked her vital signs.

"She's not breathing!" Kate performed a round of CPR. And another.

While Kate tried to revive Maria, Pete was yelling at Sean. "Did you see Matthew?"

"No! I'm going back over to the boat. Get the light on me." Pete pulled himself onboard, and Sean swam back into the darkness. While Pete maneuvered the boat behind Sean, Parker held the light on Sean's path as he reached the rowboat in a dozen strokes. There was no sign of Matthew.

Back on the boat, Kate was counting compressions between blowing into Maria's mouth. The girl coughed.

Kate choked on a sob of joy and rolled Maria on her side as she coughed up lake water. She opened her eyes to see Mrs. Eaton and her father looking down at her. She mouthed, *Matthew. Matthew. Matthew.*

Off toward shore, they could see three, four, now five lights. Other locals and a few rangers had returned to the camp, and now their small fishing boats were moving toward them. Pete got on the bullhorn. "Slow down! Slow down!" He blinked the searchlight in Morse code: *slow, slow, slow.* He followed with:

Man overboard. Man overboard. The boat captains slowed and spread out, their searchlights scanning the water in all directions.

Sean dove repeatedly in a controlled pattern, knowing the chance of finding his baby brother in the dark lake water was slim, but he had yet to fail a mission, noble or ignoble. He held to the side of the rowboat to catch his breath. "I did what I had to do, even when it seemed wrong, to keep you from getting hurt, kid. You'll find out one day. Don't drown on me now." He dove again. When he surfaced, his voice took on a haunting tone. "Damn-it, where are you?" He then began to laugh. "Besides, I need you to finish the research. With the Jacksons gone, everyone will be depending on you." He chuckled and said, "Wouldn't it be a hoot if you had the research in this boat. Wouldn't that curl *their* turbans? You would have to start from scratch, but you know what? Only *you* could."

Sean went down again and resurfaced a few minutes later, he choked and cussed. "I had nothing to do with what happened in Miami. That was all on him. He should have sold his father's research and walked away. Instead, he created an enemy of the month club. I've always regretted taking out his old man. Unlike Dad and me, Tremont was close to his father, and I know Cameron was your hero. It was a hell of a shot though, over 1,800 meters. One hell of a shot."

The sound of metal against metal shook Sean out of his psychosis. Under the light of two or three spotlights, he turned in the water to see Pete holding onto the side of the overturned rowboat.

"What the hell are you talking about, Sean? You killed that old scientist in DC?"

"Just talking crazy, Pete, that's all. The boys at the Pentagon keep saying I haven't recovered from post-traumatic battle syndrome or something. But I'm fine. Just talking a little crazy."

Pete didn't seem to be listening. He smacked a hand against the boat. His watch made that metal on metal sound again. "Now I remember. *Jackson.* That was his name, *Jackson.* A day after he was shot, you showed up in town. You were in the old saloon spouting off about all the crazy radical Muslims you killed in the Middle East and how you could take out a terrorist at 1,800 meters. And the paper said Jackson was taken out at 1,800 meters."

"Like I said, Pete, you never knew when to keep your mouth shut. Remember when you had to tell the coach how much we drank before practice, and he had us running and puking after dark."

Pete tried to laugh. "You got me back for that one, Sean. I could feel the burn off that wedgie for weeks."

"Help me look for my little brother, Pete. We'll talk about what you think you know when this is all over."

"Sure, Sean, sure."

Sean took a deep breath and went under the water. He came up right behind Pete.

Sean began to swim toward the speedboat. Something in the water away from the shore caught his attention. It was more of a sense of something, like the way he could sense a Taliban warrior approaching his camp well before he could be heard. He stopped and stared into the distance. He turned northeast out into the wide-open lake.

The waves were ever higher and the exhausted crew strained to see through the stinging wind and rain. "Where's Sean going?" Floyd yelled.

Parker shone the light in Pete's direction. Not seeing him, he yelled, "Hang where you're at, Pete!" Parker turned the boat in the direction Sean was swimming and pushed its throttle. Sean had crossed the two hundred yards or more in a few minutes, and everyone in the boat could see his target – a red and white metal cage on top of a white buoy bouncing on the waves.

Floyd was holding tight to the side of the boat. "What is it, Mr. Eaton?"

"It's a warning beacon the rangers use when there's something boaters need to avoid, like rocks or a shallow area. The red light's either burnt out, or it was just being used when the water levels were low last summer."

Sean grabbed onto the buoy and said, "Damn good thinking, little buddy. Damn good thinking." Matthew had tied himself to the beacon; blood was seeping from the old wound in his head. He was unconscious but appeared to be alive.

Floyd jumped in the water with Sean. It was all they could do to get Matthew's limp body onto the boat.

Parker signaled the other boats that were just leaving the dock by blinking his searchlight: *Success. Both Alive. Success.* They soon converged on the beacon.

Above Millinocket Lake, the news went out from radio to radio that the famous kids from Millinocket were alive. The crowd began to build between the North Woods Trading Post and Big Moose Inn. Soon they were all watching as four of five bright white searchlights headed into shore.

An hour later the ambulance holding Matthew and Maria disappeared south toward Millinocket into a curtain of rain as down on the shore the last boat limped into the dock. Later, the news was grave. Pete's body lay on a gurney; the med tech covered his head with the white blanket and tightened the buckles on four straps across his body. Thunder boomed and they all looked up to see a long flash of lightning that seemed to touch and linger at the peak of Mount Katahdin.

EPILOGUE

summer 1995

Genesis

THE BALANCE OF summer would prove to pass quickly. After three days in intensive care, and another three recuperating, Matthew stood on the front steps of Millinocket Regional Hospital. He had ten stitches in his scalp where he must have hit the side of the boat when they flipped, expanding the old wound. During the first few days after he was released, he only left the hospital to get a change of clothes and have an occasional hot meal with his family.

Matthew had not noticed a slim, balding man who edged up next to him on the steps. He said, "Hello, Matthew, I'm Kip Ackerman, from – "

"I know who you are," Matthew said, with a little more acid in his tone than he intended. Mr. E had warned him about Ackerman.

"You must be getting awfully tired of us reporters. I know things are touch and go with Maria, so I just wanted to give you my card; and when things settle down, I'd like to either meet you up here or fly you to New York. You, and Maria if you like, will get the red carpet treatment." He squinted as if he was thinking of what to say next. Instead, he turned and trotted down the steps, waving without looking back. Matthew felt sure he would see Kip Ackerman again. Somehow, he didn't get the same impression as Mr. E. He sensed genuine concern in the reporter's tone.

On another such break from the hospital, he drove past a late model white Thunderbird – with a red convertible top. He spun the Jeep around but lost the T-Bird around a bend in the road. He went back to the hospital and searched the small parking lot. He alerted the security guard on duty, and on the way back to his Jeep touched the still tender wound on his head. "I know what I saw," he said, trying to convince himself.

Matthew stopped at the nurse's station and asked, "When do you think Maria will be released?"

Nurse Reed said, "Matthew, honey, you know she is suffering from severe hypothermia. It could be a while."

Matthew stayed at her side the maximum hours the nursing staff would allow and slept in the waiting room the rest of the night.

One night after he left the hospital, he sat in his Jeep and opened a stack of mail his mother had given him that morning. One envelope caught his attention; the return address was the Federal Bureau of Investigation. He tore it open and inside was a business card of Patrick R. Flannigan, Special Investigator. On the back of the card was scribbled "Call me if you need me." As he put the card in his wallet, he bumped into a man who pulled his baseball cap down over his eyes. Besides a notable cleft in the man's chin, he could have passed for any one of the locals. The man jogged up the steps to the hospital. Matthew followed but lost track of him. He slipped off his backpack and took out a familiar black leather pouch. He removed and loaded a magazine and snapped it into Jackson's .45, slipped past the nurse's station, and stayed the entire night in Maria's room.

Matthew tried Sean at their house, but his mother said he had been staying in town. Matthew had hoped his father and Sean would bury the hatchet after all that happened, but he guessed that was too much to ask. He knew John St. John had a room over the Blue Ox Saloon, and tried calling. Bingo. John said Sean was sleeping off a four- or five-day drinking binge. John would not let him drive and that was the main reason he did not go home. He said Sean rambled on about Pete Marks and kept repeating something about the angry spirits and nightmares. "I'll have him call you at the hospital, Matt," John said and hung up.

The call came through the hospital an hour later, and Matthew was surprised to find Sean quite coherent. He said he had extended his leave from his position with Defense Intelligence. They agreed that once Maria was stable, they would meet a couple hours a day at the old Eaton Logging and Forestry mechanics shop, where they first worked on the VW bus. Matthew never left Maria without first making sure her father or a family member was in the hospital. Floyd, who had been staying at Matthew's house since the night of the storm, stood watch as well. Matthew didn't think anyone interested in the Jackson's research would hurt Maria. What would be the point, he thought wryly. But kidnapping was a possibility. Matthew would give up anything to keep Maria safe, even the research.

Once they started working together on the barn and VW bus, it appeared that Sean had cut back on his heavy drinking. But it was hard to tell for sure. After a few days, Sean informed Matthew he'd received orders to report to the Pentagon. His superiors said he had to take a desk job for a while or suffer a forced discharge. Sean was working with three agencies in the Department of Defense: DIA, NRO, and MCID. Military doctors said he suffered from battle trauma and PTSD or Post-traumatic stress disorder. He told Matthew that was ridiculous.

This day, Sean picked up Matthew at the hospital in the mule, their father's GMC Dooley six-wheel truck. They drove northwest on Millinocket Road, took a left onto Fire Road 13, a right to Fire Road 15, and soon turned north into a dirt road taking them through a thick of pines. The woods opened up to a clearing where the abandoned mechanics shop sat between four other Eaton Logging and Forestry buildings.

All day they drank cold Sea Dog Old Gollywobbler Ale, painted, and repaired the barn. The next day they patched the war-torn VW bus with Bondo, *lots of Bondo.* Matthew told Sean he was thinking about setting the barn up as a place to work on his research. But he didn't tell him anything about the extent of the research just that he needed to keep it secure and secret. Sean liked the idea, and the next day he mapped out a plan to make the barn more secure than Fort Knox . . . bullet-proof. Literally.

When they weren't working on the VW bus or stringing wire for the security system, Sean seemed content to sit, drink ale, and talk. "So now you're battle trained?" Sean asked his little brother. "Most folks in the military train and never engage in an actual firefight. As a civilian, you survived a pretty dangerous mission."

"I don't know about that. Can you call spring break a mission?"

"It was more than a field trip."

"I can't get over the people that have been hurt or killed. How do you ever get used to it?"

"You just do."

"I can't believe your old friend Pete drowned trying to save us. I set rocks out for him yesterday at the lake and at the funeral. When Maria gets out, we are going to go to the mountain, over by Sandy Stream Pond, and put out more rocks. His mother believes it will appease the great spirit . . ."

"Put a couple out for me too, bro," Sean said quietly.

Matthew shook his head and said, "In high school, he used to kick your butt in the summer mile swim on Millinocket Lake. How could he have drowned?"

"Sometimes, regardless of the reason, a man's number is up and there's nothing anyone can do about it. That's all there is to that."

Not for the first time, Matthew thought his brother responded coldly. As if it wasn't a living, breathing, close relationship but instead simply an unfortunate statistic. Is this what the years on the front line had done to his brother?

Sean walked over to the VW. He ran his hand along the side of the bus and all the bullet holes. "Maybe I should sign you up. Survival is what being a marine is all about. Look here, a very high caliber bullet was fired on you, and over here someone was shooting at you from close range with low caliber bullets from handguns. By the way, they caught the guy with the Sopwith Camel."

Matthew couldn't hide his shock. He hadn't mentioned the strange altercation with the biplane to anyone.

"I'm military intelligence, little bro. The story in the *Miami Herald* said some wealthy military aviation collector was let out of the psych ward too early and was off his medications. It seems everyone uses that excuse these days. When they caught up with him, he swore someone stole the plane and that he was home alone in Boca drinking himself into a stupor. He's being charged with murder. They locked his ass back up and probably threw away the key."

Matthew doubted an old man was flying that plane. "What else have you heard?"

"Nobody knows anything about the shootout in Miami Beach. I'm still checking into that. I read a report where this bus was involved in a sting in South Carolina and was at the scene of two homicides in the Bronx Park. Former secret service agents, of all things."

"Coincidence?"

"Nice try, junior. You know what I always say about coincidences."

"There's no such thing."

"Exactly. Then there's the whole Katahdin Sporting Lodge episode. I don't care what the papers say; you were kidnapped because of something you knew or something you had. I can't say I trust your buddy Estebanez for a lot of reasons, but he and Fazio took care of business at the lodge. But you never did say how you got out to the lake."

"There was a door in the back of the cellar. We broke the lock only to find it opened to a cliff. We were about to give up; but Maria noticed a rabbit run along the side of the mountain, as if it was suspended in air. I held on to the door and some bushes, and sure enough, there was a trail. I jammed a few tree limbs against the door. The trail led us around to the south side of the lodge and down to the lake where we found some small boats and canoes." He decided not to mention putting a bullet in Weaver's shoulder as they escaped.

Matthew opened the side of the bus and pretended to search for something. He didn't know what to say next to his brother. He could trust him, couldn't he? But he had promised Cracker Jack he would keep CJ Energy Cells secret. From everyone. Even family.

"What's so damn valuable in those bags that someone is willing to kill you over it?"

"What bags?"

"Don't treat me like an idiot, kid. I can find out what Clinton is having for breakfast and change the menu before he takes his first bite, so I can find out what a teenage kid and his Spanish princess were up to on an excursion to Miami Beach and back. You have some serious characters on your trail. Your guardian angel knows it; that's why he's been watching over you all these years."

"My guardian angel?"

"I can offer you some protection, but you have to level with me."

Matthew came to a decision. He would have to be unwavering in his answer as he knew Sean could read him like a book.

They sat on a couple stools by a work desk and the tool racks in a corner of the mechanic shop. Matthew began, "I don't think they intended to kill me. Just scare me and steal this scientific work I came across. The truth is, it had been entrusted to me."

"It must have incredible value. I understand the Saudis, U.S. government, and organized crime backed by powerful industrial giants are zeroed in on Millinocket, Maine. It's the most attention we've received since the train wreck of '79. You're quite a celebrity."

"I would prefer it to all go away. I could get down to going to school and working on my own research . . . Now that the other research is at the bottom of the lake."

His brother stood up so fast he startled Matthew and knocked over his stool. "What?" he exclaimed.

"I had everything in the boat. There's no use trying to retrieve it. It was all computer drives, journals, and well, paper. Most of it was paper."

Sean began pacing and cussing. He asked, "Do you think you can replicate the research? If anyone can, you can, right?"

Matthew knew he was winging it now, and decided a half-truth would be better at this point. "I think so, Sean."

"We are going to help you do just that!"

"We?"

"You have more friends than you know." Sean stood up and walked around the shop. "Like I said, I can help you make this place as secure as Fort Knox."

"That would be great," Matthew said, light-headed and confused. "I figure I can get up here every other weekend. I'll probably have to quit the swimming and rowing teams. They don't seem as important."

Sean seemed to change into another person. The brother he used to know. Sean said, "Don't quit. Work them in. I gave everything up to serve my country, and I have no regrets, but *you* gotta live. Life is too short. I've seen more kids your age take a bullet before they even had a chance to enjoy a good cigar, expensive whiskey, and the bed of a passionate woman."

Matthew felt safe being with his brother, but the things he wasn't telling him were ringing in his ears.

"Sean?"

"Yeah?"

"Back when you were finishing at Yale, you brought a friend with you to the house. What was his name?"

"Tree."

"I know, but what was his real name?"

"John Imbrognio," Sean lied. "We called him Tree and, sometimes, Little John. Why?"

"I remember his visit and how interested he was in my drawings. That's all. He's the one who gave me the books on solar energy, right?"

"Yeah."

"What's he doing now?"

"Who?"

"Your friend, Tree. John Imbrognio."

"He was killed in the Middle East."

"I'm sorry."

"Yeah, it was a great loss."

Matthew thought his brother didn't sound sorry.

"Do you have a picture of him?"

"I might. I'll take a look around. Hand me that oil rag over there."

The day after Sean left for Washington, Nurse Reed told Matthew that Maria would be out of the hospital earlier than expected. He was exhilarated, but made sure Maria's father and Officer Dubois were staked out at her room before he drove to his house to retrieve one of the four kayaks they had in the shed.

A creepy dread spread over him when he reached the shore of Millinocket Lake just south of where he and Maria almost drowned. He knelt on the water's edge only half in his wetsuit and thought he might be sick. Knowing what was coming next, he cussed realizing he did not bring his pillbox with him. He held out his hands and they were shaking. He could hear his crew coach in his head saying, "Got to face your demons, got to get back on the horse." He repeated this aloud as he stood to finish slipping his arms into the wetsuit.

"I haven't been called a demon since my third wife filed a restraining order against me," a voice behind Matthew said.

Matthew turned, and when he saw the man with the sharp cleft in his chin, bright blue eyes, and a Dallas Cowboys cap holding a gun on him, he put his hands up at half-mast. Mr. E and Flannigan said this man was Lomax and he was very dangerous.

"Where is the research kid?"

"At the bottom of the lake – lost in the storm."

"You're lying," Lomax said calmly, taking a step toward him, and placing the muzzle of the 9mm an inch from Matthew's temple. "Turn around."

Matthew complied, closed his eyes tight and said, "Look, I'm tired of this crap! I'm glad the research is gone, it nearly cost Maria and me our lives, more than once." The man was quiet, probably deciding whether to blow my head off, Matthew thought. "It's gone I tell you!" Matthew took a deep breath, opened his eyes and slowly turned around. The man was gone.

Matthew sat hard and cross-legged into the tall grass and buried his head between his knees. Then he let himself fall to his back, arms spread. Looking up into the white puffed blue sky, he watched a large "V" of Canadian geese pass overhead. "God? Is this ever going to end?" He knew he did not have to wait for an answer.

On the day the hospital released Maria, the reporters swept in like firefighters responding to a three-alarm fire.

"Before I take you home, I have something to show you," Matthew whispered. Doting on Maria like a mother hen, Nurse Reed helped her out of her wheelchair at the top of the front steps of the hospital. Matthew had convinced Maria's father to let him drive her home. First, they had to deal with the reporters. After telling and retelling most of the events at the lodge, and their chilling experience on the lake, they were on their way.

Matthew and Maria had survived the trip to Miami and back, imprisonment by the crazy Dennis Weaver, Lomax – at least for now – and the worst northern Maine summer storm on record. Now they had survived the barrage of reporters; at least . . . for now.

Twenty minutes later Matthew parked in the Willow Run Cemetery. He looked about to be sure the old caretaker was not nearby, and shot up the steep hill along the cobble stone path.

Maria gave him a quizzical look. They had not been to her mother's gravesite together since that dismal rainy night when they were barely seven years old. Today, the sky was a cloudless rich baby blue.

Matthew reached into the back seat and picked up an old familiar book and one of two bouquets of flowers. They walked hand in hand over to the western end of the hill and both knelt at Mrs. Valdeorras's bright white Italian marble gravestone. He laid the flowers below the headstone and began clearing branches from her grave as Maria said a prayer, spoke to her mother, and then silently wept.

Matthew left her alone and leaned up against a tall thin poplar about ten feet away. Maria came over, put her hands around his waist, and lay her head on his chest.

She sniffed and he took a handkerchief out of his pocket and wiped the tears from her eyes. They both laughed when she blew her nose. She attempted to stuff it back in his pocket.

"You can keep it," he said.

"You said you wanted to show me something?"

He led her over toward the northeast corner of the hill where stood the largest and perhaps oldest oak tree in the area.

"The old mill doesn't look as ominous, does it?" Maria asked. "I used to think it looked like a huge monster daring anyone to try and go past it to the mountains."

They held hands and stared north over the river and above the Great Northern Mill and on toward Mount Katahdin. Matthew said, "I thought of the mill as a great big bear looking out for its cubs. Now that the big bear is dying, I fear for the people of this region. Maybe one day we can come back and start businesses that will help revive the area."

"When you finish CJ Energy Cells, you can bring to north-central Maine a new form of industry, like manufacturing energy efficient products," she said.

"I will if and when I can safely get back to the research. With all the attention, I don't imagine it will be anytime soon." They sat on one of the mammoth oak tree roots.

They were quiet for some time. Matthew stood and said, "So look over here." He bent down to the base of the oak, brushed the bark with one hand, and growled. He took out his old pocketknife, the same one Sean had given him so many years before, and scraped and cut with meticulous precision. He stood up to reveal his handiwork:

M&M
WERE HERE
1984

"Hmm. I always wondered what you were up to that night. You knew, didn't you?"

"Knew what?"

"That we would be together."

He opened the book and handed it to Maria. Pressed into the very center page, in a chapter on Quantum Secrets of Photosynthesis, was a flattened, once yellow, rose. Maria recognized it immediately and looked at Matthew with wide eyes. Now *she* was speechless. Matthew took her hand and they walked back to the Jeep.

The Jeep bounded down the cobblestone walkway and out onto the Golden Road. Around the first bend, Matthew had to swerve to miss an oncoming white sedan. He frowned noticing the *Channel 9* emblazoned on the door. While he was studying the sedan, he barely missed hitting a large news van complete with satellite dishes and more *Channel 9* decals.

"They won't find us up here," Matthew said.

"You hope," Maria added. The two lay snuggled together on an old wool blanket in the hayloft above the old mechanic shop. The shot-up, patched-up bus rested in the shadows on the far side of the barn. They ate fried chicken and drank iced tea.

"It's hard to believe we'll be at UMaine worrying about tests in a just a couple weeks. I'm not sure I'm ready to go back," Matthew said.

Maria sighed and then said, "I'm excited to start college. But no more spring break trips. I think we'll spend the break in our dorm rooms. It'll be a lot safer."

“You think I’m safe?” He tickled her side.

“I’m the one to be afraid of. Very afraid.” She sat up. “And you should be excited to get going on your research now that you have the CJ Energy Cell research.”

“If they’ll let me.” He thought about the photographs Donna and Darma had delivered to him in the library; and then seeing the T-Bird at the hospital; and then there was the man at the lake with the cleft chin. The danger was far from over.

“They don’t know you have the research. At least, I don’t think they do,” Maria surmised.

“That’s the thing. We won’t know unless someone attacks us again. I don’t know if I can subject you to a world where we’ll be looking over our shoulders every minute of every day.”

“I’m in your world to stay, mister. And don’t you forget it.” She twisted the skin on his side until he yelped.

“At the very least, we’ll leave the research where we hid it for a while. I have enough information to keep me busy for the next few semesters. When we feel like all the fervor has died down, then we can plan out how to keep CJ Energy safe. That’s about as far out as I can think. Especially since there’s nobody we can trust.”

“There’s Mr. E.”

“If we knew where he was.”

“He’ll get in touch with you.”

“Perhaps.”

“And then there’s Sean, if it wasn’t for him – and poor Pete, of course – we wouldn’t be here today.”

“True,” Matthew agreed, though something nagged at the back of his mind about that harrowing time on the lake.

“My father said that after Weaver was killed, his oldest son moved back from California to take an extended leave from his teaching position at Stanford. Did you know that?”

Matthew nodded and said, “He’s running the lodge and also putting it up for sale. The wine and antiques are up for auction.”

“My father said the wine in the cellar is far more valuable than the building and the land.”

"Weaver's son came to the hospital to apologize for his father. He figures his senility turned psychopathic. No one knows it was all about money. Anyway, I asked him to look up addresses for Estebanez. He did, and I mailed a letter to his post office box in Panama City. It came back undelivered."

"I have a feeling he'll turn up."

"Yeah, I hope so. Sooner than later."

"You said you and Sean were working on this barn. What were you doing? It looks the same to me."

"We had only finished the wiring and basic security system when Sean was called back to Washington. Sean had some ideas on how to set up a hidden lab. I think I talked him out of hiding booby-traps around the perimeter. I don't want old Mr. Johnson or someone else from town coming up here and getting blown to smithereens. Hopefully we'll be able to make this old place a practical lab and workshop."

Matthew remembered something his mother handed him this morning and walked out to the Jeep to retrieve a small UPS box. It had no return address. He took out a penknife and cut through the thick tape. Styrofoam peanuts fell out and blew away in the wind. They really need to outlaw those, he thought. Inside he found, surrounded in bubbled wrap, a beautiful multicolored ceramic flask engraved with the name of one of the most notable scientists of the century, *Wolfgang Pauli.* The short note taped to the bubble wrap read:

> My nephew would like you to have this. The rest of the story is in Cameron's journals. Pauli, back in the fifties, gave it to Tremont's father. He always felt that it was charmed.

The note was not signed. For the briefest of moments Matthew thought it could be Felix Estebanez. But the note said *nephew* and there was no possible way the purely Cuban Mr. E was related to the lanky, sandy-haired Jacksons. He looked back at the note. *Would like? Would like!* He tried to shake the thought from his mind. That would be impossible, he thought. Impossible. The note was a mere scribble and whoever wrote it was probably in a hurry.

He now had three personal mementos from Cracker Jack's father; the gun, the flask, and a signed copy of *Capturing the Sun,* and, of course, his *complete* life's work, he thought.

Maria called from the barn snapping him out of his reverie. "Did Sean ask again where the research was stored?" She came out and put the trash from their picnic into the back of the Jeep.

"No, but I told him it was lost in the storm. I'm not sure why I lied about it, but it seemed the right thing to do at the time. Before he drove back to Boston to fly to DC, he said he's a phone call away, and would bring an army if I needed it. I could tell he's genuinely interested in what I'm doing, but I swear he has a twisted excitement about all the danger we're in."

"Like being protective of a baby cub but still pushing him out to look for his own food."

"Something like that. I guess what we think as danger is just a day in his life."

"And the picture of – what was his friend's name – Tree?"

"I asked my mother to dig out his yearbook. It wasn't where she knew she put it in Sean's room. I'm thinking of ordering one from Yale."

They went back into the barn. Matthew went up to the loft to retrieve their backpacks and she followed him up. He wrapped her in his arms and they fell onto a hay bale.

"I agree."

"Agree to what?" He pushed her thick black curly hair back to kiss her neck.

"I agree everything else can wait."

"Good thinking," Matthew said.

She put her hands on his chest and pushed him back. Her left eye closed slightly.

This time Matthew thought, *that* look took on a new dimension.

"Then you're going to focus on saving the world, right?"

"Absolutely."

AUTHOR'S NOTE

I HOPE YOU enjoyed the first novel in the *Perpetual* series. For those that are like me and go straight to the back of the book, I wish you well on your upcoming *Perpetual* journey. I originally intended for the first three manuscripts to become one novel. Fortunately, the characters (in my imagination) assisted me in creating three separate endings – endings that are also beginnings. Each of the three novels is intertwined, driving toward an ultimate climax.

Somewhere along life's path, writing replaced my childhood dream of becoming the next Walt Disney or Charles Schulz. According to his son Monte, in *Snoopy's Guide to the Writing Life,* Charles Schulz always wanted to be a writer. Near the last years of his life, he was astounded to find that many great writers were in awe of *his* ability to put so much in so few words or frames. For me, the crossing from writer to novelist has been quite rewarding (if you wonder if you are a writer, go with Stephen King's advice, "a writer writes"). And for you latent novelists, granted; it's not easy, as Rob Petrie experienced in *The Dick Van Dyke Show* episode, "A Farewell to Writing." Laura (Mary Tyler Moore) convinces Rob to finally write the novel he's always talked about. Sequestered at his friend's cabin with a traditional typewriter, a set of six-guns, and a paddleball set, Rob types one sentence in three days, but he does become a paddleball expert. He concludes, "When I'm ready to write a novel, I'm not going to have to have a cabin or a quiet house; I'll be able to write it on the subway . . ." Though the only subways we have in Charlotte are sandwich shops, the time was right to begin – and more importantly to finish – *Perpetual.*

Many prolific writers believe there is no excuse for not writing and that writer's block is truly a myth. I have to agree, since more stories abound in my heart and mind than I can hope to ever write. So what keeps us from finishing? I think that a plethora of distractions become convenient excuses. James Joyce often wrote in the crowded pubs which I liken to our busy coffee shops, less all the drunks. Joyce's stories and colorful characters, which became *Dubliners, Ulysses,* and his other marvelous works, came from what was happening all around him. His distractions became his subjects.

Just now, while I was writing the previous paragraph, two young families, complete with a tandem stroller as large and equipped as a Klondike sled (the stroller wheels replacing Alaskan huskies), laboriously settled around one small table. I daresay inclusion of eight sled dogs would make this an even livelier scene. That incident is now indelible. Perhaps it will show up again if Matthew and Maria happen to get stranded near a deplorable oil-drilling site within the nine million-acre Yukon flats wildlife refuge.

Finding time to write while managing a business and focusing on the family seemed, at one time, an impossible undertaking. For many years, I've been in front of the customer, marketing and selling my products and services with unabashed enthusiasm. As a parent, coach, and athlete, interpersonal interaction has been as natural to me as waking up in the morning. The act of writing, on the other hand, occurs in a different spectrum – a sequestered state of reclusiveness. When the business demands seem to be under control, I open my writing tablet (currently a Dell X300 notebook) at my favorite Caribou Coffee shop, at home on the deck, or at a picnic bench on a beautiful spring or autumn day at Freedom Park. From there, the greatest challenge is overcoming disruptions – none greater than the ever ringing contemporary electronics. Once settled, phone on mute, I begin to retreat into my subconscious zone, where Matthew, Maria, Cracker Jack, and so many others take over. All in all, over the last few decades, what seemed to be a daunting pursuit has become *Perpetual.*

Though *Perpetual* is fictional, it also intended to depict a historical snapshot of our times as we face depleting supplies and increasing demand for energy, causing environmental, geopolitical and economic imbalances. Soon all individuals, governments and businesses, will have to take energy and natural resource conservation more seriously. Google, the mega-internet search company, announced in November of 2007 that it will spend hundreds of millions of dollars on low-cost energy solutions (bravo). Perhaps when business can make a profit on renewable, clean, safe energy, we will be able to see the solution out on the horizon rather than just in our dreams. *Perpetual* is as much about the entrepreneur up against the establishment as it is about accelerating research (*Perpetual* book I), development, (book II) and implementation (book III) of alternative solutions. I don't think we can afford to wait for the release of *Perpetual X 2060* (still in my head).

Michael Crichton's tantalizing epigraph, "This novel is fiction, except for the parts that aren't," nicely applies to *Perpetual.* In 1978, I knew I would write parts of this story – having had a parallel encounter with a fellow who called himself... let's just say, an unusual pseudonym. It was not until 1993 that I was confident the initial *incidents* would evolve into a series. Reality truly is stranger than fiction. A few years ago, writing well past midnight at Mickey & Mooch, I typed "The End" to what is now the third novel in the *Perpetual* series. (I subsequently deleted the words "The End" as *Perpetual* never ends.)

The *Perpetual* main character represents the goals of the dreamer and his noble quest to achieve ultimate success – like the classic search for the holy grail or a mysterious crystal. I believe one person with a vision – given the opportunity, contacts, and resources – can make a dramatic difference in the world. The barriers to success along the gauntlet often deflate the entrepreneurial spirit. Great ideas can be scrapped by not raising enough capital or not overcoming costly government regulations. In addition, the entrepreneur needs to have a strong constitution in order to fend off the naysayers and skeptics. Many times, risking their own demise, inventors like Dr. Cameron Jackson are driven to act upon their passion in the face of deceitful, covetous enemies. Fortunately, in real life, dreamers and inventors continue to believe, strive, and achieve in the face of adversity. We are seeing an increase in alternative energy solutions, green products on the market, vaccines to prevent diseases, and corporate efforts to solve pervasive poverty and hunger around the world. There is hope. *Perpetual* hope. Stay tuned as Matthew and new allies – pitted against more subtle, but no less devious foes – attempt to bring CJ Energy Cells, the final solution, to the world.

And he shall separate them one from another, as a shepherd divideth his sheep from the goats: And he shall set the sheep on his right hand, but the goats on the left.

– Matthew 25: 32, 33 (KJ Version)

TIMELINE & LOCATION

Chapter	*pp*	*Title*	*Timeline*	*Location*
Part One		**PERPETUAL *Sun***		
Prologue	15	Revelations	March 17, 1995	Miami Beach FL
Chapter 1	23	Invent	1955-1973	Indiana Dunes IN
Chapter 2	29	Threat	1973	Vienna, Austria
Chapter 3	38	Anguish	1983	Millinocket ME
Part Two		**PERPETUAL *Journey***		
Chapter 4	46	Resolve	August 1989	Indiana Dunes IN
Chapter 5	51	Spirit	Summer 1994	Millinocket ME
Chapter 6	70	Bond	1981	Yale University
Chapter 7	75	Ramble	March 15, 1995 10:00 a.m.	Orono ME
Chapter 8	88	Patriot	1981	Gauley River
Chapter 9	93	Security	1981	Indiana Dunes IN
Chapter 10	104	Quest	March 16, 1995 Noon	Jacksonville FL
Chapter 11	115	Remember	1981	Indianapolis IN
Chapter 12	118	Genius	1981	Millinocket ME
Chapter 13	124	Honor	1982	Khyber Pass, Afghanistan
Chapter 14	129	Terror	1983	Vienna, Austria
Chapter 15	135	Transfer	March 17, 1995 1:00 a.m.	Miami Beach FL
Part Three		**PERPETUAL *Tragedy***		
Chapter 16	149	Tutor	Spring 1987	Millinocket ME
Chapter 17	169	Suspect	Summer 1988	Millinocket ME
Chapter 18	176	Declare	1989	Middle East/ Indiana Dunes
Chapter 19	191	Free	May 21, 1989	Camp Lejeune NC
Chapter 20	204	Chill	May 22, 1989	Destin FL

ACKNOWLEDGMENTS

THROUGH THE FIRST phase of the *Perpetual* journey, friends and family have contributed to this novel making its way to you. Love and thanks to my mother, brothers, and sister for their belief in me, specifically to my brother Keith (http://www.HueysFineArt.com) for the artist he is, and for the countless hours reconnoitering the highs, middles, and lows of this canvas called life. To my Dad, for he is the most avid reader I know. When he liked *Perpetual,* I knew there was hope.

Special thanks to my wife and partner in life, Lisa, for putting up with my *proclivities and idiosyncrasies* (spell-check is a modern-day miracle). Anyone who can put up with me for more than a quarter of a century deserves more than a volume of accolades. A lifetime of thanks goes out to her fabulous parents Frank and Gilda. I can't imagine my life without my multitalented son Justin (http://www.myspace.com/seahorsesmusic) and my precious daughter Kristen. The animal kingdom is a better place because she exists. From the day they were born, I have been gaining a better understanding of the scripture, "Children are a gift from the Lord; they are a reward from him." (Psalm 127:3 NLT). To Katie "Kates" and Lacey "Lace," my writing companions, if you could only read . . . It will *never* be the same without you, Kates.

To my friends who offered their critique and whom I hold in great esteem – Marsha Donahue (http://www.artnorthlight.com), Paris Edward Booth (the poet), Mort Nickell, Phillip B. Joyce, Estelle Vera, Deborah

Grzybowski, Jim Cotton, John Rego, Richard Bertrand, Rick and Debbie LeVasseur, Kenneth Huey, Alis Woodard, Chris Gibson, Gwen Vincent, my friends at Baxter State Park and throughout the Katahdin region – thank you all. And if I missed you, I shall fall on my sword . . . speaking of weapons, thank you, Mike Meacher. And to my grand friend – "Tha goal againn le cheile air Alba" – Shirley Reading.

Endless appreciation goes out to my literary guides: Heather Collings, thespian and poet; Maureen Ryan Griffin, her name rings with teacher, writer and poet; and Patricia "Trish" Benesh, EdD, who selflessly sets writers on the right path.

Kudos goes out to Carolyn Souther, photographer and friend – thanks *a lot* for the horse. And Jacob Bigham for the striking cover design.

In gathering the details to scribe Matthew's quest to bring CJ Energy Cells to the world, any mistakes remain my own.

Above all, I thank my Lord Jesus Christ, "the *author* and finisher of our faith" (Hebrews 12:2 NKJV).

Brian

Visit the Perpetual Writer: http://*www.BrianHuey.com*